MILLIONAIRE UNDER THE MISTLETOE

BY
TESSA RADLEY

AND

HIS HIGH-STAKES HOLIDAY SEDUCTION

BY
EMILIE ROSE

D1080031

MILLS & BOON

Callum gazed at the woman he'd been fighting to ignore all evening. Without success.

In a plain black dress, her hair up in a knot and no glitter in sight, Miranda should've looked plain and drab.

She didn't.

The black only served to highlight the creamy perfection of her skin. No jewelry adorned the delicious smooth line of her throat.

Desire leaped within him, quickly followed by disbelief. This couldn't be happening to him.

He narrowed his eyes. This was the same girl who had once screamed at him like a banshee, accusing him of murdering her father…so why the hell couldn't he stop looking at her? He had his life—his future—all mapped out. And it didn't include Miranda Owen.

MILLIONAIRE UNDER THE MISTLETOE

BY
TESSA RADLEY

Published in Great Britain 2010
Harlequin Mills & Boon Limited,
Eton House, 18-24 Paradise Road, Richmond, Surrey TW9 1SR

© Tessa Radley 2009

ISBN: 978 0 263 88185 1

51-1110

Harlequin Mills & Boon policy is to use papers that are natural, renewable
and recyclable products and made from wood grown in sustainable forests.
The logging and manufacturing processes conform to the legal environmental
regulations of the country of origin.

Printed and bound in Spain
by Litografia Rosés S.A., Barcelona

Tessa Radley loves traveling, reading and watching the world around her. As a teen Tessa wanted to be an intrepid foreign correspondent. But after completing a Bachelor of Arts and marrying her sweetheart she became fascinated by law and ended up studying further and practising as an attorney in a city practice.

A six-month break traveling through Australia with her family re-awoke the yen to write. And life as a writer suits her perfectly: traveling and reading count as research and as for analyzing the world…well, she can think 'what if' all day long. When she's not reading, traveling or thinking about writing she's spending time with her husband, her two sons—or her zany and wonderful friends. You can contact Tessa through her website, www.tessaradley.com

For my beloved Sophie—
The world has lost an angel
I will remember your love forever

Dear Reader,

Romance readers have a power that never fails to move me.

A dear friend of mine would catch the bus to work and home. To pass the time she read romances on the bus. Short romances that fit easily in her purse. It didn't take long to discover other romance readers. Soon several women were sharing the names of favorite authors and swapping books. A bus book-reading club had been born.

One woman changed her bus after mistakenly catching an earlier bus one morning and discovered the group. Another was barely literate but wanted to read the books that her newfound friends were chatting about. Friendships were forged between women who would otherwise have remained strangers, sharing a daily commute and nothing else. Instead their lives were enriched by the joy of friendship...and the love in stories they discovered together.

Have a wonderful Christmas.

Tessa Radley

One

Callum halted at the threshold, his attention riveted on the woman pacing in front of the reception desk. The slanting rays from a lofty skylight caught her hair and turned it into a nimbus of glowing gold.

He took a step forward.

"Callum Ironstone demanded my presence here at three o'clock." She cocked her wrist and glanced at a serviceable watch. "It's already ten past. How much longer does he intend to keep me cooling my heels?" Her husky voice held an edge of impatience.

Callum stilled as her words penetrated. *This* was Miranda Owen?

Not possible.

His gaze tracked up from slender ankles encased in sheer black hose along the sleek lines of the narrow black, hip-hugging skirt. A black polo-neck sweater emphasized the indent of her waist and a saffron-colored coat hung over her arm.

Callum stared.

Digging deep into his memories produced an image of a plump teenager, more at home in a baggy sweat-shirt, jeans and muddied yellow Wellingtons. The sunlit locks held no resemblance to the long, untidy ponytail. No doubt the braces were gone, too.

He cleared his throat.

She spun around. Wide caramel-brown eyes met his. His stomach tightened as he took in the lambent hostility.

One thing hadn't changed. Miranda Owen still blamed him for her father's death.

Callum didn't let the knowledge show as he crossed the marble tiles, toasty from the state-of-the-art under-floor heating system. "Miranda, thank you for coming in."

"Callum."

That one snapped-out word hinted at long-held re-sentments.

He stretched out a hand. For a moment he thought she was going to refuse to take it. Then with a small sigh she relented.

Her fingers were strong, her grip firm, yet her skin was soft against his. Before he could come to terms with the interesting dichotomy of her touch, she pulled away.

"Why did you want to see me?"

A woman who got straight to the point—he liked that. Callum shook himself free of the bemusement that this grown-up Miranda evoked. "Let's talk in my office. Would you like a cup of coffee?"

A picture flickered across his mind of a three-year-younger Miranda spooning several teaspoons of sugar into a cup of hot chocolate at her father's funeral.

"No, thanks." Her reply was clipped.

He glanced across to the receptionist. "Bring Ms. Owen a hot chocolate and I'll have coffee. Bring some extra sugar," he tacked on before placing his hand under Miranda's elbow and steering her along the corridor and into his spacious office.

"I'm not a child." She slanted him a look from beneath ridiculously long lashes, and a frisson of awareness startled Callum. "And I no longer drink chocolate."

"I can see you're not a child," Callum drawled, giving her a slow, sweeping perusal. "You've changed."

"You haven't." Miranda broke free of his hold and stepped away.

Still truculent. The heat of desire receded. "Maybe I'm mistaken," he mused. "I'd gotten the notion you'd grown up."

Chagrin filled her face. "I'm sorry."

Callum doubted she regretted her lack of courtesy. Yet when her gaze met his again, he read apprehension in the wide eyes. What was she frightened about? Even as he watched, she straightened her spine and the moment of vulnerability vanished.

He waved to the two boxy leather sofas facing each other under an immense wooden bookshelf packed with books. A tall Christmas tree covered with red bows and silver balls reminded Callum that it was the season of reconciliation. But Miranda's frozen face warned him that reconciliation was the last thing on her mind. And how could he blame her? Feeling carefully for words, he said, "Look, let's start over."

Ignoring him, Miranda passed the cozy seating arrangement heading for a round walnut conference table beside a wall of glass, where she slung her coat and black bag over the closest of the four chairs in a militant fashion.

Okay, so she was going to play this tough, all business. Callum gave a mental shrug and seated himself opposite her. "I asked you to come in because I have a proposition for you."

"A proposition?" Confusion clouded her features. "For me?"

He rocked his chair back. "You're a chef, right?" Hell, he knew she was—he'd paid for every cent of her exclusive training. Though he'd been surprised to learn she'd used her qualifications to gain employment at a popular pub chain rather than some fashionable, up-market café or boutique hotel. Before she could question how he knew she was a chef, he added, "Adrian told me you work at one of The Golden Goose outlets."

He'd stopped to inquire how young Adrian was getting along as a temporary driver for the company. The young man had been grateful for the vacation job and had revealed that Miranda dreamed of one day starting her own catering business. That had given Callum the perfect solution…a way to wipe Miranda Owen from his conscience forever. He gave her his most charming grin.

"Yes," she said guardedly.

She certainly wasn't blowing him away with an effusive response. Tipping his chair back to earth, he leaned forward and planted his elbows on the conference table. "Here's the deal. I plan to invite the outgoing chairman of a company Ironstone Insurance has recently taken over to a private dinner party at my home on Saturday night."

"He'll come?"

"Oh, yes. Gordon's staying on as a shareholder and I want to introduce him to the other directors. It's a celebration."

The melting brown eyes hardened. "I suppose that makes sense. Your brothers will want to get on side with a significant shareholder."

Callum stopped smiling. The merger had been *his* initiative—a successful one that would give Ironstone Insurance a strategic advantage over their competitors for years to come. And Gordon Harris had been even hungrier for the merger than the Ironstone family. Gordon wanted to retire, to take it easy. But Miranda's words stopped Callum from confessing that there was another, more celebratory reason for the dinner. That would only lead to a dig about protecting his assets.

Two fine lines furrowed her brow. "When you say Saturday...do you mean this week?" At his nod the lines deepened. "That doesn't leave much time."

He'd intended to railroad her into agreeing...and not leave any time for second thoughts.

"You don't think you can do it?" he challenged.

Angry fire kindled in the caramel eyes. "How many people?"

Hiding a grin of triumph, Callum rose to his feet and retrieved a manila folder from the polished expanse of his desk. Returning to the conference table, he dropped the file in front of her. "The details are all in there."

If he could start Miranda on the road to success, introduce her to some people, perhaps he'd be able to forget the hatred a pair of eighteen-year-old eyes had once held....

Or at least that had been the plan.

But having met Miranda again, he had a suspicion it wasn't going to be nearly that simple.

Standing behind her, all too conscious of the subtle fragrance of warm vanilla she exuded, Callum watched her elegant fingers flip the file open to the first page of the agreement his PA had prepared. Her shoulders stiffened as she read the figure he proposed to pay for a one-night job.

Satisfaction swept through him. She wouldn't refuse. His offer was too good. Helping Miranda get started in a business that must presently be nothing more than an impossible dream would be the perfect way to excise the disturbing memory of the wild accusations she'd flung at him.

You killed my father.

Of course he knew he hadn't, didn't he? Thomas Owen had killed himself once he realized there would be a trial—where he would almost certainly be found guilty on the overwhelming evidence against him. The courts showed no mercy against employees who stole from their employers. Thomas Owen would have known he was facing prison.

Yet Thomas's suicide had shaken Callum more than he cared to admit, leaving him haunted by a long shadow of guilt.

A legacy that he was determined to shake.

The black-and-white print on the paper in front of her blurred. Miranda was no longer aware of the maplewood furniture, or Callum's spacious office. Instead she experienced again the hot ball of misery that had burned constantly in her chest from the moment her father's PA had called with the news of her father's arrest.

Impossible.

But her father's assistant had insisted it was true: the police had been, and had taken her father away. Miranda needed to get hold of her mother urgently. Callum Ironstone would be issuing a press statement soon.

At barely eighteen, Miranda's first sighting of Callum Ironstone on television had swung rapidly from interest in the handsome devil with dark hair, a sensual mouth and eyes that held a mesmerizing intensity, to hatred when she'd heard what he had to say. The press statement had been brief but damning.

All of it lies. By the time it came to an end, Miranda was numb with disbelief.

There had been a mistake. Yet Callum Ironstone clearly didn't believe that. Rage had set in. Her father was *not* a thief.

Her father was granted bail, and emerged from the courthouse pale, shaken, but determined to clear his name. He had done nothing to justify the indignity the Ironstones had heaped upon him after two decades loyal service. Miranda had been confident it would all be sorted out.

But what followed had been traumatic. And, in the end, Thomas Owen simply gave up. Miranda could still remember the set, serious face of the policewoman who'd knocked on the door to break the news that her father was dead.

Then came the funeral. Miranda's hands grew clammy

and nerves fluttered in her stomach at the memory of the last terrible occasion she'd seen Callum Ironstone— it still made her cringe. Devastated by her father's death, her white-hot hatred boiling over, she'd confronted him in the stone-walled forecourt of the church.

The men beside him moved to cut her off. But she barged past them. Standing in front of Callum, she inspected him with angry eyes. "How could you take a good man's life and destroy it?" she'd challenged.

His jaw had set, and his face had grown harder than the marble tombstones in the churchyard. "He stole money from me."

"So you decided to teach him a lesson and humiliate him?"

A flush seared his carved cheekbones.

A man who resembled Callum—a brother perhaps— stepped forward. "Wait a minute, young lady—"

She brushed him aside, focusing all her emotion on Callum. "You killed him. You know that?" Tears of rage and pain spilled onto her cheeks. "He worked for you for twenty years, you gave him a gold watch, yet you never gave him a chance?"

Her father had been given no opportunity to avow his innocence. Callum had relentlessly pushed the police to the conclusion he'd wanted.

"You're overwrought," he said dismissively.

That made the ball of anger swell inside her. "And what's going to happen to my mother, my brother?" *Me?* "Now that you've destroyed our family?"

Callum gave her a stony stare. He raised a dark, devilish eyebrow and asked sardonically, "Finished?"

She hadn't been. Not by a long shot. But before she could vent any more he'd cut her off, snapping "Grow up" in a supercilious, condescending way that made her feel childishly inadequate.

Callum's words had been unkindly prophetic. She'd *had* to grow up, and quickly. Much as Miranda loved her mother, she knew Flo could never be practical. Overnight Miranda had become the adult in the home. There'd been no choice.

And now that same man was trying offer her money. A bribe?

"No."

Miranda felt Callum Ironstone start as she spoke. The sensitive skin of her nape prickled. A moment later a pair of bright blue eyes glared down at her. She'd never noticed their color before.

"What do you mean 'No'?"

Closing the folder with a snap, Miranda slammed it down against the glossy wood. "I mean I have no intention of accepting your blood money."

"Blood money?" he said softly, dangerously, and his gaze narrowed to an intimidating glitter.

She refused to be cowed. "Yes, blood money for what you did to my father."

"Your father *stole* from Ironstone Insurance."

Miranda shook her head. "You got the wrong man."

"Give me strength." Callum made a sharp, impatient sound. "You're not a child anymore."

"Stop it!" She put her hands over her ears.

Blue eyes bored into hers.

Feeling foolish, like the immature child he'd accused her of being almost three years ago, she uncovered her ears and dropped her hands out of his line of sight into her lap and curled them into fists.

With hard-won composure, Miranda said, "I'm sure being wealthy beyond belief means you've gotten used to throwing money around to make all your problems go away. But not this time. I won't take a cent."

His jaw had hardened. A shiver closely allied to fear feathered down her spine as he bit out, "Don't you think it's rather late for fine principles?"

Miranda stared at him blankly. "What do you mean?"

"You've conveniently forgotten?"

"Forgotten what?"

His lips compressed into an impatient line. "Taking money from me."

"That's a lie—I've never taken a cent from you."

She'd die of starvation before she did that. He'd caused her family so much grief.

After the funeral, the house where Miranda had grown up with its apple orchard and paddocks had, by necessity, been sold along with her horse Troubadour and Adrian's expensive racing bicycles. Her mother had never gotten used to the cramped terrace house in a rundown street south of the Thames that the three of them had moved into. Even with Adrian away during the term at the exclusive boarding school Flo had refused to countenance him leaving, space was tight.

Thankfully the lump sum Ironstone Insurance had paid out after her father's death had been invested wisely, the interest paying for Adrian's and Miranda's education as well as a modest retainer to support her mother, though it left Flo only a shadow of the lifestyle she'd once taken for granted.

Yet as Miranda's gaze remained locked with Callum's, a deep sense of foreboding closed around her heart.

"So where did the funds for Greenacres come from?" he asked, naming the exclusive culinary school she'd attended. He held up two fingers. "Two years. And your brother's schooling at St. Martin's…"

No, please God.

It had been a shock to discover her parents' precarious financial position after her father's death. But at least her father had kept his life insurance up-to-date.

Voice trembling, she said, "My father's life insurance policy paid f—"

"Your father's suicide voided the policy."

"No!" She realized she was shaking her head wildly. "That can't be true."

Yet even as she denied it, her brain worked furiously. What he said sounded perfectly logical. From the stories her father had told about repudiated claims she knew about fine print. So why had the company paid out the policy after his death when they'd fired her father…had publicly branded him a criminal? And why had she never questioned the settlement?

Because she'd trusted her father not to do anything that would leave her…them…so horribly exposed. Surely he would never have killed himself, cutting them off from the last lifeline available to them?

But he had.

Why had he killed himself, and abandoned them when there'd been so much to live for? It wasn't as if he'd been guilty. Yet Thomas Owen had left his family vulnerable. And this man, a man she detested, had bailed them out.

Why?

She must have said it out loud. Because Callum shifted from one foot to the other and discomfort flashed in his eyes. Her gaze sharpened. He thought she'd been asking why he'd supported them…and that made him uncomfortable. The next *why?* popped into her head: what did Callum have to feel guilty about?

The answer hit her like a bolt of lightning, filling her with icy shock. Had it been a payoff? So they wouldn't sue Ironstone Insurance? No. Her mother would never have accepted that.

Or would she have? Miranda wavered. Things had been pretty dire after her father's death. Had her mother been tempted?

"You can't have paid for everything." *Please, please, let it not be so.*

Something like pity softened his gaze. "Do you want to see the invoices?"

Trepidation made her mouth go dry. "And the allowance my mother receives every month?" She paused. But she had to ask…had to know. "Are you paying that, too?"

His eyes told her yes.

It was too much. Miranda's stomach started to churn again. The sick feeling that had unsettled her earlier swept over her like a tidal wave.

She turned her head away and stared out the sheet-glass window over the cloud-shrouded city where the light was rapidly waning. Miranda shivered. How much had Callum paid? How much did her family owe the man responsible for her father's death? And how was she ever going to pay it back?

Just trying to figure how much money was involved made her feel all weak inside. Jerkily, she staggered to her feet and yanked her coat on, hugging its warmth around her. Slinging her bag over her shoulder, she faced him, her head held high. "I don't want this job— I don't want anything from you. And you can stop the allowance to my mother from today—she doesn't want your money, either."

She stumbled across his office. The expanse of carpet stretched forever and the door seemed a long way away.

As she grasped the doorknob, he spoke from behind her. "If I were you, I'd check that your mother feels the same way you do—you may be in for a surprise."

Two

Outside the towering glass world of Ironstone Insurance darkness had fallen. Huddled in her coat, Miranda hurried toward the bus stop. Not even the festivity of the Christmas lights twinkling through the winter gloom could lift her spirits.

A chill wind swirled around her legs as Callum's words reverberated though her head. *If I were you, I'd check that your mother feels the same way you do—you may be in for a surprise.*

Her mother couldn't have possibly known...wouldn't have hidden this from her.

Homeward-bound traffic rushed past, and Miranda fumbled in her bag for her cell phone before punching the call button with an icy, shaking finger. "Mum?"

"Hello, darling." Flo sounded cheerfully vague.

"I'm home from my tea with Sorrel. What are we having for dinner?"

The mundane thought disoriented Miranda for an instant. Dinner? Who cared? She gathered her scattered thoughts together.

"I just saw Callum Ironstone. He says Dad's insurance never paid out and that Callum paid for my studies and Adrian's schooling himself." Reaching the deserted bus stop, Miranda halted and held her breath as she waited for her mother's denial.

Instead, an ominous silence. *Her mother had known.*

"Mum?"

Nothing.

"Flo—" Miranda resorted to her mother's name as she'd been doing more and more recently "—please tell me it's a lie." Unable to stand still, she took a few unsettled steps out of the shelter and paced restlessly along the sidewalk. Miranda closed her eyes, willing her mother to deny it.

"Darling…"

As her mother's breathy voice trailed away, Miranda knew Callum had told her the truth. There had never been a life insurance payout. Her gloved hands tightened round the phone and despair set in. The same evil little wind whirled around her ears, and she shivered. Opening her eyes, she glimpsed her bus trundling past the stop.

"Wait," she called, running after it.

"What did you say, darling?" Flo sounded alarmed over the open line.

"I just missed my bus." Miranda slowed to a standstill. Her next bus wasn't due for half an hour and she would be freezing by the time she got home. She wanted to howl to the dark sky. Or burst into tears. But what would that help? The phone pressed against her ear, Miranda backed up and sagged tiredly against the bus shelter, staring bleakly into the shadows.

"Darling, the Ironstones owed it to us."

"I don't want money from them." *Especially not from him.* "I want them to take responsibility for what they did to Dad." *To us.*

"This is their way of taking responsibility, by paying us money."

But it was Callum who had paid.

The chilling thought that had occurred to her in Callum's office resurfaced. Sucking the cold, damp air into her lungs, she plunged on. "Mum, was it supposed to be a payoff from the company so that we—and Dad's estate—wouldn't sue?"

"Darling, no!"

The tension that had tightened her stomach into knots eased a little. "So you didn't sign any settlement agreement?"

"There was a document," her mother admitted, "but it wasn't anything important."

"Are you sure?" Miranda prompted urgently.

"Only that I'd use the money for your and Adrian's education…and for housekeeping."

"That's all?"

"And there was a little something for me each month, too," Flo added reluctantly.

"Perhaps I should look at that agreement," said Miranda darkly.

"Oh, darling, I don't even know where it is anymore.

It's nothing important. Let it go. The Ironstones took responsibility for what happened."

"Not the Ironstones. Callum Ironstone."

It had become important to make that distinction. And Miranda wished she had seen that missing agreement. She strongly suspected that Callum had rushed to the grieving widow with a contract that precluded legal action—against him, his family and their company.

And no doubt the cash had been the price of his guilty conscience. Money had freed him from what he'd done.

It made her see red.

But how could she make Flo understand she wanted Callum Ironstone to sweat blood? And his brothers, too. *And* his father, who'd been chairman at the time Miranda's father had been framed.

But more than anything it was Callum she wanted to see suffer—because he'd been her father's boss. It had been Callum who'd made the decision that had ruined her father's life. He had summarily dismissed Thomas Owen, an employee with twenty years' service to Ironstone Insurance, had him arrested, charged with a crime he hadn't committed, and then had publicly humiliated a humble, gentle man.

"Darling, Adrian says he needs a word with you."

Her mother's voice brought her back to the dark London street. Miranda shivered again. A second later her brother's voice came over the line.

"Mir?"

He sounded so young. He was the reason she'd set foot in Callum Ironstone's moneyed world today. It seemed an age since her only worry had been about what Adrian might have done. In less than an hour, Callum had turned her world upside down.

How was she ever going to find the money to pay back Callum?

"What is it?" she asked dully. The long day on her feet in The Golden Goose topped by the meeting with Callum had sapped her strength. All she craved was a warm home and a hot meal that she hadn't had to cook. And someone to hold her, to tell her that everything would be okay.

None of that would happen. She'd been cutting the heating to a minimum to save money, so the terrace house would be barely warm, and there would be no hot meal unless she cooked it herself.

Adrian interrupted her musing. "Listen, sis, I need you to lend me some money. Can you draw it out on your way home?"

"*More* money?" Only last night she'd given him fifty pounds for a night out with his friends. At least he was due to be paid on Friday. It galled her that she was actually grateful for the job he had with Ironstone Insurance, but she needed that money back. Desperately. "How much do you need this time?"

"Uh…"

A sharp edge of unease knifed her at his hesitation. Her voice rising, she asked, "How much?"

The amount made her breath catch. "Good grief, Adrian, I don't have that kind of money." Even the monthly housekeeping fund was almost empty. "What have you done?"

"Nothing, I promise you. Nothing major. I'm just helping—"

"You haven't been gambling again?"

A couple of months back Adrian had developed an addiction to blackjack, and had started frequenting casinos. His talk of developing a system that couldn't lose had struck terror into Miranda. Now images of bull-necked debt collectors threatening to break her baby brother's fingers crowded her mind. "You promised not to go back there." A promise he'd resented, but she'd insisted on it before she'd agreed to pay off his debts. "Are you in danger?"

"No!" He gave a half laugh. "I haven't been gambling. Honestly, you should hear yourself, sis—you're worse than Mum."

Flo was too soft on him. That was part of the reason he'd gotten so close to trouble. Miranda knew it was time he grew up.

"I can't just keep giving you handouts, Adrian. You still owe me the money I lent you last ni—"

"I know, I know. You're the best sister in the world."

Miranda hesitated. "So what's this money for?"

"Oh, don't nag, sis. It's to help someone in trouble," he said cagily.

What had happened to being the best sister in the world? "Hardly nagging, given the amount you want. Can't this person find someone else to help them?"

"I've promised." Adrian sounded impatient. "It's going to be hard to back out now."

"You should've thought of that before you pledged my money."

Then wished she'd bitten her tongue when he said, "Just forget it, okay. I'll find someone else to help me—maybe I can get an advance against my pay."

And place her further in Callum's debt? Over her dead

body! Miranda contemplated the amount in her savings account. Every cent she'd squirreled away for the past fourteen months. The extra jobs. The overtime. All painfully accumulated to allow her a few months of breathing space when she finally handed in her notice at The Golden Goose and started her own catering business.

It was a pittance compared to the overwhelming amount she needed to repay Callum. Her dream was already history.

She suppressed a sigh.

But at least Adrian wasn't gambling. He wasn't in trouble. Despite her fears, she hadn't been called in to Ironstone's because he'd done anything stupid. And now he'd promised to help a friend. Weren't those precisely the kind of values she'd tried to instill in him?

The time had come to start trusting his judgment; otherwise he'd never grow up.

But, oh, boy, it was hard.

"Let me see what I can do."

A pause. Then, "Thanks, sis."

"But it will be a loan, Adrian," she cautioned. This wasn't going the way of all the other sums she'd "lent" her brother. "Your friend needs to understand that. When will I get it back?"

"Soon," he replied, with a worrying vagueness that reminded her uncomfortably of Flo. "He'll get paid— probably at the end of the next fortnight."

"I'll hold you to that." Hitting the end-call button with unaccustomed ferocity, Miranda noticed that it had started to drizzle. She shivered in the gloom. Her dream had just received a death knell, so why bother about a bit of rain?

Headlights cut through the drizzle, tires hissing as a

sleek car veered toward the curb. Miranda turned away, not in the mood for unwelcome harassment.

A window lowered. "Jump in."

Callum!

Miranda hunched her shoulders and ignored him.

A door slammed, and a moment later an arm landed across her shoulders, surrounding her with warmth and comfort. Miranda was tempted to lean into his broad chest and draw the strength she could. She squared her shoulders. This was Callum Ironstone. Her enemy.

"I'm parked illegally. Let's go before I get ticketed."

She shrugged him off. "I'll wait for my bus, thanks."

He glanced up at the electronic information board above the bus shelter. "Looks like a long wait. Or would you rather freeze on principle?"

She hated that he managed to make her sound like a petulant child. Reluctantly Miranda allowed him to take her elbow—ignoring the sudden prickles of sensation—and steer her to his car, a ghost-gray Daimler. Opening the door for her, he stood back while she clambered in.

A delicious frisson rippled down her spine as the warm interior embraced her. Turning her head away as if in rejection of the seductive comfort Callum's wealth offered, Miranda stared blindly out the side window as he settled in the driver's seat beside her.

"Where to?"

The weight of Callum's gaze settled on Miranda.

"Home."

"Not The Golden Goose?"

"I've finished for the day." No point revealing what a tussle she'd had getting time off.

Instead of starting the car, he said, "I'd have thought you'd have used your qualifications to land something better than a job at a place like that."

She shrugged and stared through the windshield at traffic that had slowed to a crawl as the drizzle turned to rain. No point defending The Golden Goose. Not when what he said was true and she couldn't wait to escape.

Although any chance of that had gone up in smoke the moment he'd told her about her father's life insurance being nonexistent.

"It was the closest job I could find to home." That meant less spent on transport, less time commuting, which gave more hours to work overtime. "It's only a short bus ride away," she said tiredly. "It pays the bills."

And that was what mattered. Making sure Adrian's future education was taken care of, repaying Callum and saving enough money to look after Flo. Until she'd repaid Callum she couldn't even think of opening her own catering business.

He must have heard her sigh because he said gently, "I know your family is short of cash. You should've accepted my proposition—who knows, you might have impressed people and gotten a few more catering jobs to ease the hardship."

Did he have any idea what kind of temptation he'd dangled in front of her? How hard it had been to refuse?

She eyed him warily as he accelerated into the stream of traffic. Yes, he probably did. "Now I believe everything I've heard about you."

"Everything? You shouldn't believe everything." She caught a lightning flash of wicked blue eyes before he turned his attention back to the road. "Some rumors are nothing more than wild speculation."

Ignoring the innuendo underlying the humor, Miranda said hastily, "That you have the ability to home in on what people want and then use it against them?" And now he was doing that to her.

Studying his profile, she took in the straight nose jutting out with masculine arrogance, quickly bypassing his generous mouth. Miranda had no idea how he'd gotten a glimpse into her soul, her deepest desire, but somehow the sneaky bastard had.

If the offer had come from anyone else…

"I'm only asking you to cater a dinner party for me. How can I use that against you?"

"I'm sure you'll find a way," she said darkly, thinking of how he'd pressured her poor mother into signing an agreement that Flo wouldn't have had a hope of understanding. No doubt it cleared the Ironstone family of all liability. Helplessness filled Miranda. How could she fight such a man?

"So why don't you prove to me that I didn't waste money putting you through cooking school?"

"Culinary school," she corrected.

"If you say so." He slowed as a light turned red. He swiveled his head, and his gaze met hers. "If it makes it easier, think of it this way. You owe it to me."

"I *owe* it to you?" The gall of the man. "I owe you nothing." *He* owed *her*. For taking her father away, for ruining her family.

Her anger and confusion trapped her. She wanted him to hurt as much as she hurt, wanted to force him to take responsibility for what he'd done. But not by making her family his pet charity. And the only thing she truly desired he could never give back.

Her father.

In the meantime, all the money Callum had given Flo had to be paid back. And once that had been accomplished, Miranda hoped the guilt of knowing what he'd done killed him.

"If you could, you'd gather what cash you could and hurl it at me right now, wouldn't you?" That rogue eyebrow quirked up again.

"Maybe," she said grudgingly, resenting the fact that he could read her so well.

He shook his head. "What a wasted effort."

"Easy for you to say."

"It will take you forever." As the lights changed, he put the car back into gear and pulled away. "You should put away your bitterness and grab this opportunity with both hands. Who knows where it could lead?"

And make a deal with this devil?

But she turned his words over in her mind. She'd already accepted it would take years to save what she owed him. And even if she did, it didn't look like his conscience would keep him awake every night of his life. Callum Ironstone probably didn't have a conscience.

So why was she tying herself into knots to pay back money he and his family wouldn't even miss? Why *not* take the bloody job?

The money was amazing. It would almost cover the amount Adrian wanted from her. Almost. If she cut corners on the household budget for the next month, she wouldn't even need to take anything from her savings.

Temptation beckoned. He'd be paying the money to

a caterer anyway. This wasn't charity. It looked perfectly straightforward.

Too perfectly straightforward.

"Why did you offer me the contract?"

"The caterer I usually use is too busy. Christmas." He gestured to the fairy lights sparkling through the rain. "And I've been too busy to hire someone else. Seeing Adrian at work this morning reminded me of you—I knew you'd have the skills. But if you don't want it, I'll find someone else."

She ought to refuse. No good would come out of this association. She even rounded her mouth to say "No."

Then she thought about Adrian, his frustration as he'd said, "Forget it." She thought about delving into her hard-earned cash to help his friend out. She *needed* the cash Callum offered.

Miranda took a deep breath and said, "Okay, I'll do it."

And when he smiled, a slow satisfied curve on his lips, Miranda hoped she hadn't made a terrible mistake.

Callum gazed across the refectory-style table at the woman he'd been fighting to ignore all evening.

Without success. Not only had Miranda cooked a meal that had made his mouth water, she'd carefully supervised the staff she'd hired, popping in and out of the dining room to check on the wine and that everything was running smoothly.

She'd even distracted him from Petra Harris, Gordon's daughter, something he'd never foreseen. Especially not tonight, of all nights.

Callum told himself it couldn't be Miranda's appearance that had him tied up in knots. Instead of a traditional white chef's jacket and herringbone trousers, she wore a plain black dress, her hair up in a knot and no glitter in sight. By rights she should've been eclipsed by every other woman in the room, and she should've looked plain and drab.

Yet she didn't.

The black only served to highlight the creamy perfection of her skin. No jewelry adorned the deliciously smooth line of her throat. And the only gold that glinted in the glow of the discreet uplighters adorning his dining room were the bits of hair that had escaped and framed her face, making her eyes look wider and more mysterious than ever.

Desire leaped within him, quickly followed by disbelief. This couldn't be happening to him.

He narrowed his eyes. This was the same girl who had once screamed at him like a banshee, accusing him of murdering her father...so why the hell couldn't he stop looking at her? He had his life—his future—all mapped out. And it didn't include Miranda Owen.

Forcing his attention back to Gordon Harris's daughter seated beside him, Callum vowed not to let himself be distracted. Hell, he'd planned to propose to Petra after dinner. In his study. Just the two of them. A quick ten-minute tête-à-tête, before announcing it in spectacular fashion to the world—he'd even invited a journalist tonight who covered the society pages. The ring box was in his pocket. Ready. Waiting. It wasn't only the merger with Gordon's company he'd planned to reveal tonight....

He gazed at the woman he'd decided would make him a perfect wife.

"The food tonight is out of this world." Petra smiled

at him, revealing sparkling white teeth, and her fingers brushed his.

"I couldn't agree more." Callum tried to convince himself that powder-blue eyes were every bit as appealing as the color of melted caramel, and failed dismally. To his consternation, there was no spark of electrical charge from the brush of her fingers, either.

"Would you like crème caramel or strawberry cheesecake?" Miranda asked.

Adrenaline surged through him. He could've sworn he'd sensed Miranda's approach even before she spoke beside him, and every nerve went on red alert as he picked up the subtle scent of vanilla. Her innocent offer of dessert made him instantly desire far more carnal pleasures. Damn, what the hell was happening?

"Strawberry cheesecake for me," said Petra, giving Miranda an easy smile. "I was just complimenting Callum on the fabulous spread tonight."

"Thank you." A flush of pleasure lit Miranda's cheeks, making her look even more downright sexy. "May I suggest a Sauterne or ice wine to accompany it?"

"Ooh, I'll have ice wine. Sounds delicious."

"I'll bring you a clean glass." Miranda stretched past Callum to remove Petra's wineglass. The tension within him twisted higher as she brushed against him. When she reached forward, the black fabric of her dress tightened across the gentle valley of her belly, accentuating the feminine indent of her waist and the rounded curve of her hip. He couldn't tear his gaze away.

She straightened. "What would you like?"

What would he like?

Thank God she couldn't read his mind. She'd run a

mile. He glanced up and connected with the melting eyes that so entranced him. Prosaically, she repeated the choices.

"Crème caramel, please," he muttered, his throat suddenly thick as a mental image of himself offering her a spoonful of the rich dessert flashed through his mind. He visualized her pink tongue delicately licking the creamy texture off the spoon, her lashes flicking up. Her eyes, glowing and golden, promising him untold delights and—

"That's all?"

"All?" he croaked, then realized his eyes were raking her body, so he jerked his attention away.

It wasn't all; he wanted so much more…

God, this was stupid! And the sparks had been sizzling ever since she had arrived earlier in the evening. He'd found himself hanging around the kitchen—he'd offered her a glass of Merlot to give himself an excuse to watch her—until the arrival of the two women he'd hired to serve his guests had sent him scuttling for his study and a shot of whiskey.

He'd been grateful when his half brothers, Jack and Hunter, had arrived with their dinner partners so that he could escape her thrall. Gordon and Petra had come soon after.

There was nothing special about Miranda. She wasn't nearly as beautiful as Petra—and she was extremely prickly and difficult—yet she intrigued him.

When last had he experienced anything like this?

Guilt ate at him. He was conscious of the ring he'd chosen lying heavy in his pocket. How the hell was he supposed to propose to Petra when his headspace was full of Miranda?

He glanced around the table, claustrophobia closing in on him. His brother, Fraser, gave him a grin.

This was his coup—he'd organized every last detail. There'd always been healthy competition between him and his brother, Fraser, and his two half brothers. Being the youngest of the four, he'd been last to make it onto the board of the company. But he'd intended to be the first to marry.

Yet now that the time had come to propose to Petra…he couldn't. Instead he wanted to bolt.

Perhaps this inexplicable crazy lust for Miranda was nothing more than a flight response to his carefully planned siege of Petra.

He drew a gulp of air in relief. Fear. That's what this was. It wasn't about Miranda at all—she was simply a convenient excuse.

He gave Petra an uncomfortable smile. "Enjoying yourself?"

Her father leaned forward. "We all are."

A chorus of agreement followed.

"Such a pity the snowed-up roads prevented your parents from joining us."

Callum seized on his parents' absence. How could he announce his engagement without them present? They'd never forgive him. He scanned the faces around the table. Everyone *was* having a fantastic time—except for him.

Under Petra's smile, he shifted. He knew Gordon had great expectations for this relationship with Petra. Callum hadn't slept with her yet, though both he and

Petra had known they were headed for the bedroom; he'd wanted the contracts signed…and a ring on her finger first.

He stuck one hand into his jacket pocket.

"Crème caramel," Miranda announced.

Just her husky tone was enough to make him start at the want that resurged. Taking his hand out of his pocket, he stared at the dessert she'd placed on the starched white-damask tablecloth in front of him. Creamy custard…and caramelized sugar the same rich golden brown as her eyes.

He picked up a spoon.

The dessert was smooth on his tongue. Sweet and silky. With a hint of vanilla. The caramel rich and tangy.

Would Miranda taste as delectable?

Hell! And he was getting hard just thinking about it. Callum shifted uncomfortably and forced himself to focus on the dinner conversation.

In the kitchen, Miranda rested her head against the cool, hand-painted Italian tiles and suppressed the urge to swear violently.

"Are you okay?" Jane, one of the women Callum had hired to help tonight, touched her shoulder lightly.

Miranda straightened. "I'm fine."

But she wasn't. Something had happened out there in the dining room—something she didn't understand. Callum had looked at her, and she had responded like a sunflower greeting the morning sun. And the realization pierced her heart like a shard of ice.

Please, not him.

She hated him.

Miranda reached with a shaky hand for what was left of the glass of red wine Callum had poured her earlier, and drained it. Jane picked up a bottle and silently topped her glass.

"Thanks." Miranda smiled at the other woman. "Believe it or not, I never drink when I'm working."

"It's a good vintage." Jane helped herself to a wine-glass out the cupboard. After filling the glass she lifted it. "Very nice."

Miranda felt a rush of gratitude. "Thank you." She took a sip and set the glass down. "I'm okay now. Let's get on with the coffees."

By the time she went out into the dining room, she told herself she had her reactions in check. The wine had warmed her, dissolving the icy chill. As she passed the end of the long dining table, an older man asked her for a card and Miranda flushed when she realized she didn't have any. Something she would remedy tomorrow.

Moving up the table, she was breathlessly aware of Callum's dark, brooding presence at the head. Given that he looked devilishly good in a black dinner jacket with a pristine white shirt, keeping her resolve was far from easy.

She smiled at the woman sitting beside him who had complimented her cooking, and tried to ignore the way the woman's fingers brushed Callum's dinner-jacketed arm when she made a point.

After one searing look from Callum, Miranda averted her gaze, and turned away, making sure to busy herself down at the other end of the table.

This powerful awareness of Callum was a complication she didn't need.

* * *

Thank God dinner was over.

After the planning he'd put into the evening, the end was an anticlimax. Callum could hardly wait to see Petra, her father and his family out the front door. The confusion in Petra's expectant eyes made him feel like an utter bastard.

"I'll talk to you tomorrow," he said, ushering her off behind her father.

Talk to her? And say what? How in heaven's name was he supposed to explain something he didn't even understand himself?

He justified that it could've been worse. What if he'd already been engaged to Petra when this urge to chase Miranda like a hound after a bitch in heat had taken hold? It made him go stone-cold.

This second-thoughts stuff must be normal. Wedding-ring fright. But he wouldn't run away. He'd deal with it the same way he did every other problem he met: head-on. Confront this inconvenient lust, the need to indulge in one last chase. Get Miranda out his system. Then marry Petra exactly as he'd planned.

Simple.

Closing the door behind the last of his guests, Callum went to find Miranda. Anticipation lent lightness to his step. He peered into the library—his favorite haunt—but it was empty. Not that he'd expected to discover her there.

He finally tracked her down in the scullery tucked away at the far end of the kitchen. Miranda was busy stacking the dirty dishes into the drawers of the state-of-the-art dishwasher.

She'd donned an apron, an absurd white bit of cotton

with a ruffle along the hem below a bib that barely covered her front. It lent the black dress she wore the naughty severity of a French maid costume.

Callum breathed deeply. "What are you doing?"

She kept her eyes down. "Cleaning up."

Given the boiling heat that simmered in him, her lack of interest irritated. He marched forward and said more stridently than he intended, "Where's the help I hired?"

"The *help* you hired?" She straightened, affront glittering in her eyes. "They have names. Emily and Jane. They're people. Emily was tired—she's been up since dawn and she has a long way to go to get home."

"So where's the other one?"

One finely arched eyebrow rose. "You mean Jane?"

He nodded impatiently. "Yes, Jane."

"Her brother picked her up."

"And even though you've been at work preparing food long before they arrived, they left you with all the mess?"

"They cleared most of it." She gestured to the adjoining kitchen. "And the leftover food has been itemized and frozen. I'm just packing in the coffee cups and dessert dishes, Emily and Jane—" she used their names pointedly "—have already run the dishwasher twice, and unpacked it."

She strode past him into the kitchen and looked around. "All nice and tidy, see?"

Callum followed and leaned back against the center island. Folding his arms across his chest, he said, "And what about you? Don't you have to hurry home?"

"Of course." She stalked across to a row of hooks and picked off her bag and a black woolen coat. Dropping the bag and coat on the center island, she unzipped a side pocket and retrieved her cell phone. "But I've been paid an astronomical amount for tonight's dinner—I'm making sure you get your money's worth."

His money's worth?

The words taunted, especially from a woman wearing such a starkly erotic outfit. With an effort he focused his attention back on her face. "It's what I always pay."

Her eyes went round. He could see her thoughts buzzing as she calculated. "And you entertain often?"

"Yes, but it's work." As well as being part of the rationale for courting Petra. He needed a wife.

And Petra would be perfect.

He only needed to propose....

Yet he couldn't imagine Petra looking so innocently erotic in the black-and-white getup that Miranda was wearing. Or having this effect on him. His erection throbbed painfully behind the concealing fabric of his pants.

Callum shut his eyes.

And opened them to find Miranda staring at him. The silence in the kitchen pounded in his ears. Her mouth was lush, her eyes meltingly seductive. Driven by an urge he couldn't resist, he took a step forward.

His hands settled on her upper arms, the flesh soft and giving under his fingers. Hoarsely, he asked, "I've been wanting to taste you all night. Are you as sweet as the crème caramel?"

Callum gave her a moment to object. Time stopped. She didn't move. Or say anything. His hands slid around her and he pulled her to him. The warm scent of vanilla enfolded him, so feminine, so seductive.

He took the phone out of her unresisting hand and set it down on the island.

Her lips remained closed as he kissed her, not accepting, but not rejecting him, either.

Callum raised his head, and looked down into her face. There was a startled awareness in her eyes. His mouth slanted as he said, "Not as sweet as I'd expected."

She started to say something, and in a flash he bent his head and took advantage of her parted lips.

His tongue sank in, and he plundered the warm, private cave. He'd lied. She tasted sweeter than sin. Of rich red wine, spicy cinnamon and seductive woman.

When her tongue swirled around his, Callum gave a moan of satisfaction.

Instantly Miranda's body softened against his, melting into him. Heat swept over him. His hands pressed into the small of her back, drawing her against the blatant evidence of his arousal.

She didn't pull away as he'd half expected.

His fingers played with the bow that fastened her apron behind her back and it came loose. "Do you know how sexy this outfit is?" he murmured against her mouth.

"An apron is sexy?"

"Oh, God…*yes*."

She laughed, a lilting sound that drove him wild. He put his mouth over hers, tasting the musical notes. Ah, but she was delicious.

Her hands came up between them and pushed against his chest. "I shouldn't be doing this."

Callum let her back away. "Why not?"

"Because."

He started to smile. "Because why?"

"You're going to make me say it, aren't you?"

His smile faded and he tensed, bracing himself for the accusations, ready to argue that actions had consequences, that wrongdoing couldn't escape unpunished, that she had to let it go.

Her eyes warred with his. "I don't like you."

Relief surged through him. They weren't about to discuss the circumstances of her father's death while desire raged through him and blood pounded in his head. He wanted her back in his arms. It was insane. "Liking me has nothing to do with *this*."

He whirled Miranda round and pinned her against the island, his thigh between hers. Miranda gasped at the pressure against a sensitive area, her fingers digging into his upper arms.

This time Callum gave no quarter, kissing her until they were both breathless. By the time he'd finished, she was clinging to him.

"You love that, don't you?" Some demon within him demanded a concession from her.

But she remained mute, her eyes sparkling with defiance, her cheeks flushed with high wild color.

He hoisted her up onto the silver countertop, ignoring her squawk of protest. One of her pumps clattered to the tiled floor.

"My shoe."

"Never mind your shoe." He stepped between her parted thighs, forcing her dress's hemline higher, and bending his head he placed open-mouthed kisses against the too-tempting smooth skin of her neck.

Her head lolled back, granting him unrestricted access. Lower down his hands ran along her nylon-clad thighs, he ruched her dress up farther, and when she didn't stop him, Callum moved in for the kill.

Stroking her thigh, his fingers encountered a lacy stocking edge…then soft, satiny bare skin. He groaned as he realized she wasn't wearing panty hose.

"Grief, woman, you know how to fuel a man's fantasies," he growled close to her ear as he caressed the tender flesh of her inner thigh.

Miranda only moaned, her hands knotting in his shirt.

Callum was past coherent thought. He stripped off first his dinner jacket, then ripping the snaps of his dinner shirt apart, let it fall on the stainless steel slab behind her.

"Oh."

The sound of wonder that escaped her as she gazed boldly at his bare chest made him feel like a god. He cupped her face in his hands and kissed her mouth with slow, deliberate intent, outlining the shape with the tip of his tongue. Miranda responded with hunger, and what had started out as a leisurely kiss erupted into no-holds-barred ardor.

Callum ran his hands under the loosened apron, over breasts and stomach still covered by her dress, down along her legs. He paused to caress the hollows behind her stockinged knees, then retraced the path to where the nylons ended.

After hesitating only a moment, he let his fingers drift higher until he encountered silky panties. His fingertips slid under the edge and slipped into her moist heat.

She arched against his hand. His fingers delved deeper. Her hips rocked invitingly. He buried his head in the valley between her breasts and tongued the soft hollow. Her fingers dug into his hair and pulled him closer. A roaring hunger surged through him.

This could only end one way.

With his free hand, Callum reached for his belt and zipper.

"So sweet."

He shoved down his trousers and briefs with impatient hands, then eased her closer, her thighs splayed around his hips.

The stainless steel was shockingly cold and hard. "You must be freezing."

She shook her head, arched back…and shivered. "Wait."

He stilled at her command. Disappointment, hot and sharp as a blade, twisted in his gut. Slowly, with aching regret, he withdrew his hand from her warmth. "Why are you stopping?"

Bewilderment made him raise his head. It changed when he saw the foil package that lay in the palm of her hand, her open bag upended on the bench. God. He hadn't even thought about a condom. But she'd had the presence of mind to protect them both.

He took it, tore it open and sheathed himself. "Are you sure, Miranda?"

She nodded, and her arms reached for him.

Euphoria filled him. Callum grabbed his shirt, bunched it up in a fist, and wedged it gently in behind her to pad her from the counter edge.

Then, unable to restrain himself another second, he positioned himself and pushed forward into the woman who'd been driving him wild all night.

Three

Miranda opened her eyes, caught one glimpse of the naked male torso she was snuggled up to, and a wave of mortification crashed over her.

Callum.

Oh, no! What had she done?

She lay rigid, not daring to breathe. Thankfully the man she'd fallen so foolishly into bed with last night was still asleep. Miranda suppressed a groan. And after that impulsive coupling up against the kitchen counter, she'd let him carry her upstairs—and make love to her all over again.

Let him? If anything she'd been a willing, totally wanton participant. It made her feel sick with guilt.

She cracked her eyes open and caught a glimpse of the dark mahogany bedhead. Beyond, pale winter-morning light spilled through sash windows into the bedroom. *His* bedroom.

Soon he'd waken. The idea of him finding her naked in his bed filled her with horror. Taking a deep breath, she inched her leg toward the edge of the bed. He stirred. Miranda froze.

After long, dragging seconds she slowly relaxed. He hadn't woken. Shifting her weight to the edge of the mattress, she was conscious of her heartbeat drumming loudly in her chest.

An arm slid over her, and a large male hand closed familiarly over the top of her breast. Miranda forced herself to keep absolutely still.

Oh, help!

What to do now?

Her first impulse to push that possessive hand away and leap out of his bed receded as the strong male fingers stilled.

Affront mixed with adrenaline. He'd gone back to sleep!

Eyes darting to and fro, Miranda formulated a plan. Her dress and knickers lay in a pile on the floor. Her shoes were nowhere in sight—probably scattered across the kitchen floor. She shuddered at the memories that evoked.

How could she have done such things with this man?

She blocked it all out and turned her mind back to what dominated her now: escape.

If she rolled out of bed, she could scoop up her clothes and make a run for it. With luck she'd be out the bedroom door before he'd wake and realize she'd gone. Downstairs she'd grab her shoes, her coat and her bag— which should be on the bench top where she'd left it the evening before. An image of the contents—emergency condoms, lipstick, hairbrush, wallet, cell phone—scattered over the countertop flashed through her mind and she groaned silently.

Cell phone, she thought. Her breath caught. Her mother!

She never stayed out all night. Flo would be worried sick, had probably left a dozen anxious messages.

But at least she'd be able to come out of this disastrous encounter knowing she couldn't be pregnant—or worse. Although right now that seemed small compensation for last night's stupidity.

Miranda hauled in a shallow breath and readied herself to flee.

"So you're still alive?" Provocative fingers explored the rise of her hip. "For a moment I thought you'd given up breathing—that you might require a little mouth-to-mouth resuscitation."

Callum's lazy confidence cast despair into Miranda. He'd probably been awake from the start. There'd never been any chance of a hasty getaway. Bastard.

She curled into a tight ball, refusing to acknowledge him.

"Come now." He tightened his hold, rolling her over onto her back. Wide-awake blue eyes stared down into hers. "It was better than that—in fact it was bloody fantastic…for both of us." Satisfaction oozed from that throaty growl.

Miranda careened between wishing she could actually expire from humiliation and a fierce urge to murder the naked man beside her.

Conceited ape!

Well, there was only one way to get out of this situation—and that was with what little dignity she could muster.

She sat up, making sure she took a large swath of the sheet with her to keep her breasts covered and tossed her hair back. "Don't flatter yourself. It wasn't *that* good."

His eyes ignited with laughter. "You've forgotten so soon? My sweet, you were *begging*."

A flush of heat stained her cheeks, then spread across her entire body. Damn. She couldn't deny it. But he was despicable.

Since when had she ever harbored any illusions about Callum Ironstone? She constrained herself to a look of disdainful dislike.

Under the sheet his hand came to life, playing knowingly over her all-too-responsive flesh as it edged onto the swell of her breast.

"Stop it." Her arm lashed out, knocking the offending hand away, and with horror she realized the sheet had fallen, too.

"Nice." His eyes turned molten. His hand came up and he stroked the underside of her breasts. "Delectable, in fact." Her nipples had peaked at his touch and now ached with piercing tingles of desire.

Delectable? A fresh wave of heat flooded her. Followed quickly by anger.

How could she have responded with such lack of inhibition to this man?

"Get out of my way." She leaped from the bed, and, taking time only to snag up her clothes, she bolted for the en suite where she locked the door and started to dress with frantic haste.

* * *

After pulling on jeans, Callum galloped down the stairs and got into the kitchen just in time to see Miranda shoveling her things off the countertop into her bag.

From behind her, his eyes lingered on the strands of gold that glowed like dancing sunbeams in the morning light and he resisted the urge to pull her into his arms, kiss her and tousle the waves into a more bedded look. Somehow he didn't think she'd appreciate passion right now.

She pushed a hairbrush into her bag with a hasty movement.

He took a step toward her unable to resist the impulse to say, "At least be honest and admit you loved every moment of last night."

She started at the sound of his voice. Her head jerked around and he saw her eyes held the look of a trapped deer. "I only did it because I owe you. Remember?"

His mind blanked out. "Because you owe me?"

"Money." She backed up but rubbed her forefinger and thumb together with bravado, her expression defiant. "For putting me through culinary school."

"Last night was payback?"

"Uh-huh." She nodded and her hair bobbed around her face.

"You slept with me because you felt indebted?" Outrage swamped Callum. No woman had *ever* slept with him to prostitute herself. What had been an amazing experience suddenly felt sordid. Annoyed, he said, "I paid a fortune. One night wouldn't begin to cover my outlay."

Her shoulders stiffened. Instead of replying, Miranda

turned her back on him and gathered the last few of her scattered belongings together before dropping them into her bag. She zipped it shut with a decisive movement.

She was leaving, Callum realized.

The rigid line of her back spelt out her intention to put as much distance between them as she could. She shoved his jacket aside with unnecessary force.

"Hey, that's my favorite Armani."

His attempt to lighten the mood fell flat. The jacket slithered over the edge and, despite her grab for it, fell to the ground.

"Sorry." She bent to pick it up and Callum heard his car keys jingle as they slid from the pocket. "What's this?"

Her eyes, shockingly close, were on the same level as his as he knelt, too. For a moment he felt as if he'd been sucked into her soft, melting center.

"What's what?" he asked huskily, unable to tear his gaze away.

"This…"

He glanced down at the dark blue velvet ring box lying in the palm of her hand.

Crap.

"It's a jeweler's box." She stated the obvious before he could reply. Already her fingers were working the catch.

Alarm electrified him. "No. Don't."

Too late.

For long seconds Miranda stared at the diamond solitaire ring inside. Then she raised eyes full of questions. "You planned to ask me to marry you?"

Callum had the disoriented sense that he'd just been catapulted into an alien world. He couldn't think. Hell, he couldn't breathe—his lungs were empty.

"Why?" Her eyes held a luminosity that twisted his gut into knots.

"Uh…" He gulped in air.

"Because you slept with me?" A puzzled frown furrowed her brow as she lifted the ring from the bed of velvet and caressed it with her fingertips. "No. That's not right. You had the ring before you slept with me. So…"

This was not going as he'd planned. He could see her thinking, coming to the Lord knew what conclusion.

Ah, hell. "Not you," he muttered.

"What?" Her full attention zeroed in on him again.

"I wasn't going to propose to you."

An indecipherable expression flashed across her face. "Then who?"

He saw the moment she put it together. Her eyes went dark and blank. "Petra."

He nodded slowly, uneasy at the way Miranda was looking at him.

"You asked Petra to marry you last night." She dropped the ring back into the box and the lid snapped shut, the sound loud in the early morning silence. Then she stood up and he heard the box skip across the stainless steel bench.

He flinched. Miranda thought—

"Hang on," he said urgently, leaping to his feet.

But she ignored him. Swinging on her heel, she marched across the kitchen, her heels tap-tapping a furious tattoo on the matte wooden floor.

"Hey, you don't understand." He reached out to restrain her as she stomped past.

She turned her head and gave him a contemptuous glare. His hand fell away.

"Oh, I understand too well. You asked the daughter of a new major shareholder to marry you. She had the sense to refuse, so you slept with the hired help—" she spat out the last two words "—in a fit of pique." She punctuated her conclusion by marching to the door into the house and slamming it behind her.

A click followed.

Callum skidded after her, only to find she'd locked the door from the hall side. By the time he'd rushed out the back door, through the mews, and around to the front of the row of town houses, Miranda was gone.

The beastly two-timing jerk.

Miranda was still fuming when she arrived at The Golden Goose shortly before noon on Sunday. Fortunately Flo had accepted her arrival home in the clothes she'd gone out in last night with no questions, glossing over Miranda's stuttered excuse about working late.

Her mother's skirting the issue hadn't soothed her as much as it should've. Nor did it help that Gianni, the longtime chef, was glowering at her over the chopping block while Mick, the manager, danced around muttering that she was late—even though Miranda knew she'd walked in the door at five minutes to midday.

The final straw came when Mick cornered her later to say that her commitment was lacking. She'd left early last week, and now she was late and she was to take this as a warning. In these tough times, he expected more.

Gianni gave her a sly grin as she passed him, confirming where the heart of the problem lay. She wished she could reassure him, tell him that she had no ambitions to take over his job. But she knew that would only make him rush to tell Mick about her lack of commitment.

She was screwed.

By the time she got home late that night, Miranda was ill-prepared for the sight of an ostentatious bunch of long-stemmed pink roses that must've cost some joker a fortune.

And she suspected she knew who the joker might be.

"An admirer from last night?" Flo arched a finely penciled eyebrow. "I thought you said it was work."

"Must be a thank-you," Miranda bit out, ripping off the still-sealed envelope and pocketing it to get it out of her mother's line of sight.

"So considerate." Flo touched the blooms with reverent fingers. "They're beautiful. I watered them. Why don't you put them in your bedroom?"

And be stuck looking at a reminder of last night's calamity? No, thanks! Stalking away, Miranda wished she hadn't said they were a thank-you; now she couldn't even throw the wretched flowers away.

"Someone rang for you earlier."

Miranda froze in the doorway, but didn't turn around. "Who?"

"A man. He had a rough voice. It was strangely familiar," said Flo slowly.

Miranda stifled an anxious groan. "Did he leave a name?" She prayed not. Her mother didn't need to know she'd been fraternizing with the Ironstones.

"No. He said he'd catch you on your cell phone."

Her cell phone had been off while she worked. "Thanks, Mum."

After setting down the unopened white envelope on

the dressing table in her room, Miranda made for the bathroom the three of them shared. After she'd showered the odors of The Golden Goose away, she changed into a flannel nightie and brushed her teeth.

Climbing into bed, she finally picked up her cell phone and switched it on. The message light flashed. She stared at it for long seconds.

No. She had no intention of giving in to curiosity and checking to see if Callum had left her a message. The man had dominated her thoughts far too much already. And she was not about to let him cause her another sleepless night.

Setting the phone on the bed stand, she turned the lamp off, refusing to let herself dwell on the reason why she'd slept so little last night....

Four

Miranda was wakened the following morning by banging on her bedroom door. She'd barely opened her eyes before Adrian barged in.

"Phone." He held out the handset. "Callum."

Her heart sank. She wished fervently she hadn't been too cowardly to check her cell phone the night before. Now she was at a decided disadvantage. "Thanks."

Adrian hovered in the doorway, clearly curious. But an older-sister scowl caused him to roll his eyes and depart. When his footfalls finally faded, she lifted the handset to her ear. "Yes?"

"What happened to good morning?" Callum sounded delighted.

She squinted at her bedside clock. "Do you have any idea what time it is?"

"Although now that I think about it, you didn't greet me yesterday, either. Maybe you're not a morning person."

He had that right. But nor did she want any reminder about waking in his bed yesterday morning. "What do you want?"

"Now there's a leading question." He'd lowered his voice to a husky drawl and at once a rush of heat filled Miranda. Oh, heavens! She couldn't let herself respond to Callum with such unfettered sensual delight.

She tamped it down. "Oh, please, it's too early in the morning for sexual innuendo."

He laughed. "Definitely not a morning person. I apologize for calling so early." That must be a first. "I'm flying out to New York this afternoon," Callum continued more briskly, "and my schedule this morning is hellish."

Miranda suppressed the urge to cheer at the thought of Callum over three thousand miles away—it would give her time to recover from the turmoil that sleeping with him had caused her.

He was still talking rapidly. "I've got tickets for *Les Misérables* on Saturday night. Do you want to go? We can have dinner afterward."

"You called me to invite me on a *date?*" she said, blank dismay settling over her.

The silence stretched. Then he said, "I suppose you could call it that."

What else did one call a show and dinner followed by whatever else he had in mind? Shivers prickled as vivid images of what he might be planning assailed her.

The last thing she needed was an affair with Callum Ironstone. She already despised herself enough for allowing him to seduce her—although to be fair she'd been more than willing. If she hadn't had those glasses of red wine…if he hadn't been so damn tempting…if he hadn't kissed her and turned her legs to jelly.

Oh, God, she couldn't believe she was letting herself relive it all. Callum had taken her to bed the same night he'd proposed to another woman. Because of him her father was dead. How could she have let him touch her? Seeing him again would be a betrayal of her very soul.

"No, I can't come."

"Another evening then?"

"No." She hung up.

The phone rang again. She glared at it. Then picked it up before Adrian—or Flo—could.

"Did you get the message I left on your cell phone last night?"

"No," she said guardedly, eyeing the phone that winked a message on the bedside table. "But whatever you said wouldn't have changed my answer."

"You believe I only slept with you because Petra rejected me."

That was only the tip of the iceberg. She was furious with herself for sleeping with him at all. Furious with him for making it so easy. "Yes? So what?"

"I never asked Petra to marry me," he said.

"You didn't?"

"That's the message I left for you yesterday."

"Oh." She fell silent. Why had he told her this? She wouldn't allow it to be important. Yet her pulse quickened. Miranda drew a steadying breath, aware that she had to tread carefully.

"It doesn't make any difference, Callum." She couldn't

afford to alienate him. He'd given Adrian a vacation job, which might lead to a permanent placement next year. If she annoyed Callum, he might fire Adrian. "I just don't think it's a good idea for me to date you."

She heard him whisper "Liar" just as she hurriedly severed the connection.

This time he didn't ring back. But before she could set foot out of bed, Adrian slipped into her room.

"What did Callum want?"

She wasn't telling him that his boss, her nemesis, had asked her on a date. "Nothing to do with you."

Adrian looked sick. "Sis, please be nice to him."

Adrian's anxiety reinforced her own worry that if she annoyed Callum he'd take it out on her brother. But there was a limit to how far she'd go—and Adrian had to know that.

"Be nice?" She loaded the meaning. "What are you asking me to do here, Adrian?"

"I mean be polite." His Adam's apple bobbed. "Nothing more. I don't want to lose this opportunity to get a good reference."

She hated the idea that Adrian thought she'd jeopardize his work. Was that how bitter she'd become?

Miranda crossed her fingers under the bedclothes. "I did some catering for Callum. We were talking about that."

His expression cleared. "That's great. So you'll be doing more work for him?"

"I didn't say that," she said hastily.

"I told him you were a good chef—that you were wasted at The Golden Goose."

"The Goose is convenient." Miranda fixed her brother

with a narrow stare. Adrian must have told Callum about her dream to run her own catering business. At least that meant her fear that Callum had been able to read her like an open book had been...relatively baseless. "What else did you tell him?"

Her brother spread his hands. "Nothing. I swear."

She studied him as she swung her legs out of bed. "Okay, I believe you. Now scoot—I want to get dressed."

But he lingered. "Uh...when will you give me that money?"

"I'll go to the bank today."

"Sis..." He hesitated, then said in a rush, "Can you add another couple hundred quid?"

She paused in front of the wardrobe. "*More* money? When you still haven't repaid me the fifty pounds I lent you last week?"

He all but ran out of her room. "We can talk about it when you're dressed," he said over his shoulder.

Adrian had made breakfast by the time she got to the kitchen. Miranda drew out one of the pine chairs that Flo had sewed yellow-and-white-checked gingham covers for and stared suspiciously at the spread on the table. Scrambled eggs. Bacon. Mushrooms. Toast. Marmalade. Her favorites. "Is this a bribe?"

"No." But he looked sufficiently guilty for her to frown at him. "I took Mum her food on a tray."

"So now it's just you and me." Miranda sighed as she sat down. "Okay, explain to me why I should pay another cent to sort out your friend's problems. Hasn't he got family of his own?"

Adrian turned a dull red that clashed with his freckles. "It's not for a friend. It's for me."

"A new pair of shoes?" she asked snippily. "You know I'm saving. Can't this wait?"

"No." He looked down at his plate for long seconds. When he looked up, Miranda was shocked at the desperation in his expression. "I'm in trouble."

All her worst fears crowded in. "Tell me."

"Last Monday night—"

"When you went out with your friends?"

He nodded. "I borrowed a car from work, but I crashed it—hit a concrete pillar in a basement parking lot as we were leaving a club."

Horror filled her. "Everyone was okay?" The pounding of her heart slowed at his nod, and relief seeped through her, turning her limbs weak. No one had been hurt…or worse. "Were you drunk?"

"No." He looked shaken. "I never drink and drive."

She relaxed enough to fork a mouthful of food into her mouth. "So get the car fixed."

"I've already had it repaired—and borrowed money from my friends to pay for it. But the amount was more than the original quote—that's why I need more money. And they're pressing me to repay them."

I don't have any more money. Not for this. Miranda bit back her wail of despair, as the extent of his deceit struck her. "You lied to me."

"I didn't want you to know." Even his neck was red now. "I'm sorry."

She restrained herself from asking what else he'd held back from her, and pondered on the fix he was in. "Wait, you shouldn't be paying—the car belongs to Ironstone. It will be insured. Just fill out an incident report and let Ironstone handle the claim."

"I can't." He looked utterly wretched. "I wasn't supposed to have the car out after work hours. There might be criminal charges for theft if anyone at Ironstone finds out."

"Theft?" She stared at him in alarm.

"Yes, for taking the car without the owner's consent." He suddenly looked very young, reminding her that he'd only recently finished school and was little more than a schoolboy. "I'm really sorry, sis."

Miranda knew exactly how Callum would react if he found out—and being sorry wouldn't help. He'd have Adrian arrested, and prosecute him to the full extent of the law. Look what he'd done to their father.

She couldn't let that happen again.

"I'll get you the money today." She thought with regret about the fantasy of her own catering business, then dismissed it. Adrian was more important.

But maybe if she explained it all to Callum he might understand. There was a chance. Today was her day off, and Callum had said he was flying out this afternoon.

If she hurried she could see him before he left.

"It won't happen again." Adrian's promise got her attention.

"Better not," she growled. "Now eat your breakfast."

"I'm not hungry." He pushed back his chair and picked up the plate, crossing to the sink. "I'm going to work."

This time Miranda arrived at the Ironstone Insurance building without the benefit of being expected, and the receptionist wasn't nearly as friendly.

"Mr. Ironstone is busy," she said.

"I only need five minutes." Miranda had to speak to

Callum before he left for New York. Had to make him see that Adrian was a good boy, that he'd made a mistake in taking the car—and that all the damage would be paid for.

Because the alternative was unthinkable. Prison. She couldn't let this ruin her brother's life. Miranda shuddered as memories plagued her. Her father had been arrested...and then he'd been dead. So final. It wasn't going to happen to Adrian.

"Mr. Ironstone is not available."

"I know, Callum's going to New York—he told me. I presume he's in that meeting," she tacked on, trying to sound as though she was privy to his every plan.

The receptionist shot an indecisive look in the direction of a closed door leading off the reception area before turning her attention back and giving Miranda a curious look.

Just then the door cracked open. "Biddy, can you make four copies of this report, please?"

The receptionist came round the counter, and Miranda saw her chance. "Callum," she called out.

He looked up, and his eyes crinkled into a smile. "Miranda, what are you doing here?"

"I have to talk to you. In private," she added urgently as she glanced past him into the occupied boardroom.

"I'll be with you in a minute." He rapidly made excuses to his board members and ushered her along the corridor into his office.

"You've changed your mind?" he asked, closing the door. His eyes were warmer than she'd ever imagined the color blue could be.

Changed her mind? She blinked at him as she settled

into the soft sofa beneath the bookshelves. Oh, the date! He thought she was here because she'd decided to accept?

"No—"

Help. He was moving closer, seating himself beside her. The heat that she'd sworn she would not allow herself to feel swamped her anew. His fingers closed on her upper arms. For a moment she was so incredibly tempted just to give in, to let him kiss her. But she couldn't.

"Uh…I wanted to talk about…"

He bent his head. That smiling mouth held her entranced. In a second it would land on hers.

"No!" She ducked away to the far end of the sofa. "You can't kiss me. You're going to marry Petra." She gabbled the first thing that came into her head.

He blinked. "I am?"

"You bought her a ring." He must've spent a fortune on it. That meant he had to be serious.

The powerful surge of adrenaline ebbed, and her brains unscrambled. Petra's father was an important figure in his life now that Gordon Harris held so much stock in Ironstone. That's why men like Callum married.

Not for love. Or even desire.

But for cold, sound financial reasons.

And Petra would accept with alacrity. Callum was a catch. An Ironstone. Not everyone held the view of him Miranda did.

In her mind she replayed that disaster on Saturday night when she'd ended up sprawled over his kitchen counter, and later in his bed. All evening she'd been conscious of his gaze following her, setting her body aflame. Even while he'd listened to Petra, talked to her father, been ribbed by his brothers…the whole time he'd been watching her.

All his brothers had been there. To meet Gordon, he'd told her here in this very office. A celebration.

Celebration…

Of what? She'd thought he'd been referring to the merger. Had it been something else entirely?

"Those two guests you told me couldn't make it because of the snowstorm up north. They were your parents, weren't they?"

"Well…yes."

Her suspicions crystallized into certainty. "You were going to announce your engagement."

The utter silence told Miranda she was right.

"But you didn't announce it…because you didn't get around to proposing to her," she said, following her line of thought through to the natural conclusion. "And you slept with me instead." Miranda tilted her head. "Have you broken up with her?"

He stretched. "Miranda—"

Callum hadn't broken off whatever relationship he had going with Petra. For some reason he'd simply decided he wanted *her.*

"Miranda, wait—"

He was despicable. She shifted farther into the corner of the couch. "Yes or no?"

He shook his head.

The phone on the highly polished desk rang twice before stopping abruptly. Callum glared across at it, then back to her. "The meeting is ready to continue. I have to go." But he didn't rise. "If you change your mind, call me."

"I won't," she stated with absolute conviction. "And don't invite me out again. Call Petra—she's still the woman you plan to marry."

There was no doubt in her mind that Petra would accept him.

Poor thing.

"If you say so." His eyes cooled further. "So why did you come?" His hard mouth bore no trace of a smile.

She hesitated, aware of the chasm that yawned between them, much wider than the distance that separated them on the sofa. Adrian had asked her to be nice. This didn't look like a man who would give her—or Adrian—the benefit of the doubt.

But she had to try. "How's Adrian getting—" She broke off.

"Adrian? Getting along?" His gaze narrowed. "He's doing very well. That's why you came to see me? Because of your brother?"

The warmth he'd greeted her with had vanished. The smiling eyes had been replaced with blue chips of ice.

She backtracked hastily. "No, no, I just asked." Now he must think her a total mother hen. Forcing a conciliatory smile, she said, "I'm pleased he's getting on well."

Callum rose to his feet. "I've been intending to suggest that he apply for one of the scholarships that Ironstone offers." His cold gaze swept her. "And before you leap to any nasty conclusions, this is an opportunity offered to any school-leavers who work for us to go to university. I don't even administer it."

She'd done it now. She'd made him mad. And if she breathed a word about the car Adrian had crashed, her brother would not only lose his vacation job and the chance of a permanent position, he'd also lose all chance of a scholarship—and it would be her fault.

To placate him, she said, "It would be the answer to my prayers." And it was true. The thought of Adrian studying toward a career. Having a chance of a successful future...

Except it would come from the Ironstone family. But she could live with that. She certainly wouldn't stand in Adrian's way.

Yet before she could say anything further, Callum continued, "So if you didn't come to accept my invitation and you didn't come see me about your brother, why are you here?"

Help. She sucked in a deep breath. There was only one thing left to say—sure, it meant she'd have to eat crow, but she could do that.

"I wanted to thank you for giving me the chance to cater for you." Her stomach heaved. "I've already had a call as a result. Look." She dug into her bag and pulled out a few of the business cards she'd had printed up yesterday. "One of your dinner guests on Saturday asked for a card. I didn't have any. So I've had some printed up. What do you think?" She couldn't restrain the lilt of pride in her voice as she passed him a card.

He studied it. "Not bad. Do you have any more?"

"Why?"

"I might be able to hand them to prospective clients." He shot her a quick glance. "In fact, can you cater a Christmas cocktail party?" Callum rattled off a sum per head. "In the boardroom here? This Friday?"

Embarrassment squirmed through her. "That wasn't a hint. I didn't mean for you to give me more—"

"The caterer we booked has fallen ill. Do you want the job? Or do I get Biddy to find someone else?"

Miranda considered Adrian's predicament. Their tight finances. "Perhaps," she said cautiously.

A rap on the door had Callum stepping away from her. "Yes or no?" He parodied her question from earlier, and Miranda flushed.

Biddy popped her head around the doorjamb. "The copies are done, and everyone's finished their coffee—they're waiting for you."

He moved toward the door. "So what will it be?"

Ignoring the receptionist's curious glance, Miranda blew out the breath she'd been holding. "Yes."

Five

The boardroom was packed.

Everywhere Callum looked people held cocktail glasses, while they talked and laughed. Waitresses in long, red sequined dresses wearing Santa hats with fur trim offered around trays of snacks. And behind the hum of conversation he could hear the festive notes of "Ding Dong Merrily on High."

He should've been pleased. Ecstatic, in fact. Yet all he could do was glare in increasing frustration at the woman who'd pulled it all off.

Miranda had chosen to wear fishnets.

Callum really hadn't needed his brother, Fraser, to point that out to him. She wore black. A snug dress that, unlike the V-neck of last week's dress, had a high collar suited to a nun and should've looked seriously sedate.

He couldn't take his eyes off her as she busied herself around the buffet table piled with mince pies and pots of whipped cream, repositioning the posies of poinsettias tied with gold bows and lit up with red candles.

Did the fishnets, too, end at the tops of her thighs?

A bolt of raw lust stabbed him at the memory of stroking the soft skin of her inner thigh. Had she worn them deliberately to drive him out of his mind?

As for that damn frilly white apron that tied with the great white bow behind her back, begging him to yank it loose...

Ah, hell.

"Back off," Callum growled as he caught Fraser smiling at Miranda for the second time in less than five minutes.

"I'm pulling rank," Fraser murmured. "I'm older. Go away."

Callum forced his attention from the woman who had him tied up in mental knots. "Forget it," he told his brother grimly. "That doesn't work anymore."

"You're warning me off!" Fraser's grin widened as he searched Callum's face. "I thought you were already attached." Turning his head, Fraser scanned the room. "Although I haven't seen the princess here tonight."

"Petra doesn't like it when you call her Princess," he said pompously, and spoiled the effect by slicing his brother a dirty look.

"Does your lack of answer mean she was supposed to be here?"

"No."

Callum shuddered at the memory of the disastrous call he'd made from New York. He should have ended it with Petra a week ago. It hadn't been fair to keep Petra on a string, not while this hunger for Miranda ate at him like acid. Petra hadn't said much, but he knew he'd hurt her. *It's not you, it's me*—he'd even used that old corny line. *You deserve better.* She did—he should've waited to break it off with her in person.

So he'd organized a string of pearls to be delivered to her, more to assuage his guilt than to offer consolation. And he was grateful Petra wasn't here tonight—although he'd noted Gordon's appearance with some relief.

Callum knew he probably had Petra to thank for that. The woman had style.

So why the hell couldn't it be Petra he craved with this deep and desperate desire?

"She's got more sense than I credited her with if she dumped you." Fraser sounded almost satisfied.

Narrowing his gaze, Callum studied his brother's mocking smile. He didn't correct his brother's mistaken belief that it was Petra who'd done the ditching. Instead he said with brotherly candor, "I don't think she likes you much. Kind of like Miranda—who hates my guts."

"Miranda?" Fraser's suddenly blank expression gave nothing away. "Wasn't Thomas Owen's daughter named Miranda?"

Without meaning to, Callum glanced toward the woman who'd been tormenting his nights. "Yes."

Fraser followed his gaze. "That same Miranda?"

This time Callum's "Yes" was terse.

Knowing his brother was examining him with keen interest made Callum feel uncomfortably exposed. The silence stretched long enough to become pointed. Finally Fraser said gently, "Ouch."

Exactly. "Just stay away from her."

"And if I don't?" Fraser asked. "Then what, little brother? You'll beat me to pulp?"

Blood rushed through his ears. "Don't…try…it." He bit the words out with aggressive intent.

Fraser hooted in disbelief. "You *would.*"

The sound of his sibling's laughter caused Callum to ask grimly, "What's so damn funny?"

"If you don't know, I'm not telling." Fraser was already off to where their half brothers, Jack and Hunter, huddled with a major stakeholder. Still smirking, he threw over his shoulder, "You always did like to do things the hard way, Callum."

You always did like to do things the hard way. Fraser's words still rang in Callum's ears as he fought his way through the crush of people that seemed to have grown larger and louder over the past hour, heading to where Miranda and two waitresses were replenishing platters of savories on the temporary bar.

She shot him a wary look as he approached.

He supposed it was foolish to have hoped for a little gratitude after all the trouble he'd taken to ensure she could do the catering tonight. Biddy had been far from pleased at having to call the catering company that had already been booked—he'd had to pay them in full for the late cancellation.

Of course Miranda didn't know that. He'd told her the caterer had been forced to renege for reasons of illness.… Nor did she know he'd broken up with Petra. He had no intention of telling her either. Miranda already had more power over him than he liked.

Talk about a tangled web.

As far as doing things the hard way, this fierce attraction to Miranda topped all. Callum wasn't even sure his motives were pure any longer. What had begun as a sop to his conscience had somehow gotten out of control since meeting the all-grown-up Miranda. He didn't know what had hit him. All he knew was that he wanted to take her back to his bed…sate himself with her.

Hell, why should she be grateful? Given her conviction that he'd caused her father's death it wasn't surprising she couldn't bear the sight of him. Callum didn't like the niggle of discomfort that ate at his stomach—the same sensation that often gnawed in the middle of the night. If he hadn't pushed so hard to have Thomas Owen arrested, the man might still be alive today.

And Miranda and Adrian would still have a father.

As he cut through the throng, he smiled and nodded to business acquaintances but didn't pause until he reached Miranda, busy setting out serviettes and fresh bowls of olives amid a crowd at the bar.

"Need any help?"

Miranda's eyelashes fluttered down, blocking her eyes from his view. White serviettes printed with gold snowflakes fanned out under the touch of her deft fingers, and he had to strain his ears to hear her response.

"It's all under control."

He dropped his gaze from those teasing fingers. Only to be confronted by the provocative white apron with its starchy ruffles and wished furiously he could as easily control his wild thoughts. Clearing his throat, he managed, "Uh…I need to update you on Adrian."

Her hands stilled. "Adrian?"

The rest of what she said was drowned out by a burst of laughter. Not even staring at her mouth helped him make out the words—although the soft shape of her lips caused another quake of lust.

Placing a hand under her elbow, he drew her away from the bar. "Sorry, I can't hear you."

She came slowly, her arm suddenly stiff under his fingertips.

It didn't augur well for the chances of assuaging the growing hunger that burned in him. He bent forward and said loudly over the music and surrounding chatter, "Let me introduce you around—we can talk about Adrian later."

He sensed her hesitation. Flicking him a quick, sideways look, she rested a hand on his shoulder and rose on tiptoe. "I'm not sure I can wait."

Callum shuddered as her breath warmed his ear with the innocently provocative words. Turning his head, he discovered her mouth not far from his. For a moment he was tempted to throw caution to the winds. To confess that Petra meant nothing to him and that she, Miranda, consumed his every thought. To plunder the soft ripeness of that sweet mouth.

But she withdrew her hand, leaving him bereft. Bringing himself back to the present, he mouthed, "Later. We'll talk when the party settles down. Right now, I ought to circulate."

She glanced around at the press of people that made it impossible to talk and nodded, but her irises had darkened with worry.

"Adrian's fine," he said. Miranda needed to think more about herself and spend less time fretting about her brother. Into a short lull he said, "Have you got your business cards here?"

She nodded. "In my bag. I'll get them."

He gave her a thumbs-up and waited for her to return.

Once it had sunk in that Adrian's secret was still safe, Miranda's heartbeat steadied and she started to relax.

Callum introduced her to an older couple, Madge and Tom Murray. On learning that Miranda was responsible for the food, Madge said, "The mince pies simply melted in my mouth. What magic did you use?"

That launched a discussion about pastry that attracted a nearby woman. After several minutes Miranda turned to Callum and Madge's husband and apologized profusely. "Sorry, I lose time when the talk is about food."

"Madge likes nothing more." Tom laughed.

The conversation moved on to favorite dishes and dinner-party disasters. Madge was amusing, and her husband clearly doted on her—even though he confessed to hating oysters which Madge vowed was grounds for divorce.

As everyone laughed, Miranda felt a stab of envy. Even though her father had adored and indulged Flo, there'd never been this sense of kinship and shared laughter between her parents.

The arrival of a tall, dark-haired man who looked vaguely familiar interrupted her thoughts. But the respite proved to be short. The newcomer turned out to be none other than Callum's brother, Fraser, whose sharp eyes assessed Miranda and missed nothing. Not the fact that his brother stood beside her, nor that his brother's arm was behind her. His arched brows rose a little, but thankfully he only added to the hilarity in their discussions about food.

"What is your secret food passion, Miranda?" asked Madge.

"Chocolate," she said. "Rich, dark and slightly bitter."

"Sounds like Callum," Fraser said with a sly grin.

Miranda didn't dare glance at the silent man standing next to her. In an instant those mad moments in his home played through her brain like a movie in slow motion.

Callum hoisting her up and stepping between her thighs. Callum soaping her in the shower afterward. Callum naked and damp with droplets moving over her before pinning her on his bed and...

She became brutally aware of the gentle pressure of his hand resting in the small of her back. And blinked. Hard.

This was Callum Ironstone, for heaven's sake. Petra's almost fiancé. Her brother's boss. Her sworn enemy. How could she allow such treacherous desires to consume her? How could she even be tempted to respond to his touch? And worse, to every breath he drew? Yet the touch of his hand on her back seemed so...right. What was *wrong* with her?

"I need to get back to the kitchen," she said desperately, shifting out from beneath his hand.

"Don't you dare say anything about a woman's place," Madge warned as Fraser looked as if he were about to comment.

He said, "I wouldn't dare. Mother would send us to our rooms for voicing such heresy, wouldn't she, Callum?"

"Without a doubt." The laugh lines around Callum's eyes crinkled, making him even more attractive.

Miranda escaped before she could be further seduced. Or, heaven help her, admit that she *wanted* to be seduced.

Drat the man.

The long night was almost over.

Miranda had been clock-watching for the past half hour, waiting for the guests to leave as the medley of cheerful Christmas carols segued into light classics. But she still started when Callum came up silently behind her, invading the refuge she'd sought behind the tall Christmas tree in the lobby where she'd hidden in the hope of avoiding him.

A quick upward glance from where she knelt beside three crates revealed that he'd discarded his jacket, and the white shirt he wore was startling in the dim lobby.

"I've been looking for you." Callum held out a glass of what looked like port. "You've done enough tonight, Miranda. Leave packing those glasses and take a break."

She glanced at the dark liquid swirling in the crystal glass and pictured—too vividly—what had happened the last time she'd indulged in wine under his roof. Her pulse quickened, causing blood to rush to her head and a wave of dizzy desire.

"No, thanks." Miranda fought to control her physical reaction. Port would only cause her defenses—already vulnerable—to crumble more rapidly. Earlier he'd promised to catch her later and talk about Adrian; no doubt that was why he had been looking for her. Not to seduce her—contrary to her wild imaginings.

He shrugged and took a sip of his wine. The lights of the tall Christmas tree overhead flashed, creating a surreal glow of silver, and for a moment she was riveted. His tie had been abandoned and the pulse in the hollow of his throat beat visibly.

She stared transfixed.

Then he surprised her.

"Tonight was a success. I want to thank you, Miranda."

His eyes were warm, the blue muted, making her wish they'd met under different circumstances—that he wasn't the man responsible for her father's death.

"I only did what you employed me to do," she said stiffly as he set his glass down on the white marble floor beside her. She ducked her head, determined not to reveal her impossible thoughts, and carried on stacking empty glasses into their crates, using the occasional ting of crystal as a warning bell to keep herself from falling under his thrall.

"No, you did far more than expected. The Christmas crackers were a success, and so were the edible Christmas tree decorations."

His voice came closer and she spoke quickly, desperate to keep him at bay. "I thought your guests might like something to take home."

"Madge Murray was raving about the chocolate angels."

"Yes, I gave her extras." She raised her shoulders and let them fall with what she hoped looked like a careless shrug. "My mother taught me how to make them when I was a little girl." Flo had always had the ability to bake fairy-tale items; it was the ordinary things like lunch and dinner that were beyond her.

At the brush of Callum's fingers under her chin, her head came up in a hurry. He pinned her under his ferociously bright gaze. As the Christmas lights flickered overhead, she imagined the glitter in his eyes revealed emotion. But the words he spoke negated that fancy.

"Her husband is one of our most important customers."

The hope she'd glimpsed died. Of course, for Callum everything was always about work. Never about emotion. Or fairy tales. He was ready to marry for corporate convenience. Unlike her, he would never believe in love…or Christmas wishes. She tried not to let her disappointment show—and hated herself for wishing it had all been about so much more, and that the emotion she'd imagined she'd glimpsed had been real.

She drew away. "I'm glad you're pleased."

"Very pleased."

"Good." She got to her feet. "Now I'd better get these glasses to the collection point. The company I hired them from will be here soon to fetch them."

Callum stared at the woman with frustration. He wasn't interested in the damn dirty glasses. Why couldn't she be one of those kittenish women who batted her eyelids and cooed her thanks? How he would revel being on the receiving end of her gratitude….

He took in the creamy skin, the soft, lush mouth and desire spiked through him.

Dark. Driving. Relentless.

Callum gave himself a mental shake. Not going to happen. Not tonight. Not ever. So he'd better get over this…this fascination she held for him.

Even Fraser had noticed.

Hell.

Would he ever be able to get that night she'd spent in his bed out his head? Or stop thinking about how to get her back there and make love to her all over again?

He must be crazy.

Especially as she was making it clear as the crystal she was packing away that she had no intention of even dating him. All night she'd been running from him, apprehension in her eyes. And how could he blame her? He'd been reduced to using his company functions as a way to spend time with her.

Once the festive season was over it would be some time before he could set up catering engagements for her without arousing her suspicion. He would have no excuse to see her, not unless he took to frequenting The Golden Goose.

He grimaced. That would be desperate measures indeed.

"What's wrong?"

He straightened at the sound of Miranda's voice. "Wrong?"

"You're frowning."

"I've no reason to frown—it's been a very successful evening."

"Good."

He told himself he'd find another way to keep in touch with her. "Oh, earlier I wanted to tell you that I spoke to your brother."

A subtle tension shimmered through her. If he hadn't been so aware of every nuance and change in her expressive eyes, he probably wouldn't even have noticed.

"After I flew in from New York I gave him the application forms for the two Ironstone Insurance scholarships and told him that I'd nominate him." His nomination would carry a lot of weight with the deciding committee, but she didn't need to know that. It would only make her believe he was merely giving charity in another guise.

Yet for once, instead of objecting, the tension seemed to drain out of her. "If Adrian could get a scholarship to university—or even a job for next year—it would be such a relief." Her lashes fluttered down. "Thank you."

It must strangle her to have to thank him for anything. He reached out and touched her arm, intending to tell her that she owed him no thanks—that it was the least he could do.

And froze.

Here was the opportunity he'd been looking for. So perfect—and he'd almost missed it. He could use her brother as a way to keep in touch—arrange meetings with her to talk about him.

All to get into Miranda's pants again, he scoffed at himself.

Was this what he had been reduced to? Miranda's brother was almost a man and Callum had always tried to treat him like an adult. If Adrian found out Callum was meeting Miranda to discuss him, the bond he'd been working so hard to forge with the youth would be broken.

But right now he couldn't care about that.

Unless he offered Adrian a permanent position at Ironstone Insurance or called in a favor to make sure her brother was offered a university scholarship, there would be no more reason to see Miranda.

No excuse to lure her into his bed....

He let the thumb resting on her arm stroke along the fabric of her dress sleeve and heard her breath catch.

Not totally unaffected then.

He couldn't help remembering how soft her naked skin had been against his, how sweet she'd tasted. His gaze rested on her mouth.

So passionate.

This craving for her confounded him. He'd been right to break it off with Petra—he couldn't marry any woman while he felt like this. And despite Miranda's determined indifference, he suspected she wanted him every bit as badly. The passion she'd revealed the night they'd made love couldn't be feigned.

If only her father's death didn't stand between them.

"Miranda, about your father…"

The lights flashed and he read anger in her eyes. "You should never have—"

"I had no choice."

"There's always a choice," she said.

She was right. He'd been determined to prove how tough he was, how merciless. The corporate tycoon. It was something he'd have to live with all his life.

"You're right."

"Thank you."

For a long moment he thought she was going to say more.

But instead she said with forced cheerfulness, "Christmas will soon be here. I'll just have to wish that everything will come right for Adrian in the coming year."

He blinked. "You think Christmas wishes work?"

She tipped her head up and stared at the tree above them. "I think one can dream…and wish…and hope."

Miranda was a romantic. For a moment he wished for her sheer, blind optimism. Unable to help himself, he asked, "What do you look forward to most at Christmas?"

"I love spending it with my family. I love—" She broke off. "You don't want to hear all this."

"But I do." And he found he was telling the truth. "Tell me what you want to see when you wake up on Christmas morning."

"The best gift?" She gave him a funny little twisted smile. "Well, I can't have that. So I'll take snow. As much as I love the lights in the city at Christmas, I love snow more. And it doesn't often snow in London for Christmas. Sleet and sludge, yes, but not pure, pristine snow that crunches underfoot in the early morning and yours are the first footprints of the day."

He heard the longing. "You miss the country, don't you?"

"Particularly at this time of the year."

The lights in the Christmas tree flashed again, revealing a wistful, faraway expression he knew she'd have hated him to see.

"I remember as a child getting up on Christmas morning, going with Adrian to check our stockings on the mantelpiece. Then I'd go and see my pony—take the biggest carrots I could find and slices of apple." She gave a whisper of a sigh. "The warm smell of horse and hay inside the stables after the crisp air outside…that must be one of my favorite Christmas memories. And by the time I got back to the house my parents would be awake and we'd all gather under the tree."

Her lashes lay in dark crescents against her cheeks, and her mouth curved up in a smile that made an unfamiliar ache tighten around his chest.

"A real tree." She gestured to the Christmas tree that towered over them. "Not a fake monstrosity with fake snow like this one."

Callum nodded, feeling a strange affinity for her. When he was growing up, his family had always decorated a pine tree, too. And each year the scent had filled his home along with the sweet aromas of baking biscuits. They still shared Christmas in the country every year.

He wanted to offer her a chance to relive the Christmas she dreamed of. He wanted to invite her home to spend Christmas in the country with him at Fairwinds. Although he suspected she would refuse his invitation.

"Miranda—"

She reached up to straighten a silver bow on the company tree. The movement pulled her dress tight across her breasts and his breath caught in his throat. He forgot what he'd been about to say. Forgot everything except the crazy hunger she made him feel.

Unable to resist, he hooked an arm around her and pulled her close. Then he brushed his lips across hers very gently.

The air grew still.

Callum wanted to kiss her again with all the pent-up passion she'd kindled in him and sweep her off her feet before carrying her to his home.

Instead he set her away from him.

She touched her mouth with two fingers. "What was that for?"

There had to be a reason for him to kiss her? Callum

gave her a long look. Instead of collapsing into his arms like most women would have, the suspicion in her eyes deepened.

Finally he said, "Blame it on the mistletoe."

She glanced upward and a puzzled frown creased her brow. "But there isn't any."

Exactly. He needed no excuse to kiss her—the fire she'd ignited burned with an unquenchable fury—but Callum doubted she'd appreciate his honesty if he told her that.

Six

Miranda didn't appreciate the way Callum was messing with her head. That feather-of-a-kiss-that-had-hardly-been-a-kiss had shaken her.

Badly.

And even a busy weekend at The Golden Goose failed to give her respite to regain her composure. All because the man in question turned up at the Goose on Saturday and ordered lunch.

Miranda had known about Callum's arrival in minutes. Kitty, the youngest, prettiest and flightiest of the waitresses, had rushed into the kitchen to share that the most gorgeous guy she'd seen in her life had just walked in.

"Tall, dark and with periwinkle-blue eyes," she gushed. "He looks like a movie star."

"In the Goose?" But despite her skepticism Miranda's heart stopped in horror. She steadied herself. That description could apply to thousands of men. Well, maybe not thousands. But it didn't mean...

Yet she hadn't been able to resist taking a peek—just to make sure.

Only to discover it *was* Callum.

He sat alone at a small round table to the side of the gas fireplace. In the middle of the day the fire flickered, but the flames still gave off much-needed warmth. Callum's dark head was bent over the menu, but he looked up almost as though he'd sensed her stare.

She drew quickly out of sight, hissing at her stupidity under her breath.

While Mick muttered about chefs who had too little work, Miranda hurried to rescue a batch of brandy snaps from the oven before they burnt to crisp and, after rolling them deftly around the handle of a wooden spoon, set about piping whipped cream flavored with Grand Marnier into the now-crisp tubes.

What did Callum want? Why was he here?

Her hands shook as she squeezed the piping bag and cream oozed everywhere. Which made her want to kill him!

"He wants steak." Kitty bounced into the kitchen. "Rare. No sauce. And battered onion rings. A real, live carnivore."

The two other girls giggled. "I'll take him some water," one said.

"Maybe he wants extra onions." And the second followed her out for a closer inspection.

Miranda stopped herself from rolling her eyes. For

the next thirty minutes she was aware of the giggles as the waitresses vied to serve him, and it irritated her beyond belief.

The final insult came when Kitty delivered his request to convey his thanks in person to the dessert chef.

All too conscious of Gianni glowering, Miranda allowed herself to be dragged out into the limelight, noting Callum's lack of surprise when she appeared.

Of course he'd known she was here.

Resisting the urge to drop a facetious curtsy, she smiled sweetly. "I'm so pleased you enjoyed your meal."

His gaze rested on her lips, causing them to tingle, before lifting to study her. "What are you doing for Christmas this year?"

Miranda gave a small sigh. "What I always do— spend it with my family."

For a moment she thought he was going to ask her something, but he only said, "My mother has a passion for brandy snaps, and these are quite the best I've ever eaten."

His sincerity took her aback. He was looking at her like he wanted to devour her. Miranda couldn't have spoken if she'd tried.

"She would love these."

"I'll let you have the recipe," she croaked at last.

Tipping his head to one side, he considered her. "I'd rather you made them for her."

Miranda thought about it, her heart quickening. What did he mean? That he wanted her to meet his mother? Then common sense kicked in. Unlikely. "But she doesn't live in London. The biscuit would go soggy. They should be eaten fresh."

He was shaking his head. "It was a dumb idea."

"What was?" she asked, puzzled, wondering what she'd missed.

"Coming here!" He gave her a lopsided smile. "But next time Mother is in town, I will hold you to that offer."

His smile widened, holding no edge or hint of seduction, and for the first time Miranda got a glimpse of the man his family saw.

And it was a different person from the man she'd grown to loathe. This man she could like. Yet she was no closer to knowing why he'd come today. And she'd turned down his offer to go to *Les Misérables* with him tonight—and maybe get to know him better. There was no point wondering if Petra was enjoying herself. Thay way lay the path to heartache. She'd sensibly refuse his invitation. The man was an enigma—she would never understand him.

The rest of the weekend was an anticlimax with Gianni stamping and snorting like a bull and glaring balefully across the kitchen at Miranda. One of the girls must have told him what Callum had said, and he hadn't liked it.

Thankfully, when Miranda finally got home late in the rainy cold of Sunday night there were no flowers to welcome her and remind her of her disturbing nemesis that she couldn't seem to keep out of her life.

With Adrian still out, the little terrace house seemed empty. Entering the dining room, Miranda saw Flo hurriedly sliding a window envelope under a file.

"Another bill?" she asked, picking up her pace as she crossed to where her mother sat at the table. "I thought I'd paid everything."

"No, no, don't you worry about this, darling."

The vagueness in her mother's tone sharpened Miranda's interest. "Let me see—I might have paid it already."

"This is mine."

"Yours?" She looked at her mother in surprise.

Flo normally gave all her bills to Miranda to pay— she was hopeless at organizing her finances. Though it tended to require the conjuring up of money from nowhere—often hard-worked overtime—to meet them.

Miranda felt sick. "Please, not more overdue bills that I don't know about."

Snagging up the corner of the file, Miranda caught sight of the name of an exclusive department store on the bill under the envelope. "Hemingway's?"

Guilt glinted in Flo's dark eyes. "I needed a new coat."

Miranda pulled out the piece of paper and then blanched. "What was it? Mink?"

"Don't be silly, darling." Her mother whipped the bill out from between her nerveless fingers. "There were also a few fripperies for my winter wardrobe. Your father wouldn't have wanted to see me dressed in rags."

"Dad isn't here anymore—and we don't have his income." She spied another bill from the same store, dated the previous month. "*Pans?* You told me your friend Sorrell gave those to you."

Her mother flushed, an ugly stain on her pale skin. "I'll deal with the bills, Miranda."

"How?"

Putting her hands on her hips, Miranda considered her mother. Apart from the allowance Callum paid her mother—the amount Miranda had been led to believe came from the carefully invested residue of her father's estate—Flo had no income.

"I'll make arrangements, darling. Don't worry about it. I'm not useless."

Arrangements? Dread curled in Miranda's stomach. "What kind of arrangements?"

"I'll call up Hemingway's and have them grant me an indulgence—they've done it before."

"Done it before?" asked Miranda, trying to make sense of why the store would grant her mother an extension on her accounts.

"Yes—last time they even gave me a bigger credit limit."

Miranda stared at her vague, sweet mother with mounting horror. "Increased your credit limit when you aren't paying your bills? Why would they do that?"

Flo looked abashed. "Because of Callum, of course."

"Because of Callum?" She must sound like the village idiot the way she kept repeating her mother. "What does Callum Ironstone have to do with your accounts?"

"He originally settled all our accounts after your father died. It was part of our agreement," Flo said defensively. "Everyone knows who the Ironstones are. Things were so difficult at the time—don't you remember? He used to pay the accounts I sent him until you took over."

Her mother fluttered her hands like a delicate butterfly but Miranda refused to be diverted. "I don't remember. It must have been in that agreement you never showed me," she said grimly. "Are you telling me you've extended your credit on the basis of Callum's name?" It was too horrible to contemplate.

"Well, it's not costing him anything," Flo said defiantly.

"But it will if you don't pay. I can't believe these stores have let the balances run on for so long."

"I call them regularly—I'm hardly some debtor they think is about to abscond. They know Callum will look after me."

This was getting worse and worse. Miranda snatched the account back, and studied it, before looking back at her mother in despair. "The interest is running at a prohibitive rate."

"I don't think *all* the stores charge such high rates, darling."

All the stores? "There are more?" Miranda stared at her mother, aghast.

So much for her stubborn determination *never* to be beholden to Callum again. There was no money to pay these accounts. Callum would be contacted by the stores eventually to be told that her mother was shopping on his credit.

Unless of course Hemingway's decided to institute legal action to recover the debt.

The shame of it.

"Oh, dear Lord, Mum. What have you done?"

It was the following afternoon—her day off—and after a spending the day walking aimlessly around the city, her brain in turmoil, Miranda finally decided to take action about her mother's revelation.

Even if Callum had paid off her parents' accounts after her father's death, he could hardly have intended her mother to continue using his name to lever credit. The time had come to see him and lay all the dead cats on his boardroom table, she decided with mordant humor. Adrian and Flo would have to put up with whatever repercussions followed.

She could no longer continue deceiving him.

Miranda paused at Trafalgar Square. Years ago Flo had sometimes brought her and Adrian here to feed the pigeons, and each Christmas, they'd come to admire the lights and Christmas tree. The pigeons had long since been discouraged, but the Christmas tree still stood. And the fountain Adrian had almost fallen into one icy winter's day.

So when her cell phone rang and she heard Callum's distinctive voice, Miranda was hardly surprised. She sank down on a bench near the fountain. To her annoyance her "Hi" was more than a little breathless.

"Been making any brandy snaps lately?"

His lighthearted comment made her want to cry. That teasing humor wouldn't last once he heard what her mother had been up to. "Not enough."

That reminded her that she needed to organize some overtime. There were Flo's accounts to pay. On the spur of the moment she said rashly, "I don't suppose you have more work for me?"

The pause echoed in her ears.

She shut her eyes. Stupid. She opened them and gazed blindly at the tall tree decorated with vertical rows of light on the other side of the fountain. "I mean real work. I don't want a donation."

"I know you don't. I was thinking."

She tried not to notice how low his voice was…how sexy…or how it sent shivers down her spine.

"Maybe we could meet and talk about people I know who might be able to give you work," he said.

It wouldn't be a date. And little as she wanted to be in his debt, what harm was there in using his social network to further her own ends? It wasn't as if she was taking money from him.

And she would use the opportunity to tell him what Flo had done. Maybe even what Adrian had done—if the meeting went smoothly enough.

"That would be great." The world seemed bright and shiny—no longer dull and gray. "I'd like that."

"Then I'll pick you up on Friday—we'll have dinner."

Friday night? That sounded suspiciously like a date. But she knew that this time she wouldn't refuse.

Callum was rather pleased with himself.

Not only had he managed to secure a date with Miranda—although he rather doubted she'd view the evening in the same light—he'd also gotten glowing feedback about the Christmas cocktail party Miranda had catered for him. Apart from the fact that everyone had enjoyed it, saying it was streets ahead of any similar event they'd attended, Hunter told him there'd been a promise of a new corporate deal from Tom Murray, and a businessman Callum had been courting for a long time had made an appointment to talk about having all his plants insured with Ironstone Insurance. He'd even heard that Miranda had catered a small dinner party for Hunter, though she'd said nothing about that.

All in all Callum had the feeling that his plans were finally working out.

When he picked her up on Friday evening, she was ready for him, auguring well for the night. He liked punctuality in a woman.

No black dress this time—he didn't know whether to be sorry or relieved. Instead she wore a pair of fitted narrow-legged black pants, high boots and a skirted coat with a wide belt that covered her curves. No matter. He had every intention of taking her somewhere warm, so by the end of the evening she would be wearing far fewer clothes if it all went to plan.

Seated opposite her at a table in the alcove of the bay window in one of his favorite restaurants, Callum smiled in satisfaction as he took in the sensual sheen of the gray satin blouse she wore. So far so good. He watched as she studied the menu, that endearing frown furrowing her brow. When she snapped the menu shut, she caught him staring. Callum raised his champagne flute and took a quick sip.

"Why are you looking at me like that?"

"You do things with so much concentration—it takes your whole being." He set the glass down on the white linen cloth.

Miranda looked down and fiddled with her fork. She looked embarrassed as she said, "Some people say I'm too single-minded."

"Nothing wrong with that."

"You think?" She abandoned the fork, and her gaze locked with his. "I've been told it's unfeminine."

He chuckled. "There's not an unfeminine bone in your body." His gaze traced the dark brows, the gentle curve of her cheek and settled on her lush mouth. Her tongue came out and moistened her bottom lip. Callum quickly raised his eyes. She was staring at him, her dark eyes wide and a little shocked.

There was no doubt that he must've revealed some of the insatiable hunger she roused in him.

To play down the moment, he couldn't resist asking, "Why are you looking at me like that?"

"No reason." She flushed and glanced away, picking up her serviette and spreading it out before laying it on her lap. The heat that smoldered whenever he was near her ignited.

Miranda was every bit as aware of him as he was of her. He wished she would give in to the inevitable. Couldn't she see they were destined to be lovers?

Then she looked up. "For some reason this feels like a date." She pointed at the tall crystal flutes and the arrangement of white roses on the table. "I told you I didn't want to date you." But a slight smile softened her words.

A waiter arrived and lit the squat white candle with a taper, before taking their orders.

Once he'd topped their glasses and collected the menus he departed, Callum took up the conversation where they'd left off. "It's not a date—it's a business meeting."

He fought back a grin at her expression of disbelief.

She snorted. "You bring business colleagues here on a Friday night?"

He raised his hands in a gesture of innocence. "I've been known to invite business associates on a Saturday night for dinner—I'm a busy man."

"I accept you'd bring your brothers here. But what about Gordon? Or Tom Murray? Tom must love the champagne, huh?" She raised her glass in a mock salute.

This time he couldn't help the grin that spread over his face. "We do celebrate business ventures sometimes."

Miranda set her glass down. "And mergers?"

Quietly he said, "I told Petra our relationship was over."

The mood changed. All lighthearted banter stilled. A sizzling tension filled the space between them.

"You broke up with her?" Dismay darkened the caramel eyes to a shade of chocolate. "I never wanted that."

"Over a week ago."

An unreadable expression flashed across her face. *"Over a week ago?"* she asked. "And you said nothing?"

"It had nothing to do with you," he lied.

It had everything to do with Miranda. He'd been very content with the notion of settling down with Petra until Miranda came along and stirred up his libido, leaving him hungering for so much more. They were so good together. Yet she stubbornly refused to acknowledge that…he could pretend, too, if that's what he wanted.

Callum leaned forward. "This is a meeting. And don't let the champagne bother you—it's tax deductible."

"Tax deductible?" Miranda scoffed, but the annoyance had ebbed and, to his relief, amusement lurked behind the shadows in her eyes.

He was winning. Time to cut the ground from under her feet while he was still ahead. "Let's get to work, and see how I can help you with your business. I hear you catered very successfully for Hunter last week."

Her features grew animated. "Oh, yes, I've been meaning to thank you for the referral."

"It was nothing." With a wave of his hand, he dismissed it. "Hunter was impressed."

"One of his guests called earlier today and asked me for a quote for a New Year's Eve party."

"Word of mouth. The best way to get known."

"It's an enormous relief. If I can make this work…" She fell silent.

He waited.

Finally she gave a soft sigh. "Things have been… tense at The Golden Goose. I'm not sure how much longer I'll have a job. With the economic climate there has been talk of retrenchments."

It surprised him that she'd chosen to confide in him. Normally she worked so hard to keep him at arm's length. "You won't be affected."

She nibbled her lip. "I wish I could be so certain."

Callum got the sense she didn't share personal fears easily. "What makes you think that? You're overqualified for that place, you're diligent." He leaned back. "And you cook like a dream."

She gave him a quick smile. "Thanks for the vote of confidence. I've stayed at the Goose because of the convenience—it's close to home. But I'm the junior chef—and the other chef makes life hard."

"I get it. You're young. You're good at what you do. And you probably don't earn what he does. I'm not surprised you threaten him."

Spreading her hands, she said, "Maybe you're right. I've wondered if it's that. But it doesn't help that whenever there are accidents in the kitchen, Gianni always manages to blame me—even if I was somewhere else.

Not to mention the times he tells Mick I'm late when I arrive bang on time."

"You don't need to put up with it. You could get a much better job if you wanted. In a place like this." He gestured to the fine white linen and sparkling silverware on their table, then waved his arm to encompass the rest of the restaurant with its elegant high ceilings, bay windows and alcoves, and the ivory curtains draped in swags.

"Can I? There's a cloud over my father. People remember scandals like embezzlement. They worry about the fruit not falling far from the tree." There was no bitterness in her voice.

"You'd have references."

"Really?" She raised an eyebrow. "What kind of a reference would I get?" Her expression was skeptical. "Gianni and the boss are friends—they even flat together."

Callum resisted the impulse to tell her that *he* would supply a reference to any restaurant she chose. He suspected she'd rather do things her own way. "Then focus on the catering business that Adrian says you've always dreamed of. You've already made a start. Have you got a business plan?"

She nodded.

"I'll look at it if you want." He drew an envelope from his pocket. "Here's a list of names with contact numbers of executives I know who would be more than happy to give you work. Go the whole way."

Hesitantly she took the list from him, unfolding it to glance through the names. From her expression he knew that she'd recognized several of them as movers and shakers in the city.

"I've already contacted most of them to let them know you'll be calling them."

"It's not that easy," she protested. "I'd planned to ease in gradually, but times are hard. Even established businesses are failing, and I have responsibilities."

Despite her confident façade, Miranda was afraid. Something inside him cracked a little. "The last name is an accountant who'll be able to steer you through the pitfalls of running a small business—she's an old friend of our family."

There was an expression in her eyes he couldn't read. Was she thinking of her family? Her father? Was she blaming him for how her father's death had landed her in this position?

Again that smothering sense of guilt closed in on him. She shouldn't have borne it all alone.

He'd tried to help—to ease the family's precarious financial position and give Miranda and her brother some sort of education. And now he was determined to help her get her catering business off the ground. But nothing could bring her father back.

He reached out and closed his hand over hers. "Let me help you."

She jerked away, clearly recoiling from the idea... from him.

He gave her a moment, then said, "You blame me for killing your father, so why is it so hard to let me sponsor you?"

"And make it easy for you? Throw money at the problem and your conscience is clean?" Her eyes sparkled with what he hoped was anger and not tears. "I don't think so."

He couldn't bear tears.

"My conscience will never be clear," he confessed.

She blinked frantically, then her shoulders slumped. "I wish Dad were here. Lately I've been wishing for that a lot."

Her raw admission caused an ache to splinter deep in his chest. He again tightened his hand around hers. She started, but didn't withdraw this time.

"I'm sorry, Miranda—more than you'll ever know."

Her eyes were full of anguished shadows. "Thank you. I needed to hear that."

He glanced at the list. "Call those names. You're going to be a success. And don't think what I'm doing for you is unique. I often give someone a break. And that's what we do with our company scholarships, too. Adrian's got a real chance to get one of those. He's hardworking and smart. No reason why he shouldn't."

Her eyelids lowered, veiling her gaze. "I appreciate your nominating Adrian. Now that he's finished school, he's going to have to think hard about his future."

"He's a big boy now. He has to make his own choices."

Her lashes fluttered up and she gave him a rapid, indecipherable glance, then sighed. "You're probably right. But I've been so used to looking out for him. Which brings me to something else I have to discuss with you tonight."

"What's that?"

"Flo."

"Your mother?"

She nodded. "She's been running up accounts all over the city. And the stores are letting her do it because they think you're guaranteeing her expenditure. You need to write to them so it can stop."

His fingers played with hers. "I can afford it."

She shook her head. "No. I'll never be able to repay you."

"I don't expect you to."

"Then I'd lose my self-respect. Please, Callum, let them know. I don't want to be further in your debt. It's going to be hard enough paying you back as it is."

"You don't have to pay me back."

"Of course I do." Cent by backbreaking cent.

A frown darkened his expression. "That's not what I ever intended."

"I know."

"So why don't you forget about it?"

She'd thought she could. But how could they ever move into any kind of relationship—even an uneasy friendship—if she owed him money? She'd forever feel indebted to him, some kind of charity case. She needed to be able to face him as an equal. The news that he'd broken up with Petra had caused her heart to leap. For a brief moment she'd entertained a wild hope of more than friendship...then she'd doused it.

She freed her hand from his. "I can't."

Originally it had been her hatred of Callum that had had her refusing his help. She'd wanted him to feel responsible—guilty even. But then she'd discovered he'd already spent so much she hadn't known about—on her, on her family—because he really had felt guilty about her father. And clearly still did. It didn't sit well with her that for almost three years she'd cursed him, hated him, wished that lightning would strike him.

Besides, if she accepted his money, Callum might

view her in the same way that he must see her mother—pretty, but fundamentally a parasite.

"There's an easy way around all this," he said.

Nothing was ever easy. She gave him a suspicious look. "What?"

"We make a good team."

Miranda snorted. "Where did you get that idea from?"

"The Christmas cocktail function was a huge success. People loved it. And it's given me the opening to secure opportunities I've been trying to tie up for a long time." He drew her hand back into his. "I need a hostess."

It was part of the reason marrying Petra would've been so convenient. But he'd never desired Petra with this raw, physical ache.

"I was hardly a hostess. I just made the food," she said dismissively.

He tipped his head to one side and considered her for a long moment. What was it about this woman that drew him? Even when he wasn't with her, all he could think about was her. She was starting to consume him. "No, you did so much more than that. It was the little touches that made the evening memorable." Even his PR officer had commented on the unique feel of the party.

He massaged her fingers and they went stiff beneath his. "You're asking me to hostess your functions?"

"More than that."

Suspicion glistened in her eyes at his throaty statement. "You're asking me to be your mistress?"

"No!" Even he wasn't fool enough to think she would accept such a preposterous proposition. But, God, he was tempted to ask. To have her in his bed, fulfilling his every desire…

Perhaps there was another option.

"So what *do* you want?"

Miranda had never been one to back away. So it was to be expected that she'd get to the crux of the matter. What did he want?

He lifted her rigid fingers to his mouth and placed a soft kiss on each fingertip, watching her eyes grow wide with shock.

"I suppose," he said slowly, "I'm asking you to be my wife."

Seven

"Your wife?"

Miranda's lips parted in astonishment and her pulse picked up. Opposite her, Callum looked almost as startled by his proposal as she. Had he meant to ask? Or was this an impulsive mistake? Her brain worked furiously. Did his proposal have anything to do with his break-up with Petra? Surely it couldn't. That had happened a week ago.

"Why on earth would you want to marry me?"

The corners of his mouth crinkled up into a heart-stopping smile. "Lots of reasons."

So he *had* meant to ask. And at least he wasn't insulting her intelligence by claiming to love her.

Tilting her head to one side, Miranda studied him. The tantalizing thought of hardheaded Callum in love was impossible to envision. He hadn't loved Petra—even though she would've made him a perfect wife. Especially considering her father was a major shareholder in Ironstone Insurance. Callum and Petra came from the same world. Whereas Callum imagined Miranda's father to be nothing more than a thief.

And then of course with her flawless oval face, blond hair and pale blue eyes, the other woman was exquisitely beautiful. The children she and Callum would've shared would almost certainly have been blue-eyed little angels. Thinking about them caused an unexpected glass splinter of pain to pierce Miranda's heart.

Callum had admitted he'd intended to marry the beautiful blonde—he'd even bought a ring.

So why was he asking Miranda to marry him? "Name one reason."

"Your cooking is to die for."

Even though mirth bubbled up inside her, she didn't laugh as he'd clearly meant for her to do. Instead, refusing to be distracted, she gave him her most severe look and said, "This is no laughing matter. Or was your proposal meant as a joke?"

She had to know.

In response his fingertips stroked across the back of her hand, and under his touch she caught fire. Her blood fizzed and a heady excitement seized hold of her. Okay, this definitely wasn't funny. It felt like he'd branded her as his.

She shook off the ridiculous sensation. Callum Ironstone couldn't make her his merely with a stroke of his fingers!

"And if I told you that it drives me mad with lust when you don your apron? That I have a yen to seduce you wearing a tall chef's hat? Would you accuse me of joking then?"

The intensity of his hot gaze told her this was no joke.

A wickedly erotic image flashed through her mind of Callum pinning her up against the counter in his kitchen....

She'd be fully clothed, wearing her frilliest apron and a toque. While Callum stood between her parted legs, naked and virile. His fingers dipping into a pot of rich, dark chocolate mousse then offering them to her. She licked the mousse delicately from his fingertips…he moaned…his blue eyes blazed, promising to pleasure her from head to toe before the night was out....

Good grief. Where had that come from?

A flush seared her face, scorching all the way down her body to her most private places. Her voice cracking, she said, "No one gets turned on by that getup."

"If you say so."

His cheekbones stood out under tightly drawn skin. He looked dark and dangerous and unbelievably desirable.

"Sex on its own is never a good reason for marriage," she told him fiercely, a warning to herself as much as him. The fantasy flash had disturbed her far more than she cared to admit.

"I can't think of a better reason."

Her breath died abruptly in her throat as he gazed at her with raw, unvarnished hunger.

Callum Ironstone wanted her.

For one wild moment she was tempted to flee. From him—and from her own riotous imaginings. She scanned across the restaurant, checking if the escape route was clear, and except for one waiter balancing a tray on his shoulder, it was.

She should run. Now.

If she stayed it might be too late to free herself from the power of his attraction. Callum posed a risk that she'd never anticipated.

Yet an overwhelming desire for an answer to the question she'd posed kept her in the chair, even as his hands caressed hers with slow deliberation.

He couldn't be offering marriage to get her into his bed—he'd already done that. There *had* to be more to it than this incomprehensible desire that leaped between them. And he'd already made it clear, love had nothing to do with it.

Questions buzzed around inside her head, multiplying into further questions. But before she could utter them, he bent his head closer to hers. In the candlelight she could see all the way into the bright blue eyes, to the black flecks that lurked like hazardous rocks in a deceptively calm stretch of sea.

"I think we could make a fantastic team."

"You and me? A team?" Was the man insane?

"Shh." He laid his index finger against his lips. "Hear me out."

Miranda found herself following that finger and staring at the beauty of the full lower lip that softened his strong features and gave an unexpected sensuality to the arrogantly handsome face.

His hand dropped back to rest on the tablecloth beside hers, and to her consternation Miranda was acutely aware of the inch of distance separating their fingers.

She hadn't wanted him reducing her to a quivering mass just by the stroke of his fingers, had she?

"You have a gift—one that complements my strengths," he was saying. "With your skills—"

"A gift? You mean cooking?" She jerked her head back in disbelief. "So you really do want to marry me for my cooking?"

"It's more than that. You have an ability to make people feel not only nourished, but also cherished on a level I cannot reach."

Warmth filled her at the unexpected compliment. Yet she realized it was true. She'd always cared for those close to her—her family were sure of her love. Nourish. Cherish. He'd articulated something that she'd only ever been dimly aware of in the back of her consciousness. "Thank you. That's a nice thing to say."

He shook his head. "Not nice. Absolutely true. And it's a talent I can use."

The warmth fizzled out.

"You would be able to take care of a side of my life I don't have time to deal with."

Of course. Everything was always about what he could use. What he could turn to profit. He must've been born with a calculator for a heart.

Miranda raised her glass and took a careful sip. Despite the rush of bubbles to the surface, the champagne tasted flat. A reflection of her state of mind, no doubt. She set the glass down. "You want to marry me so I can sort your business entertaining."

He didn't deny it.

What had she expected? Callum was running one hundred percent true to type.

"Gee, you must be patting yourself on the back for the wise investment you made paying for my culinary training."

His mouth compressed into a tight line. "Don't be so cynical. You'd be far more than a chef. You'd be my *wife,* for God's sake. You'd run my life."

"Mrs. Callum Ironstone. A useful wife with no identity of her own." The idea chilled her. There would be no room for nourishing or cherishing in such a life. "And what about love and romance and all the reasons people usually get married?" What about all *her* dreams and hopes?

Flags of color scorched his cheekbones and his eyes sparked. "I have every intention of sleeping with *Mrs. Ironstone,*" he said between clenched teeth. "This won't be some platonic marriage. We've already proved we're a very good fit."

Fit? It made her sound like a damn suit that he could shed when she'd outworn her use.

After a quick glance around revealed no one was looking their way, she lowered her voice and said, "I spoke of love, Callum. Not sex."

An unreadable expression flitted over his face. "Love is an emotional complication neither of us need."

"Speak for yourself. I don't see love as an emotional complication."

He gave her a superior smile. "Of course it is. Look at you—just talking about love is getting you wound up. Sex will allow you to relax, unwind." His fingertips crossed the inch of tablecloth that had become no-man's land to play along the tender skin of her inner wrist, and Miranda quivered in reaction as tingles exploded up her arm. He paused, exploring the fine lilac lines of her pulse, and the smile became reckless. "But if romance is so important to you…I can take care of that."

Despite her madly racing pulse, Miranda went down fighting. "Your idea of romance is roses and hot sex."

His hands, damn them, cradled hers with a tenderness that she knew meant nothing.

"What's wrong with that?" He truly did look puzzled. "It would be far better to keep our relationship straightforward. We both know we set each other on fire in bed— I've never experienced anything like it," he admitted with a raw honesty she had no choice but to believe. "That's why I had to end it with Petra."

He leaned closer across the table. She could smell the crisp, clean scent of him—so male with a hint of bergamot and musk underpinning it.

It would be so easy to give in—it would solve all her problems.

She wouldn't have to worry about Gianni or Mick at work. Or her family. All her financial worries would become a thing of the past in an instant. Callum would take care of everything. She'd be able to resign from The Golden Goose and she'd simply present him with Flo's debts to settle. His wealth would mean Adrian's and Flo's debts wouldn't make a dent.

Dent…

Help! He still didn't know about Adrian's accident, and she suspected Callum wouldn't be quite so sanguine about her keeping him in the dark. Yet Adrian had asked her not to tell Callum. How could she betray her brother?

Oh, this was dreadful.

A wave of shame swept her that she'd even considered accepting his proposal for such superficial reasons. She'd be using him. Marrying him for his wealth.

Hadn't he admitted that he intended to use her, too? But that was no reason to stoop to his level. When she married, it would be because she loved a man so much she didn't want to live without him.

Miranda stopped herself from sighing aloud. It was better this way. They didn't even share the same life views. And she wasn't likely to change him.

She shook her hands free from his. "I can't marry you."

"You can't?" He looked utterly surprised.

He'd expected her to say yes? But Miranda found that she had no urge to laugh at the stunned expression in his eyes. Instead a curious hollowness settled in the space beneath her heart. "I want more, Callum." *Much more.*

"I see."

But she doubted he did. And it was too hard to explain.

Putting her elbows on the table, she dropped her face into the cup of her hands, feeling utterly wretched.

The touch of a finger under her chin caused her to lift her head. It was only the pad of his index finger yet she was aware of his touch through her whole body.

When she met his eyes, she could read little there. But then he was hardly the kind of man a woman could read like a glossy gossip rag. And that enigmatic quality was part of what drew her to him again and again even though she knew it was downright self-destructive.

"Look, I really do need your help."

"What help?" she asked with more than a little suspicion. After all, he was an Ironstone.

"Our family always spends Christmas at Fairwinds."

At the height of her hatred for Callum, she'd pored

over *Country Life* images of Fairwinds, the Ironstones' country retreat set on Lake Windermere's bank in the Lake District. A long tree-lined lane cutting through a grassy park, a forecourt edged with neatly clipped box hedging, and a flight of stone stairs leading up to the imposing house with its mullioned windows and a steep jagged roofline. The photos had oozed old wealth and gracious living.

And she'd raged against how unfair life was.

Miranda shook herself free of the memory. "Why are you telling me this?"

"I'd like you to spend Christmas with us," he said, "as my partner for the weekend."

Miranda sucked in a breath.

"It's my mother's birthday," he continued, "the day after Christmas. We're planning to throw her a surprise birthday party—and Gordon and Petra have already been invited."

Callum didn't need to add that he'd originally planned to take Petra along to his mother's birthday as his fiancée. That his break-up with the blonde had caused a horrible complication. It was written all over his discomfited face. And that knowledge caused an unexpected wash of bittersweet sensation to engulf Miranda.

"You're asking me to come along and *protect* you?"

Heavens, men could be so *obtuse*.

"Something like that." The barely imperceptible tension that had been coiled within him eased a little, and his eyes smiled into hers. "You could take over working the kitchen on the weekend. I'd make it worth your while."

Miranda itched to slap him.

"My mother always goes to a great deal of trouble over the festive season—works herself half to death, which makes us all feel guilty. This year she turns sixty." His expression held a tenderness she'd never seen. "We want to spoil her rotten. We'd planned to get some help with the Christmas preparations, but we've all been involved with the merger and no one's gotten around to organizing it. Neglectful sons, aren't we?"

There was something inherently sweet about the thought of four grown men—five if you counted his father—coming up with such an idea. It made her turn to marshmallow.

"We'd even pay you—top rates, given that it will be over the Christmas weekend."

For a moment she thought of her family. She'd never spent Christmas away from them. But how could she possibly resist? The commission Callum was dangling in front of her would enable her to put something toward the deposit Adrian wanted for the pre-owned BMW he'd already agreed to buy from a friend before the expense of the accident—and maybe even buy her mother the new microwave she desperately wanted. And she had to admit to a yearning to see the home in the country that he'd spoken of with such affection.

The only thing that concerned her about his request was Petra. How did the other woman feel about Callum? Miranda suspected Petra would be wounded to be faced with her supposed successor. It made her feel uncomfortable.

Callum must have seen her hesitation because he asked, "Will you come?", giving her a charmingly lopsided smile. "Will you make my mother's life, my life—all our lives—so much easier?"

Faced with his love for his mother, how could she refuse? He cared for his mother, loved her. That was beyond doubt. She was discovering a side of Callum she'd never seen before.

Or had she?

Even though he barely knew Flo, he'd taken care of her since her husband's death. More than Miranda had ever realized. He'd misjudged her father with tragic results...but he hadn't walked away and abandoned them. Anonymously he'd tried to make amends in the best way he could—by making sure she and her brother received a top-class education, and by looking after the widow of the man he'd wronged.

Perhaps it was time for her to let up on him a little. He'd done wrong, but he'd clearly regretted the consequences his actions had produced.

She'd intended to throw all his money back in his face once she scrimped it together. Yet here was something he was asking her to do, something that could ease her burden of the debt.

Their food arrived before she could answer, the two waiters whipping off the silver covers of the plates with a flourish.

After she'd made the expected noises of approval, they departed. And, drawing a deep breath, Miranda said, "I think it's a lovely gesture. Your mother will adore a birthday celebration. Of course I'll come."

"Toothbrush. Shampoo. Perfume."

Miranda packed the final items into her toiletry holdall

and tossed it into her overnight bag. Then, crumpling up her list, she dropped it into the bin beneath her dressing table.

"You're all packed?"

She hadn't heard her mother come in. Miranda turned her head to smile at Flo. "Only my cooking stuff left to pack—at least Callum's Daimler has plenty of space. I'm going to miss you and Adrian, Mum."

"You'll be back after the weekend on Boxing Day." Flo patted her arm. "Not that long."

But it would be over Christmas. "With Christmas falling on Friday this year, Boxing Day seems so far away."

Flo gave her a kiss on the cheek. "I'll keep you some Christmas pudding, darling."

"That would be lovely." Her mother made the best Christmas pudding in the whole world.

"Adrian's already up. Should we open our presents before you go?"

Miranda studied Flo. "Wouldn't you prefer to wait until Christmas tomorrow?"

"It will be so strange without you. Let me see what Adrian wants to do."

Flo waltzed out, and Miranda gathered up the modest gifts she'd bought for her mother and Adrian, before making her way to the small lounge.

Adrian and Flo were already waiting, Flo all but dancing with excitement as she pushed a package into Miranda's hands. "We're doing it now. Save mine until last."

Miranda laughed. "I will, I will." She handed Adrian the bottle of aftershave she'd bought him—one she knew he liked. "This is yours. When I get paid for this weekend's work, I'll give you a check to put toward the BMW—that way your friend will at least continue to hold it for you. I'd like to get Mum a microwave, too."

Adrian's face lit up. "Thanks, sis. That's awesome. One day I'll repay everything you've done for me."

Miranda felt a niggle of misgiving. "Pay me back? You don't need to. It's a gift."

Her brother looked uncomfortable. "One you can't afford—not if you want to get out of The Golden Goose."

Had she become so tight about money that her brother couldn't accept a gift from her anymore? It reminded her of her own determination to pay Callum back come hell or high water.

But Adrian was family. It was different.

Before she could say anything more, he handed her a flat parcel. "It's a boring gift. But I think you'll enjoy it."

It was a book by a chef she admired. She hugged him, then she settled down and tore the wrapping from the package her mother had given her. Her fingers peeled back the paper to reveal a red woolen scarf. She drew it out. It was as soft as the silk she'd collected from the silkworms she'd reared as a child, the wool fine and warm against her fingertips.

How much had it cost?

She bit back the question. "It's beautiful. Thanks, Mum."

Flo's eyes glowed with happiness. "Take it with you. That color does marvelous things for your skin. I knew it was yours the moment I spotted it. And here's something else."

A second, much larger, package landed in her lap.

"Mum, you didn't need to…" Her voice trailed away as she saw the ivory trench coat that lay inside.

"They're very in this season, darling."

Miranda felt as if she'd been turned to stone. She stared at the coat. But instead of seeing a garment, all she could see were bills.

Unpaid bills.

"Mother…" She looked up. "Please don't tell me that you've extended your credit further. Tell me you won a lottery. Anything. Just not more debt."

The happiness on her mother's face subsided. "Oh, Miranda, don't spoil it."

Beside her mother, Adrian fidgeted.

"We can't afford this, Flo."

She'd have to face Callum, tell him that her mother was still using his name. Then she'd have to pay him back. The debt stretched ahead of her like an un-scaleable mountain. "Oh, Mum."

"Don't 'Oh, Mum' me." Her mother stood up abruptly. "You're not the only one allowed to give nice presents."

"What do you mean?"

"You just promised Adrian you'd help him with the deposit on his car—and possibly buy me the new model microwave I've been wanting. But we're not allowed to give you anything nice?"

Adrian looked like he wished he was far away.

"It's not the size—or the expense—of the present that counts. It never has been." Miranda folded the wrap-pings over the coat. "You need to take this back. Get the account credited."

Her mother's shoulders sagged. "But you'll keep the scarf?"

She took in her mother's dejection. With an inward sigh Miranda conceded, "Yes, I will."

Flo perked up instantly. "And wear it this weekend. That red lipstick of yours will match it perfectly."

Miranda crossed over to her mother and hugged her. Flo stood quietly in the circle of her arms, and Miranda noticed that her mother had become as fragile as a butterfly; she was thinner than she'd ever been. "I love you, Mum."

How she wished that things were different. For Flo to be more reasonable. For her father to be here.

Ah, what did it help to wish for the impossible?

Her father wasn't coming back.

And she was spending the weekend with the man who had caused his death. A man who'd asked her to be his wife.

What a traitor she'd become.

Eight

Everything was packed and ready to take to Fairwinds. There was some baking that with Flo's help Miranda had prepared in advance, a selection of herbs and spices that she never traveled without—and extras that she intended to gift to the family—as well as a plethora of laborsaving devices and utensils.

Unfortunately it had been raining since they'd opened presents, making it impossible for her to stack it all outside, and now Callum was due to collect her.

Deciding she had to get moving, regardless of the weather, she kissed her mother goodbye and moved to hug Adrian.

He pecked her on the cheek. "I'll give you a hand with all your junk." Picking up her overnight bag, he held the front door open for her. "I'll make a second trip for the bigger boxes."

Miranda smiled her thanks up to him. "What would I do without you?" she said teasingly, then realized it was true—she loved her brother, would do whatever she could to protect him.

Outside the rain had eased off. Droplets dripped from the eaves, while the wind whistled through the bare branches of the lone potted silver birch.

"Look after Mum," she told her brother on the step.

Adrian set down her bag. "I will."

He was back in a jiffy with her boxes and stacked them at the bottom of the steps beside her luggage. "It's going to snow again," he said, studying the sky.

"Maybe." Miranda squinted at the heavy clouds overhead. "Remember how we used to make snowmen in winter? With an old pair of Dad's gumboots? Once we borrowed Mum's pink scarf and she was so cross."

Adrian chuckled beside her. "Remember the time you pulled my carrot nose out and gave it to Troubadour? We had such a snowball fight after that."

"You stole the horse's carrot. And anyway, you started it. You put a handful of snow down my shirt." Miranda grimaced. "You hooligan."

"And you clobbered me with your riding crop, so I hit you back."

"And then Dad came and gave you a lecture about how boys should behave with honor always." A lump thickened her throat. "I'd forgotten about that. We were a right royal pair of brats sometimes."

Adrian stopped laughing. "Miranda—"

His eyes were full of turbulence, and her heart sank. "What's wrong?"

"I'm sorry to have to add this to everything, sis."

Oh, no. What had her talk of honor provoked? "What? What's happened now?"

Adrian flinched.

She tried to temper her impatience. "Callum will be here any minute. Tell me."

"The panel beater who fixed the car—"

"What did he do wrong?" That was the last thing they needed. Had the car been shoddily repaired. Or worse?

"Nothing—he fixed it. The car's been back at work for days—otherwise it would've been missed."

"Then what's the problem?"

"He's threatening to tell my supervisor I borrowed the car without permission unless…"

"Unless what?"

"Unless I pay him more money."

She stared at her brother aghast. "This man's blackmailing you?"

"He says if I pay him, he'll stay quiet."

"You're actually considering paying this lowlife hush money?"

Adrian shrugged. "I don't exactly have a choice."

"And where *exactly*—" she said with emphasis "—is the money going to come from? Please tell me you're not going to rob a bank—that would hardly be honorable."

He recoiled at her sarcasm, then shot her a quick look. "I thought—"

Miranda shook her head and said grimly, "No, you can unthink that idea right now. I'm not giving you the money. Not even as a loan. If you pay him once, it will never end."

"So what am I supposed to do?" Adrian had gone pale beneath his freckles.

"Report him to the police. But first come clean to

Callum about what you did—it's hardly as bad as extortion."

Adrian looked horrified. "I can't."

"You must." At the glimpse of ghostly gray in her peripheral vision she added flatly, "He's here. Why don't you talk to him now?"

The sight of Callum's Daimler pulling up at the curb caused Adrian to blanch further. "Please, sis, I'm begging you—don't tell him."

"He should know."

His eyes darted around. "Not now. Not yet. I need time to think about what I'm going to say—and I really should be going to work."

His eyes pleaded with her.

After a moment, Miranda caved in. "Okay, but you *must* tell him—otherwise you'll leave me no choice but to do it myself."

She shuddered at the thought of it.

"As soon as you get back," he promised, giving her a sick smile. "I don't want to spend Christmas in jail while you try to arrange bail."

"It won't come to that." At least she hoped not. But she still shivered as Callum got out of the car and came round to greet her.

Her brother acknowledged Callum with none of his usual confidence and quickly sidled away, saying, "Drive carefully, and have a merry Christmas both of you."

Despite the fact that there had been heavy snows a few days earlier, the roads were clear and they were making good time.

Callum glanced over at the woman beside him.

Apart from a few monosyllabic answers, Miranda hadn't spoken much in the past three hours. After trying to engage her in conversation a couple of times, he'd shrugged and flooded the car with music, negating the need for conversation.

Right now she was scribbling in a notebook, a frown of concentration wrinkling her brow.

"Don't worry, everything will go like clockwork."

"I'm not worried." But the way she gnawed the end of her pencil refuted the statement. And so did the closed, withdrawn expression that had been etched on her face since he'd collected her earlier.

"Try to relax, my family won't bite."

"If you say so."

Callum fell silent.

She must be nervous. That would explain her behavior. They'd spoken several times over the past few days. At first she'd made panicked calls to him about logistics, but each time they'd spoken, she'd sounded more and more like the Miranda he knew. Smart. Confident. Totally together. After consultation with his brothers, and with his parents' housekeeper, he'd approved all the menus she'd produced—and given her carte blanche to buy whatever she needed.

With the housekeeper's help, Miranda had decided to employ three women from the local village to help with the birthday party, and to hire the majority of the crockery and cutlery needed from a firm in Ambleside. Much of the produce would come from local suppliers, too, which she'd already organized.

As late as last night, there'd been no problem. So why was she so withdrawn and tense now?

Or was he imagining problems where none existed?

Callum shrugged his concern off. It could be that Miranda simply wasn't a morning person—he'd teased her about that before. Or maybe she needed sustenance.

So fifteen minutes later he pulled off the M6 and headed for an inn set well back from the main road.

She looked up with surprise as he turned into the car park. "Where are we?"

He gestured to a large sign in front of the inn. "The Rose and Thorn."

She groaned. "That much is evident—I can see the sign."

His mouth twitched as he sensed her rolling her eyes.

Switching off the motor, he unclipped his seat belt. "I often break the journey here. They serve a good breakfast." He went round to her side and opened her door. "If you don't want breakfast, my mother swears by their cream teas."

She hesitated.

"Come on." Miranda was shivering as the cold air drifted into the warmth of the Daimler. "There's a warm fire inside," he coaxed as she drew her red scarf more tightly around her neck and emerged from the car in a flurry of denim and a bright red woolen coat.

Inside the dining room, the low wooden beams and a fire in the hearth gave the inn a welcoming ambience. Once a plump, smiling woman had taken their orders, Callum watched Miranda's gaze settle on a large Christmas tree in the corner. Her shoulders sagged imperceptibly.

"What's the matter?" he asked.

Miranda shook her head.

"Don't fob me off." He waited, but she still said nothing, though shadows lingered in her eyes. "This is me, Callum. When have you ever not been able to tell me exactly what you think?"

She gestured to the Christmas tree. "This will be the first time I haven't been with my family for Christmas." She slanted him a glance from under long, dark lashes and the expression in her melting eyes caught at something deep in his chest. "Nothing you can do about that."

He exhaled in relief. "That's all?"

"All? What do you mean 'all'?" The fire was back in her eyes. "No one is as important to me as Mum and Adrian. Since Dad died we've always roasted a Cornish hen—a turkey is too big for the three of us—and prepared all the trimmings. And this year I won't be there."

Callum cursed silently as he filled in the unspoken blanks. There probably hadn't been sufficient money for a turkey after her father's death. Remorse tugged at him that Miranda would be missing out on precious time with her family because of him.

Because he was prepared to go to any lengths to get her back in his bed.

God, he'd been selfish. If she ever learned how he'd manipulated her, she would be furious. So she had better never learn the truth.

The egg and bacon pie they'd both ordered from the special-of-the-day board arrived, distracting them both for a few minutes.

She continued with a wan smile. "Next year Adrian will probably be gone—out making his own life."

"That happened for a while with my family. It's part of growing up. But Adrian will return to the fold." He thought of his own family. "These days all my brothers go home for Christmas each year. It's rare that one of us doesn't make it."

"Four boys! Your poor mother. It couldn't have been easy. Isn't Hunter your stepbrother?"

At the glint of curiosity in her eyes, he explained, "Hunter and Jack are my half brothers. Dad married Mother after his first wife died. He already had Hunter and Jack. Then he and Mother had Fraser and me."

"I knew you were the youngest, but I wasn't sure who were your real brothers—you all seem so close."

"We are close. Hunter and Jack are every bit as much my brothers as Fraser is. And Dad had a busy job so most of the task of bringing us up landed on Mum." He waited for Miranda to make a comment about how privileged they all were, but she didn't. "Once Dad retired, Mother was very relieved. She's always wanted to live in the country—although I don't think she expected it to be quite so wet in winter."

Miranda's eyes were full of longing. "I can understand that—I wouldn't care about the wet though."

She'd grown up in the country, he knew. "You miss it, don't you?"

"I have fond memories of living there. Just the—" she broke off "—the ending wasn't so nice."

Callum knew her home had been auctioned off after her father's suicide—along with most of the furniture and valuables. He'd done what he'd could to help patch up the shambles of her parents' finances but it hadn't been enough.

"I think one of the worst things was saying goodbye to Troubadour."

"Troubadour?"

"My horse. I'd had him since I was thirteen and he was rising three. I loved that horse."

Another loss.

Her father. Her home. Her horse.

Everything she'd loved. Everything dear and familiar to her. Gone.

Callum fell silent and dug into the bacon and egg pie as if he was waging a battle.

"Look, I don't know how we got into such distressing topics." She made a dismissive gesture with her hand. "It's too depressing—especially so near to Christmas."

He laid down his knife and fork. "I think we do need to talk about it," he said gently. He wanted to reach out and touch the hands he suspected would be ice-cold despite the warmth of the inn's fire.

"I'd rather not." She inhaled audibly, and gave him a very fake and, to his mind, a very brave smile. "It's not practical to live in the country. London is where the work is."

Her deliberate changing of the subject warned Callum that the past still affected her deeply.

Would she ever be able to let it go?

A restless edginess shook him. He faced the fact that she might never do so. And that would leave them forever estranged. The realization was akin to looking down into a long, dark tunnel, one without a glimpse of day at the other side.

He wasn't ready to exist in perpetual darkness. He'd find a way to see the sunlight on the other side. Because the notion of never holding her again, never making love to her, was one he wasn't ready to accept.

It left him with no choice. She was going to hate him

for reopening the wounds, but if he didn't, he might as well kiss any chance of having her back in his bed goodbye now. Without resolving the past, they had no future.

However, now was probably not the best time to address it. Taking the conversational olive branch she'd offered, he gestured around. "The big money might be in London, but surely there are enough places like this where you could have the country lifestyle you want?"

"Maybe, but I never wanted to be an innkeeper—" she pulled a face that he found rather endearing "—or a café owner. I'd be perfectly happy catering for an array of the rich and famous."

He laughed but his eyes remained fixed on her. "Is that what you really want?"

Her lips firmed. "What I really want isn't possible, so I live with what is."

She wanted her father back. "Look, about your father—"

"You've already apologized. Let's leave it there." She glanced down, her lashes forming dark shadows against her creamy skin, and her body had gone very still.

Callum couldn't leave it—it pervaded their whole relationship.

Three years ago he'd been appointed to the board as financial director after returning from five years of working in Australia. He'd worked all hours, day and night, to get on top of the chaos after his predecessor— a good friend of his father's—had resigned with a colon cancer scare. The cruel whispers of nepotism had infuriated Callum—particularly as he didn't want to hurt his father's friend with the truth.

Callum had been unknown and unproven, and that had fueled his fierce desperation to prove to his brothers, to the management team and to the skeptical naysayers that he could do the task his father had set upon him.

He'd probably gone over the top.

He'd certainly adopted a take-no-prisoners management style.

How best to explain the climate against which his actions had played out? Whatever he said was going to sound like justification for his arrogance.

He chose his words carefully. "If I could have that time of my life over again, I would have handled things differently."

Miranda met his gaze. "*Handled things differently?* You mean you would've done a decent job of investigating before you issued a statement to the press that damaged a good and honorable man, before you called the police in to arrest my father?" The eyes that had seduced him were full of pain. "The humiliation of that was what killed him."

"Wait a moment!" He leaned forward. "Even if no statement had been made to the press, your father would still have been arrested—just perhaps not so publicly."

Her expression grew closed, shutting out anything he could say. "My father didn't steal anything from your company," she bit out.

She still believed her father had done nothing wrong. Callum sighed. "Miranda, you need to face the truth."

"It's *not* the truth. Let's just agree to disagree." She picked up her bag and rose to her feet.

God, but this woman was stubborn!

He snagged her elbow as she tried to force her way past his chair and pulled her to him. Ignoring the startled looks from the only other couple in the dining room, two gray-haired women, he murmured close to her face, "Your parents were living way beyond their means. I can only assume your father meant to pay back the money he took."

She tossed the gold, tousled hair that always gave him bedroom fantasies. The gesture made him want to haul her into his arms. He wasn't sure what he'd do next—shake some sense into her...or kiss her stupid.

"He never took it—he left us letters telling us that."

"Letters?"

Callum had never heard anything about any letters.

"Before he shut himself up in the garage and gassed himself, he wrote letters to me and Adrian and Mum telling us that he loved us. He said he could *never* have done such a thing—that he'd been convincingly framed for his predecessor's mistakes, and that the humiliation of living with it was too much for him. He apologized for being weak."

Her eyes filled with tears, but her pain and anger glittered through the moisture. "The whole charge was a fiction to cover administrative blunders from the financial department. You know that—you've already said you were sorry for framing him."

"No!" Jeez, how had this happened? He couldn't let her labor under such a misunderstanding. "I never said that. I was apologizing for making your father's shame so public—I didn't need to have been quite so gung ho, but my appointment was still fresh and I thought I needed to stamp my authority. I've never said his arrest was unjust. I believe people should be held accountable for their actions—"

But Miranda pulled her arm free. "I'm not listening to this garbage. You're lying! I'll wait for you at the car."

By the time Callum stalked out of the Rose and Thorn fifteen minutes later, Miranda's teeth were chattering.

She supposed it served her right. She could've waited in the warm hallway, but she'd been so angry, all she'd wanted was to get out of the space Callum occupied. She'd needed to breathe the clean, crisp air outside to cool down.

Without glancing in her direction, he pointed the key fob at the car and the doors unlocked. She scuttled in and Callum climbed in beside her.

When he didn't start the car, she swiveled her head to see what the holdup was. And nearly wilted under the blast of his blue gaze.

He said softly, with lethal contempt, "I'm going to say this once more and never again. I would never have a man I believed to be innocent arrested."

Maybe Callum didn't know the full extent of it. "The evidence was falsified. He was framed."

"The written admission from your father was not falsified."

The quiet menace of his statement silenced Miranda like nothing else could have.

"And no one tampered with the evidence he produced that showed what he'd done with the money he'd misappropriated."

Her lips parted, but the shock of what he was telling her had frozen her vocal cords. At last she stuttered, "That's a lie." *It had to be.*

A muscle flexed high in his cheek but no emotion crossed his face. "You must believe what you will."

Bile burned bitterly in the back of her throat as her stomach clenched in fear. She'd been lied to before. In the past few months, her mother and brother had both lied to her, but Callum never had. She'd even believed the lie her mother had been spinning for years about the life insurance policy paying out. Callum had debunked that myth. And he'd been telling the truth.

"You're lying," she said without hope.

He looked pained—as if he was hurting. Miranda leaned her head back against the head rest and closed her eyes, shutting him out. A few seconds later the car started, and soon they were back on the main road.

She pretended to sleep, but her mind ticked over.

Callum was nothing if not honest. Even when he'd asked her to marry him, he'd never iced what was essentially a practical request—albeit garnished with lashings of sex—into a romantically pretty proposal.

What if he was telling the truth this time, too?

The hurt that seized her was unbearable. Her father wouldn't have lied to her. It was important to believe that, to keep faith lest her whole world come tumbling down around her like a pack of fraudster's cards.

Yet even while she clutched onto that belief, deep within her most secret heart, something withered.

Near the town of Windermere, they turned off onto a road with breathtaking views of the lake dotted with sailing craft tied up for winter. Another turn took them into a narrow lane flanked with low stone walls while snow-covered fields lay beyond.

Their speed had slowed, and Miranda knew they must be approaching their final destination.

Now that they were nearly there, Miranda wished she hadn't let Adrian's latest bombshell depress her, since it was that mood that had gotten her into the bridge-burning fight with Callum. There were a thousand questions she wanted to ask as he nosed the Daimler through a set of imposing wrought-iron gates and onto a drive that wound through a park.

She sat up, squinting against the bright light. The snow, the absence of livestock, the leafless trees with their bare crisscrossing branches all gave the landscape a bleak, monochromatic beauty.

Loneliness swept her.

Huddling down, she pulled the scarf Flo had given her for Christmas tighter around her neck.

She already missed the cramped terrace house and the merry music Flo played in the evenings. She longed for the funny, bent Christmas tree Adrian had salvaged after a Boxing Day party a couple of years ago.

Why the hell had she agreed to come? Because of an inexplicable yearning to see the place Callum called home. And, to a lesser extent, for the cash incentive he'd offered.

Because they needed the money.

Miranda gave a silent sigh. It always came back to money. A predicament *he* had put her family into. If she didn't maintain that belief, she might go mad. And while she wouldn't accept his charity, she was going to use every commission, every lead he offered, to get herself out of this financial quagmire.

At least she hadn't given in to her urge to unload the burden of Adrian being blackmailed. Judging by Callum's black-and-white statement about accountability, he would expect Adrian to face charges.

Callum was a rigid autocrat who gave no quarter. There was no doubt that he would have her brother convicted of using the car without permission.

Adrian's concern about spending Christmas in jail was too real to dismiss.

Nine

They rounded a bend and unexpectedly Fairwinds rose up against the sky ahead of them. Fingers of winter sunlight pressed through the cloud to caress the rugged blocks of hewn stone, and the mullioned windows winked in the brightening light.

"It's exquisite," Miranda breathed softly. The house was more beautiful than the spread in *Country Life* had promised.

"Every time I come home, it takes my breath away." Callum's voice was full of pride.

The Daimler rolled to a stop in the cobbled forecourt. Instantly the heavy wooden front door swung open, and a crowd poured down the stone stairs behind two black, barking Labradors.

Before Callum could come round to her door, Miranda was already out of the car.

Callum reached the dogs first. "Mojo, Moxie, be quiet!"

The pair of dogs stopped barking and came forward to sniff Miranda. She stood still, giving them a chance to become accustomed to her scent.

"Don't be afraid. They don't bite." A woman with an elegant silver-gray bob smiled warmly at her. "I'm Pauline, Callum's mother."

The rest of the group separated themselves into his father, Robin; two of Callum's brothers, Fraser and Jack; Jack's girlfriend, Lindsey; and the housekeeper.

Once Miranda had gotten everyone's names sorted out and their luggage had been brought in, Pauline showed her upstairs to a lovely guest bedroom decorated in shades of pale blue and lilac with views over the home paddocks to the park beyond.

"There are towels as well as a range of toiletries in the en suite if you'd like to freshen up." Pauline opened a door. "If you need anything more just sing out. With the exception of Hunter, who's coming later, the whole family is here now. I'm so pleased you came with Callum. Hunter's also bringing a girl he's recently met."

Of course Pauline didn't know that more guests would be arriving on Saturday for her surprise birthday party.

It discomfited Miranda to realize that Pauline truly believed she was Callum's girlfriend. What she had thought a deception only for the benefit of the Harrises was clearly not the case. All the brothers seemed to be bringing dates home for Christmas.

Except apparently for Fraser, which prompted her to say, "I don't remember meeting Fraser's girlfriend."

"He didn't bring one. There doesn't seem to be

anyone special in his life right now—or at least not one he's telling his mother about." Pauline smiled at her. "My sons keep us in the dark. We'd actually thought Callum was about to—"

The older woman looked suddenly flustered. "What am I saying? I talk too much."

So Callum's parents had known about Petra—that Callum was going to propose to her.

Before Miranda could say anything, Pauline said, "I suppose you'll think I'm a nosy mother when I say this, but I hope you don't mind that I put you in separate rooms. I'm still a little old-fashioned that way. I like to know a couple is committed to each other before they fall into bed together. My upbringing," she explained.

Miranda felt herself flush hectically. What would this sweet woman think if she had any idea of the wild no-strings night Miranda had spent with her youngest son? There'd been no thought about commitment, only stark pleasure on the spur of the moment. She'd hated Callum—but he'd ignited a fierce blaze in her that had scorched them both without thought of tomorrow.

For sure his mother wouldn't approve.

Although Miranda feared she could hardly claim to hate Callum any longer. "Callum and I are still getting to know each other," she said, before her mother imagined the peal of wedding bells. "Our connection started with business."

Connection? What a word to choose. She groaned inwardly at the image it conjured up.

"And Callum said you're a chef?"

Miranda nodded. "I'm helping with tomorrow's catering." While Callum's mother was still in the dark about the birthday party planned for Saturday, the brothers had told her that Miranda would be preparing Christmas lunch to explain her calls to Millie, the house-keeper, and the tons of supplies she'd brought. Millie had already been given Christmas Day off.

"Thank you. It will be wonderful to have you here for Christmas, Miranda."

Miranda smiled uncomfortably at Pauline's warm words, all too conscious that she'd come to Fairwinds under false pretenses.

Under the guise of playing Monopoly, Miranda spent the next two hours closeted in the study downstairs with Callum, Fraser, Jack and Lindsey, coordinating the ar-rangements for Pauline's party. Three women would be coming up from the village to help with the preparation, do all the serving and clean up afterward.

Robin had been co-opted to keep Pauline occupied, but Pauline still managed to wander in from time to time to check whether they needed anything—causing Miranda to hastily cover her notes while everyone else frantically shuffled Monopoly money and moved houses around the board that was spread out on the card table.

When Hunter arrived with a tall redhead he intro-duced as Anna, he handed Callum a large, white envelope. "The documents you requested."

A look passed between the two brothers. Miranda tensed. What was going on? A shiver feathered down her spine.

The meeting broke up when Pauline came to remind them that they would need to eat soon to give enough time to make the Christmas Eve carols in the nearby village. Everyone dived for the doors to ready themselves for dinner, but Callum caught Miranda's arm, restraining her from following the others.

"I have something for you." He handed her the envelope Hunter had brought. "I called Hunter from the inn and asked him to bring this."

She knew from the set of his jaw she wouldn't like whatever that envelope contained.

"Open it."

For a brief second she contemplated refusing and shoving it back at him, unopened. But curiosity got the better of her.

She lifted the flap and drew out the sheaf of papers stapled in the top corner. Her heartbeat accelerated. "What is this?"

"It's a copy of your father's confession—the original is in the police file. He signed it. I know I said earlier I wouldn't raise this again, but it's clear we've been talking at cross-purposes for some time."

No triumph glowed on Callum's face in the deathly silence that followed. Instead deep lines of concern cut into his forehead.

Miranda dropped into the chair beside the table where they'd plotted his mother's surprise. All the light-hearted camaraderie of earlier had evaporated, leaving her drained.

She was suddenly quite sure she didn't want to read the confession.

But she knew she had no choice. Not after the accusations she'd flung at Callum almost three years ago. Not after her hostility and resentment over the past few weeks.

It hurt unbearably to read of her father's desperation. Of his admission of stealing—

"One million pounds!" Shocked, her eyes flew to Callum's. *"How?"*

"By a false claim on a bogus life policy."

She bit back a stream of questions. Drawn inexorably back, she read the confession through to the end, her heart clenching when she reached her father's familiar signature at the end of the document.

Had he written that sweet, loving note absolving himself of all responsibility after this stark admission of his guilt?

She'd never know.

"In case you think that's a forgery—the police have the original along with a certificate of identification. Once your father died, they dropped the criminal charges against him—and the company chose not to pursue civil action against your father's estate after the bulk of the funds were recovered."

The slim thread of hope that Callum had been mistaken or misinformed snapped. The charges against her father had never been unfair or trumped up. And Callum was clearly in no way responsible for her father's death. "Where did you find the money?"

"From accounts in your father's name."

Callum stood a few feet away, arms folded, offering none of the support she'd become accustomed to. And Miranda knew she deserved none. The distance between them yawned wider than it had ever been.

She said nothing. There was nothing to say.

"And before you point out the confession could have been forced, the bank manager identified your father as the person who'd opened an account in the name of the fictitious deceased. When the large deposit arrived, he became suspicious. And when he discovered that your father's name—the only contact telephone number on the account—didn't match the account holder, he notified the bank's fraud department. His statement was corroborated by video footage showing Thomas entering the bank on the date that the fictitious account was opened." Callum related the facts in a remote tone that gave no comfort. "There are other equally damning statements on file. No way such a body of evidence could be falsified."

Her father was guilty.

For years, hatred for Callum had sustained her, given her someone to blame for the hopeless sense of loss and disorientation after her father's death. The unanswerable questions that had haunted her.

Why, Dad? Why kill yourself? Why not endure it and clear your name?

Now she knew. Her father couldn't clear his name. And he hadn't been able to face up to what he'd done. Hadn't been able to face a prison term.

She pushed the pages back into the envelope, feeling as if she'd opened Pandora's box. Her life would never be the same again. "He had a family. A home. A great job. Why would he have done such a thing?"

"Thomas lived to a certain standard of living and he wanted to maintain that. He told me once that his wife was a real lady and he was her humble servant, that he would always give her everything she wanted."

"I remember him saying that, too." She'd thought it wildly romantic. "But I wouldn't have wanted him to commit fraud for our family to have such a lifestyle. We could've sold our house, found a cottage. I could have hired Troubadour out to the local riding school. There were so many expenses we could have saved." *If he'd only told us.*

But it was true, Flo had always liked to maintain a certain lifestyle. With her husband gone, Flo had simply moved on to make free with Callum's largesse.

"That reminds me—you never did stop Mum's accounts, did you?"

He shook his head.

"She's been running them up again with Christmas spending." Miranda sighed. "We're going to have to pay that amount back to you." Perhaps she should just become his hostess indefinitely without pay to offset the debts her family owed him, she thought blackly. And Flo would simply keep running them up. She would never be free of Callum.

When she got back to London, she was going to have to take Flo in hand.

"You can't take responsibility for what Flo owes."

"She's my mother."

His brows jerked together. "Flo is an adult."

"I'm not sure she's ever been treated like an adult in her life."

The housekeeper popped her head around the doorjamb. "Sorry to interrupt, but dinner is served."

"Give us a few minutes to clean up and we'll be there." Callum's frown had vanished abruptly.

When the housekeeper had gone, he took two steps closer.

Feeling unaccountably nervous, Miranda gestured

with the envelope between them. "I'll run upstairs and put this away."

"Miranda…" A strange, almost hesitant expression flitted across his face. "I hope we can start afresh—put the past behind us."

The veil had been ripped off what she had believed for years, revealing a truth so sordid it had shaken her to the roots of her self. "I hope so, too. But I need time to absorb this. I don't even know if I can ever be the same person I was this morning. My whole life has shifted."

The winter night air was crisp and cold.

Miranda closed the door of the Daimler behind her and hitched her scarf more snugly around her neck as she gazed around. After the shock of reading her father's confession earlier, she'd expected the world to look different.

But it didn't. It was still winter. That hadn't changed. Even though her world had tipped upside down around her, the seasons had at least remained constant.

Only she had changed.

Wrapped up in a warm coat and her new scarf, Miranda trudged through the snowy sludge beside Callum, past homes lit with merry Christmas lights, to a village green beside a little church.

She took a proffered song sheet with small smile of thanks before hurrying to catch up with Callum. In the glow of the flickering tree lights, they found his family near the village Christmas tree, where a brass band had set up. Minutes later the bells in the church tower pealed out, heralding the arrival of the carolers.

The crowd pressed closer and as the band launched

into an overture, a tall man moved in front of them, blocking Miranda's view.

Callum's hand pressed against the small of her back, guiding her to a place where her view was unobstructed. "Better?"

"Much." She threw him a quicksilver smile over her shoulder. "Thank you."

In the light of the lampposts she watched his gaze soften. She'd hated the sense of alienation between them. The first notes of "We Three Kings" struck up and she turned to watch the carolers, acutely conscious of Callum's bulk behind her.

As more people arrived, the crush shifted forward and he pressed up against her. The heavy warmth of his body crept into hers and a delicious, unfamiliar contentment stole through her.

He said something she couldn't hear.

"What?" She tipped her head back and the top of her head brushed his chin.

"Your hair smells of vanilla and cinnamon," he said into her ear. "It's a heady fragrance."

The heat of his breath in the whorls of her ear caused tingles to ripple along her spine. Her awareness of him, never long absent, rocketed up.

"Just ordinary shampoo," she said, tilting her head so she could see his face.

"There's nothing ordinary about you," he said.

The moment stretched. Tension built within her as their eyes held. Her breathing quickened.

She forced herself to look away.

No.

She didn't want this.

Not now. Not with Callum.

Even though it felt so right. Even though she'd accepted he wasn't to blame for her father's suicide, there was too much history between them. An affair with him would only bring unhappiness—especially once he found out that while he'd always been brutally truthful, she'd been less honest.

She shivered, and a wave of ever-present loneliness swamped her.

Callum wrapped his arms around her from behind and pulled her to rest against the length of his body. "I'll keep you warm."

She let herself sag into the safe refuge of his arms. It felt strangely like coming home.

A dangerous dream.

The band was playing "Silent Night." All around, Miranda was aware of couples, young and old, of families, and the joy of Christmas Eve surrounding them.

She wanted that joy. That love. It came to her in a moment of clarity that she'd been a fool to turn down Callum's proposal.

If she'd agreed to marry him, it all would have been hers—companionship, great sex and a life with a man who did his best to consider her and solve all her problems.

"Tomorrow morning, I'll take you for a walk in the snow. There won't be time for a ride, but the horses will be out in the field in the morning and you can meet them."

How could she have been so dense?

While she'd been intent on hating him, fighting him, she'd been falling in love with Callum. How she wished…

Then reality kicked in. Callum would never *love* her. He might desire her with fierce passion, but that wasn't love. He'd told her point-blank he didn't want the emotional complications love entailed.

Her Christmas wish would never come true.

It was early and the rest of the household still slept when Callum pulled the front door open and stood back for Miranda to pass.

She halted just ahead of him and he heard her gasp as she took in the bright beauty of the morning sunlight on the pristine blanket of fresh-fallen snow.

"This is the gift you said you wanted," he murmured behind her.

"It's so beautiful—so peaceful—it makes my heart hurt." Her voice was husky. "What a perfect start to Christmas Day."

He knew what she meant.

She stepped forward and the sun caught her hair, turning it to gold. Callum followed and her scent stayed with him. Vanilla. And a hint of honey this morning.

"Old Jim will already have put the horses out in the paddock." He led her through the silent, snow-encrusted garden, their Wellingtons crunching on the snow that covered the cobbled pathways.

Mojo and Moxie padded up behind them, looking expectant. Callum eyed the dogs. "You can come but you need to behave. No running off." Opening the gate set in an archway in the stone garden wall, he paused for a moment to let Miranda take in the vista before them.

"Wow." She sounded awed.

"Come on." He snagged her gloved hand in his. "Let me show you."

They entered a lane lined with post-and-rail fencing and leafless trees, their boughs forming ghostly shapes that fragmented the stark landscape.

"It feels like we're the only people in the whole world."

He glanced down at her. "Maybe we are."

With a hint of bravado that had been missing since he'd produced the proof of her father's confession, she said, "You and me? That could be interesting."

"Very," he said drily and watched as color washed her cheeks.

She tried to wiggle her fingers free but he tightened his hold. "There are the horses," he said to distract her.

Followed by the pair of Labradors, they headed for a five-barred gate set in the fence. A rugged-up chestnut came toward them, whickering in greeting, followed by a big bay.

The chestnut nuzzled delicately at Miranda's gloves and she laughed. "This one's gorgeous. What are their names?"

The melancholy that had hung over her yesterday had lifted. Her skin was bright and clear, and a slight flush lay on her cheeks. God, but this woman was gorgeous. His chest squeezed tight.

"The chestnut is Red, the bay Cavalier," he said hastily, before she caught him fawning. "The gray mare at the back is Lady Anne. She's shy. It may take her a while to come forward."

"Oh, I feel so bad—I've got nothing for them."

Callum drew a plastic bag from his coat pocket. "Luckily, I came prepared." He passed her a carrot.

Miranda pulled off her glove and tucked it under her other arm. Holding her hand out palm up, she offered the carrot to Red. The chestnut lipped it up.

Cavalier bumped Callum's elbow and he fed the bay a piece, too.

"Here comes Lady Anne," he warned. The gray had edged up on the far side of Miranda.

Miranda stretched her arm out and Lady Anne took the offered morsel. Red's ears went back and the gray mare skittered out of reach with her carrot.

"Not nice, Red," said Miranda reprovingly.

Too soon the carrots were gone.

"I enjoyed that," said Miranda.

Her eyes glowed and Callum's throat grew tight. "At a quieter time, you must come again. We'll go for a ride." The words were out before he could stop them.

She looked as surprised by his impulsive offer as he was.

"That would be nice. Thank you."

She hadn't refused. Callum gave her a broad smile. It gave him a chance to see her again in the New Year, without having to rely on their connection through Adrian. Before she could put her glove back on, Callum snatched her hand. A sizzle of electricity seared him.

"Your fingers are cold."

"Freezing," she said cheerfully.

"I'll warm them." He held her hand between his and gave them a rub, all too conscious of her long fingers dwarfed between his but strong from molding dough. The short, square nails had been painted with clear varnish. Leaning forward, he brushed a kiss over her lips.

They both froze, then broke apart.

Miranda pushed her hair back and Callum stared at her. What was happening? What was her power over him? It was as if he was in the presence of something he'd never felt before—and that he hadn't seen coming.

Ten

The rest of Christmas Day passed in a rush of laughter and joy. Miranda barely had any time alone with Callum, which only reinforced that her decision—not to ruin the day by dwelling on her problems with Flo and Adrian—had been the right one.

After breakfast the family gathered in the living room to open presents beside the Christmas tree. Miranda was astonished to find she was expected to join the family.

Everyone had brought small gifts for each other. CDs of favorite bands. Books. Aromatherapy lotions. Each carefully chosen. Callum gave her a lacy white apron that made her blush and everyone else giggle, and Miranda was relieved that she'd thought to bring a CD as a gift for him. Thankfully no one had any idea of the significance of his choice.

Her own gift to the family of a selection of small pots of herbs for the kitchen and a huge tin of mouth-watering iced biscuits cut into snowflake shapes was met with cries of delight.

As soon as that was over, Miranda belatedly called Flo and Adrian to wish them a merry Christmas, keeping the conversation deliberately upbeat, then headed for the kitchen. After a hectic, busy morning spent preparing the turkey for the family's Christmas feast that night and the more time-consuming dishes that would be eaten the next day, Miranda whipped up a light lunch of roasted pumpkin soup with pesto and sour cream stirred through, served with freshly baked rolls on the side. It caused oohs of delight. And Miranda flushed with pleasure when Callum's father commented, "You picked a winner, Callum." Her gaze met Callum's then skittered away under the heat and intensity she read there.

Don't make more of it, she warned herself. She was only here because Callum had wanted a date to provide a distraction from Petra's presence tomorrow.

That afternoon she focused on their Christmas dinner, and preparing what could be done in advance for Pauline's party the next day. Although with the help she'd had from Callum's mother as well as Lindsey and Anna, Miranda was starting to feel like a fraud. Even Callum and his brothers wandered in through the course of the afternoon to give a hand, the kitchen ending up full of action and much hilarity. It had been incredibly fun.

The hardest part had been keeping a straight face when Pauline looked around in bewilderment at all the food and demanded, "Who's going to eat all of this? It's far too much."

"Have no fear, Mother," Fraser said. "We're growing men—there won't be a crumb left."

Miranda caught Callum suppressing a grin, and Hunter immediately marched his mother out on the pretext of needing her advice about how to best dry the Italian loafers he'd saturated the previous night.

"You shouldn't have worn them to the carols, Hunter," they heard Pauline say as she followed him out the kitchen, completely diverted.

"You're fortunate to have such a wonderful family," Miranda murmured to Callum.

"I know."

It wasn't only Callum who held Miranda enthralled… she was dangerously close to falling in love with his family.

And that she couldn't afford.

His mother's utter, unfeigned surprise the next day when the first of her birthday guests arrived made the whole loving deception worthwhile, Callum decided as he exchanged looks of satisfaction with his brothers.

"How did I not get the smallest whiff of this?" Pauline asked as cars crowded the forecourt in front of the house.

"It was supposed to be a secret," said Callum.

"Though Dad nearly let the cat out of the bag five minutes after we arrived on Thursday," said Fraser with a mock glare at his father.

"Never could keep a secret, your father." Pauline gave her husband a fond smile, and Callum looked away to give them a private moment.

"I managed to keep it in all of yesterday," said Robin, and everyone laughed.

But when Petra arrived with her father, tension filled the air as Callum stepped closer to Miranda. Petra gave Miranda a quick glance, and aside from the hurt in her eyes, showed little reaction.

But Callum was aware of Miranda shifting away from him, distancing herself. She didn't like the deception he'd asked her to perform, Callum realized.

It grew even more sticky when Callum discovered that Gordon and Petra had been invited to stay with the family for the balance of the weekend and wouldn't be leaving with the other guests.

"Trouble?" Fraser asked a little while later with a meaningful look in Petra's direction.

Callum resisted the urge to snap at his brother. "Nothing I can't handle."

"Good. Because despite the fact that Petra had the sense to dump you, Gordon remains important to our business."

"You invited them to stay?" Callum stared at his brother in disbelief.

"Yes." Fraser narrowed his gaze. "It shouldn't be a problem, should it?"

Callum sincerely hoped it wouldn't become one—but he had already detected Gordon's coolness toward Miranda.

When all the guests had arrived, everyone assembled in the large formal dining for a buffet-style birthday lunch. Callum stopped dead at the sight of Miranda. She'd changed into a red dress that clung softly to her curves. Everything about the dress shrieked *touch me!* He swallowed. How the hell was he supposed to resist such an invitation? In desperation he forced himself to focus on the spread she'd prepared. Miranda had surpassed herself. An ice sculpture dominated the centre of the table and she'd carried the winter wonderland theme through in the snowflake decorations suspended around the room, with masses of tall, white tapered candles lit to give an impression of glittering Christmas tree lights.

After lunch Pauline opened her gifts, and with every card she read out, her eyes grew increasingly dewy. Callum was surprised to see Miranda hand his mother a box lightly wrapped in tissue paper.

"Happy birthday," Miranda said.

His mother pulled off the wrapping to reveal a half dozen brandy snaps filled with cream, and a finger lick at the end of one had her whimpering with delight.

It stunned Callum that Miranda had taken the care to make the sweet he'd told her his mother loved. But her consideration warmed his heart. For an instant he was guiltily conscious of the fact that she should be spending Christmas with her own mother and brother—not his.

As the afternoon passed, Miranda was supremely aware of Callum's every move whenever they were together, and she grew increasingly uncomfortable with the number of times his fingers would brush hers, or his hand would settle on her waist, the fine, soft jersey fabric of her dress failing to present any substantial barrier to the warmth of his touch. She knew he was making certain that Gordon harbored no hopes of a reconciliation between his daughter and Callum. But she disliked the deceit and the flare of pain in Petra's eyes. And on top of that, it troubled her deeply that she was deceiving Callum. He still had no idea of the damage Adrian had done to an

Ironstone car…and more significantly that she hadn't disclosed it to him.

Yet how could she? She couldn't have gone against Adrian's wishes. And ultimately it was Adrian's problem. How would he ever learn to take responsibility for his life if she fixed all his problems for him? Look what a mess Flo made simply because she expected everyone to leap around and fix things for her. Her father treating Flo as a china doll had only worsened the problem.

But now Christmas was over. Adrian's worry about being locked up over the holiday with little chance of bail was no longer valid. And every time her gaze connected with Callum's, Miranda wished she hadn't agreed to keep quiet until she returned to London. As much as she hadn't wanted to raise something controversial on Christmas Day or his mother's birthday, she now needed Callum to be in the picture.

Then maybe they could finally advance their strained relationship. But would he still even want to be friends when he found out she'd deceived him?

Tea had been served in delicate china cups. Miranda sneaked out to take a five-minute break in the downstairs study and decided she would call Adrian. Maybe he would agree to let her tell Callum the truth—presuming she got the opportunity.

Adrian answered his mobile on first ring. "What's up, sis?"

She told him, and when he spoke again the breezy note had vanished. "No," he said adamantly. "I'll tell him when I'm ready."

"On Monday when I get back, you said," she reminded him.

"Maybe."

He was trying to wriggle off the hook. Her brother must be truly scared of the consequences.

"It's not going to get easier—and if you leave it too long, I'll tell him myself."

"I know that." Adrian sounded so despondent she felt like an absolute witch. Then he said, "I've been getting threatening calls. I've managed to put them off because I told them you were away."

"It doesn't make any difference whether I'm there or not. I've told you—they're not getting my money. Absolutely not." She breathed deeply. "Look, Callum will give you a break."

Adrian's sin wasn't anything like what their father had done. They couldn't use that as a yardstick for judging Callum's likely reaction. "I'm sure Callum will understand." Miranda hoped that he would live up to her brave claim.

Adrian muttered something she was grateful she couldn't make out, and then hung up.

Well, she'd handled that just beautifully!

"Why the frown?"

She started at the sound of Callum's voice and discovered he was standing in front of her. Had he overheard her conversation? She hoped not.

She forced a smile. "Nothing much."

"You were on the phone. Trouble? Is it your mother again?"

At least Callum hadn't homed in on Adrian. "A little."

"She takes advantage of you." Callum held her gaze.

"And you," she said.

"And me," he conceded. "We're not doing her any

favors. By always fixing her problems, we've allowed her to become totally irresponsible."

Miranda had reached that conclusion herself, but it still stung to hear it from Callum. It took sheer will-power to stop herself from defending Flo.

"I suppose I should butt out," he said when she didn't answer.

"No, you're quite right. I need to stand up to her."

There was sympathy in his eyes. "It won't be easy."

That was an understatement. Flo was going to rail against it, Miranda suspected. "No, it won't be easy. And I don't want to hurt her feelings."

"Sometimes one has to be cruel to be kind," said Callum.

And Miranda suspected he was thinking not of Flo—but Petra.

After seeing the last of the guests off, Callum and his brothers trooped back into the house with his parents. Gordon had gone up to his room already.

His mother had been thrilled by the unexpected party and was still looking overwhelmed. "I should check on—"

"The kitchen is fine," his father said firmly. "There are four women taking care of it, and one is a trained chef."

"Then I suppose we can go to bed, then."

Callum pecked his mother good-night on the cheek, and wasn't surprised when his father quickly followed her up the stairs. He had a feeling his father was going to reap the benefits of the celebration.

A lull fell over the big house. Anna, Petra and Lindsey were helping Miranda tidy up, and his brothers had gone out to the stables to feed and rug up the horses, because Old Jim had gone home to spend the day with his even more elderly mother.

So Callum made his way to the kitchen to find Miranda. There had been worry in her eyes earlier—he wanted to check that she was okay. And he wanted to make sure that putting her into close proximity with Petra hadn't made her too uncomfortable. She clearly didn't like the deceit—despite his explanation that by his dating another woman, Gordon would forget all thoughts of a match between him and Petra.

Or at least that's what he told himself right up until the moment he reached the kitchen and halted in the doorway.

She'd pulled a long double-breasted white chef's jacket on over the red touch-me dress. He supposed he should be grateful that she wasn't wearing the sexy apron he'd given her...

Seeing her rubbing down the black granite bench tops and steel-fronted appliances reminded him of the night in his town house and involuntarily his body hardened.

Even wearing that jacket, she was the sexiest woman he'd ever known.

He stuck his hands in his trouser pockets and glanced around. There was no sign of Petra—or his brothers' girlfriends—so he sauntered forward. "Hey, Cinderella, looks like the elves have been busy."

"You're mixing Christmas with fairy tales."

"What's wrong with that?"

She thought for a moment. "Nothing."

"Where are Petra, Lindsey and Anna?" he asked.

"Probably in the bath by now—where all good prin-cesses should be." She smiled at him—and a blast of heat spread through him to settle low in his belly, building mercilessly on the arousal he already felt. "I think they're both a bit shell-shocked by how tired you can get just from standing on your feet all day. I'm used to it," she added quickly.

"Come and sit with me—I might even rub your poor abused feet." He shot her a smoldering look from under heavy eyelids and watched with satisfaction as she colored.

Freeing his hands from his pockets, Callum led an unusually pliant Miranda into the sitting room, where flames licked at the logs in the grate and the lights of the Christmas tree twinkled.

He paused to fill up two glasses with tawny port and crossed to where she'd sunk down on the squashy couch with her feet tucked under her, the folds of the dress draped around her.

She looked so right here in his family home. His family liked her, he could tell. By the way Fraser teased her. By the way his mother had almost burst into tears when Miranda had given her the brandy snaps.

She fitted in.

He'd almost forgotten the deception of her accompanying him as a "fake" date. It felt so real.

When he'd decided weeks ago to help her attain her dream—and more financial independence—it had been so he could salve his conscience. He hadn't expected the hunger that ate him every time he looked at her. He hadn't expected to like her. And he certainly hadn't expected his family to be so charmed by her.

When had his connection to her started to become so…emotional?

"What is it?" Miranda had taken a sip of the sweet

port, but now she examined him standing in front of her, his legs apart, and male enough to make her forget all about the rich, nutty flavor of the liqueur that had delighted her only seconds earlier.

Callum wore a strange, bemused expression. The intensity in his eyes unfurled a restlessness deep within her.

He shook his head and laughed. "I think I'm going crazy."

"You? Crazy?" She raised an eyebrow. "Never."

But he didn't laugh as she'd intended. Instead he stared at her until she shifted under that intimidating gaze.

"What is it that makes me forget about everything else when you're around?"

"Now it's *my* fault you're going crazy?" She tried to laugh again, but found that her voice had dried up. His admission made her toes curl.

"Maybe not." He crossed to a wall unit, where he pulled a drawer open and extracted a box. "You said once that your only weakness is dark chocolate."

Her gaze lingered on Callum's broad shoulders and trailed down to the long legs clad in dark trousers. Chocolate was no longer her only weakness....

"I couldn't eat another thing," she protested as he came toward her brandishing a bar of Lindt.

"Indulge me." He tore the wrapper off. "Have you ever tasted dark chocolate and port together?"

Wordlessly, she shook her head.

"Then you haven't lived."

His voice was deep and throaty, and Miranda's pulse went through the roof.

"Open your mouth."

She never considered not obeying. Her lips parted. He placed a morsel on her tongue and the chocolate melted in her mouth. It tasted sublime.

"Now the port."

He held the glass for her, and Miranda set her lips to the rim. Their eyes locked. He tipped the glass ever so slightly. The liquid mingled in her mouth with the rich sweet and flavor exploded on her tongue.

Callum set the glass down, and when he leaned forward to stroke her hair back from her face with gentle hands, her heart dropped.

"It's been way too long since I've kissed you, Miranda."

The moment had finally arrived. He'd brushed her lips too briefly yesterday morning during their walk, leaving her hungering for more. All day yesterday and today she'd waited, tension winding up within her.

Which made her feel even worse about not telling him about Adrian. He'd done so much to help her family, and all they'd been was Trouble with a capital *T.*

"You're not going to stop me this time, are you?"

Was she so obvious? Tongue-tied, she shook her head.

"Good," he purred.

His lips were firm on hers. He pulled her up against him and she became aware of the power of his body under the cotton shirt. His arms were strong around her.

He was all man.

She parted her lips and he devoured her. All *hungry* male. He gave a groan that turned her weak. She wanted him.

"That's how to taste dark chocolate." He brushed a kiss over her lips. "But if we continue this, someone might walk in on us." His laugh was breathless. "My brothers only went to feed the horses. One of them could return any second."

She ran her fingertips over his jaw, pausing to rest them against the soft pad of his lower lip. His eyes ignited with passion and he sucked a finger into his mouth, his tongue swirling around it.

Her breathing quickened.

Removing her hand, he took her mouth, plundering it, filling every crevice with his tongue. He tasted of port, chocolate and aroused male, and when he'd finished, he lifted his head and she gazed into eyes heavy with desire.

"I don't want to wait anymore." His voice was hoarse. "Come up to my room with me."

Unable to speak, she nodded.

Callum shoved his bedroom door shut with his foot, and—holding Miranda's gaze—locked the door.

Her pupils darkened, consuming the caramel gold of her irises, and causing his body to shudder and harden in anticipation.

He shrugged his tie off, crossed the room, and dropped the tie across the railing of his huge four-poster bed.

Miranda followed more slowly.

He waited for her, unbuttoning his shirt. She stopped at the bottom of the bed, her eyes huge.

The edges of his shirt fell open. He reached for her and brought her close. Letting his fingers caress her nape, he speared them into the silken mass of hair and tilted her head back. Scanning her features, he saw no sign of resistance.

He had her. Alone. At last.

With a sigh of relief he unbuttoned the double row of buttons and pushed the chef's jacket from her shoulders. His shirt, trousers, underpants and her sinful dress all followed, then he tumbled back onto the bed, taking her with him. She landed sprawled, all soft skin and tousled curls against his nakedness.

A moan of satisfaction shook him. "Kiss me, Miranda."

She obliged, and her hair caressed him, tresses scented with the vanilla that teased his dreams. He played his hands over her shoulders, along her back, and his fingers encountered her bra strap. He undid the clasp. She lifted her torso, and as the halter-neck bra fell away she wriggled free.

Callum gasped.

Her breasts hung above him. Full, ripe curves that tempted him to touch…to taste.

He reached out reverently and caressed the berry nubs with gentle fingers. She arched sharply, and a keening sound broke from her throat. Seeking to taste her, he closed his mouth around the dark tip and sucked it. It hardened further, and he knew she was as desperate for him as he for her.

Keeping his mouth on her breast, he slid a hand down over the swell of her stomach and dipped between her legs—and found her moist and ready.

Before he could take the next step, her legs wrapped around his hips and she pushed herself upright, breaking the contact of his mouth on her.

Miranda rubbed herself along the rigid length of his erection. Callum nearly came apart. Only a brief bit of satin separated them from the final sweet connection they both sought. Impatiently he pushed the thin thong of her panties aside and, the delicate barrier gone, she sank down on him.

Pure ecstasy.

He growled in delight. Miranda moved above him and heat consumed him in a bright white flash. Clasping his hands over her hips, he fought to control the pace. But when she bent forward and outlined his mouth with her tongue, laving his lips, Callum moaned, his resolve crumbling. Then she sealed the caress with a kiss. And all the while he drove fiercely, desperately upward into her.

Callum shuddered, his body full of tension. She fell forward, boneless, breathless, on top of his chest, her hair silky against his cheeks, her fragrance embracing him.

And the heat exploded around them, tumbling them into the hot vortex of desire.

Eleven

Callum woke to a sense of supreme satisfaction.

Miranda lay curled up beside him under the covers, one hand resting on his bare chest, spreading warmth through him. It felt so right. Her hand belonged there, against his skin. Over his heart. He wanted to wake every morning to her touch, to the softness of her body tucked against his, her golden hair tousled around her face.

She was his.

The strength of emotion that surged through him awed him. Reaching out, he brushed a silky curl away from her cheek. She stirred.

Her eyes opened, and in the pale morning light that spilled through his bedroom window Callum saw something warm and wonderful in their golden-brown depths.

Then alarm took over, chasing the glow out and filling her eyes with shadows.

She was about to withdraw from him. He couldn't—wouldn't—allow that to happen. Not after last night.

"Don't move," he demanded.

She blinked up at him. "Why?"

"Because I want to look at you."

Miranda gave a breathy laugh and shifted away, leaving a cold space in the bed beside him.

"You're making me feel uncomfortable."

"Don't feel uncomfortable." He rolled closer and cupped his hand under her chin, forcing her to meet his gaze. "You better get used to it. I'll never tire of looking at you."

Something flickered in the caramel eyes that melted his heart. "Oh, yes, you will."

He shook his head. "No, I won't." *Not ever.* But he wasn't ready to confess that yet. Instead he let his fingertips caress the soft skin of her cheek. "What we had last night…I want more."

Yet he couldn't put the unfamiliar emotions and desires that churned inside him into words. All he knew was that he wanted to savor this…thing…that bound them together. Driven by an impulse, he leaned forward and pressed his lips fiercely against hers, determined to make her acknowledge the power of his need.

Last night's wild heat returned in a rush. Swirling through him, racing through his bloodstream, quickening the passion that had ignited at the first touch of his lips to hers. Her lips parted, his tongue plundered the warm depths of her mouth.

And words became unnecessary.

It was the sound of the dogs barking, a shout from Hunter and the lilt of feminine laughter outside that brought Callum abruptly back to his senses. He stared down at the woman who had made him forget everything. His family. His work. He caught sight of the clock on the bed stand. Even the time.

He gave a husky laugh. "My God, I was ready to take you again."

She was breathing quickly, and her eyes had gone dark with desire. The covers had shifted, revealing a pale, creamy shoulder and the slope of one breast. Want surged through him, and he hauled in a ragged breath.

"We better get up." With heavy reluctance he sat up and shrugged the bedclothes off. "Breakfast will be ready—and I don't want anyone coming searching for us." He wanted to keep the intimate joy he'd found with Miranda a secret from the world.

"No, we don't want that."

Miranda moved away, and this time he let her. Her cheeks were stained a rosy pink from the kiss they'd shared, and she took care to keep her nakedness covered. "Your mother told me she was old-fashioned, and didn't approve of us sharing rooms. I feel like I've abused her trust."

There was a strange expression in her eyes.

Callum resisted the impulse to pull her back into his arms, tumble her against the rumpled sheets and possess her with the desire that burned so hotly within him. Instead he said, "I wouldn't worry too much about that. My mother will be only too pleased that I've found someone."

Uncertainty glimmered in her eyes. "I don't want to deceive your mother—your family—any further."

"I wouldn't ask that of you."

Her shoulders stiffened, and her eyes grew wary. "So what are you asking?"

Callum hesitated. Hell, what was he asking? For a moment fear closed around him. He shook it away. This was no time to get cold feet. But he tempered what he meant to say. "I want to make this fake relationship real."

He thought he glimpsed joy in the gold-brown eyes. Too quickly it was gone. For a moment he thought she was going to object. Then she smiled. "I'd like that, too."

An overwhelming relief settled over him. Miranda hadn't refused outright as he'd half expected. She had said yes.

And he had no intention of letting her escape.

Miranda floated downstairs after a quick stop at her room to pull on something more suitable than the red halter-neck dress she'd been wearing last night. She was unable to suppress the silly smile that curved her lips, all too conscious of the man padding down the stairs beside her, his fingers loosely linked with hers.

No doubt she was heading for heartbreak, falling for Callum. It was stupid. Totally insane. Yet she couldn't help herself.

And she would allow herself no regrets.

This was her last chance to seize a slice of happiness for herself. It wouldn't last. But she would enjoy it while it did. Because it would be over too soon—she knew that. As surely as she knew that Callum Ironstone would not fall in love with someone like her. He would find someone with the class and the social connections he needed. Not an embezzler's daughter living under the fog of her father's notoriety.

They entered the dining room, and her gaze settled on Petra. Someone like Petra Harris.

The blonde glanced across at them.

Miranda read the bruised hurt in Petra's pale eyes as she took in their interlinked fingers. For Petra it had never been about business interests. The woman really had loved Callum, she realized. Then her gaze shifted to the man seated beside Petra at the breakfast table. She took in Gordon Harris's tight lips. For Petra's father it had been about business. And he looked none too pleased.

Hunter greeted them first. "We started without you. Mother decided you two must've gone for a walk again and lost track of time."

Miranda felt herself grow red. Thankfully Pauline wasn't in the dining room, and she didn't have to answer any polite questions about how their walk had gone. She didn't dare look at Callum as he held a chair out for her before sliding into the empty seat at her side.

"I promised to take Lindsey down to the craft fair in the village." Jack rose to his feet.

"Can we go, too?" Anna turned to Hunter. "Please?"

Hunter rolled his eyes. "What have you got me into?" he demanded of his brother as he pushed his chair back.

Within minutes the dining room had emptied. Only the Harrises—and Fraser—remained.

"Gordon wants to schedule some time with you this morning, Callum," Fraser told his brother as he, too, got to his feet.

"We can talk after breakfast," replied Callum, lifting a pot of aromatic coffee. After Petra had refused the offer of a cup, he said, "Coffee, Miranda? Or would you prefer tea?"

Or me?

Miranda could've sworn the invitation was in his wickedly glinting eyes. "Coffee," she said huskily, all too conscious of the effect he had on her as he filled first her cup then his.

Gordon's mouth was suddenly grim. "After breakfast will do. I was starting to think you might be otherwise occupied." He glanced meaningfully at Miranda.

Callum stilled, then carefully set the coffeepot down.

Petra put a hand on her father's arm. "Daddy—"

"No, Petra." Gordon shook his daughter's hand off. He turned in his seat. "Callum, I had hoped the relationship between our families would be more than business. I had hoped…" He paused.

"Daddy, *please.*"

Petra looked mortified. A shaft of pity for the other woman pierced Miranda. Wasn't it enough that she was hurting already? Did her father have to humiliate her, too?

She shot Callum a pleading look. Couldn't he do anything to stop this? His arm came across the back of her chair, and his hand rested possessively on her shoulders. "Gordon, I think—"

"Petra would make you a very suitable wife. Much better than *she* ever would."

The anger in his gaze stupefied Miranda.

"I can't believe that you broke it off with Petra for *her.* Think whose daughter she is. The fruit doesn't fall far from the vine. Will you ever be able to trust her?"

"Daddy!"

Callum's body had coiled tight, and Miranda could

feel the tension radiating from him. Suddenly she felt decidedly ill.

"Yes, I can trust her," Callum bit out.

Oh, heavens. Miranda grew cold. *Trust her?*

Callum's free fist hit the edge of the table with a loud bang. Both Miranda and Petra jumped. Callum glared at Gordon. "Frankly, I wasn't intending to spend the morning closeted in meetings. And, yes, I had intended to spend the day with Miranda, who is one of the nicest women I've ever had the fortune of dating."

Miranda sighed. Poor Petra.

"So you can be the first to congratulate us, Gordon."

"First to congratulate you?"

Gordon's shocked expression echoed Miranda's own shock.

Callum's hand tightened on her shoulder. "We're getting married."

"Married?" A gasp of delight came from the door.

Miranda closed her eyes as Pauline hurled herself across the room.

"Oh, Callum, I heard a thump and thought something must have broken. But this is wonderful. Just wait until I tell your father."

Oh, help. What in heaven's name had Callum done?

As Callum closed the door of the study behind them ten minutes later, Miranda wrenched herself out of his hold. "What possessed you to say such a dumb thing to Gordon in there? I feel like such a fool."

"Hey, it's not that bad," he said, the protective streak that he hadn't known existed still strong as he crossed the room to stand beside her. "I—"

"I told you that I didn't want to lie any further to your family." She covered her face with her hands and her curls bobbed. "Now your parents think we're getting married. At least your brothers haven't heard. You can tell *them* it's a stupid misunderstanding."

"Why?" Callum could see his bald question had thrown her.

She dropped her hands and stared at him. "Your parents like me. Once they hear that you only said it to protect me from Gordon's nastiness, they'll understand." Then her mouth formed an *O*. "Of course, you can't do that, can you? Gordon is an important shareholder. That's the whole reason your brought me along this weekend—to stop exactly the kind of scenario that just occurred in the dining room from taking place."

Callum crossed the distance between them in two long strides. Catching her by her shoulders, he growled down at her. "Listen to me. I wouldn't allow anyone to talk to you like that—and I don't care that he's a shareholder."

She tipped her head back. "That's very noble, but—"

"It's not noble. I—"

He stilled. He'd almost said, *I want to marry you.*

Callum froze. He couldn't propose marriage just to stop Miranda feeling humiliated by Gordon's attack—even though he'd been tempted to punch the man in the jaw instead of banging the table.

Yet in the past he'd asked her to marry him to be his hostess....

That reason was no better. Damn it, he wanted her to marry him for himself.

The bombshell thought shocked him rigid.

Why?

Because she was special. Like no other woman he'd ever met.

"Of course it was noble." She was looking at him like he'd done something heroic.

He shook his head to clear it. "I was angry. He was insulting you."

"No one has ever defended me like that before."

He didn't suppose they had. Miranda had always protected her mother and brother. There'd been no one to protect her. His chest expanded with emotion. "That's about to change."

She laughed, and the bittersweet sound caught at his gut.

"Callum, he didn't say anything that both you and I know isn't true. Petra would make you a fabulous wife. And given the fact that my father stole from you, then committed suicide, it's true that will make me a scandalous girlfriend."

"That doesn't matter."

"It does matter." Her eyes had gone dark. "And how can you trust me?"

"Miranda—"

A knock sounded on the door.

Callum marched over and yanked it open. "What?" he demanded of Fraser.

"Have you seen Petra?"

"No," he snapped, and started to close the door in Fraser's face.

His brother stuck a foot in the crack. "You let me believe she broke it off with you."

"Not now." He glared at this brother. "Leave us in peace."

Fraser removed his foot, and this time Callum closed the door with a determined thud.

Miranda had moved to the window. She stood looking at the view over Lake Windermere down at the bottom of the property, the sag of her shoulders revealing how troubled she was.

Tenderness filled him. "Stop fretting."

She turned to meet his gaze over her shoulder. "Trust me, I have reason to fret. Every single thing that Gordon said was true." She shook her head as she started to object. "I like your parents so much. I was looking forward to coming back with you, riding the horses." She gestured at the paddocks visible to one side of the house.

At the yearning in her voice, cold fingers of dread danced over his skin.

Did he want this? A woman who loved his horses, his home, his family…but not him? Out in the corner of the paddock he could see Red pawing through the snow. In a flash of insight he saw what marrying him would mean—it would give Miranda back everything she'd lost and finally assuage his guilt.

And he'd get the woman he wanted more than he'd ever wanted anything in his life.

Callum sucked in a breath. He crossed the room, and slid his arms around her shoulders from behind and drew her to his chest.

Beneath his palms the woolen cardigan she wore was soft, and he could feel the rise and fall of her rib cage as she breathed. His fingers crept forward. Below the cardigan, the edge of her wraparound dress had parted and his fingertips brushed her bare skin. Need swamped him. *God.* Just by breathing she made him desire her. He resisted the fierce urge to yank her up against his hardening body. Now was not the time.

The thought he'd had when he'd woken with her in his arms this morning returned.

This woman belonged with him.

He stared blindly over her shoulder at a red-breasted robin chirping in the undergrowth beneath the window.

If she married him, he would have her in his bed each night instead of seeing her only through functions she catered for him—or through communications about her brother. Surely this was a win-win situation?

So why wasn't he asking, begging, her to marry him?

Because this wasn't what he wanted.

He wanted Miranda to love him.

And there was no chance of that ever happening.

With a hop, the robin he'd been staring at vanished into the undergrowth, bringing Callum back to life. His hands dropped from her shoulders. He felt the loss of the softness of her skin acutely.

He loved her.

God.

Despite the success of his parents' marriage he'd always known that love wasn't easy or straightforward, and that it would make an emotional mess of him—and he'd been right. Good thing she didn't know how he felt.

But he had to ask again. Give her the opportunity to accept what he could give her. Because then he'd get what he wanted more than life. Her.

Callum drew a shuddering breath. "Miranda, you really could marry me—and make my dumb suggestion a reality." He directed the words at golden curls that

cascaded down the back of her head, relieved he didn't
have to meet her eyes. This way she would never know
how desperately he craved to hear her say yes. "We
would go downstairs and celebrate our engagement.
What do you say?"

Miranda spun around.

Callum was asking her to marry him? There was an
expression in his eyes that caused her heart to ache.

A flutter of hope made her stretch out her hand to touch
his chest—to check he was real, that this wasn't a dream.

The tension of the moment was shattered by the jazzy
"Jingle Bells" ringtone of her phone in her cardigan
pocket. Definitely no dream. Life had intruded.

Miranda hesitated. It might be Adrian, calling her
back after terminating their call yesterday, but she didn't
want to speak to him. Not now, not while Callum was
asking her to marry him. Not when she knew Gordon
was right. She had been less than trustworthy. Her
stomach clenched.

"Answer it."

Reluctantly she hauled it out of her pocket, but by
that time the ringing had stopped. She stared at the
screen and her heart sank. "It was Adrian."

"Do you want to call him back?"

She shook her head. "I called him yesterday—he's
probably just returning my call." No point telling
Callum her brother had hung up on her because she'd
wanted permission to tell Callum the truth.

As she was about to pocket the phone, it started to
ring again, loud and intrusive. Faced with no choice
under Callum's expectant gaze, she answered it.

* * *

Impatient now, Callum thrust his hands into the pockets of his trousers and turned away to stare back out the window, trying not to listen to Miranda's conversation with her brother. He searched for the robin but couldn't find it.

Miranda was going to accept his proposal. He'd seen it in her eyes.

The corners of his mouth turned up as he anticipated Fraser's surprise. Callum would be the first of the Ironstones to marry. For once he would've beaten his brothers at something life-changing. There was some small masculine satisfaction in that.

Behind him Miranda's voice lowered, catching his attention.

"I can't talk about that, Adrian. Not now."

What was going on? What did she need to speak to her brother about that she couldn't say in front of him?

Frowning slightly, he swiveled to face her.

She gave him a fleeting, sideways glance from beneath those long, dark lashes and turned away. "Thank you for that. I appreciate it more than I can tell you." A silence. Then, "Yes, I know it's hard for you, but it has to be done. I must go. I'll call you later."

Was Adrian in some kind of trouble? Callum told himself the suspicion was unfounded.

Except...there was that air of discomfort.

When she clicked the phone shut he asked, driven by a compulsion he couldn't name, "What's wrong?"

Her lashes fluttered down. She drew a deep breath, looked up and said in a rush, "Adrian's being blackmailed."

Twelve

"What?" Callum's eyebrows jerked together into a ferocious frown. "What do you mean Adrian's being blackmailed?"

Miranda forced herself to hold his gaze. Inside she was trembling. *I can trust her.* Callum's words rang in her ears. He wouldn't want anything to do with her after this. She wouldn't blame him for reneging on his proposal.

"The day you called me to see you, I found out after our meeting that Adrian had crashed—" she hesitated "—a car."

"Yes?"

"I didn't want to tell you because you'd said you were pleased with him." Miranda spread her hands in a gesture of helplessness. "I was afraid it would jeopardize his chances of getting a great reference from a vacation job."

"But what does that have to do his job? Or being blackmailed? Was someone killed? Did he fail to report it?" Callum looked bewildered.

"No, no one died." Thank heavens! "But he'd borrowed the car without permission." She bit her lip. "It was one of your company's cars."

Callum's eyes turned to slits. "Why didn't he tell me?"

"He was scared you would fire him…and have him arrested and charged with theft."

He didn't blink.

Unnerved by the relentless stare, she blurted out, "So he found a panel beater who could fix the car in a hurry and managed to get it back into the car yard before anyone noticed."

Still Callum said nothing.

Miranda started to tremble. "And now the panel beater says if Adrian doesn't pay him more, the man is going to blow the whistle on Adrian and tell his supervisor."

"And you've known about this all the time?"

The lethally soft tone caused Miranda's throat to close. She nodded, unable to speak.

His relentless blue eyes bored into hers. "You believed I would have had him arrested?"

She thought about that. Did she really believe he would have Adrian arrested?

"You've done it before," she pointed out in her own defense. But her father's crime had been so much worse. "And you must remember I believed that you'd had no reason back then. And this time I knew Adrian had actually taken—" she couldn't bring herself to say *stolen* "—your car. At the start I didn't think you'd have any compassion for him."

Callum turned away. "Thanks for the vote of confidence."

Had that been pain she'd glimpsed in his eyes?

But that would have to mean that she was capable of hurting him and she knew she wasn't. He saw her merely as someone who would make his business life easier—a memory from the night before came to her—and someone he desired.

She blinked back the tears that threatened. This wasn't going to work out. Ever. Better she cut her losses and leave.

"So I suppose that means you aren't going to marry me after all." His mouth was compressed.

"I don't think it would ever work," she said, and the ache of loss spread through her, drowning her in sadness.

The drive back to London took forever.

Miranda was conscious of Callum's hands gripping the steering wheel. They'd stopped twice—briefly—but neither lingered; both of them were eager to get back to London.

There was a constant ache below Miranda's heart. Christmas was over. And so was any brief accord she and Callum had shared. Heaven help her, she'd enjoyed playing Callum's girlfriend. She had come so close to a chance to make it real. And she suspected the ache eventuated from her knowledge that it could never be real. Any relationship between her and Callum had been doomed before it could get started.

Finally the car turned into the narrow street where she lived. As soon as it drew to a halt, Miranda leaped out. "Thanks—"

But Callum was already at the trunk, taking out her overnight bag and the baskets, now filled with a collection of empty containers and kitchenware.

"Let me take that." He relieved her of the handle of her overnight bag. At the top of the steps, he paused. "Miranda—"

The door swung open and Flo fell out, her eyes wild. "Oh, darling, I'm so glad you're here. Adrian is in such trouble. He's taken my car to sell it because he needs to get his hands on some cash."

Nosing his car into one of London's seedier suburbs the morning of Boxing Day, Callum was grateful for being given the opportunity to talk some sense into young Adrian's head—when they finally found him. They'd driven around London most of last night and been unable to locate Flo's car, either with or without Adrian in it.

Miranda was beside herself. "What if he's hurt?" She unfolded arms that she'd folded less than a minute ago. "This man's a criminal. He might kill Adrian. Though I might just kill him myself," she said darkly. "What is he thinking?"

He glanced at her. "We'll find Adrian. There are only so many places that'll be open today where he could sell the car. But surely Adrian doesn't think that'll make this blackmail problem go away? He'll have to keep paying this crook money forever."

"That's what I told him." She looked utterly miserable, curled up in the passenger seat. "But he still didn't want me to tell you. He hero-worships you, you know. I should have taken matters out of his hands and told you earlier—but I didn't want him to end up like Mum, evading responsibility for his actions, getting someone else to do the dirty work. I'd already had to find the money for the panel beater the first time. So I told him I wouldn't give him any more money, thinking that would mean he'd have to tell you. But all he did was keep putting it off—and beg me not to tell you. I never thought of him trying to sell Mum's car."

If he could get his hands on her brother right now all hero worship would end. Didn't Adrian realize what he was doing to his sister?

He could understand why she hadn't dobbed Adrian in—she had a fierce loyalty to her family and she was right about it being Adrian's job to 'fess up. None of this could have been easy on her. He said, "We'll find him. He'll be okay."

Whether Adrian would still be fine after Callum had gotten through tearing a strip off his hide was quite another matter.

"You must be regretting giving Adrian that job." It was four hours later and Miranda knew Callum must be gnashing his teeth, but he showed no sign of it as they pulled up at their third car fair, facing the now-familiar sight of hundreds of cars being examined by backpackers and students all looking for a bargain. And the equally familiar trawl up and down the lines in the slanting drizzle, searching for Flo's Kia.

Except this time they found it in the second row.

When Adrian saw them approaching, his shoulders sagged. "I suppose I've wrecked my chances of ever landing that scholarship now?" he said to Callum as the three of them huddled under the shade cloth.

"You should have come and told me—young men often do silly things."

Adrian flushed under the older man's scrutiny.

"Do you realize how much worry you've caused your sister?" Callum put his hands on his hips and stared Adrian down. "She's got enough on her plate without having to run after you all the time."

Her brother looked sheepish. "I didn't think."

"No, I don't suppose you did. Nor did you think when you rushed off with your mother's car. You're going to be going off to university or to work and you're going to leave your mother—and sister—without a car?"

Adrian lowered his gaze and stared at the floor, thoroughly chastened.

After a pause he looked up and met Miranda's sympathetic eyes. "I'm sorry, sis. I shouldn't have done it." Turning to Callum, he asked, "What will you do about—"

"About the reparation for the car you crashed?"

Adrian swallowed, and his eyes flickered nervously from side to side. "Uh, yes."

Callum inspected Adrian, then said, "I have a social welfare project I'm putting together—I'd like you to be involved."

Adrian looked astonished. "Me?"

"Yes." Callum started to smile. "I rather suspect that you're going to have a busy year. I know that the scholarships committee is going to want to meet you. You're going to have to work hard to impress them. I can't get you in on my recommendation alone."

Adrian appeared about to fall down with relief. "Oh, no, I understand that. I'll do my best."

"Good."

That one word told Miranda of the high expectations Callum had of her brother. Her brother would be in good hands—the best.

Flo nearly wept when Callum, Miranda and Adrian returned to the little terrace house with her car. But it became clear that Callum had plans for her, too.

"Miranda is going to be very busy with her new business." He gave Flo a meaningful stare. "She's going to need help."

"I can help."

Miranda started to object. What could Flo do—aside from spend money like water? But Callum held up a hand, halting what she'd been about to say.

"I could help her with baking—as I did last week."

That was true, her mother had been a great help in the time leading up to Pauline's birthday.

"You could also probably take charge of hiring the crockery, cutlery and glasses that Miranda needs."

"Yes, yes." Flo looked animated. "I know a couple of places that would give me very good deals."

Callum was brilliant.

Miranda could see what he was doing: giving her mother's life meaning. And giving her responsibility. If it worked, it would be fantastic.

Callum had insisted on taking Miranda out for dinner. She needed a break from the mayhem that her family had caused. And afterward he took her to his town house for coffee.

The lights were blinking on the Christmas tree in the drawing room, giving his home a welcoming ambience after the cold and drizzle of the day. As they sat in two comfortable armchairs in front of a roaring fire, their cups of coffee untouched, Miranda said apologetically for the umpteenth time, "I'm terribly sorry for all the inconvenience my family has caused you."

He waved a dismissive hand, not wanting her to take responsibility for her mother and brother. "Don't worry about it. Everything is sorted out."

She gave him a hesitant smile. "Not quite everything."

"What have I overlooked?"

"I never answered your question."

"Which one?"

But he knew.

Miranda looked suddenly anxious, and tension filled him.

"You mean my will-you-marry-me question?" he asked, on the remote chance he'd gotten it wrong.

For a second he thought she was going to turn and run. But she stayed. Her chin went up. "Is it still open for consideration?"

"I thought you said it would never work."

She lifted her chin. "It will work. We'll make it work. I want to marry you."

"You want to marry me? Why?"

"Why do you think?"

Callum started to enjoy himself. "Because I have a family you like?"

Her teeth snapped shut. "No."

"Because I have a country house you like…which even has horses?"

He knew the moment she sensed that he was teasing. The caramel-colored eyes he loved so much began to sparkle. "No—but I definitely want to visit again."

"It must be because I lust after your body?"

She swallowed. "We-ll, that might be part of it."

"Or because I love you?"

"What?" Her eyes went wide.

"I love you." He started to laugh. "Don't you know that by now?"

"I hoped but…I wasn't sure."

"Of course I love you—I think the whole world knows it."

"How long…?"

"Well, it certainly wasn't the first time I met you."

"Nor the time I responded to your summons," she said firmly.

"I just wanted to get that girl who'd called me a murderer off my conscience. But I hadn't anticipated the effect a grown-up Miranda would have on my libido." He rose to his feet and pulled her out of the armchair into his arms.

Miranda's eyebrows lowered as she peered up at him. "You nearly married another woman."

"Almost," he said, grinning unrepentantly down at the woman he held in his arms, "but I didn't. Actually, that was when I fell in love with you, though I didn't realize it at the time. I just knew there was no way I could marry Petra—anyone—when all I could think about was you. It was only later that I realized it was love."

"Look." Miranda pointed. "Is that what I think it is?"

Callum peered up. "It's mistletoe."

"I thought so," she said with supreme satisfaction.

His arms came around her. "You don't need an excuse to kiss me. Just do it anytime you want."

She linked her arms around his neck and drew his head down.

"I fully intend to kiss you plenty. Because I love you, too," she whispered against his mouth, thankful that all her Christmas wishes had been fulfilled.

Callum Ironstone would forever be her Christmas love.

* * * * *

There were times in a girl's life when she just had to prove a point.

It didn't necessarily have to be smart or even right, but the situation demanded Paige take action and teach Trent Hightower a lesson. He couldn't get away with using and discarding women the way he had her.

Her pulse blipped erratically as she gathered her resolve and decided to not only make him remember every second of the night they'd spent together last year, but also make him sorry he'd walked away without calling.

She would make him want her, and then she'd dump him like he'd dumped her.

Bad idea, her conscience warned.

But what did she have to lose?

HIS HIGH-STAKES HOLIDAY SEDUCTION

BY
EMILIE ROSE

Published in Great Britain 2010
Harlequin Mills & Boon Limited,
Eton House, 18-24 Paradise Road, Richmond, Surrey TW9 1SR

© Emilie Rose Cunningham 2009

ISBN: 978 0 263 88185 1

51-1110

Harlequin Mills & Boon policy is to use papers that are natural, renewable
and recyclable products and made from wood grown in sustainable forests.
The logging and manufacturing processes conform to the legal environmental
regulations of the country of origin.

Printed and bound in Spain
by Litografia Rosés S.A., Barcelona

Bestselling Desire™ author and RITA® Award finalist **Emilie Rose** lives in her native North Carolina with her four sons and two adopted mutts. Writing is her third (and hopefully her last) career. She's managed a medical office and run a home day care, neither of which offers half as much satisfaction as plotting happy endings. Her hobbies include gardening and cooking (especially cheesecake). She's a rabid country music fan because she can find an entire book in almost any song. She is currently working her way through her own "bucket list," which includes learning to ride a Harley. Visit her website at www.emilierose.com or e-mail EmilieRoseC@aol.com. Letters can be mailed to PO Box 20145, Raleigh, NC 27619.

To my boys for allowing Mom to live her dreams and for sometimes sharing yours.

Dear Reader,

Who hasn't fantasized about visiting Las Vegas?
For me, the allure isn't the bright lights, big-named
performers or the casinos. I want to go because Vegas
is jam-packed with roller coasters. I love the thrill of
these rides.

Any city with a motto like "What happens in Vegas
stays in Vegas" has to be chock full of fun, right? But
for Paige McCauley finding fun in Sin City proves
elusive until she meets sexy CEO Trent Hightower—
again—or so she thinks.

When Paige confuses him for his identical twin,
Trent is forced to spend time with her to protect his
family's assets. They end up exploring more than the
region's amusement parks and discover a steamy sexual
attraction worth gambling on.

I hope you enjoy the ups and downs of Trent and
Paige's roller-coaster relationship as much as I did
researching for it.

Happy reading,

Emilie Rose

One

Paige McCauley stopped dead in her tracks. Her heart banged like gunfire on the CNN news, and her face felt as if someone had pointed a heat lamp at her.

The beauty of a one-night stand was that once it ended it was supposed to be *O-V-E-R*. That went double if it had been a humiliating experience.

She'd spent a good part of the past twelve months worrying about this day, looking over her shoulder and flinching at the sight of every tall tawny-haired businessman. That wasn't good considering her job routinely required her to deal with conventions and men in suits. But there was no mistaking that the face and body purposefully striding toward her belonged to the man who'd found her so lacking he couldn't even—

She flinched away from finishing the thought.

The memory of that night made her want to run clear

back to South Carolina and hide behind the counter at her parents' hardware store. But she couldn't do that. Not only did she have a job keeping her in Las Vegas, but going home meant facing the gossips and worse, admitting to her family that she'd exaggerated about her new and wildly exciting life in Sin City.

Curling her toes in her shoes, she held her ground and prayed she'd get through the next five minutes without totally disgracing herself. Perspiration dampened her palms as she watched Trent Hightower's handsome face and waited for him to recognize her.

He gave her a slow once over, then when their gazes collided he nodded with no sign of recognition and walked right past her, leaving a faint trail of cologne behind.

Her lungs deflated like a blown tire. Was she invisible with her clothes on? The man had seen her naked. Didn't she at least deserve a hello?

Ticked off, she snapped her gaping mouth closed and spun on her heel to visually track him. He didn't look back. "Trent?"

He stopped and slowly pivoted. Only mild curiosity lit his eyes. "Yes?"

She'd spent her entire life being the invisible middle sister until she'd taken drastic steps to change that—steps including Trent, her first and only attempt at a one-night stand.

And he'd *forgotten* her?

She fisted her hands, squared her shoulders and strode toward him, determined not to let him know his dismissal had ripped the scabs off old wounds. Not that she'd imagined herself in love with him or anything. In fact, the entire episode in his suite last year had been awkward and embarrassing and hadn't lived up to her expectations. But she had her pride, and at the moment she wound it around herself like a razor wire prison fence.

"Weren't you going to say hello?"

He looked a bit impatient, as if he had to be somewhere else. "Hello."

"Are you in town for the aviation convention again this year?"

She waited for the less than subtle hint to ring a bell in his memory. Judging by the polite mask of his handsome face, he wasn't hearing any chimes. The realization pierced her skin like slivers of glass.

Discarded and forgotten by yet another man.

"Yes, I am. Is there something I can do for you?"

She wanted to slink away and pretend this encounter had never happened, but she'd taken the easy way out when she'd packed her Jeep and driven twenty-three hundred miles west to start over in Vegas fourteen months ago. And she'd been paying for her cowardice ever since.

Her fingernails bit into her palms. "We met last year."

His eyes narrowed.

"And spent time together…upstairs…in your suite," she prompted uneasily.

His entire body stiffened. Seconds ticked past. The muscles in his square jaw flexed and relaxed. "Yes. Of course… um…"

"Paige." She forced the word through teeth clenched so tightly she could probably bend metal with her molars. Clearly, he didn't have even a faint memory of her. But then, could she blame him for wanting to block the unpleasant incident from his mind?

They'd been having so much fun flirting harmlessly in the bar. He'd been attractive, funny, smart, and he'd made her feel feminine and wanted. Then he'd issued his invitation.

Going upstairs with him that night had taken two appletinis and every ounce of courage she'd been able to dredge up. And then with the way it had ended…

That had to be tough for a guy.

But not as tough as it had been for her to be found lacking. Again.

"Of course. Paige. I'm sorry. My apologies for not recognizing you. I'm a little preoccupied."

Previously, he'd been a smooth-talking charmer from the moment he'd offered to buy her a drink to when he'd put her on the elevator after…the disaster. There wasn't anything inviting or charming about him today. He flashed No Trespassing signs like a strobe light.

Crawling under a rock appealed tremendously. She couldn't believe what she'd done with him, couldn't believe she'd been such an idiot, couldn't believe what a disappointment her first and only walk on the wild side had been. She'd been too mortified and disillusioned to try again.

But that didn't stop you from faking it for your sisters, did it?

She cringed inwardly. One of these days she would have to take her medicine for the stories she'd been telling. But better to embellish her boring, lonely, work-filled life than let her family worry, or worse yet, pity her.

She'd deal with the fallout if and when it happened. But how was she going to salvage *this* encounter?

Coolly. Calmly. Politely. She forced her fingers to uncurl. Everybody made mistakes. Trent Hightower had been one of hers—a big one. And the fact that he'd never called afterward made it clear he felt the same way about her.

Trent's eyebrows dipped. "There were no repercussions from our…meeting, were there?"

Another wave of shame rocked her. She had been a

little concerned that someone from work had seen her go upstairs with him, but no one had, and she hadn't been tagged as *loose* the way she would have been if she'd been caught slipping into the local motor lodge back home. "No."

"Good. Nice to see you again…Paige. If you'll excuse me." He nodded and resumed his path across the mezzanine. Speechless, she watched him go.

Something struck her as off. She studied his back, trying to pinpoint the difference in him. There was no mistaking the man with whom she'd had her only no-strings-almost-sex encounter. Some things a girl just didn't forget. Like those incredible light eyes, that square jaw and his deliciously carved mouth. She'd been drawn by his looks immediately.

But something nagged at her. Trent's stride seemed more confident, more decisive. His shoulders looked broader. He must have been working out. His voice seemed a little deeper and firmer, but that might be because he was as uncomfortable as she about the way things had ended and that made him sound gruff.

She'd tried to forget that night. But it looked as though she'd have to suffer through a reminder for the rest of the conference. One thing was certain. She'd never let Trent Hightower know how much he'd rattled her or that he'd killed her fantasy of an exciting life in a big city, a life that involved getting over the guy who'd dumped her instead of proposing the way she'd expected.

She glanced at her watch and winced at the time. Another moment wandering down bad memory lane and she'd be late for work. Her curiosity about the man from her past would have to wait until their next encounter, and since they'd both be sharing the same piece of real estate for the next week, she didn't doubt there would be one.

* * *

Damn his conniving, lying and apparently adulterous twin.

Trent Hightower veered away from his path to the conference room and stepped into a crowded elevator. He needed to talk to his brother and the conversation didn't need to be overheard by others in the aircraft industry.

Who was the woman? And why had his brother risked his marriage to be with her? Hadn't Brent learned anything from their mother's numerous sordid affairs?

The second his hotel suite door clicked shut behind him Trent hit speed dial on his cell phone. He paced impatiently, waiting for Brent to pick up.

"Hey, bro. How's Vegas? Have you checked in yet?" his brother answered.

"Brent, what in the hell did you do while you were here last December?"

"Good crowd?" His twin ignored his question. Typical.

"Who is she?" Trent all but growled into the phone.

"I don't know what you're talking about." The overkill on the too innocent tone made Trent's ears burn with fury.

"I ran into a woman in the hotel who says she spent time with *me* in my suite at this convention last December. I wasn't here, Brent. *You* were. And you used my name. Again. Didn't you? You're too old for that impersonation crap."

"Using your name was easier than changing the reservations and registration. You backed out at the last minute, remember?"

"I had to handle a work crisis. *Remember?*" One his twin as sales manager had caused by promising a client more than Hightower Aviation could deliver. Trent had pulled all kinds of strings and called in numerous favors to avoid violating that promise. In business, reputation was everything.

"Who is she and how badly did you screw up?"

"That depends. Is she a blonde, a brunette or a redhead?"

Trent's anger grabbed him by the throat, threatening to choke him. "How many women are we talking about?"

"At that conference? Hmm. Let me think. Three. One of each hair color."

"This one's a blonde named Paige."

"Oh. Her."

His brother's odd tone caused the muscles in the back of Trent's neck to seize with tension. "What?"

"Nothing."

"Did you or did you not take her to your suite?"

Silence seconds ticked past. "I did."

"And?"

"None of your business."

"Brent, you are an idiot."

"If you remember, Luanne and I were having marital difficulties at the time. I was exploring my options." Brent's defensive tone set Trent's teeth on edge.

"Your marriage is a combat zone. You're always fighting over something, and your wife is always going home to her momma about something. But this? What were you thinking?"

"Get rid of Paige before Luanne and I hit town next week."

"Stay home."

"No can do. My wife has her heart set on seeing Vegas."

"It's too risky."

"Just deal with Paige and any other women who might come out of the woodwork. If this gets back to Luanne there'll be hell to pay."

"And deservedly so. But somehow *I* always end up footing the bill for *your* mistakes. Your wife would filet you and Hightower Aviation's assets. She's likely to leave your ass for good this time and take a chunk of HAMC with her. You should never have given her half your company stock."

"I had to prove my love. Fix this, Trent, the way you fix everything else."

"Damn it, Brent, I can't keep cleaning up your mistakes. You're thirty-four. When are you going to grow up?"

"Save your breath, bro. I can recite this lecture by heart. We both know you're not going to let disaster strike. You value Hightower Aviation Management Corporation over everything—including your identical twin's happiness."

"Don't try to twist this and make me the bad guy."

"Luanne and I aren't changing our plans. She's determined to renew our vows in front of Elvis before the baby arrives, and we don't want to upset the delicate mommy-to-be or ruin my second honeymoon. By the way, I'll want you to be best man again."

"Why? So I can object this time like I should have the first time? You were too damned young to get married."

"But I did. Can I count on you?"

"Don't change the subject. We're talking about your screwup and the potential disastrous consequences."

"Were we? I thought we were discussing me renewing my vows."

Trent clamped his jaw shut on the string of vicious curses battling for freedom. The pregnancy was probably the only reason his bitch of a sister-in-law had dropped her threat of an extremely expensive and very public divorce. Discovering her husband had screwed an attractive, brown-eyed blonde with a sweet Southern drawl would drive Luanne right back to her overpriced attorney's office, and that would stir the tabloids into another Hightower feeding frenzy. The last two had barely died down.

"Trent, you could always leave and skip the conference."

The suggestion didn't surprise him. Brent lived by the "why fix what you can avoid" motto—the opposite of Trent's "why avoid what you can fix" strategy. They might look identical, but their philosophies on most things were polar opposites.

"I'm the speaker for three of the seminars. I won't leave the organizers in the lurch."

"Guess you're stuck then."

"Who is this woman?"

"Just some chick I picked up in a bar. She probably snags a new man every conference. Get rid of her. *Please.* I'm finally going to be a daddy, Trent. I don't want to blow that."

Trent scraped a hand across his knotting neck muscles. Brent knew exactly how and when to pull the ace from his sleeve.

"You should have thought about that before unzipping your pants."

"Then think of the board meeting you've called for the week you get back. This news won't help your cause."

Damn it. Brent was right. Trent's plans for Hightower Aviation would never get off the ground if his family didn't quit making asinine decisions and drawing negative publicity. Every time one of the Hightowers made the gossip columns Trent's credibility as CEO went down a notch. If he couldn't control his family, then the board would not believe he could control a multibillion-dollar company or endorse the financing for his proposed expansion plans.

His grandfather had wisely instigated a convoluted board approval process for large cash expenditures as a safeguard back when Trent's father had been blowing big bucks on gambling. The policy had not yet been overturned because his mother, as president of the board, had dug in her designer heels. She might not work for the company anymore, but she liked to flex her muscles and maintain as much control as possible.

Trent paced his suite, irritation, frustration and fury warring inside him. He had to strike now while HAMC's smaller competitors were struggling. In this down economy he could buy them for a song and gain territory and assets. But to get board approval he had to avert this latest potential catastrophe.

Brent had him over a barrel and knew it. "I'll see what I can do. But Brent, this is the last time I'm hauling your ass out of the fire."

"Yeah, yeah, that's what you always say. But I know I can count on you, big brother. Hey, gotta go. Luanne's coming." Brent disconnected.

Trent crammed his phone back into his pocket. They both knew he would do anything to save the family business—a fact he'd demonstrated repeatedly, first by forfeiting his dream of becoming an air force pilot to join HAMC after college and clean up the mess his father had created and then most recently by not correcting Paige downstairs.

Priority one: Get rid of the woman.

Two: Formulate a damage control plan.

But to do either of those he required more information.

Who was this Paige person? Was her presence at the convention again this year a coincidence? Or was she part of the aircraft industry? Did she work for a vendor or the competition?

An affair within the aircraft community would be harder to keep hidden—especially if she worked in the executive offices of a competitor. Private aviation was by necessity a cutthroat business. Corporate espionage wasn't unheard of.

He hit Redial on his phone to grill Brent, but the line immediately dumped him to voice mail. His idiot brother had likely turned the thing off to avoid future calls. Again, typical.

Trent pocketed his phone. Finding a pretty blonde whose last name he didn't know in a hotel of this size wouldn't be easy, but once he did he'd make damn sure Paige *whoever-shewas* would be long gone before the parents-to-be arrived—even if he had to encourage her departure by sending her on an all-expenses-paid vacation elsewhere.

What good was having a fleet of jets at your command if you couldn't use them?

After running into Trent earlier today and having her audio-visual tech call in sick the first day of a major conference, Paige decided her day had to get better. It couldn't get worse.

Great. Jinx yourself, why don'tcha?

Grimacing, she grabbed the work request slip and headed for the banquet hall to tackle the first problem on her roster for the conference. Her title might be Assistant Event Coordinator, but she'd learned that at the Lagoon Hotel and Casino that translated into chief troubleshooter and jill-of-all-trades. Luckily, because of her summer jobs at the hardware store during school she was qualified.

She entered the room and spotted an annoyed-looking Trent Hightower beside the podium. Her shoes stuck to the carpet for the second time that day. *He* was the speaker having microphone troubles? Just her luck. She wasn't ready to face him again so soon. But what choice did she have?

Just because you've seen him nearly naked doesn't make him special. Treat him like any other guest.

She took a bracing breath and approached the stage. His head jerked up. His eyes tracked her steps, making her stomach swoop as if she'd taken a plunge on the Goliath roller coaster at her favorite Atlanta amusement park.

It's only nerves.

But then his gaze dropped to her chest. Her nipples tightened and her stomach quivered. Funny, she didn't recall that happening when he'd looked at her last December. Then they'd been more relaxed and fun…like her relationship with David—her ex.

"You weren't wearing a name tag earlier."

He was looking at her name tag? Not her breasts? That was a bit…humbling, especially considering her intense reaction. "You might remember I like to walk through the hotel before I clock in."

"Of course." That he didn't remember was clear on his handsome face and in the hesitation before his reply.

"What's the problem?" Goody, her voice sounded normal.

"Too much feedback."

She wasn't a sound technician, but she'd picked up some experience. She tried to go around him. He simultaneously moved in the same direction and then the opposite. The awkward little dance resembled the clumsiness they'd shared in his suite. Only this time it felt…different, as if static electricity arced between them.

Weird. Had a short in the sound system wiring leaked current into the metal-framed stage platform?

Trent caught her shoulders, stopping her, then he moved aside and gestured for her to go ahead. Her heart skipped and her shoulders tingled with residual pressure from his big, warm hands. Wow. His touch hadn't affected her that way before, either.

Tucking that thought aside to hash over later when he wasn't scowling at her, she forced her unsteady feet into motion and spoke into the microphone. Her words echoed off the walls of the large room. She winced, hating the sound of her voice. The other hotel employees teased her unmercifully about the low country drawl she hadn't been able to completely erase despite a year of trying.

She left the stage and adjusted a few knobs on the base unit tucked in the corner, aware of Trent's gaze boring through the back of her head the entire time. When she straightened she realized the platform's height put her eyes right at his crotch level. Had he talked to a doctor about his problem?

Or had the problem been her and only her?

She averted her gaze and cleared her throat. "Try it now."

Trent confidently resumed his position behind the podium, as if he were accustomed to addressing large crowds and didn't mind hearing his magnified voice. "Testing. One. Two. That sounds better. Thank you, Paige."

His deep tone reverberated loud and clear, vibrating down her spine like calloused fingertips. She shivered in a way that she definitely had *not* when he *had* touched her in his suite. How odd. Was she coming down with something?

"You're welcome."

"You don't wear a hotel uniform," he said as she rejoined him on the stage.

"Never have. You know why." Or at least he should. She'd explained the night they'd first met in the bar that the hotel management expected her to dress to blend in with their high-end clients.

He's probably forgotten that the way he's forgotten everything else about you.

Doesn't that make you feel special?

Hardly.

She suppressed another wince. "Is there anything else I can do for you, Trent?"

His eyes cooled, the color going from warm blue-green Caribbean to silvery arctic ice, startling her back a step. "Paige, what happened between us at the last convention won't be repeated during this one."

She flinched. *Ouch. That stung.*

But she wasn't known as the family peacemaker and mediator for nothing. She'd never cowered simply because a situation turned ugly or uncomfortable.

Except for running to Vegas, her conscience jeered.

Digging deep for the fortitude to get through the next couple of minutes, she held his gaze and forced a sympathetic smile.

"Trent, I don't blame you for being…embarrassed about our previous encounter. We were both disappointed in…well…um, the episode. But that doesn't mean you have to be rude. There were two of us in that suite. I was incredibly nervous. You were my first one-night stand."

He jerked as if the microphone had shorted and shocked him. "You were a virgin?"

Mortification broiled her skin. "No. But…I didn't— I *don't* make a habit of going upstairs with hotel guests."

"You don't?"

Wow. That said a lot about his opinion of her. She ignored her burning cheeks and forged on. "No. As I was saying, I accept half the blame for our…less than wonderful time, but the other half is yours. I can understand that you wouldn't want to repeat the experience. Trust me, I'm not crazy about the idea, either. But it would be nice if we could put the past behind us and be civil since I expect we'll run into each other quite often during the conference. Have a good day."

Relieved to have gotten that off her chest, she pivoted and hustled away as fast as her trembling legs would carry her. Too bad she couldn't find a way to avoid him for the remainder of his stay, but hiding wasn't an option. She had too much pride to be a coward a second time.

Two

Embarrassed?
  Disappointed?
  Less than wonderful?
  Didn't want to repeat the experience?

Trent's pride shot up a series of distress flares. He'd wanted information, but he didn't like what he'd learned.

He took great satisfaction in the skills he'd developed since his first fumbling adolescent affairs. And even though it hadn't actually been *him* with Paige, the idea that she believed *he* had failed to satisfy her in bed chaffed like a cheap, overstarched shirt.

He yearned to correct her. But he couldn't. Not without shooting his expansion plans for Hightower Aviation out of the sky and risking his brother's marriage and the subsequent consequences—monetary and otherwise.

Part of him—the intelligent, thinking-with-his-brain

part—warned him to implement damage control and walk away from Paige.

But part of him wanted to make her eat her words.

Not smart, man. Let it go.

What in the hell had happened between his brother and the hotel's assistant event coordinator? Trent didn't want to know, and yet he couldn't afford not to. Diffusing the situation would be impossible without knowing what he was up against. Whatever it was couldn't have been good.

Damnation. He wanted to wring Brent's neck. Short of fratricide Trent had to find another way to avoid certain disaster. But how?

His intention of getting rid of Paige before Brent and Luanne arrived in town had hit turbulence the moment Trent had read her name tag and realized Paige *McCauley*—or so the engraved brass bar pinned to her breast stated—worked at the Lagoon.

There had to be another solution. And he would find it.

He visually tracked her retreating form, taking in her stiff spine, small waist, curvy hips and sleekly muscled legs atop sexy high heels. She had great legs. Hell, who was he kidding? Her hourglass shape in a green figure-skimming dress had caught his attention the moment he'd spotted her, but he'd ignored the call of his libido because he had a tight schedule, and because he *never* mixed business with pleasure.

For once his brother had great taste—without resorting to poaching. But Trent had always had a serious aversion to his brother's leavings, a remnant from high school and college when Brent had relished playing tricks on Trent's girlfriends to prove he could fool them out of their clothes and into the sack. Then Brent would tell Trent about his scores in graphic detail. Brent's deceptive, juvenile actions had killed more of Trent's relationships than he could count. Any woman who couldn't tell the difference between him and his brother wasn't worth his time.

The memories left a bad taste in his mouth, but if he wanted to derail disaster and keep Paige from discovering Brent's deception, then Trent had to find a way to get her out of the hotel before next weekend.

"Paige," he called out and pursued her. She kept walking. Either she didn't hear him or chose to ignore him.

She turned a corner. He followed. At the sight of the dark casino with its garishly lit machines flashing even at this time of the morning, repugnance swept through him. He halted short of the entrance. If she kept going he'd have to let her escape. Given his father's gambling addiction, a weakness that could be hereditary, Trent avoided casinos at all costs—a circumstance that made attending the annual aviation conference in Vegas a challenge.

"Paige," he called again, louder this time.

She turned. Arms folded across the clipboard hugged to her chest, she looked less than thrilled to extend their discussion. "Was there something else?"

"I apologize for my rudeness. Let me make it up to you by buying you a drink."

The obvious lack of interest thinning her lips and furrowing her brow blew a hole in the fuselage of his ego. "That's not necessary. But thank you."

"I insist. I'll finish here by seven this evening."

"I'm sorry. I have other plans after work."

"Then lunch tomorrow."

She shifted in her sexy shoes and glanced toward the exit—her desire to escape him as clear as crystal in her expressive brown eyes. "Trent, you don't owe me anything."

"We need to talk about what happened." He had to find out how many people had seen her with Brent. Had the witnesses known it was his brother or had they, too, believed Brent's pretense?

Paige frowned. "We had a good time. And then…we didn't. I'd prefer to forget it."

So would he, but then she might put two and two together when Brent arrived and detonate like a scorned woman. He had to find a way to circumvent that, and the only way to do that was by gathering enough facts to formulate a plan.

"I insist. What time is your lunch break tomorrow?"

She swallowed, looking as if someone had given her a dose of bad medicine. "I can't leave the hotel during my shift."

Meeting with her in the hotel was risky, but a risk he had to take. He considered his options. The top floor seafood restaurant was pricy enough to discourage most convention-goers. "I'll make reservations for us at The Coral Reef."

Indecision flickered across her face before resignation settled in, taking another sharp jab at his ego. He wasn't used to having to work this hard to get women. His wealth had always brought them to his door whether he had time for them or not, and he'd made Knoxville's most eligible bachelors list often enough to know his looks weren't slowing them down.

"Sure. Fine. Whatever. Lunch tomorrow. Upstairs at noon." With a dismissive flick of her wrist, she turned and departed, flaying him with her lack of interest.

Failure—even if it wasn't actually his—didn't taste good. *Brent, buddy, you are going to pay for this one.*

From her corner table in the hotel's seafood restaurant Paige had a clear view of Trent Hightower swaggering into The Coral Reef like he owned the place.

He hadn't been that arrogant last year. Sure, he'd been confident, but also fun and flirtatious in a harmless, nonthreatening way. This year he appeared driven and serious, like a man on a mission. He emitted an I-can-handle-anything-you-throw-at-me vibe that she found quite sexy.

What could have happened over the past twelve months to change him so drastically?

Not your problem.

But a lifetime of being her sisters' sounding board and problem-solver was a hard habit to break. Her momma claimed it was because Paige was "a born fixer" who couldn't stand to see others out-of-sorts. Paige knew better. She hated unanswered questions and the unexpected chaos that usually accompanied them, so she tended to probe where others wouldn't dare to go.

Trent's gaze met hers across the linen-draped, crystal-topped tables. Her heart blipped erratically. Cold water splashed over the rim of her glass, wetting her fingers. She set down the goblet before her unsteady hands gave away her agitation.

Trent waved off the maitre d' and made his way to the table alone. Heads turned as he crossed the room. The women were no doubt as drawn as Paige to his charismatic black-suited form. The men were probably envious. Who wouldn't want a body that looked as though it had walked off the cover of a fitness magazine? Trent possessed power-ful shoulders, lean hips and all the good bits in between capped by a drool-worthy gorgeous face.

His attitude wasn't the only thing that had changed. She'd thought him handsome before, but they hadn't had this potent attraction that hit her like a triple-shot of espresso each time he came near, making her skittish, breathless and her heartbeat irregular. If they had, then maybe things would have turned out differently and her walk on the wild side wouldn't have fizzled like a dud firework.

She had to admit the combination of his attitude change and their sudden sizzle had snagged her curiosity. There was nothing she liked better than a puzzle, and trying to figure him out was going to be more interesting than the crosswords she did alone on her treadmill each night rather than face the scary Vegas singles scene alone.

Excavating the cause of Trent's transformation should keep her entertained during this duty lunch. Afterward, once he'd satisfied himself by making whatever amends he believed he needed to make, she'd go her own way and relegate him and the memory of that miserable night to the past. If she didn't, she'd never find the courage to try again, and she really had to do that before her sisters decided to make good on their threat to visit Vegas.

Trent lowered himself into the seat across from her. A faint whiff of his cologne drifted across the table to tease and tempt her. Had he changed cologne? Funny, she'd forgotten the scent and taste of a jaw she'd kissed. As big of an impact as he'd had on her year you'd think she wouldn't forget any of the details.

"So how's the airplane biz?" she asked even before he'd unfolded his napkin.

"Still profitable despite the economy. How has event managing been?"

She mentally rolled her eyes at his deflection. Apparently, he wanted to chitchat before getting to the point of the conversation. Two of her sisters were that way. The other two blurted out information like avalanches. Before you knew it you'd been buried under too many facts and had to dig your way to the point.

"It turns out I'm good at event management since I'm used to juggling multiple crises simultaneously."

His focus sharpened. "A trait we share."

"Probably because we both worked in our respective family businesses with our siblings. But unlike home, now I get a paycheck for handling catastrophes instead of a soggy shoulder, and I don't have to loan anyone my favorite earrings to cheer them up."

Amusement flared in his eyes, jump-starting her pulse. "Remind me which part of the South you're from."

Had he forgotten everything she'd told him? "South Carolina—a very small town on Lake Marion about halfway between Charleston and Columbia."

"Are any of your siblings still there?"

"Yes. All of them. Kelly, my oldest sister, left for a while, but she came back." Single, two months pregnant and dumped by her lover. Tongues had wagged, making starting over all that much more difficult for heartbroken Kelly.

Failure in a small town provided entertainment for the gossips—something Paige had learned firsthand when David had dumped her after seven years together. It hadn't been one of her finer moments when she'd taken the cowardly way out and run clear to Vegas to avoid being fodder for the rumor mill. But as her granny always said, she'd made her bed and now she had to lie in it.

"And the rest?" Trent prompted.

She pushed down a twinge of homesickness and focused on her lunch companion. "Jessica and Ashley still live within thirty miles of my parents. We'll see where Sammie ends up when she graduates from USC in June, but my guess is she'll teach in the same elementary school we attended. I suppose we McCauleys like to stick close. Even when I first left home I was just over an hour away in North Charleston. Are your brother and sisters still working for the family?"

She would have missed his sudden stillness if she hadn't been looking directly at him. "Most of them."

"Most? You told me before that you had a younger brother and two younger sisters. Which one moved on?"

A closed expression shuttered his face. "My newest sister."

Her eyebrows hiked at his odd word choice. "Your *newest* sister? I've called my sisters a lot of things, but never newest. You're going to have to explain that one."

"You must be the only one in the country who missed the tabloid stories. Have you decided what you'd like to eat?"

If he thought she'd be deflected that easily, he'd better think again. "I know what I'm ordering. Your family is featured in tabloids? Mine only stars in the grapevine. It's amazingly efficient. But I don't read the gossip rags. What happened?"

Resignation anchored the corners of his mouth and formed a crease between his eyebrows. "A few months ago my mother introduced us to Lauren, a daughter she'd given up for adoption twenty-five years ago. Lauren worked as a pilot for us for a while, but she recently returned to Florida to run her father's charter plane company. She's engaged to my best friend."

His tense tone raised flags. "Not happy about that, huh?"

"Lauren's an excellent pilot and a hard worker. She's made Gage happy."

"But…?"

He lifted one broad, tense shoulder. "I don't like surprises."

"Have you had many of them this year?"

He flicked open his menu. "A few."

That could have contributed to his changed demeanor. "Anything interesting?"

"No." His clipped voice warned her not to pursue the subject. He signaled for the waiter. "Would you care for a glass of wine?"

"I can't. I'm working. But the hotel's cellar is top-notch,

so I suggest you try something." If she was lucky, it might loosen his tongue.

The waiter arrived with a bread basket, took their orders and departed. She noted Trent didn't order alcohol.

"What does Hightower Aviation do again?" She remembered, but she didn't want him to think she'd attached more importance to their night than she should have. The details were locked in her brain because their time in his suite had been a lightbulb moment for her.

After David dumped her she'd vowed that she'd only have temporary affairs from that moment on. She didn't intend to invest her time and her heart in a guy only to have him ditch her when a more exciting opportunity came along.

Meeting Trent, a handsome stranger in town for only a short while, in the Lagoon's bar had seemed like fate. She'd convinced herself she was ready for the first step of her new plan, and she'd allowed Trent to coax her upstairs. After she'd left him that night with her fledgling wings singed to a crisp she'd decided that maybe the exciting, romantic, sexually fulfilling life she'd hoped to find might not be worth the effort or the embarrassment.

"Hightower Aviation Management Corporation sells, leases, rents, staffs and maintains more than six hundred aircraft worldwide primarily for business travelers, but also for celebrities and political dignitaries. We have four global operating centers and service one hundred fifty countries. Our four thousand pilots are the most qualified in the business aviation industry."

The pride in his voice as he tripped out his spiel hadn't been there before. Or maybe *she* was the one with the faulty memory, but she didn't think so. Being the middle of five meant she'd learned to read people pretty well. As for recalling details…keeping her sisters' soap opera lives straight had been excellent training.

"And you're the boss?"

"The CEO and vice president on the board of directors."

She nabbed a sourdough roll from the basket and wished she had a hush puppy instead, but the crispy, fried, sweet cornmeal nuggets hadn't made it to menus this far west— at least not in the fashion to which she was accustomed. If she ever found a steady boyfriend and took him home to show him off to the family, she'd stuff herself with calabash shrimp and hush puppies before coming home. But that wouldn't be this year.

She debated cutting into the fancy seashell shaped pad of butter on her bread plate, but decided it was too pretty to destroy. "You were the convention's opening speaker. I guess that makes you an industry expert?"

"We run a tight ship at HAMC. There's no room for error at forty thousand feet. If other companies choose to emulate us, that's their decision." A corner of his mouth lifted, drawing her gaze like nectar draws a butterfly, and making her pulse skip. "A wise one, I might add. We are the best at what we do."

His smile morphed into a frown. "But we could be better."

She knew for a fact that previously Trent hadn't used the words *we* and *our* when describing his work. He'd always said *my* or *I* very much like her oldest sister, who as the princess of the family and the first McCauley to graduate college, had always focused on herself until she'd gotten dumped and been forced to return home and beg for help.

It usually took something big to humble someone enough to make them aware of the world around them— not that Trent seemed at all defeated. But what had turned him from being the center of the HAMC universe to part of a whole? Had it been the surprises he mentioned?

Wishing he'd smile again, she tilted her head and studied him. Come to think of it, there'd been something different about his smile, too. He still had the same carved mouth and straight, white teeth, but there was something… "Tell me about your year, besides the new sister, I mean."

"It's been productive. Tell me about yours," he said.

She wanted to groan in frustration. Getting information out of people was her specialty, but he was a tough nut to crack. Given he was footing the bill for this party, she'd let him lead while they ate their shrimp cocktails. She'd have plenty of time to delve into his psyche over entrées and dessert.

"I've spent most of the past fourteen months learning the job and slowly taking on more responsibility."

"Sounds like you could use a vacation."

She was due one after the current conference, but she'd plead work again and skipped going home to her family to rest here.

Coward.

She shrugged off her discomfort. "Couldn't we all?"

"My private jet is sitting idle at the airport. I'll loan it to you for the duration of the conference. All you have to do is choose a location—or a series of them—and pack. Within a few hours you could be parked on a beach, a tall cool drink in one hand and a thick beach read in the other. Or you could hit the slopes and do a little skiing."

She chuckled at his humor. Then she noted his serious expression. "You're joking, right?"

"My plane and crew are at your disposal."

Wow. "Trent, as generous and tempting as that sounds, I can't leave now. This convention is my baby, the first event my boss has let me handle alone. If I screw it up, my job could be on the line."

"Do you like living in Vegas enough to want to keep it?"

Strange question. "My job? Absolutely."

Vegas might not be as socially fertile as she'd hoped, but her career was far more stimulating than standing at the cash register at her parents' hardware store. She hadn't gone to college for four years to work at a small hotel like the one in Charleston. She'd always wanted to work in a big city...but she'd expected to do so with David by her side.

Their appetizers arrived. She popped a chilled shrimp into her mouth and chewed. The Coral Reef might be a five star restaurant, but it couldn't compete with the East coast fresh catch seafood she'd been raised on. There was no comparison to seafood that had been caught in the morning and cooked the same evening.

She tried to hide her disappointment. "I like Vegas, although I've seen very little of it. My sisters keep threatening to visit. I really should hit some of the tourist spots so I'll know what to show them if they can ever synchronize their schedules. But thus far, the only list of attractions I have is of the roller coasters I plan to ride...if I ever find the time."

His eyes zeroed in on hers and his body tensed alertly. "Roller coasters?"

A little embarrassed by her obsession, she wrinkled her nose. "I'm an addict. I love them."

"So do I." He sat back in his seat, an odd look on his face. "Or I used to. I haven't ridden one since college."

The image of this polished version of Trent screaming his lungs out on an amusement park ride wouldn't form on her mental movie screen. "Why haven't you?"

He hesitated as if mulling over his reply. "Heading up

a company as large as HAMC doesn't allow for a lot of downtime."

She filed away another clue to his personality change. All work and no play—an apt description of her life at the moment—could sap the energy right out of you.

"Now's your chance. There are about twenty roller coasters in Vegas. You'll be here for what…a week? Ten days? The conference can't take up all of your time. You should ride a few…unless you're a sissy like my sisters who would be too afraid to ride even the tamest of the bunch."

His jaw jacked up at her jibe, and the fire of competition flamed to life in his eyes. "How many have you ridden?"

She grimaced. "None yet."

"Why?"

Another pang of homesickness hit. "Riding alone is no fun. I used to ride with my father. Love of roller coasters was the one thing he shared with me, but none of my sisters."

"Invite him for a visit."

"He won't leave his hardware store for more than a day or two, and with the current airline schedules…it just wouldn't work."

"My offer of a plane stands. Let me fly him out next weekend. That'll give him time to find someone to cover the store for him. Surely you can take a few days off to show him around."

She shook her head at the absurdity of his offer. Rich people who could jet off at the spur of the moment didn't think like working folks who had regular jobs and bills to pay. "Thanks. But no. This close to Christmas he wouldn't dare leave. People buy a lot of tools during the holiday season. And as I said, I can't take the time until after the conference. Back to the roller coasters…I dare you."

His dark golden eyebrows lifted. "Excuse me?"

"You heard me. And you have siblings, so you know what a dare means."

He leaned forward and laced his fingers on the table. "Enlighten me."

She wished she could forget those hands had once touched her and had little to no effect. Today, simply looking at his long fingers with their short-clipped nails made her mouth moisten and her pulse trip. *Go figure.* Last year when she'd desperately needed him to make her feel feminine and desirable he'd failed. But now that she wanted nothing to do with him he rang her chimes like a handbell choir playing "Hallelujah" with almost no effort.

She peeled her gaze from those hands and forced herself to look into his beautiful teal eyes. "What I meant, Trent, is that talk is cheap. I dare you to enjoy a few rides while you're in town."

A cool predatory smile curved his lips as he eyed her speculatively. "I will on one condition."

She knew she'd regret asking, but she couldn't stop herself. "And that is…?"

"Ride with me. Unless you're chicken."

She had stepped right into that snare, hadn't she? So much for clearing the air then saying goodbye to her second most mortifying memory. But she'd never been one to back down from a challenge. Middle kids learned to hold their ground early on or get lost in the shuffle.

On the positive side, going out with Trent would give her a chance to actually see some of the sights she'd told her sisters about.

On the negative side…

She took a deep breath and squared her shoulders. There would be no negative side. One date in a public place was no big deal. What did she have to lose? The worst had already happened. Trent had taken her to bed and been so turned off he couldn't get an erection. She wasn't dumb enough to repeat that experience.

"Talk is cheap," he quoted back at her.

His jibe crushed her resistance. "I guess we have a date to ride a roller coaster."

"Name the time and the place, and we'll see who begs for mercy first."

She hoped it wasn't her.

Three

Trent's new jeans were stiff and uncomfortable. His conscience wasn't in any better shape as he waited outside Circus Circus's indoor amusement park for Paige.

He blamed his discomfort on the dishonesty. It couldn't be anything else. What he was doing was no different than his brother's childish pranks. It didn't matter that he was trying to save Brent's marriage and HAMC's reputation rather than have a laugh at someone else's expense. Good intentions or not, any way he tried to whitewash it, he was lying to Paige.

The verbal scrimmage they'd played over lunch had been a test of his skills. He'd had to tread carefully because he hadn't known what information Paige and Brent had shared, and Trent didn't want to contradict anything his brother might have said, but for his plan to succeed he needed to ferret out as many facts about their past as he could. Then he'd craft the perfect breakup scene—one that wouldn't have negative repercussions for Brent or HAMC.

When Paige had mentioned roller coasters, despite his reservations, Trent had jumped on the idea for two reasons. First, getting her out of the hotel meant avoiding other industry professionals who might mention his absence at last year's event. Second, he'd known he could relax his guard while fact-finding. She couldn't have ridden coasters with Brent because Brent couldn't stomach thrill rides of any kind.

Unfortunately, the rides weren't without the substantial risk of kicking off an adrenaline craving—a risk Trent had avoided since taking the helm of HAMC by staying out of roller coasters and cockpits. He shut down that line of thought and focused on his goal of getting rid of Paige rather than the concerns gnawing at the edge of his subconscious.

He hated uncertainty and being unprepared. Tonight's date perfectly illustrated the pitfalls of lying. Normally, he would have planned their date from beginning to end, but in this case, he'd had to follow Paige's lead. He couldn't offer to pick her up because he didn't know if his brother knew where she lived, and he couldn't ask because Brent, the numbskull, still wasn't answering his phone or e-mails or returning messages Trent had left with his brother's PA. Luckily, Paige had suggested meeting outside the hotel for their first outing.

Given the only reason Trent attended the annual aviation conference was to network, promote HAMC and view the vendors' latest products, he couldn't believe he'd blown off the opportunity. And yet here he stood, wasting valuable work hours doing damage control and playing mind games with a doe-eyed blonde.

Resenting his brother for putting him in this position, he shifted in his new shoes—yet another reminder of the cost of Brent's lie. Trent had had to purchase casual apparel from the hotel boutique this afternoon because he never allowed himself downtime at a convention and therefore hadn't packed anything except suits. In the past he'd always worked each day from the moment he left his hotel suite at dawn until he fell into bed around midnight. If there was a beneficial connection to be made for HAMC, he made it. But not this time.

He scanned the sidewalk again. At six in the evening the foot traffic had begun to pick up. Then like some clichéd movie scene, the pedestrians parted and he spotted Paige striding through the center of the crowd. A breeze lifted her long hair off her shoulders. She'd changed from the dress she'd worn earlier in the day into denim. Her jacket, zipped-up to her chin against the evening's chill, embraced her breasts. Faded jeans hugged her rounded hips and long, slender legs. His heart rate increased. It was easy to see why Brent had been tempted. But the idiot should have had more control.

Her steps faltered when she saw him, then tucking her chin, she charged in his direction with determination. She halted in front of him, tense and wary, hands in her jacket pockets.

His gaze dropped to her lips, and an almost over-whelming urge to kiss her hello the way a lover—*former* lover—would rose inside him. Would Brent have greeted her that way?

Eyes widening, Paige fell back a step, giving him his answer. He wasn't disappointed.

Hell, yes, you are. Who are you trying to fool?

The insight stunned him. He wanted to kiss her. Where was the aversion to Paige he should be feeling? He'd always been repelled by his brother's discards. But his prickling skin and sudden spike in temperature weren't difficult to identify. Desire.

He crushed his response. As much as he would love to rectify Paige's incorrect appraisal of his bedroom skills and prove his prowess between the sheets, he had no intention of sleeping with her. Sex would only complicate matters. Brent had left enough of a mess for Trent to clean up already.

She tilted her head back, her eyes glinting with pure challenge. "I half expected you to chicken out."

He shook his head. "I'm not the one who's lived here for over a year and found excuses not to ride. I expected you to be the no-show."

She scoffed in disbelief. "We'll see who screams first and loudest."

He pulled the wristbands from his pocket. "It won't be me, brown eyes. I've bought unlimited ride passes. I'm here until they shut the place down and throw us out. You can leave whenever you've had enough."

What in the hell? He even sounded like Brent. Cocky. Childish. Selfish.

Her wicked grin hit him like a punch in the gut. "My money says you won't last that long."

"That's a bet you'll lose. Give me your arm."

She extended her right forearm. He took her fist in one hand and shoved up her sleeve with the other, revealing pale skin and a fine-boned wrist. Her flesh warmed his palm. He had to fight the urge to trace his fingertips along the blue veins to test her softness. At thirty-four he was long past the juvenile stage of getting turned on by holding hands. But damned if a familiar tingle didn't start behind his fly.

He shut it down, quickly fastened her wristband with

hands that weren't as steady as he'd like, and released her, then tried to apply his own, but wrapping the slippery, limp paper around his arm proved to be trickier than putting on a watch even though the principle was the same.

"Let me do that." Lightning fast, she snatched the strip from his fingers before he could react and stretched it between her thumbs. He laid his wrist across the cool band. The tips of her fingers danced over the sensitive inside of his wrist as she removed the adhesive backing then snugly secured the flaps. "You're good to go."

The breathless quality of her voice drew his gaze to her flush-darkened cheeks then her wary, dilated eyes. Knowing she was as affected as he by the contact thickened his throat and increased the urge to erase her memories of his brother. The idea of threading his fingers into Paige's thick, straight hair, pulling her close and covering her mouth with his assaulted him like a Technicolor film streaming through his head.

No. No unnecessary entanglements. No more complications.

He refocused on the appetites he could satisfy. "Dinner first or rides?"

She gave him a you've-got-to-be-kidding-me look. "Rides. We can eat afterward—if your stomach can handle it."

Her taunt ripped a laugh from his gut. Damn, she was sassy. Had Brent had any clue what he'd bitten into? Or maybe Paige's sweet girl-next-door manner had been the attraction. As far as he could tell she was as different from Brent's bitchy, moody, manipulative wife as possible. Paige seemed too smart to have fallen for Brent's dubious charms.

You wouldn't be here if she hadn't.

Something he better not forget. "My stomach is not an issue. Do you want to start with the main attraction or something tamer?"

"I'm ready for the Canyon Blaster, but if you need to work up your courage, we'll ride the gentler stuff first."

Her baiting tone and the mischief in her eyes made his lips twitch. He didn't want to like Paige McCauley. He wanted to do his job of convincing her she'd slept with him during the previous convention then find a way to make her wish she'd never met him. That way when Brent and Luanne arrived next week Paige would avoid all of them. Trent just hadn't decided how to accomplish his goal yet.

He pivoted on his heel and headed toward the entrance of the hotel's indoor amusement park. Inside the Adventure Dome, Paige scanned the circus-themed space with the enthusiasm of a child while he inhaled the aromas of popcorn, cotton candy and hot dogs. She paused to read a map then hustled toward the roller coaster, leaving Trent to follow. The quick swish of her tush in her snug jeans drew his gaze like a train wreck.

"Come on," she called over her shoulder.

He lengthened his stride, then kept pace with her until they reached the short line for the double-loop, double corkscrew track. She bounced on the balls of her feet beside him. Her contagious excitement quickened his pulse.

If his family could see him now, goofing off and fighting a smile at Paige's antics, they'd think *he* was the imposter. His siblings accused him of being all business all the time, but somebody had to be focused on the future of Hightower Aviation.

For the past thirteen years he'd been too busy busting his ass and trying to hoist the family business from the financial crater his father's gambling addiction had created to have fun. He'd finally gotten the company on firm ground and ready to expand, then this year…everything had hit the fan.

His gaze followed the twists and turns of the roller coaster track—a track that bore a resemblance to his life over the past twelve months. Hell, even HAMC's top-notch PR team hadn't been able to find a way to put a positive spin on the discovery his mother's secret daughter or one of his sisters getting inseminated with the wrong donor's sperm at a nationally renowned fertility clinic. Luckily, his new half-sister wasn't half-bad, and his pregnant sister's situation had turned out well when she'd married her baby's biological father last month.

But he still had challenges ahead of him—the first, getting through this ride without triggering a downward spiral. But he'd worry about handling the adrenaline rush when it hit, or more correctly, if what his father claimed was true, Trent's problems would start when the adrenaline ebbed and the lack of excitement drove him in search of another kick.

"You look anxious," Paige taunted him. "Afraid?"

He blanked his expression. "Just wondering if I'm going to have to hold your hand or your hair."

Her exaggerated eye roll made his lips twitch. "*I* won't be the one getting sick."

The line inched forward. She grasped his elbow, held him back and motioned for three couples to go ahead of them. With a sinking stomach he recognized the tactic. Paige was waiting for the next ride and positioning them to be first in line for the train. In the past, he'd done the same thing countless times.

Sure enough when the gate opened, she tugged on his sleeve, dragging him toward the front car—the one guaranteed to give the wildest ride—and leaped into the two-seater. Clamping his jaw against what lay ahead, he climbed in beside her and slid into the seat. The compartment forced him into hot contact with Paige from his shoulders to his knees. His heart rate accelerated, and a familiar rush surged through his veins even before the overhead restraints descended and locked into place, preventing his escape.

He used to get this kind of buzz from flying, but he hadn't taken the yoke of an aircraft in years—not since the day his father had confessed he'd gambled away hundreds of thousands of dollars because games of chance gave him the same high as flying. His father had claimed he couldn't stand the dead feeling when he wasn't flying in the air or in the casinos.

His father was an adrenaline junky. Trent had known plenty of those and he'd been one. The MOs might be hot planes, fast cars or motorcycles, but one thing remained constant—most junkies ended up dead, broken or bankrupt. The scariest part was, when his father had rattled on about the excitement flying and gambling gave him, Trent had understood completely. Flying had once fueled his soul in exactly the same way.

The Hightowers couldn't afford another addict in the family, and given Trent was like his father in countless other ways, he couldn't risk discovering he had the same lack of willpower when the adrenaline ebbed. He didn't want to cost the family Hightower Aviation the way his father almost had.

Paige shifted in the narrow seat, branding her thighs and upper arms against his. Another jolt rocked his system. He attributed the powerful pumping of his blood solely to the anticipation of the ride, but then Paige wiggled again and he experienced a fresh power surge. Could his energy overload have something to do with Paige's proximity?

She turned her head and gave him a wide grin. "Hope you can hold your cookies."

The car rocketed out of the station before he could reply. A quick ninety-degree turn slammed Paige against him. Her body heat penetrated the layers of their clothing, burning him clear to his bones. Arousal hit him just as hard. The only other times he'd had a woman resting this heavily on him had involved sex.

The car rose then plunged and barreled into a series of loops and corkscrews. Each change in direction shifted the momentum, alternating between flattening Paige against him then him against her. He tried to hold himself off her, but it proved impossible. The contact was definitely like sex—the hot and sweaty, rolling-across-the-mattress, who's-on-top-now variety.

The coaster stuttered to a halt and the overhead restraints lifted. Surprised, Trent glanced around the loading station and sucked in a much-needed breath.

Over? The ride was over?

He'd missed it. He'd missed the whole damn thing.

Because of Paige?

He'd ridden a lot of roller coasters in his life. Next to flying, coasters had always been his favorite pastime. But he'd never been so focused of the passenger beside him that he'd failed to notice the thrill of the ride.

Until now.

Rocked by the realization, he turned to his seatmate. Paige's brown eyes sparkled like mica. Her pink cheeks, the windswept tangle of her hair and her enormous grin made him ache to lean down and kiss her.

What in the hell kind of crazy reaction is that?

Fighting to keep from following through, he drew in a ragged breath and her lemony scent filled his nostrils.

"Let's ride again. This time in the last car," she gushed in a breathless voice and shot to her feet. Unbalanced by his visceral reaction to a woman he planned to deceive and dump, he remained immobile.

"C'mon, Trent." She reached into the car, grabbed his hand and pulled as if determined to drag his lagging butt along. Her slender fingers laced with his, sending another shock through him. He rose, and for the first time, let himself be led by a woman.

He recognized trouble when he crash landed in it. His plan was in serious jeopardy. The vicious cycle of adrenaline addiction wasn't all he had to worry about. Avoiding sleeping with his brother's former lover had jumped to the top of his priority list.

Amusement parks had always excited Paige, but before tonight they had never aroused her.

Okay, so the park didn't get all the credit.

She stopped on the brightly lit sidewalk outside the Adventure Dome and turned to the most likely culprit—Trent. "I'm impressed. You stayed until they closed."

"Can't say I didn't warn you."

His short, blond hair stood in wind-whipped spikes and a five o'clock shadow darkened his angular jaw. He looked too sexy for words in his jeans, black polo and a tobacco-brown leather bomber jacket, which he'd left unzipped despite the cool night air blowing Paige's hair across her face.

He lifted a hand toward the errant lock, but lowered his arm before making contact. Her skin tingled as if he'd followed through.

"I'm glad you finally loosened up. I thought I was going to have to pour liquor down your throat to get you to enjoy the rides." It had taken at least an hour's worth of riding for the stiffness to leech from his muscles.

He looked down at her from his superior height. "So you said."

She'd hoped tonight's exposure would cure or at least make her understand this overwhelming new attraction she felt for him, but it hadn't. Instead she was more confused than ever and wondered if maybe, just *maybe* her psyche had recognized a kindred spirit the night when she'd let him charm her out of the Blue Grotto Bar and up to his suite.

But if that were the case, then why had that night been such a dismal, embarrassing failure? Had the problem been his? Or hers?

Pedestrians bustled past them on the sidewalk, buffeting her closer to Trent like waves pushing her to shore until scant inches separated them. Her synapses crackled at his nearness. During their rides tonight she hadn't been able to distinguish which lost breaths, belly whoops and skipped heartbeats had resulted from the coaster's drops, turns and twists, and which had been a reaction to Trent's big, solid body jarring her at irregular intervals.

One thing was certain; being hurled against him bore no resemblance whatsoever to similar contact with her father or David, who even after being her boyfriend throughout high school and college, had only tolerated thrill rides for her sake. David had never loved them the way she did.

The realization startled her enough to make her break eye contact. If she'd missed that, what other facets of their relationship had she ignored?

She checked her watch and did a double take. "Midnight! I can't believe I stayed out this late. I need to go. I have to work tomorrow."

"I enjoyed this." Surprise laced Trent's gruff voice. Their gazes locked and held and her lungs locked up.

She swallowed and gulped air. "Me, too."

Say good-night and leave.

But she couldn't. Blame her Southern upbringing or call her crazy, but for some inexplicable reason she wasn't ready to end what had easily been her most fun evening since arriving in Vegas. "Do you need a ride back to the hotel?"

"I don't want to take you out of your way. I'll hail a cab."

Wise up, Paige. Go. You wanted one date and closure, remember?

She ignored the voice of reason. "I drive right past the Lagoon on my way home."

He shoved his hands into his jacket pockets and rocked back on his heels, his narrowed eyes searching her face. "Then thanks. I'll accept your offer."

He kept pace beside her to the parking lot. A big black Cadillac shot out from the curb. Trent grabbed her arm and hauled her against his lean, hard frame. Even after hours of similar contact on the rides, his strength and the combined scents of his cologne and his leather jacket filled her nose and hit her with a death drop of want like she'd never before experienced. Not even naked. With *him.*

What was up with that?

She tipped her head back and stared into his eyes. Inertia gripped her muscles and electricity charged the air as they stood frozen in place. It took several pulse-pounding seconds to shake off his mesmerizing effect, but she did, then hustled to her vehicle.

"Are you all right?" he asked.

"Of course." But her keys slipped from her trembling

fingers as she tried to unlock her Jeep. She hoped he attributed her clumsiness to the Caddy's near miss.

Trent bent, scooped up her key ring then opened her door for her. She climbed in and tried to unravel her puzzling reaction to him while he rounded the hood and joined her. The confines of her vehicle seemed even more cramped and intimate than the closer quarters of the rides they'd shared, ratcheting up her awareness of him several notches.

He dangled her keys from his fingers, and she snatched them from him, being careful to avoid touching him, and shoved them into the ignition. She put the car into motion. Thankfully, traffic wasn't its usual stop-and-roll awful, or she'd probably plow into a bumper. Her concentration seemed shot to pieces. Aware of his every breath and shift in the seat, she kept glancing at him instead of the road. The short distance to the hotel passed all too quickly. She pulled up to the front doors and stopped, ready to drop him off and bolt home to the safety of her apartment.

Trent twisted in his seat. His gaze searched her face and the silence stretched between them. Would he kiss her good-night?

Did she want him to?

Yes.

Shocked, she leaned against her door. She must have lost her mind. How could she be attracted to a man who'd already rejected her in the most basic and humiliating way? Was she so desperate for a date that she'd risk rejection twice?

Apparently so.

"Join me for dinner."

She didn't realize she'd been staring at his mouth until his lips moved. His invitation made her stomach dive. Torn between the intelligence of leaving and the mistake of lin-

gering, she levered her gaze upward and shook her head.
"It's late. I should go."

"We need to plan our next outing—unless you've had
all you can handle."

His eyes gleamed with a challenge she couldn't miss
even in the shadowy interior of her car. Her competitive
hackles rose despite the alarms sounding in her subconscious. "Our next outing?"

"You said there were nearly twenty roller coasters in
Vegas. You don't think I'm going to let you off the hook
after one amusement park, do you?"

His half smile was almost irresistible. *Almost.* But she'd
had enough of his brand of humiliation to last a lifetime.

Hadn't she?

"I guess not." Whether she was answering his question
or hers, she couldn't be sure. Her stomach definitely felt a
little queer. Maybe it was hunger pains instead of desire.
"Maybe I can come in for a quick bite."

She put her car in Park, shoved open the door and
accepted a ticket from the valet. When she joined Trent on
the sidewalk, he splayed a warm hand against her lower
back, and she got a little woozy. She blamed her sudden
light-headedness on the fact she hadn't eaten since lunch.
It had nothing to do with Trent's touch urging her toward
the entrance or the fact that he tempted her tonight ten
times more than he had when she'd let him coerce her up
to his room.

You are the Queen of Denial.

The voice in her head sounded a lot like her older sister
Jessie's. Jessie, the pretty one who went through men faster
than she did panty hose. Paige had intended to model
herself after her heartbreaker sister when she had that total
makeover before moving to Vegas. She'd even used her

sister's hairdresser to add the highlights to her usually dishwater-blond hair.

Trent escorted her through the opulent, nearly deserted lobby and across the sand-colored marble floor between giant coral sculptures, multiple saltwater aquariums and a spattering of Christmas decorations. At this time of night most guests would be in their beds, out seeing a show or in the casino. The wine bar-slash-coffee shop in the lobby had closed. She recognized both the security guard and the night manager behind the registration desk and waved at each.

"What are you in the mood for?" Trent asked.

Her addled brain couldn't come up with the names of the restaurants she walked past every day at work. "We could always go back to where we met. You said it was your favorite of the hotel bars."

He gestured for her to lead the way. "After you."

With each step she took toward the Blue Grotto her heart pounded harder and her mouth became drier. History was not about to repeat itself. Tonight wouldn't end the way it had last year—in humiliation. She wouldn't let it.

But maybe, a nagging voice in her head insisted, maybe this crazy, wild chemistry between them hadn't been there before because it had been too soon after her breakup with David. Maybe she'd still been hurting and healing three months after getting dumped. And maybe this year would be different. It certainly felt different.

But that didn't explain Trent's lack of…interest then. Had it been a physical issue on his part or that he didn't find her desirable?

She was so preoccupied with her thoughts she almost passed the bar and had to turn abruptly. She'd taken a couple of steps toward the cavelike entrance before she realized Trent hadn't followed.

He'd kept walking a few more steps, staring straight ahead with his attention apparently on the noisy group of suit-clad men leaving the Black Pearl Cigar Bar, then he glanced back, his gaze finding her by the archway. His quickly concealed confusion as he changed direction sent a mortifying chill slushing through her.

Had he also been preoccupied? Or had he forgotten where they'd met the way he'd forgotten everything else about her?

"Do you remember *anything* about that night, Trent?"

His expression turned guarded. His chest rose and fell on a deliberate breath. "I'm sorry. I was under a lot of pressure at work. I don't recall much of that conference."

A rising tide of anger melted her mortification.

Forgotten.

Again.

The way David had forgotten her the moment he'd been offered an exciting Manhattan job.

Trent gripped her upper arms and her traitorous pulse, darn it, skipped like crazy. "Paige, you are a beautiful woman who deserves better. Let me make it up to you," he said with all the smooth charm of last year.

Normally, she was the type to let small annoyances roll off her back. In a house filled with five girls sharing a bathroom, cosmetics, shoes and clothing and pretty much everything else, she'd had to become extremely tolerant. But on the heels of the fun and simmering awareness she and Trent had shared tonight, discovering he'd forgotten where they'd met was too much to bear.

There were times in a girl's life when she just had to prove a point. It didn't necessarily have to be wise or even right, but the situation demanded she take action and teach Trent Hightower he couldn't get away with using and discarding women the way he had her.

If the majority of men were like her loyal, devoted dad instead of faithless, fickle scum who led women on then dumped them, she'd let this go and walk away. But that wasn't the case. She'd seen this scenario or a variation of it played out too many times to count via her four sisters. She'd been the shoulder on which Kelly, Jessie, Ashley and Sammie had cried out their broken hearts after each nasty breakup.

Guys were jerks because women let them get away with it, and while she knew she couldn't save the world from all self-centered men, she could hammer a few lessons home on this one.

Why not go into this with the same agenda as last year? She'd pull a Jessie, have the brief, wild fling she'd wanted then—only this time with the benefit of sexual chemistry. She'd use Trent to see some of Vegas and make truth of the little white lies she'd told her family. Then she'd say goodbye with no regrets.

But she'd have to be smart. Suddenly throwing herself at him wouldn't work. He'd already said their previous encounter wouldn't be repeated. But she wasn't stupid. She could tell when a guy wanted her, and Trent definitely wanted her. The attention he'd showered on her tonight had been as thrilling as the roller coasters they'd shared.

She had never needed her sisters's advice more than she did now. But thanks to her own stupid pride and the stuff she'd made up to protect it, she couldn't ask for help.

She'd only really had one lover—David—throughout high school and college. Because of that she'd never learned the art or skill of fishing for men. Her sisters knew all about trolling. But she'd figure it out or bluff her way through it. Asking for help never had been her forte anyway. She excelled at giving advice, but taking it…not her thing.

Her mouth dried and her pulse quickened as she gathered her resolve. *You can do this.*

But she needed a plan—a plan to seduce Trent Hightower. And while she was at it, she decided, she would not only make him remember every second of the night they'd spent together last year, she'd also make him sorry he'd walked away without ever giving her a second thought. He should have agonized at least half as much as she had. It was only fair.

Bad idea, her conscience cautioned.

But what did she have to lose? She'd already faced the worst—naked rejection—and survived.

Four

Paige glanced at her watch. "On second thought, it's late. I should go."

Trent scrambled to find a way to salvage the situation. Had he given up the game? He'd been so focused on one of his rivals on the opposite side of the mezzanine that he'd missed Paige hanging a right into the shadowy bar.

"What about scheduling our next roller coaster ride?"

"We can do that another time. It's not like either of us is going anywhere for a few days."

Relief coursed through him. It would have served him right if she'd told him to go to hell and walked out. But he didn't feel the least bit triumphant that she'd bought his overworked excuse.

Needing a stiff drink, he scanned the bar's shadowy interior beyond her, but decided against trying to convince her to stay. He couldn't afford to drink and let his guard down with Paige. He had a job to do. Find Paige's weakness and exploit it to obtain the desired result.

His conscience needled him, but he ignored it. The strategy was the same one he would employ with any other business opponent. And in this instance, Paige wasn't just a woman. She was an adversary who could cost him. Big-time.

A hand descended on his shoulder, bringing his head around. Donnie Richards. The shark. Damn. So much for avoiding the bastard.

"Hightower, good to see you again. Introduce me to your lovely companion."

Trent gritted his teeth on the *go to hell* he wanted to snarl as he processed the good news. The jerk didn't know Paige. That meant he probably hadn't seen her with Brent.

The perfect opportunity to ditch Paige stood before him. Donnie had always wanted anything Trent possessed. Territory. Employees. Clients. Women. If he paired Paige with this carnivorous loser—

Revulsion severed the thought. Apparently, there were limits to how low Trent was willing to go to lose Paige. No woman deserved Donnie, whom Trent trusted about as much as he would a used car salesman who'd scrubbed the VIN numbers from his merchandise.

"Paige, Donnie. Donnie, Paige." He deliberately omitted Paige's title and last name. He wasn't giving the bottom-feeder any help in tracking her down later.

"I didn't see you at the vendors' reception tonight," Donnie said without taking his eyes from Paige.

He ground his teeth on the reminder of the business opportunities he'd missed. "Paige and I went sightseeing."

"Too bad. Paige would have brightened the room."

She smiled. "Thank you, Donnie. I hope you're finding everything to your satisfaction."

"It would have been better if Hightower hadn't stolen the most beautiful woman in the Vegas. May I buy you a drink?"

Paige blushed and dipped her chin. Surely she wasn't buying that crap? Trent slipped his hand around her waist, staking claim—but only to get Donnie to back off. "If you'll excuse us, this is a private party."

Donnie's predatory and assessing eyes flicked to Trent, then skated over Paige's curves again as if the toad were gauging his chances of success with her. "Surely you have time for one drink."

"Actually, I'm about to call it a night," Paige said.

"Perhaps I'll see you tomorrow?" Donnie continued to address Paige as if Trent weren't glowering at him.

Her lips curved. "I'll be here."

Trent's frustration climbed another notch. He couldn't glue himself to Paige's side for the entire conference and still do his job for HAMC. The only consolation was that Donnie would be tied up in the same events as Trent.

"We both will," he added.

Donnie raked Paige with another lingering glance that made Trent clench his fist behind her back, then slunk out like the lowlife he was.

"You weren't very nice to him," Paige chastised.

"He's not someone you want to know."

"Says who?" She moved out of reach and folded her arms. The defiant posture accentuated her breasts.

"Me. Don't trust him, Paige."

"Trent, you don't have the right to tell me how to spend my time or with whom."

No, and he didn't want the right. But the idea of her with Donnie made him want to hit something. He had to keep Paige and Donnie apart—not only because the guy was a prick who'd screw anybody, literally and figuratively, but because Donnie could blow the subterfuge wide open. Not many of the convention goers could tell Brent and Trent apart. But Donnie could. Donnie would know Trent hadn't attended last year.

"I'll walk you to your car."

It only took a couple of minutes to reach the entrance. Paige handed the valet her ticket. The young man jogged toward the parking deck, leaving Trent alone with Paige.

She tilted her head back. The bright lights shone down on the pulse fluttering at the base of her pale throat. "Thanks for tonight. I had fun."

His gaze focused on her mouth, and his libido kicked in anticipation for a craving he had no intention of satisfying. A roller coaster's seat was all they'd share—if his brain had any say in the decision. "Tomorrow night we'll hit the next stop on your list."

"Maybe." A small smile played across her delectable mouth.

Delectable? Have you lost your mind?

"Definitely." The sound of her Jeep's engine starting in the distance caught Trent's attention, and in that split second of distraction Paige wrapped one of her hands around his nape and rose on her tiptoes.

He could have dodged the kiss. *Should* have dodged the kiss. But he didn't. Masochistic fool that he was, he wanted to endure one and in doing so, prove the passion couldn't meet his expectations. There was no way a simple kiss could be anything but anticlimactic after the way she'd kept his hormones simmering all night.

Her lips touched his, butterfly soft and tentative. But damn, she packed a punch that breached his defenses and cinched every muscle in him tight. The strength of his whole-body response rattled him. While her lips fluttered over his he struggled to justify and rationalize why this woman got to him in an attempt to prevent himself from responding.

Hers wasn't an experienced woman's kiss. Her claim that she didn't make a habit of going upstairs with hotel guests contradicted Brent's accusation that she probably picked up men in the bar on a regular basis. He believed Paige. Her lack of expertise showed.

Not that she couldn't kiss.

He was used to women who knew what they wanted and went for it without hesitation. So while Paige had initiated this kiss, she'd done so with a lack of confidence that was strangely…endearing.

Endearing? What kind of crap is that?

Determined to push her away, he grasped her waist. But then her tongue eased across his bottom lip, and hunger hit him like a strong crosswind, blowing him off course. One taste wasn't enough. He had to have more—if only to understand and evaluate her appeal.

Against his better judgment he angled his head and opened his mouth. When she tried to retreat he pursued, chasing her tongue with his, tightening his grip and yanking her closer. She startled at his aggressive move, and her squeak of surprise filled his mouth.

Her short nails dug lightly into his neck as he engaged her in a hot, slick duel, then with a cheek-steaming sigh, she sank against him. Her soft breasts pressed his chest and her heat penetrated their layers of clothing, making his skin suddenly hot and damp. Desire drove a spike into his gut. He drove his fingers into her hair. The soft, silky strands entangled him as he tilted her head to deepen the kiss.

Brent's leavings, his brain cautioned.

But Trent ignored the warning. He wanted her. Paige. Brent's lover. *Ex*-lover.

The slam of a car door overrode the pounding of his pulse in his ears and knocked some sense into him. He fought off the need clawing his skull, peeled himself away from Paige and stepped back, trying to drag air into his laboring lungs.

Paige's dazed brown eyes, flushed cheeks and the quick rise and fall of her breasts told him he wasn't the only one left wanting more. He could feel the push toward her still-wet lips like a strong tailwind. But the parking brake of his common sense slowly engaged, and he held his ground.

He should never have let her kiss him. Because now that he knew how she tasted and how she felt against him, for the first time since his childhood when his father had pitted him and Brent against each other regularly, Trent coveted what his brother had already possessed.

Never again. He silently repeated his vow not to compete with Brent.

Mentally distancing himself, he shoved a hand into his pocket, peeled a twenty from his money clip and tipped the valet.

"Good night," he ground out and pivoted on his heel. He'd never been one to retreat, but as far as he was concerned tonight had put him in double jeopardy.

He'd enjoyed the rides and the adrenaline rush and wanted more. But not nearly as much as he wanted more time with Paige.

A smart man would avoid both hazards, but he couldn't afford to opt out.

He needed a new strategy. And he needed it now.

Late. Late. Late.
Paige jogged toward the hotel's employee entrance,

cursing herself and trying not to break an ankle in her four-inch heels.

Trent's kiss had kept her awake most of the night. And then she'd hit the snooze button one—okay, *three*—times too many this morning.

She swiped her ID badge and opened the door. Day one and her plan for seduction had already gone awry. She hadn't had time to wash her hair and had only applied minimal makeup. Her basic black dress was too boring to tempt Trent, and she'd forgotten her earrings and watch, which left her feeling naked. Not in a good way.

So instead of tracking down the object of her indecent intentions, she had to avoid Trent until she could pop into the hotel's salon on her lunch break and beg for emergency assistance.

Checking the hall in both directions, she breathed a sigh of relief on finding it empty and quickly tiptoed to her office. After turning on her computer, she shoved her purse into her desk drawer and slumped in her chair to catch her breath and gather her shattered composure.

A masculine throat cleared, startling her into opening her eyes. Her boss stood in the doorway. Fiftysomething and distinguished with his thick crop of white hair, Milton Jones frowned at her.

She bolted upright. "Good morning, Milton."

He looked pointedly at the clock on the wall beside her desk. "You're late."

He should cut her some slack since she'd never been late before. In fact, she was always at least fifteen minutes early. But Milton was old-school. No excuses. "Yes, I'm five minutes late. I'm sorry. My first time, but it won't happen again."

"Have you walked the floor yet?"

Funny how the practice she'd started on her own had become an expectation. She pasted on a smile and rose. "I'm going to do that now."

Argh. She'd hoped to duck into the ladies' room and take another stab at her makeup and hastily twisted-up hair first—in case she accidentally ran into Trent. But that would have to wait. She'd simply have to be vigilant enough to dodge him until she'd prettied-up.

She gathered her clipboard and radio. She'd learned early on at home and on the job that occasionally she had to sing her own praises unless she wanted to be overlooked and taken for granted. "The aircraft conference is going well."

"It's only the third day," he pointed out drily.

"And we're off to a great start despite a few glitches with the sound system and the missing strawberries. Are you going to join me on my walk-through?" she asked when he didn't move out of her path.

"No time. I have to negotiate the conference fee for a podiatrists' convention. Report back on any irregularities after you've dealt with them." He pivoted abruptly then headed down the hall and into his office.

She sagged in relief. Milton was an amazing mentor. He'd taken a chance on hiring her from the small hotel where she'd been working since graduating from USC's School of Hotel, Restaurant & Tourism Management, and he'd taught her more than she could ever learn from a textbook. But she really couldn't handle his nitpicking this morning. Her nerves were already frayed because of Trent's kiss.

Okay, *her* kiss. *She'd* kissed *him*.

Her sisters would be proud. She grinned.

But she couldn't tell them. The smile faded and an empty ache filled her belly.

During her tossing and turning last night she'd reached

for the phone countless times to call one of them for a chat. Not that she could actually reveal the real reason behind a middle of the night call, but she'd needed to hear a familiar voice, and Ashley was usually up before dawn for her shift at the hospital.

Shaking her head, Paige picked up a small stack of messages. Not even calling home to talk about the weather was safe. Her sisters would guess something was up even if she didn't let one word slip about that stupendous, knee-melting, brain-mushing kiss.

Perceptive. Yep. All four of them. Except when it came to handling their own problems. Then they relied on Paige, their relationship GPS, to talk them through the romance jungle. How she'd ended up being the "expert" with only one affair under her belt was a mystery. Then again, time-wise she and David had outlasted all her sisters' relationships combined. But she'd still gotten dumped, hadn't she?

Her sisters' ability to pick up even the slightest nuance in Paige's voice meant she had to limit most of her family communications to e-mail or calling home on Sunday evenings when the entire family gathered at her parents' house for dinner. Only then was it too noisy and chaotic for anyone to hear more than minimal conversation, let alone interpret her tone. And the phone got passed around so quickly that no one had time to dig deep.

Her family's ability to sniff out her moods was also the reason why she hadn't been home for a visit since moving to Vegas. That didn't mean she didn't miss her boisterous, dependent, interfering relatives. But it looked as though she'd spend another Christmas vacation week solo this year. And she had nobody but herself to blame.

She could practically hear the gossips already. *Still alone, poor thing. Do you think she'll ever get over David?*

The thought quickened her step. Multitasking as usual, she shuffled through the pink message slips, prioritizing the pages as she walked the service corridors between the meeting rooms. She poked her head into each, checking to make sure the urns of coffee and pitchers of iced water had been set up per her specifications.

When she came across a sheet containing nothing except her name and a phone number she didn't recognize she stopped. She'd never received an anonymous message before. Who could it be?

The puzzling aspect intrigued her. Too impatient to wait to get back to her desk to make the call, she ducked into a quiet corner, pulled her cell phone from her pocket and typed in the number.

It rang twice before someone picked up. She heard what sounded like a crowd in the background, then, "Trent Hightower."

The deep voice made her stomach do a loop-de-loop. She huffed out a breath then wheezed it back in again. "I— it's Paige. I received your message."

"What time will you finish your shift today?"

"Six."

"I'll meet you outside then. We're going to Buffalo Bill's."

Her mouth went dry. The hotel was twenty-five miles outside of Vegas in Primm, Nevada. "Trent, I'll have to go home and change first."

"We'll stop by your place on the way."

"What about my car? I can't leave it here. I'll need it to get to work tomorrow."

"I'll follow you."

The idea of him in her apartment or even waiting outside made her want to hyperventilate. "But—"

"See you tonight, Paige." A click followed by dead air told her he'd already disconnected.

The pink slip crumpled in her hand. This was not good. She needed to be dressed for her seductress role to bolster her confidence. There was so much more at stake. Last year she hadn't had nearly the same reaction to his kiss and his lack of interest or ability had devastated her. As strongly as she felt the attraction this time around, she hated to think how bad another rebuff would feel.

But it was a risk she had to take to wipe the slate clean and start fresh.

Getting into Paige's home was the best way to discover her weakness, Trent had decided some time during his restless night, and he'd planned tonight's outing around getting access.

Judging by the way she fidgeted uncomfortably beside him in her living room with her white teeth pinching her bottom lip and her fingers fussing with the handle of her purse, he suspected Brent hadn't been here.

"Paige, we're short on time. Get changed."

"Right. I'll just…go do that." Her reluctance to leave him alone in her space couldn't have been more obvious. She must not bring men home often. She slowly backed away, then pivoted and hurried down the short hall.

Beyond her shoulders he spotted a wide swatch of dark purple satin. Paige's bed. His abdominal muscles tightened. He abruptly averted his gaze. Where and how Paige slept was none of his business. But he wouldn't have pegged her for the satin bedding type. And he'd prefer not to have the image of her blond hair spread across the purple pillowcase in his head or think about being sandwiched between her cool sheets and her hot skin.

He pushed aside the prohibited thought. Taking advantage of her absence, he scanned her space, hoping to discover more about her than the neutral decor and standard apartment layout revealed. Framed photographs dotted nearly every flat surface. There had to be at least thirty scattered about.

He stepped closer to the cluster on Paige's dining-room sideboard. An older couple standing in front of a shop labeled McCauley's Hardware, Bait and Tackle smiled from the largest frame. Her parents, he guessed. Paige had inherited her father's blond hair and brown eyes and her mother's curvy build.

In another Paige stood on the beach in the center of five women. She wore leg-revealing shorts and a bikini top. Great body. Tanned skin. She wasn't tanned now.

The other women's shapes, hair and eye colors varied, but their features were similar enough to imply a familial relationship. Probably her sisters. Paige wasn't the prettiest, the shortest or the tallest, but there was something about her smile, the glint in her eyes and the challenging tilt of her chin that made her easily the most interesting of the bunch.

All of the photos were candid shots primarily of the same people in different groupings and locations, but each gave a clue to the subject's personality unlike the stiff, formal poses his family preferred. His family didn't do casual photos. Only studio portraits or oil paintings graced the walls of the Hightower home. This unpretentious collection made Paige—and her family—seem very real and made his deception that much more untenable. He turned away.

A pile of cards on her coffee table caught his eye and pulled him across the living area. The top one had a firefighter on the cover and the words, "Hope your birthday's a hot one."

Trent glanced down the hall and on seeing no sign of Paige flicked open the card. He blinked in surprise at the stripped-down, oiled-up version of the fireman inside holding a cake to conceal his groin.

He skipped to the hand-written inscription.

Happy 28th. We miss you. Hope your latest beau shows you a hot time. Don't do anything I wouldn't do—but of course that leaves the field wide open, doesn't it? Love you, Jessie.

Your latest? If Trent were a betting man—and he wasn't— he'd put money on Paige not having a lover currently. Not with the way she kissed. Sweetly. Tenderly. Tentativ—

For pity's sake. Forget it already.

There were no men in the photographs other than her father, so if she had a significant other, she didn't have a picture of him around. Unless it was on her bedside table. That whipped his thoughts back to those purple satin sheets. Not good.

He checked the second card. It featured similar beefcake on the cover of the first card.

"What are you doing?" Paige said behind him.

Caught red-handed. No point in denying it. He dropped the card and faced her. She'd changed from her black dress into jeans again, this time topped by a snug, red, low-cut pullover sweater that accentuated her breasts and narrow waist almost as well as the black number had. He tamped down his appreciation and focused on his fact-finding mission.

"When was your birthday?"

She blushed and rushed forward to scoop up the cards and shove them in a drawer. "Last week."

"Belated happy birthday." The bed down the hall snared his attention again dammit, but he dragged his gaze back to her and gestured to the closest group shot. "Your family?"

"Yes."

"I'll bet you're looking forward to seeing them over Christmas."

She broke eye contact and straightened a frame. "I'm not going home for Christmas."

His family might not be the closest or the most traditional, but they always celebrated Christmas together somewhere around the globe. He made a mental note to find out where his mother planned to gather this year and to make sure his sister found him a pilot who didn't mind working the holidays for a little extra pay.

But the idea of Paige being alone bothered him for some reason. "You're spending the holidays alone in Vegas?"

"I'm planning to do some of that sightseeing I've been neglecting." She'd infused her voice with false eagerness, but the shadows in her eyes and the quiver of her lips before she mashed them tightly together told the truth.

Afraid he'd provoke waterworks if he continued that line of conversation, he pointed to the picture of five women. "Your sisters?"

"Yes."

"Who's who?"

"I thought you said we were in a hurry."

"Talk fast."

She choked out a laugh and headed for the door. "We have a ways to go and your chauffeur is waiting."

He'd hired a driver and town car because he wanted to focus on his goal of decoding Paige tonight. He hadn't expected to find the solution so quickly. "He's paid to wait."

She rolled her eyes. "The Desperado is supposed to be the best coaster in the area. *I* don't want to wait. Come on."

He shrugged and followed. Her sisters' names didn't really matter. He'd found what he'd come for. Paige's family was her Achilles' heel and the perfect way to get her out of the hotel before Brent and Luanne arrived. If he could get the women here, they'd get Paige out of the hotel and monopolize her time.

Now all he had to do was put his plan into motion.

Five

"I thought you said you liked roller coasters," Paige said as she and Trent made their way through Buffalo Bill's Casino toward the arcade to board Desperado for the third time. Her heart still raced from the excitement of the steep drops and double helixes, but Trent's restraint dampened her enthusiasm.

He transferred his attention from the two-hundred-plus-foot-high first hill of the track rising above them to shoot straight through the roof of the casino to her. "I do."

"You have a funny way of showing it. You don't look scared. You look…tense. You were a lot more relaxed the first time we met. Honestly, you almost seem like a different person."

He inhaled sharply and paused. "It's a good coaster. One of the best I've ridden. The designer made good use of the space by going through the casino, under the lobby and over the parking lot. Anyone gambling, checking into the hotel or even driving by outside will be lured into shelling out the price of a ticket."

There he went again, deflecting the conversation away from his feelings to a less personal area. She'd never figure out how his mind worked if he kept that up. And call her crazy, but she needed to know someone before she slept with him—even if she planned on this only being a short-term encounter.

"Leave it to a CEO to make this about money."

"In business, every decision is about money, Paige."

"True. But why are you fighting so hard not to enjoy this?"

His eyebrows dipped. "What makes you think I'm fighting?"

"You could gamble with that face, you know? No expression. If I wasn't so practiced at pulling details out of my sisters, you'd probably get away with it. But the blank look doesn't work on me. I can see in your eyes that you're holding back tonight."

"You have an active imagination."

She sighed. "I'm not the creative McCauley. Tell you what. I'm starving. I missed lunch. You can elaborate over dinner. Tony Roma's looks good."

"Does your bossiness work on your sisters?" His amused tone combined with a half smile made her toes tingle and curl. He guided her toward the restaurant without touching her, but he didn't need to. His proximity was enough to spike her pulse rate—not that it had slowed much since she'd met him outside the hotel after work.

Having the big black car follow her home had been eerily like something out of a mob movie—and this was Vegas, a town once owned by the mob. "My sisters claim I'm a lot like a river. Over time I can wear down even the rocks."

That earned her a wide smile and a deep, rumbling chuckle. Her belly swooped in response. He really was something else when he turned on the full wattage of that smile. Whatever hormones or pheromones the man possessed were certainly effective on her. It didn't hurt that he looked absolutely yummy in his black cashmere sweater and jeans. He had a confident "I'm rich, I'm gorgeous and I don't care" swagger going on that made her mouth water.

She waited until they were seated to start chipping away again. "I'd like to try the log flume ride before we go and maybe even the Turbo Drop. But only if you're up to it."

"I am. We should have time and still get you home by your self-imposed deadline."

"I can't do too many late nights or I'll drown in my coffee mug." She could only think of one cause for the distance in his behavior today. "Is this about the kiss?"

His jaw jacked up. "Is what about the kiss?"

"That you're not comfortable with me. Because you were okay until I kissed you last night."

"I am not uncomfortable with you. My mood has nothing to do with the kiss—which shouldn't have happened."

Her cheeks burned. "You kissed me back."

His gaze held hers, and from the look in his eyes, she knew she wasn't going to like what he had to say. She braced herself.

"Paige, I'm not looking for a relationship."

"Are you married?" She'd checked his ring finger both this year and last, but not all guys wore rings.

"No. Not married. Never have been. Never will be."

"Wow. Tell me what you really think." After David's sudden change of heart, she understood Trent's bitterness completely. She wasn't sure she'd ever be ready to trust a guy enough think about marriage again. "Is there an interesting story behind your vehemence? A broken engagement? A wounded heart? A lying, cheating, deadbeat ex?"

"None of the above."

When his eyes twinkled that way she could stare into them all day. How silly was that? But that was her neglected hormones' fault. It didn't mean anything.

"Are you seeing someone?"

"No."

"So if the kiss isn't making you uncomfortable, then what's the problem? Because we don't have to ride roller coasters together. If you remember, dating was your idea."

Of course, not going out would kill her plan to get him in the sack and try to right the wrong they'd committed last year—assuming he was…up to the task. Maybe she'd better shut up. She was jeopardizing her own intentions. Sometimes her sense of fair play got her into trouble.

One golden eyebrow hiked. "I remember this starting with *your* challenge."

"Which you accepted and then broadened to include me."

He nodded to concede her point. "Judging by the pictures of you and your family, you look very close. What made you move all the way across country?"

His unexpected query made her shift uneasily. She liked it better when she was the one asking the questions. "The job."

"That's it?"

"People relocate for work all the time. It's the American way. Besides, we were talking about you."

"You were talking about me, and while I'm sure that's a fascinating subject—" his tongue-in-cheek delivery kept the comment from sounding conceited "—I'm more interested in you. Where did you work before the Lagoon?"

Okay, she could play this verbal chess game. "Before high school graduation I worked for my parents, and after college in a small hotel in Charleston, if you must know. The city was close to home, but far enough away to discourage family from dropping in unexpectedly too often.

"Then I had an amazing opportunity to work in a hotel three times the size and with more amenities than my old one. So…I cut the apron strings and moved." Thank goodness Milton had been in a pinch and hired her right away.

"How did your boyfriend feel about your decision?"

She flinched. His narrowing eyes warned her he hadn't missed it. "What makes you think I had one?"

"You're smart and attractive. Why wouldn't you?"

The compliment lit a glow inside her. "He was moving to Manhattan for his new job anyway, so it wasn't an issue. Back to you. What's keeping you so uptight tonight?"

He shook his head. "You don't let up, do you?"

"Persistence is a virtue, or so my momma tells me."

He scanned the restaurant, stalling, in her opinion, before meeting her gaze again. "I used to get the same kind of rush from flying that I get from riding roller coasters."

"You don't now?"

"I don't fly anymore."

"You run an airline company, and you said your plane was waiting at the airport. Of course you fly."

"I mean don't *pilot* aircraft anymore."

"Why not?"

His lips compressed into a thin line. "Flying myself is a time-consuming luxury I can't afford. I work en route."

"You couldn't fly as a hobby?"

"I don't have time for hobbies." He kept his gaze fixed on a spot beyond her shoulder when he said it, then he gestured for the waiter who rushed over to take their orders. "What would you like to eat, Paige?"

She shrugged. "Ribs. That's what the restaurant is famous for. Might as well decide if they've earned their reputation. The small sampler platter, please."

As soon as the server departed she tilted her head to study Trent's stiff posture. "To paraphrase you, does that too-busy-to-fly story work on other people? 'Cause I'm not buying it. What's the real reason you quit flying?"

His eyes widened slightly in surprise, then narrowed. Bracing his forearms on the table in front of him, he leaned forward into her space as if trying to intimidate her into silence. "Have you considered working for the FBI?"

She grinned. "Be paid to pry, you mean? My youngest sister Sammie might have suggested something similar one or two dozen times. And you're dodging the question."

Sitting back, he shook his head and wiped his mouth, but she thought he might be hiding a smile given that spark in his eyes making her tummy fizz like Alka Seltzer in a glass.

"So you're not going to answer?"

"That was my answer."

She shook her head. "How long since you flew yourself somewhere?"

"Does it matter?"

"Yes. You said you hadn't ridden roller coasters since college, and you gave up flying. You claim to love both. I'm trying to figure out the correlation between them. Did you quit cold turkey on flying and coasters at the same time?"

"You are like a mosquito—always buzzing around."

"It's my special gift. But asking questions is the way to get to the heart of a problem, so I ask rather than just speculate. Why give up your two favorite things?"

"Why stay away from your family when you're obviously homesick?"

Ouch. Direct hit.

They stared at each other across the checkered table

cloth while she debated her answer. If she wanted to solve the puzzle of Trent Hightower, get into his head and his bed, then she was going to have to give a little. She took a bracing breath.

"My family lives in a small town where gossip, fishing and boating—in that order—are the favorite forms of entertainment. Moving to Charleston wasn't far enough away to remove me from the persons of interest category. When I got dumped by the man everyone thought I'd marry—" her cheeks burned with humiliation "—who also grew up there, I might add, I ran rather than face the whispers behind my back. That first night with you was sort of a…rebound thing. Your turn."

Paige's eyes never wavered from Trent's during her confession, giving him a front row seat to her pain. Her willingness to show vulnerability rocked him. In his family the policy was never show weakness, but Paige did so and it didn't make him think less of her. Instead, it made him respect her on a whole different level.

He fisted his hands against the urge to reach across the table for hers. But he'd learned from the women who'd passed through his life that offering sympathy usually evoked waterworks. He didn't do tears.

She'd been dumped. Then Brent had picked her up like a cheap one-night stand while she was still reeling. Anger stiffened Trent's muscles, making him want to punch the bastard who'd hurt her, then tackle Brent for taking advantage of her. Paige couldn't be blamed. His brother could be quite the charmer when he set his mind to it. The trait made Brent a damned persuasive salesman.

Trent was used to solving his family's problems. He didn't share his own or tackle an outsider's issues in any way other than a business sense. But how could he be any less candid than Paige had been?

He wouldn't tell her that she gave him that same adrenaline punch as flying, or that her proximity made it difficult to concentrate on the ride, and that the first trip around the track was more about being aware of the feel of her, smell of her and heat of her against him than in marveling at the mechanical engineering that comprised the journey. The second was a battle to control his reaction to that awareness. It wasn't until the third pass that he noticed the roller coaster's unique qualities. An admission such as that would take them in a direction he had no intention of traveling.

He stared into her face. Her genuine interest in him, someone she barely knew, astounded him. Why would she care about solving his problems? In his world it was every man for himself. Something about Paige's openness made him want to share the secret he'd told no one else. Not even Gage, his best friend knew the whole truth.

"Taking the yoke of an airplane, especially a small one, is like sitting in the front car of a coaster."

"No wonder you love roller coasters. Maybe I should take up flying. Of course, I'd need to win a jackpot to finance the fees, but that's another story." Then confusion darkened her eyes. "But how does that explain you sacrificing your two loves?"

He hesitated. But what the hell? Neither his father's gambling nor HAMC's past financial struggles was a secret. Anyone who had access to a computer could do a Google search on William Hightower's name and come up with the sordid details.

"My father has a gambling addiction. I quit flying the day he told me gambling was the only way he could fly with both feet on the ground. He claimed he'd land his plane and drive straight to a casino, because coming down from the natural high of flying made him want to crawl out of his skin. The casino gave him the same rush. His addiction almost cost us Hightower Aviation."

"And that's related to you…how?"

"I can't risk repeating his mistakes."

"You're a gambler?"

"No. But I get high from flying. I feel the rush. And I crave more of it. I used to love to push a plane to its limits, to test its strengths and my abilities. I lived on the edge. Skydiving, boat racing, bungee jumping, hang gliding. You name it. If there was a thrill to be had, I did it."

He could practically see the wheels of her brain turning and wished he hadn't revealed as much as he had. "Did you have trouble walking away from the coaster tonight?"

"No."

"What about last night?"

"No."

"Did walking through the casino to get to the rides make you want to stay and try your hand at the tables?"

He didn't need to have a borderline genius IQ to see the point she was trying to make. But she posed a valid argument. He had walked through the casinos with her to board the rides and hadn't even noticed the games of chance going on around him. He'd been more focused on his destination and the woman beside him—especially the woman beside him. Her energy and excitement were addictive.

"It's not that simple, Paige."

"Maybe it is. How old are you?"

"Thirty-four."

"So you abandoned the two things you loved the most over a decade ago, and you haven't been sucked back in. It sounds like you don't share your father's lack of willpower. And yes, your hobbies were a little dangerous, but I hate to tell you, most kids—even some of us girls—go through that invincibility phase and do crazy stuff. I know my sisters and I did. Ask my parents. My mom blames us for every gray hair. It's normal to test your limits, Trent. It's how we define who we are. I'd worry more about someone who never tested himself and always accepted status quo."

"I can't take the chance that you might be wrong."

"Then why torture yourself by becoming CEO of High-tower Aviation and in charge of an entire fleet of airplanes? That's like a dieter taking a job in a bakery. Why not do something else?"

"Someone had to get us out of the financial hole my father had dug."

"What about your brother or your sisters? Couldn't one of them have taken on the role? Or were they too young?"

Brent must not have told her he had a twin. "My brother and I are…close in age, but he doesn't have the aptitude for seeing the big picture. As for my sisters, one had just started college, and the other was barely sixteen. I had double-majored in aeronautical science and business, I was the most qualified."

"It sounds like your education prepared you to be HAMC's CEO. Did you always intend to assume that position?"

"No."

"Then what did you want to do? Something with planes, obviously."

The woman defined tenacious. "I wanted to be an air force fighter pilot."

"Are you too old to enlist now?"

"Age is irrelevant. That part of my life is over. My family is counting on me to keep HAMC profitable. The point you're missing is that I was willing to die to fly, to get that rush."

"How is enlisting in the military any different than becoming a firefighter or a cop? The risk of getting killed on the job is a given. And let me tell you, plenty of cops and volunteer firefighters come into the hardware store. They're certainly not doing the job for the money, because the salaries are atrociously low. They are committed to what they do, and they must enjoy the adrenaline rush or they wouldn't last long. Why shouldn't you have a job that excites you and makes you eager to go to work each day?"

Her oversimplification contradicted everything he knew and believed, knocking him off balance. But he wasn't going to waste his breath trying to explain. Besides, he didn't need a woman who would be gone in a matter of days crawling around in his head.

"Why did you go into hotel event planning instead of training to take over your parents' store? From the picture in your living room, it looks like a successful business, and if you worked there for years, you're qualified."

She blinked at his abrupt counterattack. "The store is doing well, but as much as I love my family and our small town, I wanted out of the fishbowl. I want to see the world. Besides, my oldest sister is going to take over when Dad retires."

She rearranged her utensils, seemingly fascinated by the task for nearly a full minute, then she offered a sympathetic smile. "You're off the hook, Trent. We don't have to ride any more coasters if it disturbs you."

Her words should have pleased him. But they didn't. She'd issued a challenge—one he was determined to meet and defeat. "This was a demon I needed to face. Thank you for forcing me to do that."

Her smile scrunched into a grimace. "I know a little something about facing those demons."

The ex-boyfriend, Trent realized on a fresh surge of anger.

However this ended, he didn't want Paige to be hurt again. That didn't mean he could afford to be a bleeding heart instead of a shark. He had a job to do—protect HAMC and Brent—and he would get it done.

He wasn't taking the high road for Paige's sake. He was merely being compassionate because it would further his agenda for Hightower Aviation. Terminating the relationship without causing her more pain or bitterness allowed for less of a chance of negative backlash on HAMC.

Paige's heart pounded and her palms dampened as the chauffeur-driven car neared her apartment.

Should she invite Trent in? Their last kiss had whetted her appetite for more, but she wasn't used to being the aggressor.

Beside her on the cushy leather seat, Trent looked completely at ease. But he didn't reach across the seat to touch her. His hands rested on his thighs, his gaze focused ahead. They'd connected during dinner, but had barely touched since.

She bit her lip and debated closing the open window between the front and backseats to give them a little privacy. But she wasn't sure which of the many buttons worked the partition. Blame it on her upbringing in a gossipy town, but she didn't want to issue the invitation where the driver could overhear.

The car turned into her apartment complex. Trent leaned forward and pointed to the fire lane in front of her building. "Pull up here," he told the driver. "Keep the motor running. I'll be right back."

That didn't sound good.

Trent pushed open the car door, climbed out and turned to wait for Paige. He didn't offer her a hand out.

She gathered her courage and stopped on the pavement beside the long, black car. "If you want to let the driver go, I can take you back to the hotel later."

Trent went still. His nostrils flared and his eyes narrowed. Then his gaze focused on her mouth and her stomach fluttered. He shook his head. "We both need an early night."

Ouch. She winced and turned for the stairs, pride stinging. Trent accompanied her to her door, keeping at least a yard between them. Why the distance? Did he regret his earlier confession?

Conscious of the driver's clear view of them from the other side of the railing of her second-story, end-unit apartment, she fished out her key and shoved it into the lock with a less than steady hand, then opened the door and crossed the threshold. Trent didn't follow inside. "Come in."

"Not tonight." He punctuated his reply by stepping back, but once again his eyes focused briefly on her mouth. But he made no move to kiss her. "I'll see you in the morning."

"Trent? Is something wrong?"

"Nothing. Good night, Paige."

Heart sinking, she watched him jog down the stairs until his blond head disappeared from view. She had a lot of work to do to get used to this seduction thing, because she sucked at it. But tomorrow was another day, and she'd step up her game.

"Hightower Aviation. Nicole speaking," Trent's sister answered the phone early Wednesday morning.

"I have a job for you. Make it a top priority."

"Well, hello to you, too, Trent. Ryan and I are fine, thanks, and our baby is growing so fast I'm starting to look like I'm carrying twins."

He rubbed a knuckle against his temple. "I'm glad your little family is well, but I'm going to have to skip the niceties. I'm scheduled to lead a seminar downstairs in fifteen minutes."

"Right. Go ahead. What do you need?"

"Contact the owners of McCauley's Hardware, Bait and Tackle and arrange for as many of the family members as possible to fly Vegas. I specifically want Paige McCauley's sisters on the flight, but if her parents can make it, get them on board, too."

"A tackle shop? Are they a potential client?"

"No. The store's in South Carolina. I don't know which city, but somewhere west of Charleston. Line up a jet for them. Arrange for hotel rooms at the opposite end of the strip from the Lagoon at HAMC's expense."

"Um…Trent, you do know that Vegas is extremely popular at Christmastime, don't you?"

"Find them rooms regardless of the expense."

"Do you have the travelers' names?"

He couldn't remember her sisters' names. "No. Ask for one of the store owners. That'll be Paige's parents. Get them to give you the information. Tell them you want to get their daughters out here to see their sister."

"What about specific dates?"

"I need them here no later than Sunday morning, the twentieth."

"Of December?" she squeaked.

"Yes."

"That's only four days away. You know we're always stretched at Christmastime. Our planes are booked months

in advance, and believe it or not, even pilots like to celebrate the holiday with their families. Vacation days are
already set."

"Nicole, you are the best client aviation manager on our
payroll. You can pull this off."

"I could put them on the plane with Brent—"

Alarm shot through him. "*No.* Whatever you do, keep
the McCauleys away from Brent and Luanne. I don't even
want them landing in the airport at close to the same time.
Brent's coming in Sunday afternoon. Keep it that way."

She groaned. "What has Brent done now?"

Nicole had done her share of fulfilling Brent's impossible promises. "After you pull this off I'll tell you whatever
you want to know. Right now I don't have time."

"You mean *if* I pull this off."

His gut clenched. "Failure isn't an option. If you can't
find anything else, use my jet and crew."

He had to get Paige's siblings out here. If he couldn't
get her out of town, the least he could do was get her out
of the hotel.

"I can't do that unless you stay an extra night. Your
crew will have exceeded its allowable hours."

"I'll stay." To make sure nothing went wrong. "Do whatever it takes."

"That'll push you tight to get back for the board meeting
Tuesday. With the upcoming holiday there won't be time
to reschedule it."

"I'll be there."

"*Yessir.* I'll call with updates as soon as I have them."

"Leave a message on my room phone rather than my cell.
I'll be in seminars and business meetings all day. And
Nicole, one more thing. Tell the McCauleys this is a surprise
gift for Paige. They need to keep their plans a secret."

"Oh, Trent, that is so sweet. She must be a very special lady for you to go to all this expense."

He recoiled at the mushy tone of his sister's voice. "It's not sweet. It's not personal. It's business."

He didn't do sentimental, and his strategy had nothing to do with the fact that he actually liked Paige. That she'd benefit from his plan was purely incidental.

Six

Having a chauffeur had temporarily derailed Paige's plan last night, but today she'd brought her A game.

She'd dressed for success in a microknit wraparound top that flattered her curves and slinky slacks that made her legs look longer. She'd even found sexy high-heeled boots in the back of her closet comfortable enough to wear on the hike to the Sahara Hotel, home of tonight's roller coaster.

Wanting to see Trent in action, she silently eased into the back of the conference room at the end of her shift Wednesday evening. He stood behind the podium wearing a dark suit that accentuated his lean build and broad shoulders. His deep voice paused and his gaze reached across the room to pin her by the door. Her pulse stuttered.

Heads turned to see who had disrupted the speaker. Paige's cheeks burned. She considered ducking out. But that would only cause more commotion. She hugged the wall and slipped into the shadows at the rear of the room.

Trent resumed his program, discussing the security issues of landing private jets on foreign soil, she quickly deduced. Not a soul fidgeted during the next twenty minutes as he flipped through riveting slides that made the dry statistics come alive even for a novice like her. He had his audience in the palm of his hand—as he'd had her last night.

She'd hoped to end their date with another one of those toe-curling kisses, especially since she and Trent had connected on a personal level during dinner. But that hadn't happened.

Tonight would be different.

When she and Trent returned to the hotel after their rides she intended to do whatever she could to make him act on those hot looks he'd been sending her way and invite her upstairs. He desired her. So why was he holding back? Ignorance might be bliss for some, but she'd found it tended to bite you in the behind when you least expected it.

Focusing her attention on the man mesmerizing his audience, she decided she actually liked this intense version of Trent more than the easygoing charmer. His confident air of authority was quite a turn-on.

Trent switched to an alarming slide of an obvious hostage situation and said, "We all remember how this tragedy ended. The subsequent lawsuits and negative publicity drove the airline into bankruptcy. What we learned from this is that regardless of the costs, ensuring the safety of your passengers and crew, not to mention your multimillion dollar aircraft, is essential. No matter how tight your budget during this economic downturn, security is not the area from which you can afford to cut corners."

Upon his conclusion, the attendees applauded then

gathered their gear and rose. Some approached the stage. Paige remained stationary, waiting for Trent to finish. She'd had no idea his business could be hazardous beyond the usual concern for crashes. How naive of her considering traveling abroad was her dream. His knowledge pointed out exactly how far apart their worlds were. He was sophisticated and well-traveled, and she was still a sheltered small-town girl despite living in Charleston for four years and Vegas for just over one.

"Hello there, Paige," said a familiar voice from beside her, pulling her concentration away from Trent.

She forced a smile and looked up at the man standing in the aisle beside her. She couldn't warm up to Trent's acquaintance. There was something about Donnie that didn't encourage trust. She'd figured that out even before Trent had warned her.

"Good evening, Donnie. I hope the conference is going well for you."

"Only one thing would make it better. Join me for dinner. There's a sweet steak place down the strip that can't be missed."

"Paige will be with me." The simultaneous sound of Trent's voice in her ear and his hand on her waist made her jump. Her skin tingled and her pulse quickened. She glanced at Trent, and the territorial stamp on his face sent a thrill through her.

"Thank you for the invitation, Donnie, but Trent and I have a previous engagement."

Donnie extracted a business card from his wallet. "Your loss, sugar, but here are my numbers if you wise up and want someone who's a little more fun than our uptight amigo here." He circled a number on the card. "That's my cell. You can call me anytime. Day or night." He nodded and strolled off, leaving Paige holding a business card she didn't want but for the sake of politeness couldn't have refused.

Trent glared after Donnie, then looked at Paige. Even though she wore heels he was still tall enough that she had to tilt her head back to meet his gaze. "I need to change clothes. Come upstairs with me."

Her mouth dried. Back to the scene of the crime— sooner than she'd expected. But she wouldn't complain. This worked into her plan splendidly. That didn't mean she didn't have an entire flock of butterflies circling her tummy. "Lead the way."

The crowded elevator forced them to stand close together. Trent had his back to the wall, and in typical fashion, every occupant faced the doors. Trent's sleeve brushed her shoulder, then someone else squeezed into the compartment just before the doors closed, forcing Paige to slide in front of Trent. She could feel his presence behind her like a magnet pulling at her. His breath stirred the hair on the back of her head, and his leather attaché case brushed her leg. She ached to lean against him. An inch, maybe two, and her back would press against those hard pectorals she'd been admiring.

An involuntary shiver racked her. She inhaled and his scent filled her nose. Funny, she could distinguish his unique aroma from the eight others in the confined space. Had she ever been able to do that with David? She couldn't remember.

Over the shoulders in front of her, she met and held Trent's reflected gaze in the polished brass doors as the elevator slowly climbed and emptied with each stop until only the two of them remained. He didn't move away.

Did he feel the current arcing between them? His dilated pupils and flaring nostrils suggested he did. But if so why was he fighting it? Hadn't she been obvious enough in expressing her interest? Maybe he thought she was looking for more than a short-term affair? According to her sisters, that would scare off any man.

The doors swished open on the thirty-sixth floor. She swallowed to ease her parched throat and forced her feet forward. He brushed past her, his hand briefly touching her waist as he moved around her and setting off a chain of sparks along her synapses. She followed him. With each step she took the knot of tension twisted tighter in her belly.

You're not going back. You're moving forward. Make new memories while nudging him with old ones.

He reached the corner room at the end of the hall, swiped his card, opened the door and held it for her. She stepped inside one of the Lagoon's most luxurious tower suites.

Although she rarely had reason to visit the guest accommodations, she knew that not only did this suite have a marble-floored entry and separate dining area, it contained an entertainment lounge complete with big-screen TV and surround sound, a private work station with every gadget a traveler might require and a luxurious bedroom with a whirlpool bath big enough for two. It was twice the size of her one-bedroom apartment and cost more per night than she paid for an entire month's rent with utilities.

She'd been alone with Trent in a similar unit before, but she hadn't been totally sober, nor had she felt anywhere near as electrified as she did now. Her skin tingled as if she'd been sprinkled with sparkling water.

He gestured to the minibar, showing no sign of remembering or worrying about their less-than-stellar past. "Would you care for a drink while I change?"

"No. Thanks." She wasn't running the risk of anything dulling her response this time around—if she could convince him to have a second go. The blinking light on the phone caught her eye. "You have a message."

He stared at the phone for a full five seconds. "I'll check it later."

He disappeared into the bedroom, firmly closing the door with a click. No subtlety in that communication. Did she even have a chance of breaking his iron control?

She strolled to the windows. The bright lights glowed beneath her as each hotel and casino vied for attention and tourist dollars. This garishly lit twenty-four-hour city couldn't be more different than her hometown or even Charleston with its historic flavor and quaint, old-fashioned streetlights.

Then she noted the whipping flags and the Bellagio's blowing fountains. The wind had picked up since she'd come in this morning. Her heart quickened with the new possibilities. Not that she wasn't having fun riding the roller coasters, but it was difficult to get intimate in a crowd.

The bedroom door opened. Trent returned to the sitting area wearing another V-neck cashmere sweater, this one in a rich cream, over a black crewneck T-shirt and black jeans. Sexy.

She dampened her suddenly dry lips. "We may have to change our plans. It looks pretty gusty outside. Many of the outdoor rides, including the one we'd intended to visit, don't operate in inclement weather or windy conditions. We should probably call before walking to the hotel."

He crossed to the phone and hit the button for the front desk. "The Sahara Hotel, please."

Paige studied his broad shoulders, straight spine, firm butt and long, muscular legs as he waited for the connection to go through. The man looked yummy in a suit, but what he did for designer denim was an engraved invitation to sin. Her fingers itched to stroke his bottom—and that was so not like her.

Last year they'd been completely comfortable with each other until arriving in the suite. Then it had been as if both of them weren't so sure they should be here, but neither had wanted to say so. The kisses had been awkward, the caresses even more so.

So why are you here?

Because this year the chemistry between them was too volatile not to give it a shot. She couldn't remember ever shaking with need or getting flushed all over just from thinking about sex—the way she was now.

She and David had begun as friends in high school and slowly—very slowly—progressed to sex. They—or at least *she*—had been happy with their comfortable, even-keeled relationship. And while the physical component of their relationship had been good, she'd never experienced an attraction as urgent or strong as the one she shared with Trent in her life.

A crazy urge to sneak up behind Trent while he was on the phone, wind her arms around him and rub her breasts against him almost overcame her. She ached to touch him, to shape those deep pectorals with her palms and taste that firmly checked mouth with a hunger she hadn't had felt last time.

"Is Speed, The Ride operating tonight?" Trent said into the receiver, then seconds later he added, "Thank you." He disconnected and faced her. "You're ri—"

She tried to wipe her desire from her face, but judging by his sudden alertness, she hadn't done so fast enough.

Their gazes locked. His pupils expanded and his lips compressed. "The ride is closed until the wind dies down."

"We could order room service and see if it reopens by the time we've finished eating."

She saw the refusal in his expression before he opened

his mouth. But she also caught a flash of heat. The latter gave her courage.

"Paige—"

"Trent, I'm not interested in more than a brief affair, if that's what you're worried about. I don't intend to fall in love again or get married and spawn a basketball team of children like my parents did. I'm devoted to my career and my dream of seeing the world—despite what I heard in your scary seminar earlier."

Her attempt at a smile wobbled and failed miserably. She took a step toward him, and when he didn't retreat, another. "You may be used to passion so overwhelming it makes it impossible to think, but I'm not. This chemistry we share…this connection…wasn't there last year, and I would like to explore it."

Still sensing resistance on his part, she continued, "Yes, I admit I'm scared and worried that like before we won't… That our…efforts won't go well. But it's a chance I'm willing to take. If you are."

When he remained silent, she wrapped her arms around her torso and glanced toward the window. "I want to know— No, I *need* to know if the problem was yours, ours…or just me."

Once more Paige's openness and vulnerability hit Trent like jet wash, tossing him into a turbulent tailspin of tangled emotions.

First, a g-force of desire so strong it nearly knocked him to his knees hit him when he considered sinking into her lush body. His core muscles tightened against it.

Second, a fresh gust of curiosity blindsided him. What in the hell had happened? The frustrating need to know versus the repelling distaste of being a voyeur to his brother's intimate life battled within him. Unlike Brent, Trent had never been one to share the personal details of his sex life.

Third, anger toward his brother. Damn Brent for whatever it was he'd done to cause the pain and self-doubt in Paige's eyes and the slight quiver in her voice.

Whatever *problem* Paige and Brent might have had couldn't have been her fault. She was so open and honest that it would be impossible for any man who listened to fail to satisfy her. She seemed like the type of woman to vocalize her needs—a trait Trent found extremely sexy.

The need to comfort her propelled him forward against his better judgment. He knew touching her could erode what was left of his resolve to resist her, and yet his hand lifted to cup her cheek almost of its own volition. She leaned into his palm, her soft skin warming his as she nuzzled against him.

"Paige, you are beautiful, desirable and so damn sexy my jaw aches from biting back the need to taste you."

She gasped. The hope and hunger on her face hit him with a one-two punch. "What's stopping you?"

His resistance wavered. She claimed all she wanted was a brief affair. What would it hurt if they did what she believed they'd done already—only this time without whatever disappointment she'd suffered? He could pleasure her until she begged him to stop and prove to her that she wasn't at fault for whatever had gone wrong with Brent.

Trent's conscience urged him to back away from temptation. But how could giving her what she wanted be wrong? And how would a brief, no-strings affair be any different than what he practiced at home?

Because you never mix business with pleasure, and you never date anyone within the industry.

But by blowing off networking to spend time with

Paige, he'd already broken both rules. She might not work in commercial aviation, but the annual convention had been held at the Lagoon for the past four years and was scheduled to be here for at least three more.

This is business. Yours. HAMC's. Brent's. Specifically, saving all three by avoiding a nasty and costly blowup.

A brief liaison would hurt nothing. If anything, it would leave Paige with a favorable impression of Trent and HAMC instead of the negative one she currently held.

Decision made, he covered her mouth with his. Her satiny lips parted to receive him, and her tongue met his at the entrance of her mouth, tangling and wrangling for supremacy the way she did with her words.

She tasted good. Damn good. He tried to hold back, to coax her slowly and prolong the foreplay, but her enthusiastic response unleashed a carnal hunger in him that was hard to control. He banded his arms around her, yanking her close. The heat of her body, the cushion of her breasts and the slick wetness of her mouth made him hot, heavy and hard in seconds.

Her arms rose, surrounding his shoulders, and her sigh filled his lungs as she sank against him, then her nails lightly raked his scalp, ripping through his restraint like a propeller slicing through damp air. He gave up the fight and stabbed his fingers into her silky hair. Tilting her head back, he deepened the kiss.

She shifted and her pelvis brushed his, sending a surge of animalistic need through him. He swept his hands over her shoulders to her waist, then he cupped her bottom. She needed to feel how badly he ached for her. He wanted to lay her down on the floor and drive into her, but he settled for grinding against her and pushing himself to the edge of control.

The stretchy fabric of her pants invited his hands to plunge beneath the waistband. His fingertips found the smooth material of her bikini panties then skin. Warm, velvety skin. But feeling her wasn't enough. He wanted to see her—every luscious curve. He tortured himself by delaying, stroking her bottom, her waist and the undersides of her breasts. Her hum of pleasure filled his mouth and his ears.

He skimmed his thumbs over her bra, finding hard nipples pressing against the lacy cups. He circled the crests until she jerked her mouth free and let her head fall back to catch her breath. Bending, he buried his face in the crook of her neck, inhaling her lemony fragrance and nuzzling her smooth skin. Her pulse fluttered wildly beneath his lips.

She raked her nails through his hair and down his back. "That feels good."

Her ragged words made his heart pound harder. He had to see her, to touch her, to taste her. He fisted his hands in her top and tugged it over her head. A black bra cupped her full, pale breasts. He bent to bury his face in her cleavage. Her fragrance, headier here in the shadowy warmth, filled his nose. He traced the lacy bra's border with his lips, then his tongue as he flicked open the front clasp and allowed the soft globes to spill into his palms. She bit her lip as he devoured her with his eyes and thumbed the tips, then she shrugged and her bra fell to the floor.

Paige had great breasts. Her nipples were tight, begging for his mouth. He didn't delay taking what he wanted and rolling first one tight bud, then the other around on his tongue. Her lashes descended and her lips parted. Clinging to his shoulders, she leaned against the arm he hooked around her waist to give him better access and cradled his cheeks to guide him. He didn't need her hands to point him in the right direction. He took his cues from each whimper, gasp and shudder to arouse her as much as she had him.

Her fingers painted a trail of goose bumps down his neck then his sides before hooking in his belt. Hunger clawed at him, once again urging him to rush. But tonight wasn't about what he needed. Tonight was about Paige. He'd get his pleasure, but only after she'd had hers.

Impatient to see and taste the rest of her, he swept her into his arms and headed for the bedroom. He planted a hard kiss on her mouth then set her down beside the bed.

With more speed than finesse, he stripped her pants and panties down her legs. Just below her knees he encountered the tops of her leather boots. He nudged her backward until she sat on the turndown sheets, then eased her loose-legged pants over her boots. From his kneeling position beside the mattress, he allowed himself a leisurely visual feast.

Her legs, naked except for black leather high-heeled boots, made his mouth water. A dense triangle of dark blond, glistening curls marked his next target. That she was already wet for him amped up his sense of urgency.

Unlike the thin model types he usually dated, Paige had rounded hips, a narrow waist and full breasts. When his gaze reached her flushed face, he caught her searching his eyes with a guarded expression.

"Paige, you are so damned beautiful I ache for you. Feel how much I want you." He straightened, captured her hand and stroked her palm up and down his erection. Hunger hammered him. He wanted—needed—her hands on his skin. But if she touched him there was no guarantee he could keep this slow. He sucked a breath through clenched teeth and quickly knelt again to tackle the zipper of one boot. He removed it and tossed it aside then dealt with the other.

Her fingertips stroked across his shoulders and up the side of his neck to trace his ears. A shudder racked him. To hell with slow and easy. Bolting back to his feet he ripped his sweater and T-shirt over his head and reached for his belt.

"Let me help." Paige rose. But she didn't reach for his buckle. Instead her hands flattened over his pecs and glided downward at a snail's pace. He gritted his teeth against the hedonistic agony as she neared his abdomen then finally, *finally* his belt. Each shift of her trembling fingers dipping behind his buckle made his heart and groin pound and his temperature rise.

Paige released the leather and unfastened his pants. She ran her fingers across the bulge of the swollen flesh tenting his briefs, and he bucked involuntarily into her hand. She wrapped her hand around him, squeezing with just enough pressure to milk a groan from him. The look she sent him from under her lashes nearly undid him.

He clamped down on the raw bite of passion, and shoved his pants and briefs past his hips. She reached for him again, but he arched out of the way.

Her smile faded. She stood before him, hands clasped in front of those damp, enticing curls, the temptress slowly transforming into lip-biting shyness.

Another dot of anger blipped on his radar. What in the hell had happened to make her this unsure of her allure?

Whatever it was, he'd wipe it from her mind before the night ended. He grasped her shoulders and gently pulled her forward until her bare skin seared his. He sluiced his hands down her back and crushed her tightly against him as he captured her mouth. Her belly cradled his hard-on, making him want to rut like a damned stallion against her. He fought the urge.

Her touch fluttered over him, her nails tracing butterfly-soft trails over his shoulders, his back, his butt. A shudder racked him. He peeled his mouth away and buried his face in her neck, back to the soft, smooth spot he'd discovered earlier.

She curled her hand around him again and stroked. "You're very hard."

"Not for long if you keep that up."

Her hand stilled and fell away. "Don't you like it when I touch you?"

"Hell, yes. Too much. Paige, if you keep that up my plan to make you beg for mercy is going to be moot."

Surprise widened her eyes then a slow grin spread her delectable mouth. The mischief in that smile spurred him into kicking off his shoes—one thumped the wall—tearing off his socks and shedding the remainder of his clothing in record time.

The wildly beating pulse in her neck quivered against his lips, then he outlined her ear with his tongue, nipped her lobe and eased back. He incrementally bent his knees, kissing, nipping, licking a path down her front, over her collarbones, her breasts, her nipples, her navel.

As he approached her bikini line her fingers fisted in his hair. "Trent, wait. That's not necessary. I'm already…um… ready."

He clasped her bottom, holding her captive when she tried to squirm away. "Tasting you is very necessary. The question is, can you come standing up?"

Her cheeks turned crimson. Her fingers clutched the edge of the mattress, then the spark of challenge entered his eyes. "I—I don't know. But I'm willing to find out."

Her fighter response sent a shot of adrenaline through him. He liked that she didn't retreat. "That-a-girl."

He bent and licked her, one swipe though her center. Her

flavor exploded on his tongue, making him greedy for more. He plied her slick flesh with his mouth, licking, sucking and grazing her with his teeth. He felt her tremors increase through his hands and against his face, then her back bowed and she jerked over and over until her knees buckled and she sagged against the bed.

He nipped her thigh and looked up at her. Her lids slowly lifted. Her breath shuddered in and out again. He kissed a return path up her body, then she started easing down his the way he had hers. Her intent jolted him with a blast of heat that nearly fried his brain.

"Save that mission for another time. Right now, I can't wait to be inside you." He scooped her into his arms. Planting one knee on the bed then the other, he lowered her into the center.

"I want that, too."

Reality took a bite out of the moment. Damn. It had been years since he'd needed to carry condoms in his wallet, but tonight he wished he hadn't broken the habit. "I need protection. Don't move."

He hustled into the bathroom, grabbed a couple of condoms and returned to the bedroom. He pitched his booty onto the nightstand, save one packet. The sight of Paige with her creamy skin and golden hair reclining on her elbows on the chocolate-brown sheets made his mouth water and his erection twitch in appreciation.

He opened and donned the latex. With her sultry gaze on him, even the stroke of his own hand as he rolled on the condom bordered on too much stimulation, but then a quick flash of nervousness across her face made him pause. She still had doubts? How could she when he was about to explode all over her and the linens?

He captured her ankle and lifted it.

She stiffened. "What are you doing?"

"This." He caught her big toe between his teeth, circled it with his tongue then sucked it into his mouth.

She gasped and fell back on the bed. "Ooh, that feels good."

He nibbled his way to her instep. Her leg muscles knotted. Her fingers fisted in the sheets. "Wow. I mean… *woooow*. I've never had… I mean, kissing feet feels so…amazing."

Her breathless voice egged him on. He savored his way past her ankle, up her calf and to the back of her knee where he teased the sensitive crease with his mouth and his fingertips until she wiggled impatiently, then he made his way up the inside of her thigh. She started shaking before he made it to her panty line. Fine tremors rattled her body and stuttered her breaths, but she arched up to meet his mouth when he reached her center. He shelved her bottom on his hands and went to work on driving her wild. It took less than a minute of stroking her swollen flesh to make her climax again.

He couldn't wait any longer. She reached for him as he climbed his way up her body, but he couldn't handle her hands on his hypersensitive erection right now. It would be too much. He caught her hands and carried them to his mouth to press wet kisses on her palms.

She opened her legs and her arms for him, then sandwiched his face between her hands and pulled him down to her mouth. He simultaneously slid into the slick glove of her body and plunged his tongue into her mouth. Hot, liquid pleasure enveloped him, lubricating each thrust. He struggled to hold back, but he couldn't stay his hips.

He tried to drag air into his tight chest, and withdrew from Paige only to lunge in again and again. Pressure and heat built in his groin. Her hands mapped his torso, bumping over his nipples and sending tiny electric shocks shooting through his limbs. He rocked back on his haunches, lifting her hips and freeing his thumb to circle her center. Sweat beaded on his torso with the effort to keep his hunger on lockdown.

He couldn't look away from her face. The rush of color to her cheeks, the way she bit her knuckle to hold in her cries and the expansion of her pupils revealing her pleasure. Then her internal muscles clutched him tight. Her eyes slammed shut and orgasm rippled through her again, bowing her torso off the bed and making her contract around him. She stifled her cries against her fist.

Her climax triggered his. He fell forward, bracing himself to plunge deeper and faster. Tension gathered in his limbs, coalescing into a hot ball that raced through him and burst from him in resurgent, mind-numbing pulses of ecstasy. A groan he couldn't contain thundered from him, shattering the quiet of the room.

Sapped of strength, his elbows buckled. He barely caught himself on his shaking arms before crushing Paige. His lungs blasted hot air against her temple. Her pants fanned his neck and her hands swept down his damp back.

Then reality returned like a dousing of de-icing fluid.

Despite the attraction between them, taking her to bed had never been part of his plan. Now that the heat of the moment had cooled, he realized he shouldn't have brought her to his suite. But he'd believed he had more control over his libido, and with that damned Donnie lusting over her downstairs he'd been stuck between two bad choices: risking Donnie exposing the truth or risking temptation.

Trent rolled onto his back beside Paige. As amazing as the sex had been, he wished he had a rewind button to undo it. Was Paige even now comparing him to his brother? Comparing this year's performance with the previous one? Could she tell the difference between him and Brent? The idea of his sexual skills being weighed against Brent's made his skin crawl.

But, Trent's pride pointed out, there was no way Paige could call this encounter disappointing.

He needed to clear his head and come up with a new strategy, because there was no way in hell sleeping with his brother's former lover would lead to anything other than a disaster if his secret broke.

Despite the evidence he'd seen to the contrary, a part of him had wanted to believe Brent's claim that Paige probably picked up a new man in the bar at every conference, when she'd said all she wanted was casual sex he'd let himself be persuaded. Big mistake.

He couldn't even blame his lack of control on abstinence. He had sex on a regular basis whenever it fit into his schedule. But on those occasions his partners were female versions of him—takers who wanted a physical release without messy ties or expectations. They were as eager to leave after the orgasms as he was. No cuddling. No pillow talk. No false promises.

Despite the fact that Paige's sensuality had totally melted his brain, he'd bet his personal jet that she wasn't the temporary kind of woman. He could tell the difference between someone focused on self-gratification and one eager to please her partner and afraid she might fail. Her vulnerability was the key. Her tentative touches and hesitant kisses combined with her earnest expression proved her a giver not a taker.

Paige was the type of woman who looked for a long-term connection, not a temporary hookup—the kind of woman he usually avoided the way he would standing on high ground in a lightning storm.

Damn. Damn. Damn. With one stupid decision he'd derailed his damage control plan and very likely worsened the potential outcome. He had to find a way to make this situation work *for* him instead of *against* him.

But how could he turn a mistake of this magnitude to his advantage? There had to be a way. And he would find it.

Seven

Paige sank into Trent's mattress with a sigh of contentment. A fine coating of sweat cooled her skin.

What a difference a year made. Making love with Trent this time around had been as wonderful and exhilarating as the previous attempt had been awful and humiliating.

She didn't know what to say to him. How could she possibly ask what had changed without reminding him of last year's disastrous failure? That would certainly spoil the moment.

Tonight with little or no coaxing from her, he'd been hard as steel even before their clothing had come off. She'd bet her upcoming week's vacation he hadn't taken one of those magic blue pills advertised on TV because he hadn't acted as if he intended them to become intimate tonight or any other night.

She hadn't changed, so she couldn't have been the reason

for his…lack of enthusiasm last year. Right? Please let that be right. She turned her head. He lay on the pillow beside hers, staring at the ceiling, a frown furrowing his brow.

A sinking sensation settled in her stomach. Did he have regrets? How could he? That had been the most amazing sex of her life. Hadn't it been as good for him? She bit her bottom lip as doubts dampened her afterglow. The cheesy "Was it good for you?" line ran through her mind, but she couldn't reduce the sublime pleasure they'd shared to a cliché.

His head turned and their gazes met. The combination of reserve and regret in his eyes winded her. "You can shower first."

"We could shower together," she said, hoping she'd read him wrong.

"You go ahead. I'm going to take a look at the room service menu."

His disinterested tone slapped her. She wanted to pull the sheets over her head. But that wouldn't solve anything. The problem would be waiting for her when she came out from under the covers.

He rose and walked into the bathroom. Her gaze fastened on the flexing muscles of his firm buttocks, and arousal rekindled in her midsection. The toilet flushed then water splashed in the sink. He returned wearing one of the hotel robes, tightly belted, and carrying another. He draped the spare across the foot of the bed. "Take your time."

He left the room, siphoning all the warmth and oxygen with him. She clutched the sheet to her chest and listened to him moving around in the sitting area. She heard the refrigerator open and the chink of ice cubes falling into a glass.

She'd driven him to drink?

Feeling more exposed and unsure than she had since last year, she clutched the robe to her chest and raced into the bathroom. Keeping a wary eye out for Trent, she tucked her hair into a hotel-provided shower cap, then showered quickly in the glass-walled cubicle. Her mind raced. Had she done something wrong? Or did he just blow hot and cold? She knew from her sisters and her experience with David that most guys weren't cuddlers. She wished she could pick up the phone, call home and ask if this was typical male behavior. But she couldn't.

She stepped from the enclosure and dried off. *Her clothes.* She winced. She'd shed them all over the suite, and half of them were in the other room with Trent. Retrieving them would take a little courage. But she could handle it.

She shrugged back into the thick white cotton robe, ventured into the bedroom and stopped in surprise. Her sweater, pants, bra and panties lay neatly on the bed. Trent must have put them there. Was he simply being considerate or was he eager to get rid of her?

She debated her options for a full ten seconds. She could take the coward's way out, get dressed and bolt...or she could try to hold the ground she'd gained. Because she had gained ground. She'd taken her first lover since her breakup and her first step toward the future she'd envisioned for herself when she'd moved to Vegas. Sure, she was fourteen months late getting the party started, but still she'd made progress.

She decided to stay in the robe. Dressing pretty much said, "Wham bam, thank you, ma'am," or in this case, "sir." Not the message she wanted to send.

Taking a bracing breath, she padded into the sitting room, her bare feet silent on the thick carpet. Trent stood with his rigid back to her, staring out the window. He held a glass of amber liquid in his hand. His thick hair was still rumpled, presumably by her fingers.

He didn't look like a guy who'd just had the best sex in

well…ever. But then he was probably more experienced than her. Maybe it hadn't been as amazing for him.

She gulped and gathered her courage. "The bathroom's all yours."

He looked so James Bond suave as he turned that he took her breath away. His gaze raked from her finger-combed hair to the toes she'd curled into the carpet. Funny, she'd shared her body with him, but she hadn't felt comfortable borrowing his comb. *Twisted, Paige.*

"I've ordered dinner from room service." His cool demeanor suggested it wasn't because he wanted to keep her in bed all night. A sense of foreboding crept up her spine. She shivered—not in a good way.

"Trent? Is something wrong?" Oh God, she was going to have to use the lame line. *Well, here goes nothing.* "Wasn't it good for you?"

He downed the rest of his drink in one gulp and set the tumbler on the nearby dining-room table. "Yes, it was good. But it was a mistake."

The firm statement sent her mentally reeling. "Why? Why was making love a mistake?"

His lips—the same lips that had driven her to unbelievable passion moments ago—flattened into a straight line. "It wasn't making love. It was sex."

She barely managed not to wince. But what he said was true. Amazing or not, what they'd share had been only sex. Not fate or love or any of that other romantic junk. "Semantics."

His scowl deepened. "How long were you with your last lover?"

Not a conversation she wanted to have. She fussed the tie belt of her robe. "Does it matter?"

"Answer the question."

He wasn't going to like her answer even if it wasn't relevant to what they'd just shared. "Seven years."

"That's what I thought. Paige, I can't be the man you need."

If she didn't have her pride to cling to, this would be a good time to run. She dug deep for a little of her big sister's chutzpah. "That's where you're wrong, Trent. You were exactly what I needed a few minutes ago. A guy who's fun to be with and good in bed."

"I can't offer you anything more than—" his gesture encompassed the room "—this. Despite what you said, I don't see you as the casual-affair type."

"Then you'd be wrong." Casual was exactly the type the new Paige intended to be. She had to find a way to convince him of that. "I love my job and I won't give it up for a man—any man. And you'll be leaving in what…three or four days?"

"Five."

"Then I suggest we make the most of those days…and nights."

His silence as his searching gaze held hers spoke volumes. She tried to blank her expression.

"Am I going to lose my roller coaster riding partner over this?"

"No. If room service arrives while I'm in the shower, the tip is on the table. The rest will be billed to the room." He turned on his heel and disappeared through the bedroom door. Seconds later she heard the shower spray.

Her bravado drained away. She'd gotten the walk on the wild side that she'd wanted.

So why wasn't she happy?

What a damned wuss.
Trent scrubbed hard enough to make his scalp tingle. He

hired and fired employees on a regular basis without a twinge of remorse. But the hurt in Paige's eyes when he'd left her in bed had speared him.

While sleeping with her and dumping her immediately thereafter might piss her off enough to make her steer clear of him and Brent, it wouldn't stop her from hooking up with Donnie. And an angry, vengeful woman was exactly the scenario he wanted to avoid. That left Trent at an impasse.

The flashing message light on the telephone extension in the bathroom nagged him as he sawed the towel over his back with enough vigor to redden his skin. He closed the bathroom door, lifted the receiver and punched the buttons to play his messages.

"Hi Trent. Nicole here. Your girlfriend's—" he grimaced "—family has reservations about hopping on a private jet and flying cross country. So…my report is that I have nothing to report. I'll call back when and if the status changes." *Click*.

That wasn't the answer he wanted. He checked the clock on the wall and calculated the time difference. Nicole should still be awake. He dialed her home number.

"Hello, Trent," she answered. Caller ID was a blessing and a curse. At least she'd decided to talk to him—unlike his brother, who was still dodging calls.

"What do you mean the McCauleys are reluctant? I'm offering them a free vacation, and HAMC has the highest safety rating in aviation."

She laughed. "You know that old adage, 'When something sounds too good to be true it usually is?' Apparently the McCauleys are firm believers. They want to research HAMC and our safety rating before loading their precious daughters onto a stranger's plane. Now that I'm going to be a mom, I can't say I blame them. I'd do the same with my baby."

Frustration tightened his muscles and made his stomach burn. "Nicole, fix this."

"Trent, I'm trying," she replied in the same impatient tone. She'd been doling out a lot more sass since marrying the father of her kid. But Ryan was a good guy, and he made Nicole happy, so Trent let her get away with mouthing off. This time.

"We're on a tight schedule here," he reminded her.

"Don't I know it? You've asked—no, *ordered* me to work a miracle, Trent. Like I said in my earlier message, I'll call when I know something. Good night." The line went dead.

He stared at the phone. His sister had hung up on him. A first. He cradled the receiver and scraped a hand over his face, searching for a quick solution. His brain echoed like an empty hangar. No ideas taxied around.

He'd have to keep Paige on a string for a little longer— at least until he was certain her family would arrive to distract her.

As if keeping her around will be a hardship.

No, it wouldn't. If it weren't for walking on eggshells and fearing he'd misspeak, he enjoyed her company. And she was damned good in bed. Not that ending up there with her again would be wise. The more involved they became the more extreme her reaction to his leaving could be come...unless what she said about wanting a temporary lover was true. He still had his doubts about that.

He opened the door and exited in a wave of steam. The bedroom was empty, and Paige's clothes were where he'd left them on the bed, meaning she hadn't left and hadn't taken his hint to get dressed while he showered. His mixed feelings over the discovery confused him. He wanted her gone. And yet he didn't.

But he wasn't going to traipse around in his robe. No

point in testing his will to resist her unnecessarily. He yanked on jeans and a T-shirt. The new clothes were yet another reminder that instead of satisfying his personal desires he should be making connections downstairs, viewing vendor products and cutting deals for state-of-the-art electronics.

He needed a Plan C. If Paige's family refused to fly out, he'd have to find an alternative to getting Paige out of the way before Brent arrived. Short of kidnapping the woman, he had no viable schemes. He'd have to take another shot at convincing her to fly home.

He returned to the living area and found Paige wedged into the corner cushions of the sofa with her legs crossed and one of the glossy hotel-provided magazines in her lap. A large room-service tray sat on the coffee table in front of her.

"Dinner's here," she said unnecessarily and set her reading material aside.

His stomach rumbled, surprising him with an appetite that circumstances should have robbed. "Let's eat."

She leaned forward to lift a stainless-steel cover from one of the plates. Her robe gaped, baring the curve of one breast. He could almost see her nipple. His pulse quickened and the urge to tuck his hand into her cleavage and cup her satiny flesh had him fisting his hands.

She scooted forward to lift another lid. The hem of her robe snagged between the seat cushions, flashing enough of her thigh and hip to let him know she wasn't wearing panties. Then she snatched the fabric free and blocked his view.

He wasn't disappointed.

Hell, yes, you are.

All right. Yes. Paige had a great body. Curvy, but toned. Any man would enjoy admiring her.

He searched her face, looking for any sign that she might be deliberately teasing him, but she seemed completely unaware that her actions had caused his blood to drain to his groin. She continued removing and stacking the domes without once glancing his way.

Then it hit him that part of Paige's allure rested in the fact that she didn't work at being sexy. It happened naturally. There was something about the way she moved. Confident. Sure. But easy at the same time, as if she were very comfortable in her skin. And then there was the way she threw herself into the roller coaster rides, lustily enjoying every second from start to finish. He'd been the same once upon a time.

His gaze returned to her pale cleavage. How could he concentrate on food with her breasts on display? He shifted to ease the tightening of his jeans. "Wouldn't you prefer to eat at the dining-room table?"

"Too stuffy. You ordered a lot of food. There are four dinners, three appetizers and two bottles of wine, plus a hunk of chocolate cake."

"I wasn't sure what you'd like."

"Any of it." She looked up at him through her lashes, her eyes glinting with challenge. "But I have news for you, Hightower, you will share the cake."

She dipped her finger into the frosting and carried it to her mouth to lick off the smudge. Again, it seemed to be a completely natural move, not one designed to seduce him. But deliberate or not, his libido and blood pressure spiked and his throat closed up.

That's when he realized the only way he wouldn't take Paige back to bed tonight was if he quit breathing.

But the affair in Vegas was all he'd allow himself. When he boarded the jet for Knoxville he'd leave Paige behind.

* * *

Paige closed her eyes and tried to hold back a moan of delight as the fat-laden, calorie-loaded dessert sent her taste buds into orgasmic bliss. The rich, moist, four-layer chocolate, coconut and walnut cake lived up to its name of Chocolate Ecstasy.

"Why didn't you go to Manhattan with the boyfriend?" Trent's question shattered her blissful moment.

She swallowed, choked, coughed, wheezed, then grabbed her glass of wine and tried to wash down the crumb stuck in her throat. When she finally caught her breath she met Trent's gaze.

"I told you. Job opportunities. His there. Mine here."

"There are hotels in New York City. I've stayed at a few." His tongue-in-cheek tone didn't lessen the sting. "You could have worked there."

She laid her fork on the table. Not even a slice of chocolate heaven could revive her appetite. "Our lives took us in different directions."

"You invested seven years with him. Why give up?"

Her skin prickled uncomfortably, and the soft robe abraded her behind as she shifted on the sofa. "Does it matter?"

"I wouldn't ask if it didn't."

She swallowed, but the bitter taste in her mouth remained. Not even another sip of wine washed it away. "Because he didn't want me to go with him. He said a country girl like me wouldn't fit in with his new urban lifestyle."

"He's an idiot."

Her lips twitched in a smile at his support. "You and my sisters share that opinion. What about you? Any lost loves in your past?"

"No."

She waited, but he didn't elaborate. "*No?* You made me spill my guts and all you're giving me is *no?* I don't think so."

His mouth twisted. "Let's just say I'm not convinced a woman can be faithful, and I don't want to always wonder whose bed my wife is in at night when she's not in mine."

She grimaced at the bitterness in his voice. "Your mother?"

He refilled their wineglasses instead of responding.

"You said you had a surprise sister. Your mother must have had at least one affair."

"More than one."

"I'm sorry, Trent. I can't imagine how that feels. My parents have been together forever. They'll celebrate their thirty-sixth anniversary this year. That's a good thing because in my home town if either of them had strayed the news would have reached home before they did."

His eyes narrowed on her face. "You miss your home-town."

How had he seen something she'd refused to acknowledge? "Yes, I do. It's hard to believe, but I miss the nosy neighbors, the local diner, the drive-in movie theater and Main Street. I even miss the crazy tourist season when the roads get clogged with people who don't know where they're going. And I miss my parents. But mostly, I miss my sisters."

Loneliness welled within her. She fussed with the hem of her robe. "We were close, y'know? We shared every-thing—a bathroom, makeup, clothes, shoes… When I moved here I thought not having to share any of those things would be great. And it was—" her voice broke "—for about a month."

"Didn't you have privacy when you lived in Charleston?"

"I was close enough to home for them to drop in for a weekend at the beach or an overnight shopping trip. I saw my sisters at least once a week. Sometimes they packed. Sometimes they just threw their purses in the car and drove over—which meant my closet was their closet."

She mashed her lips together over the aching emptiness and struggled for composure. Crying all over a guy was not the way to end an intimate evening.

"If you miss them that much, why not go home? And don't throw the convention center crap at me. There are convention hotels in South Carolina."

"For several reasons. First, because the people back home never forget. Kelly, my oldest sister, will always be the unmarried McCauley who got knocked up. I'll always be 'poor Paige' the one who got dumped by her high school sweetheart. I'm more than that. That was only one small part of my life, not the sum total of it. And if you keep this up I'm going to need Oreos."

"The cookie?"

His confusion was adorable. "You can't have a pity party without Oreo cookies, the ultimate comfort food. Surely you've had them before and understand the healing power of a chocolate, cream-filled treat?"

"No. But you just had chocolate cake."

"You've never had an Oreo? You poor, deprived man. My sisters and I always devoured a bag when one of us had a crisis."

"Did you have many crises?"

She grimaced. "We're talking about a houseful of emotional women. There is always a crisis. That was the second reason I wanted out. I was Miss Fix-It and the family mediator. Whenever something went wrong, my sisters expected me to talk them through the situation and help them make the difficult decisions. I got tired of being the scapegoat when things didn't turn out well. I wanted them to learn to handle their own problems. It was really hard, but I had to risk letting them fail."

He frowned. "The consequences of failing couldn't have been that great."

"Of course they were. I don't mean to be overly dramatic, but we're talking life-or-death decisions. When my oldest sister got pregnant she wanted *me* to tell her whether to keep her baby or abort. I couldn't have lived with her hating me for the rest of our lives if she'd followed my advice and then later decided that my suggestion was the wrong one. There were other, smaller issues, too, but Kelly's pregnancy was the turning point in my decision to be…less accessible."

"What if they make mistakes?"

"They will, and I hope they'll learn from them and that the lessons won't be too painful." Enough about her. "Are you and your siblings close?"

He picked at a lobster tail. "We work together."

"What about outside the office?"

He shrugged. "We're not a social bunch."

"But…you're family."

"We gather for Christmas somewhere around the globe." She noted his lack of excitement. "Somewhere?"

"My mother chooses a location—usually some place she's heard about or discovered during her travels. We show up."

"Where are you going this year?"

"I don't know yet."

"But reservations— Wait, I guess if you own your airplane company you don't need to make airline reservations."

"No. Our pilots fly on four hours or less notice to wherever we tell them to go."

Such unbounded freedom sounded thrilling, and yet… sad and isolated despite having the world at his fingertips.

"You live in the same city as your siblings and yet only get together for Christmas?"

"And board meetings. Now that one of my sisters is pregnant, she's trying to force us to gather more often."

"Force?" She had to force herself to stay away. "It's too bad that you don't enjoy each other's company more."

Paige realized Trent didn't get together with his family because he didn't care. She cared, but she'd been dumb enough to willingly walk away and break or at least fray the bond. It had been for her sisters' own good, or so she'd told herself. But was that really the truth?

She'd accused him of abandoning something he loved— flying and roller coasters. What she'd done really wasn't any different. The acknowledgment disturbed her. She rose and crossed to the refrigerator to get a soda. If she kept drinking wine, she was going to end up a soggy mess. She'd already shared more than she'd intended.

When she turned around she caught Trent studying her with a speculative expression. "What?"

"I was watching the way you move. It's…"

Her muscles snapped taut. She braced herself for an insult. She'd never been a girly girl. She left that to Jessie and Sammie.

"I don't know the exact word. Unique. Deliberate. Powerful. Sexy."

Warmth rushed over her. "My mother made us take gymnastics and ballet from the time we turned five until we turned sixteen. She claimed it was the only way a houseful of tomboys had a chance at being graceful."

"You're a tomboy? From your sexy dresses and do-me heels I never would have guessed. The roller coasters should have been a clue." The upward twitch of one corner of his mouth made her stomach pitch.

Something inside her that had been dead since David told her she wasn't good enough for New York blossomed to life. She'd tried very hard to eradicate any remaining traces of small-town girl from her looks and demeanor. That's why her Southern accent bothered her so much. It was the only part she hadn't been able to shake. But she wasn't finished trying.

"Remember the McCauley girls grew up working in a hardware store. We can handle anything from power tools to fishing and camping gear." She wrinkled her nose. "I used to be a lot less…girly. I kind of gave myself a make-over before I moved west."

"I can't imagine you needing one. You're a beautiful woman, Paige."

Her breath caught. He couldn't have said anything more perfect. She dug deep for the worldly attitude she'd fought so hard to acquire. "I dare you to say that from over here."

She pointed to a spot on the floor in front of her, and when his eyebrows shot up she mentally kicked herself. Trent Hightower wasn't the kind of man to take orders from a woman. And while he had been watching her every move for the past half hour and making her very aware of her near-nakedness while they ate, he'd also kept to his end of the sofa as they passed the dishes between them, sharing servings of each.

His gaze raked over her from head to toe. Desire kindled in his eyes. He uncoiled—she couldn't think of a better word—from the sofa with an alertness of a snake ready to strike, and made his way across the room slowly, deliberately, with his eyes assessing her. "You're changing the subject."

She licked her dry lips. "I am?"

"We were talking about you."

"We were?" Her brain couldn't seem to catch gear.

"What do you hate most about being away from your family?"

She blinked to try to break the mesmerizing spell of his eyes and tried to think. No matter how much fun he might be or how good in bed, he was only going to be a part of her life for a short time, and he'd never meet her family, so what could it hurt to be honest?

"I hate having to watch every word I say when I call home."

He circled behind her. "Why would you do that?"

Her pulse pounded heavily in her ears. She wanted to make up something pretty or flippant, but she couldn't think of anything. "I might have misled my family a teensy bit about how much fun I've been having out here."

He circled in front of her again, snagging the belt of her robe as he passed and tugging hard enough to loosen the knot. "Why?"

The fine hairs on her body rose and her nipples tightened. How could she be embarrassed and turned on at the same time?

"Back home my sisters and I traveled in a pack when we went out. Safety in numbers, et cetera. Here…the singles scene is daunting. I tried going out alone for a while, but I wasn't comfortable. And then there was…us. After the way that turned out…let's just say I decided to take a break and focus on my job. But I don't want them to think 'Poor Paige is sitting at home alone.' So I, um…spend a lot of time talking about the cool places in Vegas."

"That you haven't visited." He stopped behind her. She couldn't see his face and had no clue what he was thinking.

"They've assumed I'd been there and I haven't corrected them. I drive by the sights often, and I read the pamphlets since they are the Lagoon's competition, so I know…some stuff. And then you walked back into my life." She inhaled deeply, smelling him, feeling his nearness. "I thought it was a good opportunity to wipe the slate clean and start over."

His body heat soaked through the fabric of her robe an instant before his breath brushed her ear. "Drop the robe."

Her heart stuttered and her stubborn side kicked in. Where had it been seconds ago when she'd been spilling her guts? Trent couldn't possibly know that middle kids detested being bossed around. She folded her arms across her chest. "Make me."

He stepped in front of her, his eyes filled with surprise that morphed into humor. "You're challenging me?"

Her pulse raced and she couldn't seem to draw enough air into her lungs. "Looks like it."

He grasped her shoulders and yanked her close. A flash fire of hunger consumed her as his lips slammed hers in a hard, not-quite bruising kiss. His thigh nudged hers apart and pressed against her center.

She couldn't remember ever getting this turned on from a kiss before—certainly not last year. Her muscles turned hot and sluggish as he worked her mouth with his tongue, lips and teeth. She looped her arms around his neck and kissed him back, trying to show how much she desired him.

She couldn't believe she could react this strongly toward someone she didn't love, someone she planned to use and discard. Maybe she and Trent could have an affair like the one in that old movie her mother loved so much, the one where the couple hooked up each year for a passionate vacation then returned to their normal lives.

He stabbed his hands beneath her robe and stroked her bare skin, shaping her shoulders, her back, her waist and finally her bottom. Grasping her hips, he pressed his pelvis to hers. His thick, long erection nudged her belly. But there was too much material in the way.

Impatient to be skin-on-skin with him again, she lowered her hands and shrugged off the robe. It slithered down her legs to pool at her feet.

She tunneled her hands between them and wormed her fingers beneath his T-shirt. The taut flesh of his abdomen heated her palms. She caressed his smooth belly and chest, and scraped her nails over his tiny, tight nipples. A growl of approval rumbled from his throat.

Curling her fingers into the fabric, she tugged upward. Trent broke the kiss long enough to discard the remainder of his clothing, then he stood before her naked, proud and fully aroused.

She dropped to her knees and ran her tongue up the length of his arousal.

"Paige," he groaned. She didn't know whether he did so in warning or encouragement, so she did what she'd been wanting to do and took him into her mouth.

His fingers speared into her hair and fisted—not tight enough to hurt, but enough to anchor her. She'd known last year he probably needed this to get hard, but she hadn't wanted to go there. Not with a stranger. Back then she hadn't felt this consuming need to experience every bit of him, to please him, to drive him to the edge of control the way he had her. Then she'd only wanted to take that first step in getting over D—

"Damn, that feels good," Trent murmured roughly.

She swirled her tongue around his engorged tip once, twice, a third time, then she raked her nails over his buttocks, down his thighs, and back up to the sensitive sacs between his legs as she caressed him with her mouth.

He muttered a curse and trembled. Then his hands hooked under her arms and he yanked her to her feet.

"I wasn't fin—"

His blue gaze burned into hers. "But I was about to. Without you. You are amazing, but I want to be inside you when I come."

He held out his hand. She laid her palm across his. He turned and led her to the bedroom where he sat on the bed, with his back against the leather headboard. He reached for the condom on the bedside table and stroked it on then extended his arms. "Ride me, Paige."

Heart pounding, she climbed onto the mattress, straddled his hips and slowly lowered. His thickness nudged her opening, then she sank lower, taking him deep inside. He grasped her rib cage and pulled her forward to capture a nipple with his mouth. He plucked the other with his hand. The combination of fingers, teeth, tongue and the suction of his mouth made her muscles quake.

She rose and fell on his slick flesh, increasing the heat and tension building inside her. Trent found her center with his fingertips, and she gasped at the burst of sensation deep in her core.

"Grab the headboard," he ordered.

She curled her fingers over the cool leather upholstery. Trent thrust upward, meeting each gliding descent by driving deeper, harder and faster, pushing her to the brink so quickly her panting breaths blended with his. Approaching orgasm wound tighter and tighter in her womb then it exploded through her, bowing her forward in spasm after spasm of rapture.

He hooked a hand around her nape, pulled her forward and muffled her cries with his mouth. Then he grasped her hips and pounded into her until his moan of release mingled with hers and his body shuddered beneath her.

She sank onto him one last time, her legs weak, her lungs burning. His arms looped around her waist, holding her close. She didn't want to move or separate from him. In fact, she thought as her lids grew heavy, she could probably fall asleep right here in his lap and in his arms.

Trent was the lover she'd always dreamed of finding—one with whom she could play and share passion. And she was very much afraid that she might be getting in far deeper than she'd intended.

She had to remember that this was a temporary affair, because if she didn't the only thing she could guarantee was heartache.

Eight

Paige paced Trent's suite in a tizzy while she waited for him to return. She passed the rumpled bed, the bathroom with its oversize glass shower—the places she and Trent had made love. Her body quivered with arousal she couldn't stamp out despite the worry that if he didn't return soon she was going to be late for the second time in one week. Milton would never forgive her.

The electronic lock beeped then the door opened. Trent entered with a dry cleaning bag hooked over his fingers. She raced toward him, snatched the coat hanger from him and ripped the plastic.

"Thank you. Thank you. Thank you. I don't know what I would have done if I hadn't left my dry cleaning in the car. I can't wear yesterday's clothes to work today, and I don't have time to go home."

"You look good in that outfit. It bears repeating."

She clutched her clean clothing to her chest and smiled. His ignorance reminded her of her father. Men didn't get it. They could wear the same suit day after day and only change shirts and maybe neckties, but no self-respecting woman wore the same clothes to work two days in a row— or so she and her sisters had declared years ago.

"Thank you again," she repeated, and retreating to the bedroom, dropped the garment on the bed. She shrugged out of the robe and Trent whistled in a breath. The passion in his eyes ignited a matching flame in her. "Don't even think it. We'll both be late."

Last night had been amazing. They'd never made it to the roller coaster. Instead they'd stayed here and connected more than just physically. Add in Trent volunteering to retrieve her dress from her car while she showered and applied the makeup she'd started carrying in her purse after the morning when she'd been late and had to do without her full war paint, and she just might fall in love with him.

Oh, no, you won't. Short-term, remember?

Too late?

Her stomach swooped as if she'd plunged from the highest roller coaster. No. It wasn't too late. This wasn't love. Love was gentle and warm and took time to ripen. This was potent, heady, *temporary* lust and the first of many affairs to come in her future. Trent was not a keeper and she would throw him back on Monday. And she'd do so with no regrets.

She reached for the yesterday's bra and grimaced. "I can wear the bra again, but I don't have clean underwear."

"Go without." Arms folded and ankles crossed, he leaned against the dresser, watching her dress. He looked scrumptious in his black suit and blinding white shirt and every inch the billionaire with his gold cuff links and watch glinting at his wrists.

"I can't walk around the hotel without panties."

"Who'll know?"

"I will. You will."

His lips twisted in the way that she'd come to know anticipated a sarcastic quip. "I'm sure the knowledge will haunt me all day."

"Funny, Hightower." She wiggled the emerald dress over her head. The fabric slid over her bare bottom.

"Meet me up here for lunch," he ordered in a husky voice.

The candle of warmth flickering in her tummy turned into an all-out blaze. "You have a luncheon, and I have a planning meeting with Milton, my boss."

"I can skip a rubber chicken meal."

She gasped in mock horror and pressed a hand to her chest. "Our chef doesn't do rubber chicken. And it'll be braised pork, fingerling potatoes and maple-glazed carrots followed by Amaretto cheesecake. I planned the menu myself."

"I'd rather have you."

She felt her heart slipping. No. This was infatuation. Nothing more. "I'll call your cell number when I finish with Milton. I might be able to squeeze you in."

His eyebrow hiked, insinuating a naughty double entendre. "Squeeze me in?"

Her cheeks heated. "That's not what I meant, and you know it."

His grin widened. He closed the distance between them, cupped her face and kissed her hard on the mouth, then stroked a hand over her bare bottom. "I'll see you in a few hours."

Her heart skidded down a slippery slope and fell with a big, messy splat.

Omigod. This wasn't infatuation at all. She was falling

in love with Trent Hightower, her transitory lover, a man who would dump her exactly the way David had.

Trent couldn't concentrate. The past four hours had been a blur.

For the first time in his career he couldn't focus on the materials being presented to him, and he didn't give a rat's ass about the state of the art electronics currently being demonstrated. Some CEO he'd turned out to be. His pilots and clients wouldn't be happy with him. They counted on Hightower Aviation having the most up-to-date equipment available.

The exhibition hall's double doors opened again, drawing his eye for the umpteenth time. He kept expecting Paige to duck in to check the status of the event.

Pantiless Paige.

His smartass comment earlier had turned out to be annoyingly prophetic. The idea of her waltzing commando through the hotel corridors had haunted him all morning.

He tugged at the suddenly too-tight collar of his custom-fitted shirt and tried to concentrate. Hard to do when his blood had pooled in his crotch.

His cell phone vibrated in his pocket, startling him and kicking his heart into overdrive. Paige. Finally. He excused himself from the vendor and headed for a quiet corner of the vast room. Eager to talk to her, he flicked open the phone. "It's about time you called."

"Well, hello to you, too, big brother."

Nicole. Not Paige. He battled disappointment on hearing his sister's voice and mentally shifted gears. "What's the news?"

"The McCauley sisters have given me a tentative yes.

If all goes according to plan, they'll be arriving on your plane with an ETA of nine Sunday morning."

That was good news, so why did his neck kink up? Because an early arrival time meant he had less than seventy-two hours left with Paige. Once her sisters arrived they'd occupy her time.

That was exactly what he wanted, and yet his chest felt as heavy as it had that day when he was eight and his father had informed him Santa was a hired employee.

But his weird mood wasn't his sister's fault. Nicole had done her job. "Good work. Thanks."

"Hey, are you okay?" A personal question. Territory the Hightowers didn't enter. But Paige did. She waded right in and wheedled information out of him he'd had no intention of sharing.

"I'm fine."

"You don't sound as pleased by the success of your plan as I'd expected."

Because he wasn't. "I'm in the middle of the trade show."

"Oh. Sorry. But I didn't think you'd want to wait until tonight to get the message on your room phone."

"Correct assumption. Thanks for calling." He clicked the phone shut and shoved it back into his pocket.

His damage control plan was right on track—albeit with a few extremely sensual detours. Detours that cost him precious networking time. But somehow he couldn't work up any concern over the missed connections even though it meant he'd have to work harder to make up for dodging his duty after he returned home. It was a fair trade-off and a necessary one if he wanted to avoid disaster.

He'd enjoy his time with Paige, then hopefully her sisters would monopolize her from the moment they touched down Sunday morning and get her out of the hotel to see some of those sights she'd mentioned. Brent and Luanne weren't due to arrive until late Sunday afternoon. That was cutting it close, but he was used to juggling tight deadlines.

He'd be leaving on Monday, as soon as his flight crew had logged the required downtime, and he'd still have time to organize his thoughts before the critical board meeting on Tuesday.

Everything was going exactly according to schedule. What more could he want? Nothing. Nada. So why did he still feel unsettled?

His phone buzzed again. This time he checked the caller's identity. *Paige.* Adrenaline shot through his system, making his pulse spike. In less than a week Paige McCauley had become as adept at throttling up his engines as flying or roller coaster rides ever had. "Have you finished with your boss?"

"Yes." Her breathless voice swept over him with the same physical punch as the scrape of her fingernails down his spine had earlier this morning.

"Meet me upstairs."

Her quiet chuckle circulated through him like an aphrodisiac. "If I meet you in your suite, neither of us will get any lunch. Meet me by the service elevator at the end of the Calypso hallway instead, and I'll show you my favorite place in the hotel."

He caught himself grinning. And for the first time since he'd taken over as HAMC's CEO, Trent walked away from work in the middle of the day, and he honestly didn't care if he made it back to the convention before tomorrow morning. The vendors could make an appointment and demonstrate their wares in his office when he returned to Knoxville.

Paige stood at the top of the world—or at least as close to it as she'd ever get.

Her personal paradise consisted of a thirty-foot-wide

circle of terracotta tiles with a twelve-by-twelve green-house parked in the center of it. The private patio on top of the hotel's tallest tower was off-limits to guests, but she often escaped here.

"I feel like I can see the world from here," she said without looking at Trent. Knowing that her feelings had crossed the line from lust to love made it difficult to look him in the eye. She was desperately afraid he'd guess, and the last thing she needed was another embarrassing goodbye scene.

She ducked her head and stubbed her toe on the tiled decking. "That probably sounds stupid to a guy who has traveled the globe."

He held the picnic basket she'd borrowed from the kitchen in one hand and turned a slow circle, scanning the city of Vegas spread out as far as the eye could see. "No. It doesn't. The view is incredible."

"When I look at the Paris Hotel's Eiffel Tower I think about the day I'll visit the real one in Paris. It's the same with the Venetian. One day I will get to Venice and ride in a real gondola."

He strolled toward her and cupped her shoulder. "You'll love both. I'm sorry I won't be there to share them with you."

Her breath caught at the sincerity in his voice and the hollowness his words left inside her. No. He wouldn't be there. A future together had never been part of their plan, and the reminder saddened her. But she didn't dare show it and frighten him away. She had a few days left of his company and she intended to make every second a good one.

She pivoted and gestured to the glass structure in the center of the patio circle. "This is our chef's private garden. I'm lucky he's willing to share it with me. He grows a lot of his herbs up here."

"You come up here alone with him?"

"Of course."

"How old is this guy?"

His bristly questions surprised and pleased her. If only it were jealously. "He's my father's age. He goes by the name of Henri, and studied in a French culinary school, but don't tell anyone his real name is Henry, and he's a Georgia farm boy with a green thumb. He lived in Europe long enough to banish all traces of Georgia's red clay from his roots."

"Is that why you like him? Because he's erased his southern roots."

Grimacing, Paige nodded. "I'm trying to lose my accent."

"Don't. It's charming."

Her eyebrows shot up. "That's only because you're from Tennessee and Southern sounds normal to you. But I notice *you* don't have an accent."

He shrugged. "Private schools and international nannies will do that."

"You had nannies?"

"My parents traveled a lot and left us behind."

How sad. "My sisters and I never had strangers watch us. We had each other. The older ones babysat me and then I babysat the younger ones. There's nothing like knowing family will always be there for you no matter how bad it gets."

He studied the horizon. "I envy you that."

She had to strain to hear his nearly inaudible comment. "I can see where you might not be close to your sisters, but what about your brother?"

"My father raised us to be competitors, not friends."

Her heart ached for him. He'd come from a large family, but from the sounds of it he might as well have grown up an only child. Paige gave his forearm a squeeze. "I'm sorry. My sisters and I can be competitive, but ultimately, we were the McCauley team. Take on one of us and you're facing the whole bunch."

His somber expression made her wince.

Way to go, Paige. Kill the mood. She crooked her finger. "Follow me. The picnic table is back here."

She led him around the greenhouse to the round iron table and chairs set up on the other side. She sat, unzipped and discarded her boots and let the radiant warmth of the tiles seep into her soles. This was as close to running barefoot through the grass or sand back home as she could get.

"Another thing I miss about South Carolina is the seasons. Here it is late December in Vegas and with the sun shining on us it's warm enough that we don't even need a jacket."

"You enjoy cold weather?"

"Sure, and even the occasional snow. Not that we had much of that in the South Carolina low country, but every few years we'd get a surprise."

"You'd like Knoxville. We get snow and have four full seasons. In the spring and summer Tennessee is so green it's like flying over a rolling emerald carpet." He opened his mouth as if to add more, then closed it again, leaving her curious as to what he'd chosen not to say.

"Knoxville's not on my short list of places to see, but maybe one day when I've checked off the rest on my list I'll get to explore Tennessee." But not with Trent.

She took the basket from him, set it on the table and unpacked their lunch of chipotle chicken, grilled vegetables, foccacia and, of course, dessert.

"Oreos?" He took the bag of cookies from her.

She withdrew a thermos and two highball glasses. "No one should miss the Oreo experience."

"Even without a crisis?"

That would come soon enough. Monday, his departure day, to be precise. "Especially without a crisis. I even brought milk for dunking them."

His gaze softened on her face, then flicked to the greenhouse. "How often does your chef come up for herbs?"

"Only in the morning. Why?"

"I'm wondering if we'll be interrupted if I take you into the greenhouse."

The passionate intent in his eyes sent arousal racing through her like a drought-fueled forest fire. "I— I don't know. But getting caught would probably get me fired."

"Willing to risk it?"

And be forced to return home in disgrace? She'd return when she was ready and not before. "No."

"Are you sure?"

Right now she wasn't sure of anything except that saying goodbye to Trent was going to hurt. "Not this time."

He cupped her face and lifted her chin. His kiss blistered her with his hunger. "You have until Monday to change your mind."

And she was tempted, tempted to abandon sanity and follow her heart right up until the crash.

Don't do it. Don't do it. Don't do it.

Paige hit the enter button on her computer keyboard Friday afternoon. The job search engine filled her screen, listing available assistant hotel event coordinator positions in the Knoxville area. There were two. Her heart pounded in panic and her hands shook over the keys.

Stupid. What are you doing? This is no better than practicing writing a married name. That was something her sisters had often done with each school crush.

She clicked her mouse and closed the window. She and

Trent would not be sharing names, cities or anything else after Monday.

But he's everything you've ever dreamed of in a lover.

Her phone rang. She grabbed the receiver. "Paige McCauley. How may I help you?"

"By getting your chef to share his brownie recipe," her youngest sister replied.

"Sammie, what a surprise. Are you home from school?"

"Yep. I'm on winter break and, of course, I am working at the store for the holiday rush. But I'm taking my dinner hour, so I decided to call. What's up?"

For once, Paige didn't have to get creative or prevaricate. "I'm dating a hot guy. We've been riding roller coasters."

"Dad will be jealous that you've replaced him. Details?"

"Trent's tall, blond, gorgeous, built, smart, fun and sexy. He has the most amazing teal eyes and—"

"You're at a loss for words, I see. So what are you two doing for Christmas?"

Paige's bubble of happiness burst. "I'm staying close to the hotel. There won't be any conventions over the holiday, but a lot of staffers will be on vacation."

All true, she told herself, but guilt twisted her stomach because she was one of the employees with a vacation scheduled to begin as soon as the aviation conference ended.

"If I have any free time I'll— We'll check out some of the hot spots. What about you guys? Same ol', same old?"

She never thought she'd see the day when she missed the tried and true, tired McCauley rituals.

"You know how it is."

"Yes." A strong wave of homesickness struck her. "Is the tree already decorated?"

"Yes. One of these days we are going to have to throw out those old ornaments and get some new stuff."

"Don't you dare. Mom would be heartbroken. Our grandmothers made some of those decorations." But when Paige had been Sammie's age she'd felt the same way. She always wanted something new and different. Twenty-one seemed like an aeon ago instead of only seven years.

"So…is there any chance you're lying and you really intend to spring a surprise visit on us?"

"No. I wish I was."

Silence seconds passed, and with Sammie, there was never silence. "Spill it, Sammie."

"There's one piece of news that I thought I might share. Kelly and Jessie are going to kill me if they find out I told you, but…you need to know. For whenever you decide to come home. And I hope that will be sooner than later."

Paige braced herself. "Okay, shoot."

"David's back."

The air rushed from Paige's lungs and a cool sweat beaded her upper lip. "For a visit?"

"To stay. He got laid off from his pretentious investment firm. He's taken a job at City Bank."

Paige turned the knowledge over in her head, trying to make sense of her tangled emotions. But the last thing she wanted was her sister's pity, so she fought to keep her feelings out of her voice. "I'm sorry to hear that. He was excited about Manhattan."

"If you ask me, the butthead got what he deserved."

Sammie's anger seeped into Paige, mixing with a large dose of resentment. She'd let David's defection run her out of her home state, and his return would keep her away until she found the courage to face the whispers about their broken relationship and the speculation about the cause or until she could return triumphantly—actually living the exciting life everyone believed she had. Because she couldn't go home and lie. Everyone would see right through her.

"Give him my best next time you see him," she said in as breezy a tone as she could muster.

"Sis, somebody needs to teach you how to make a guy pay for hurting you. Revenge keeps a body warm. Hey, I'm still in school and I already know how to bring the bastards to their knees."

Paige forced a smile to her face and hoped it carried over through her voice. "Sammie, look where I am now. I work for a top-notch Vegas hotel. I have the job of my dreams, and I've reached step two in my ten-year plan. Life is good. David did me a favor."

Her breath caught as she realized the truth in her statement. If she'd married David, she would have taken whatever job she could get that would allow her to live with him. His dreams and his career would have always come first, and her goal of working her way around the globe and up the hotel ladder would never have launched. And her plan to have ticked off all the cities on her must-see list by the time she hit forty in twelve years wouldn't even be part of the equation.

A weight lifted from her shoulders. She was in a good place right now. Sure, come Monday, she had a feeling she was going to need a case of Oreos, a gallon of milk and a shoulder to cry on. But until then, she was exactly where she wanted and needed to be.

Nine

Trent shifted on his feet in the Lagoon's aquarium-filled lobby Friday evening and checked his watch again. It read two minutes later than it had the last time he'd checked.

"In a hurry to go somewhere?"

Donnie. Trent harnessed his irritation and turned. "I have a dinner appointment."

"With our pretty blonde?"

Trent took umbrage at *our,* but refused to acknowledge Donnie's successful hit. "Yes."

"Paige is a sweet little morsel. But then I've always been partial to Southern girls. Your brother is, too, apparently."

Alarm pricked Trent's nape. Donnie knew Brent had been with Paige last year, and the bastard was toying with him. "Don't let me keep you from dinner. The comedian slated for tonight's entertainment is a good one."

"I don't care about the comedian. I have enough jokers

as clients already. So you're keeping your women all in the family, eh? Is Paige into the twin thing?"

Trent's fists clenched. It took everything he had not to punch the dentures right out of Donnie's smirking mouth. "That's none of your business."

"I could have sworn I saw Brent wearing your name badge last year."

"You might want to mention your vision problems to your optometrist."

Donnie looked ready to launch another verbal volley, but then his gaze shot toward the far side of the lobby. He clicked into alert mode. His jackass demeanor switched over to smooth operator mode, putting Trent on guard.

"Here's our girl now," Donnie taunted.

Trent's mental gears clanked. Would the devious bastard spill the beans? Trent decided to use a tactic he'd refused to employ in the past. Previously, he'd lived by the rule that what other people did—other than his family, that is— was their own business, but tonight he'd use the weapons in his arsenal. He had to.

"Does your wife know about you and Sapphire Electronics' product demonstrator? Benita has worked the past three conferences, hasn't she?"

Donnie stiffened and panic flashed briefly in his eyes, then his lips curled in a wily fox grin. "Well played, Hightower."

Their gazes held, but Trent refused to back down. If this asshole hurt Paige, he would pay. Dearly.

"Good evening, gentlemen."

Donnie broke eye contact first and looked at her. "Well, aren't you a sight for these tired, Texas eyes? Evening, Miz McCauley."

"Hello, Donnie." Paige was as innocent as a lamb being led to slaughter. Either he or Donnie could hurt her and she wouldn't even see it coming. The protectiveness surging inside him surprised him. But it was his own interests he was protecting and not just hers, he assured himself.

Despite his leverage, Trent didn't trust his adversary. He stepped between Paige and Donnie. "Donnie needs to get to the banquet hall. Let's go."

"I'm sure I can make time for a drink in the bar," Donnie added.

"We can't." Trent grasped Paige's elbow and hustled her toward the door, only just then noticing the dry cleaning bag on her arm. "You retrieved your clothing from my room."

"I had the maid let me in. I hope you don't mind, but with the twice daily housekeeping service in your level of suite, the maid would have folded my dirty underwear and moved them off the bed where I left them. The thought of a stranger handling my dirty panties grossed me out."

That reminded him she wasn't wearing any. But a more urgent issue superseded that knowledge. Paige had been in his suite without him. He didn't like anyone invading his privacy. He'd never given a lover a key to his home or even allowed one to stay overnight in his wing of the mansion he shared with his parents. It was bad enough that he'd let Paige spend the night in his suite, but the idea of her—or anyone other than his personal housekeeper—having free range of his space disturbed him.

He searched his mind for anything he might have left laying out that might clue Paige into Brent's identity and give the deception away, but he couldn't come up with anything. "You could have called me."

"I would have if you hadn't been leading a seminar when I remembered and had time to go upstairs. I'm sorry if my invading your space makes you uncomfortable. I won't do it again."

The incident was over and couldn't be changed. But he would make sure it didn't happen again. "Forget it. Let's go to your place, then we'll tackle The NASCAR Café and the roller coaster."

He accompanied her to her car and opened her door for her. She backed up to the high Jeep seat to hop in, once again reminding him that she wasn't wearing panties—not that the thought had strayed far from his brain all day. His blood took a southerly trajectory. He scanned the parking deck around them. Walls screened two sides of the car. Paige had backed into the space. Her Jeep's door blocked the view from the front. The structure was well lit, but deserted.

"You need to park closer to a security camera. There are none in this corner," he said as he stepped between her knees and placed his hands on her bare legs.

She gasped and her rounded eyes searched his. "What are you doing?"

"Do you know how hot it makes me to know I can touch you here? Like this?" He swept his fingertips up the inside of her thighs. The higher he ascended, the warmer her skin became until she almost scorched him.

"Trent," she scolded in a scandalized whisper.

He found her curls—damp curls—and dipped between her folds. "You're very wet. Did being bare all day arouse you?"

She bit her lip and swallowed hard. "Maybe."

He stroked her moisture over her sensitive flesh, circling again and again until her cheeks darkened, her lids descended and her breaths quickened.

She slapped a hand over his. "We can't do this here."

They shouldn't. Public displays had never been his style. Until now. Paige had him breaking all kinds of rules. He didn't know what in the hell she'd done to him, but he wanted to make her come. *Now.* "You want to."

She stared at him through thick eyelashes. "Yes."

"No one can see, Paige. Let it happen." He continued his caresses until her muscles bunched and her thighs quivered, then clamped hard on his. She shoved a knuckle to her mouth, but couldn't completely stifle her whimpers as an orgasm ripped through her, making her bottom lift off the seat.

He was so hard he ached. But he would wait until he got her home and naked. He pressed a quick kiss on her lips then carried his fingers to his mouth and tasted her essence on his tongue and smelled her arousal on his skin. Hunger exploded inside him. "Let's get to your place."

She sighed with a sleepy, satisfied smile on her face. "I think you'd better drive. My legs are too weak."

He was going to miss that smile, he realized with a shock.

She braced herself on his forearms and scooted from the vehicle, sliding against him. Rockets of heat launched through him and he groaned. Clinging to his biceps, she wobbled on her heels. He didn't know or care whether she did so to tease him or because she was genuinely unsteady. He had to rein in his desire before he made a bigger fool of himself than his brother had. Getting arrested for indecent exposure in the Lagoon's parking deck wouldn't help Trent's cause with the HAMC board.

But he had to admit Paige tempted him to say to hell with the consequences, drop his pants and drive into her wet heat right here, right now.

And that was probably how his brother had ended up in trouble. Paige had worked her magic on both of them. And for the first time in his life, Trent was jealous of his brother—and whatever it was Brent had shared with Paige twelve months ago.

* * *

Paige's body still hummed with arousal despite the orgasm. Would Trent finish what he'd started in the parking lot?

She held her apartment door open for him, hoping for one more opportunity to soak up as much of him and his lovemaking as possible. "Come in."

He seemed oddly reluctant to enter, given he'd made her melt ten minutes earlier. "Trent, I'm not a black widow spider. I don't kill my mate after he's given me what I need."

His lips twitched. "I'm glad to hear that."

"I have a bottle of South Carolina Riesling in the fridge. Would you like a glass while I change?"

"No, thanks." He scanned the photos in her living room. "Which sister is which?"

She followed him across the room and lifted the picture he'd indicated. She tapped the glass. "This is Kelly, the oldest. That's her little boy, Nate."

His gaze found hers. "The one she almost didn't have?"

He remembered. "Yes. Nate's another thing I miss. He's growing like a weed." But a man didn't want to hear a woman yap about babies. It made them nervous. "Next in line is Jessie, the real-estate agent, then Ashley, the nurse, and finally Sammie."

"The soon-to-be school teacher."

"Yes. Do you have any pictures of your brother and sisters?"

"No."

"None? Not even on your laptop computer?"

"No. I imagine that will change when my sisters and sister-in-law give birth."

"You have three pregnant women in the family?"

"Yes."

"You'll definitely need to keep a camera handy. Babies grow up so fast." Oops. The baby thing again. "I make a mean fettuccini Alfredo. We could relax and eat here and save the roller coaster for tomorrow night."

"No. We'll try the NASCAR Café as soon as you change."

"You're sure? I wouldn't mind having you for dessert." Her cheeks burned over her boldness, but the flare of passion in his eyes made her glad she'd taken the leap.

"We'll revisit that after we ride the coaster."

"Okay." But that didn't mean she'd accept his refusal easily. She'd promised herself she'd be more like Jessie and ask for what she wanted. Might as well start now. She turned her back to him. "Unzip me?"

After a moment his knuckle brushed her nape. The zipper descended, allowing air to cool her spine. She shrugged her shoulders, and the dress slid to her ankles, leaving her naked except for her bra and boots. Reaching behind her back, she flicked open her bra, removed it and then bent over very slowly to scoop up both items. Hooking them over her fingertips, she straightened and pivoted.

Trent's hot gaze raked her from head to breasts to hips then legs and back. The rising bulge behind his fly rewarded her bravery. She smiled. Maybe Jessie had been right when she'd claimed seducing a man was more fun than shopping. "I'll be right back."

She strolled toward her bedroom, putting as much sway in her walk as she could muster. She heard movement behind her then his hand clamped on her wrist. He spun her around and backed her against wall so quickly she lost her breath. His pelvis pinned her in place.

"You are a tease, Paige McCauley," he said without malice, but with a dangerous glint in his eyes that sent her blood humming.

"Oh, please, you made me come in a parking deck. Consider it payback."

His hands briskly brushed down her body, over her breasts, her waist, then found the sensitive spot between her legs. "Is that a complaint?"

A moan squeezed past her tightly mashed lips as he unerringly circled with exactly the right pressure and tempo to rekindle her desire. With a few deft strokes he created a knot of tension low in her belly.

"No. But Trent, I want to please you, too. Only you're playing hard to get."

He caught her hand and carried it to his erection. "Definitely hard."

She rubbed him through his jeans and he thickened even more. Trent slammed his mouth over hers in a kiss of pure hunger and aggression. She wiggled her fingers between them to unbutton his jeans, then slid down his zipper and slipped her hand inside. His heat burned her through his underwear. She shoved his jeans and boxers out of the way and curled her fingers around his hot, satiny flesh.

He broke the kiss to whistle in a breath, then covered her fist with his and guided her with long, slow strokes. She used her other hand to smooth the slick droplet over the engorged head.

He threw back his head, straining the tendons of his neck. "The way you touch me is…damned good."

His hoarse words filled her with satisfaction. He wouldn't dare forget her by this time next year. Nor would she forget him. Trent Hightower had gotten under her skin as permanently as a tattoo.

He stabbed a hand into his back pocket, withdrew a condom and quickly applied it. "Dessert first tonight."

His hand hooked her leg behind her knee, then he

lifted her leather-booted calf to his hip and drove in, forcing her breath from her lungs with the delicious depth of his penetration. She clung to his shoulders as he plunged and withdrew again and again. Her back skidded against the wall with each powerful thrust. With his eyes tightly shut and his jaw clenched, his face twisted as if he were in agony—the same wonderful agony she shared of wanting satisfaction and wanting to make the pleasure last.

His hands cupped her breasts and tweaked her nipples. Her head tilted to the side as a delicious sensation washed over her, making her skin hot and weighting her eyelids. His breath steamed her neck then he nipped her. The sharp love bite sent a shock through her and pushed her toward the edge of release. He thrust deeply and swiveled his hips, sending her body into spasms of pleasure.

His pace increased. She held on tight, fisting her fingers in his T-shirt, then raking her nails down his back. She matched every push and then he groaned against her neck and hammered even harder. His back bowed. He jerked once, twice, a third time, then his weight settled on her, a heavy, heaving blanket that she never wanted to let go.

She ran her hand over his hair, cradling his face to her neck. She loved him and she was going to lose him.

Unless you do something about it.

The voice in her head sounded a lot like Jessie taunting her. Paige's heart pounded harder. She'd lost David because she hadn't cared enough to fight for him. She wasn't going to let Trent go as easily. Tomorrow she'd pull up the job Web site again and contact the Knoxville hotels to test for interest.

Then she'd find a way to convince Trent not to let a great relationship slip through his fingers.

* * *

The familiar rush working its way through Trent as he unlocked the door to his suite Saturday evening had nothing to do with flying airplanes or riding roller coasters and everything to do with the curvy blonde monopolizing his time and thoughts.

Waking in Paige's arms this morning had felt good—*right*—as though he was finally where he was supposed to be. He'd woken before dawn and lain in her bed, watching her sleep. Despite the staggering amount of work waiting for him at the hotel, he'd wanted to say to hell with work, kiss her awake, make love to her, then spend the rest of the day alone with her in her apartment.

That staggering realization had sent him running. Nothing came between him and work. Especially women. He'd worked double-time today, attending seminars and networking during the breaks, trying to make the connections he'd missed during his evenings away from the hotel with Paige.

He dropped his briefcase by the workstation and loosened the necktie choking him. He didn't know what in the hell had come over him yesterday. He'd lost control: first the parking deck, then against wall of Paige's hallway. After the roller coaster and a shared bottle of her South Carolina wine, he'd give her a serious case of rug burn by taking her on her living-room floor and then again in her bed. He hadn't been able to get enough of her.

Despite yesterday's frat boy actions, a strange urgency still rode him today. It was more than just being horny. It was the knowledge that he had only fifteen hours left with Paige before her sisters arrived. Fifteen short hours to soak up every drop of her Southern charm. One more night. Then she'd be gone.

Just as he'd planned.

It wasn't enough. He wanted more. He wanted—

Paige. He wanted Paige.

He'd fallen in love with his brother's ex-lover.

Warning sirens screeched in his skull. A chill enveloped him and a crushing sensation settled on his chest. He stabbed a hand through his hair and headed for the minibar where he poured an airplane bottle of bourbon into a glass and knocked it back straight. The liquid burned a path down his throat and settled like a pool of lava in his belly.

He'd taken a bad situation and turned it into a freaking disaster by lying to Paige. Not even his siblings could bungle something this badly.

To have Paige in his life for more than one stolen week he'd have to risk everything by telling her the truth. But coming clean also meant risking his goals for HAMC, the family's financial coffers and his brother's marriage if his greedy sister-in-law learned the details of Brent's affair.

Was the steep price worth it?

He poured himself another drink and stared into the amber liquid.

Yes. The prize—Paige—outweighed the risks.

His life was empty, and he had no one but himself to blame. He'd *made* it that way by cutting out all the things he enjoyed. He worked, slept and worked more. He had only one friend whom he saw infrequently, and he didn't speak to his family unless it pertained to work or because one of them had screwed up, and then he talked at them rather than with them.

He didn't have to worry about killing himself with his adrenaline pursuits. He'd already died in every way that counted. He'd become a robot programmed with an unfeeling get-the-job-done mentality.

Paige had changed that. She'd made him feel more than ambition and anger toward his father for forcing him into this job and his family for always needing to be bailed out. Paige had brought him back to life by challenging him to leave the cell he'd locked himself in. Sure, his father's addictions would always be an issue lurking in the background like a genetic predisposition toward cancer, but with Paige beside him he could monitor it and control it.

But to have a chance with her he needed to convince her to forgive him for deceiving her. On the pro side, if anyone could understand his reasons for lying, Paige would. She shared the clean-up role in her family, and she would appreciate the relationships that drove him. Like him, she didn't back away from the tough topics.

On the con side, Paige was the most honest person he'd ever met. She'd revealed things to him and shared her pain with an openness he'd never encountered.

Telling her the truth was a risk he had to take. But not yet. He'd wait until after her sisters' visit. Paige needed the next four days to reconnect with the ones she loved. Having her family here would make her holiday.

He hadn't intended flying her siblings in to be a gift, but he knew he couldn't have chosen a better one if he'd racked his brain for months.

For now, he'd keep his secret. Monday he'd fly out for Tuesday's board meeting as planned, then he'd return to meet Paige's sisters before they flew home Wednesday night. He'd give himself the two days before Christmas to win Paige's heart.

Warm lips trailed down Paige's spine, weaving in and out of a hazy dream of lying on a tropical beach with Trent.

"Paige, wake up."

"Mmm."

Teeth nipped her butt, jolting her awake. She flipped onto her back. Trent lay grinning beside her in the bed of his hotel suite. "I have a surprise for you. You need to get dressed."

"A surprise?" She swept her hair out of her face. Excitement trickled through her. "What is it?"

His boyish flash of teeth and sparkling eyes quickened her pulse. "Something you'll like. But first you need to hit the shower."

"I have to be dressed for this surprise?"

"Yes."

She loved him so much the words bumped against the back of her teeth like a battering ram, wanting to escape. But she bit her tongue. It was too soon. He wasn't ready for a soul-baring declaration. The look in his eyes tempted her to throw caution into the winds.

But not yet.

How had it happened? How had she allowed this man who was supposed to be nothing more than a transitory phase of her life and a way to heal the past so she could move forward sink deep into her heart? She couldn't find the answer as she looked up at him. "Are you joining me?"

"Not this time. You shower first."

She threw back the covers and rose, relishing his hungry gaze raking her body and the hiss of his breath. "It's Sunday. The conference is over. I'm free to spend the day with you."

A secretive smile twitched his lips. "Good. Go. I'll order breakfast for us."

She rushed through her shower, drying her hair and applying her makeup all the while trying to figure out what kind of surprise Trent would give her. Would it be the first or the last? The odds of the latter were slim given what he'd said about never wanting to marry. But she couldn't let the odds keep her from trying to win him over.

She joined him in the living room. The smell of bacon and eggs and toast made her stomach growl, but the pot of strongly scented coffee on the table made her hustle forward. Trent handed her a filled mug.

She could get used to mornings like this—waking late and sharing breakfast with Trent. She burned her tongue trying to wash the lump from her throat and reached for a slice of chilled pineapple. She'd just taken a bite when her cell phone rang. Chewing and swallowing quickly, she raced across the room and snatched it from the dresser.

Caller ID said The Lagoon. She groaned, "Work."

"Answer it."

She grimaced. "This is Paige."

"Hi, Paige. It's Andy at the front desk. We have…an issue that we need you to come down here and deal with."

Her heart sank. She didn't want anything to rob even one second of her time with Trent today. "An issue?"

"Yes."

"What's the problem?"

"I, um…can't say exactly."

Argh. It must be a difficult customer. She glanced at Trent, but he'd turned his back. "I take it the problem is standing right in front you?"

"Yes, ma'am."

"Isn't Janice the manager on duty?"

"She said this was your specialty."

Paige sighed. Even in Vegas she'd earned a reputation as a peacemaker when problems with clients or employees escalated. At the moment her gift of diplomacy seemed more like a curse.

"I'll be right there." She disconnected and joined Trent

by the window. "I have to go. I'm needed downstairs. Can your surprise wait until I get back?"

A smile he couldn't quite suppress played about Trent's very talented mouth, and he had a look in his eyes that she couldn't quite decipher. "It'll keep."

"Then I'll see you soon. I—" *Love you.* "Bye for now." She raced out of the suite before she could say anything crazy.

The elevator arrived almost instantly and descended blessedly fast. She hurried across the mezzanine. Keeping a ticked off customer waiting only exacerbated the situation.

A familiar face caught her eye. Trent? Already dressed? But that was impossible. She'd left him upstairs in his robe, and there was no way he could have gotten dressed and down here faster than she had. Her elevator hadn't made a single stop.

The woman beside him hooked a hand around his nape and pulled him down for a passionate kiss. He wound his arms around her, kissing her back with enthusiasm. A queer feeling Paige couldn't described snaked through her as she stared, unable to look away. Then she noticed his weird posture. He'd bowed his back out to accommodate the woman's very pregnant belly.

A frisson worked its way up her spine. Trent had said he wasn't married, but from the ring on his finger to the pregnant woman on his arm he looked very married.

He looked up and Paige's heart stalled.

That was Trent's face. But that wasn't Trent.

That was the man she'd almost slept with last year.

Ten

Trent Hightower had an identical twin.

Paige's body went numb, but her feet kept carrying forward, and her brain kept churning. The differences between the men were slight, but now that she'd met both, the dissimilarities were impossible to miss.

The man who had introduced himself to her as Trent last year had narrower shoulders and a less muscular build. He was still good-looking, but he didn't have the same sense of power or charisma as the version she'd left upstairs.

This Trent spotted her and his eyes widened. Even the unique shade of teal seemed muted. Her gaze dropped to his mouth—a mouth she had kissed. His bottom lip had a petulant set rather than one of sensual promise.

No wonder the one upstairs had walked past her as if he didn't remember her. He hadn't met her before that day a week ago when she'd stopped him in the hotel conference center. She couldn't make a man recall something that he'd never experienced. She'd called him Trent, and he hadn't corrected her.

One of the Trents had lied. But which one?

A confusing mix of emotions stirred inside her. Anger. Hurt. Betrayal. Sadness. Loss. She'd thought she'd found the man of her dreams. Instead, she'd found a liar or maybe a liar and an imposter.

But she wasn't going to run, and she wasn't going to hide. If she'd learned nothing else over this past year, she knew that taking the coward's way out only delayed the inevitable confrontation.

She stopped two yards from the couple. Part of her yearned to do as Sammie said and bring the bastard to his knees. But for all she knew, he might not have been married last year, and *he* might not be the liar.

But you've seen his brother at work. He's respected by his peers and he knows his stuff.

But this one was with those same people last year, wearing that same name on his conference badge.

The silent argument in her head only confused her more. She didn't know what to believe.

Determined to solve this puzzle, she confronted the man who'd supplied her most humiliating moment ever. "You must be the other Hightower brother. I feel as if I know you already."

This copy paled and shifted on his feet, then his gaze shot past her shoulder and his eyes filled with relief.

Before Paige could turn, a familiar hand settled on her waist. Her pulse did that crazy thing—the chaotic one it hadn't been doing in the presence of last year's guy, she noted absently.

"Paige, I see you've met my twin, Brent, and his wife,

Luanne. They've come to Vegas to celebrate their twelfth anniversary."

She didn't miss the warning in his voice, and one look at the tense, watchful expression on his face and she realized he'd known what had happened all along.

She stepped away from his hand and numbly nodded to the couple's hellos as she digested the unsettling fact that last year she'd almost had sex with a married man.

The good news: the man she had slept with wasn't an imposter. His name was Trent. The bad: he was still a liar. She'd been falling in love and he'd been playing a game— a lying game.

Had anything he'd said or done with her been genuine? Or had it all been faked to cover up his brother's attempted adultery? She felt used and manipulated.

"I take it this is my surprise?"

Regret darkened Trent's eyes. "No. Aren't you needed at the front desk?"

The front desk. She'd been called down to solve a crisis and she'd forgotten all about it. Grateful for the excuse, she nodded.

"Yes. If you will excuse me, I will leave you to your family reunion." She pivoted away and stalked toward the lobby with her heart breaking, but an underlying anger gave her the energy to keep functioning.

"Paige," Trent called from behind her. "Wait."

Not knowing what she'd say or even if she could speak without bursting into tears, she quickened her step and ducked through the casino for a shortcut. So much for her vow not to run from her problems anymore. It hadn't lasted five minutes. But she couldn't face him now. Not until she'd made sense of this fiasco.

"Paige," he called again. The front desk was in sight.

She'd almost made it when he grasped her elbow, forcing her to stop yards shy of the casino exit. She jerked it free and he sighed. "Let me explain."

She looked into the face she'd inexplicably and unexpected fallen in love with. "No explanations are necessary, Trent. We had a brief, no-strings-attached affair. That's all I wanted from you."

The words she'd uttered a few nights ago raked her throat raw. How could she know her feelings could change so drastically in such a short time?

"I want more." His gravely words launched her heart into a crazy rhythm.

She shook her head and edged toward reception. "There was never going to be more. Even if there was, how could I trust anything you said ever again? Go home, Trent. We've had our fun. Now we're done. Goodbye. Have a nice life."

Behind her a squeal shattered the quiet lobby. She knew that squeal. *Sammie?* Paige turned in time to see her sisters descending on her. Emotion welled in her throat, carrying with it a monsoon of tears. She blinked furiously and her vision cleared enough for her to recognize the exact second her perceptive sisters read her face. Almost as one, their arms opened.

She rushed into their loving embrace.

It was time to tell the truth.

All of it.

The McCauley sisters circled Paige and led her away.

Trent ached to go after her, but the raw hurt in her eyes had gored him. He'd let her talk to her sisters and calm down. Tomorrow, before he left for Knoxville and his board meeting he'd find her and explain. She'd understand.

She had to.

"Hey, bro," Brent said, coming up beside him. "What'd I miss?"

He wanted to punch his brother in the mouth—something he hadn't done since he was twelve. Afterward his mother had pulled him aside and explained that Brent was weaker and needed Trent's help and his protection. Trent had been playing watchdog ever since.

"Where's Luanne?"

"She went upstairs to rest."

"You weren't supposed to arrive until this afternoon."

Brent shrugged. "Luanne got impatient. What's the big deal?"

"Paige didn't know about you yet."

"You didn't tell her?"

"No, I was covering your ass."

"Wait a minute. You lied? *You?* Mr. Honesty-is-the-best-policy, Mr. Head-off-any-problem-before-it-starts? And you got caught pretending to be me, pretending to be you? That's rich." Brent's laughter only made Trent want to hit him more. And harder. His fists clenched by his side.

"It was stupid." Paige was right. You had to let your siblings learn from their mistakes or they'd be doomed to repeat them. Brent was a perfect example. He screwed up. Trent cleaned up. There were never any consequences for Brent.

Trent should have been honest with Paige and let Brent sweat out his own problems.

But it would have cost you.

Not as much as losing Paige would.

Brent shifted on his feet. "Yeah, okay, fine. But what's the harm? You're leaving Vegas tomorrow anyway, and you won't see Paige again for at least a year."

"I love her." Trent wanted the words back the second he

said them. He didn't do emotional displays or share personal secrets. But apparently Paige's brutal honesty was contagious.

Brent stopped his fidgeting. "Aren't you the one who told me twelve years ago that nobody could fall in love in a couple of days?"

Trent remembered the conversation well. He'd been trying to talk his brother out of getting married. "I might have been wrong."

"What? You? Wrong? Do you want to repeat that?"

His irritation with Brent rose a few more degrees. "Not particularly."

Brent's sarcastic smile turned into a sympathetic grimace. "I know a little about being in love and wanting a woman so much nothing else matters. And I know what it's like to want to make someone happy so badly that you'll do anything. Even ask your brother for sperm."

That caught Trent's attention. "What?"

"Can we go to the bar? I need a drink or three."

"It's 9:00 a.m."

"Back home it's lunchtime."

Trent pivoted and headed for the Blue Grotto, the closest bar. The place reminded him of Paige because she'd met Brent here. After they placed their orders—his for coffee he didn't want or need in his already burning stomach—he turned to his brother. "Explain."

The bartender set down the drinks. Brent downed his Scotch in one gulp and signaled for another. "I didn't sleep with Paige."

Muscles unraveled that Trent hadn't realized he'd tensed.

Brent fingered his empty glass. "I wanted to. I mean, she's hot and cute and everything. But…I love my wife."

"You and Luanne fight all the time."

"That's just our way. You know. Fight and then have blazing hot make-up sex. Haven't you ever had make-up sex?"

"No." He didn't keep women around long enough for that.

"It's killer good, man. Kicks it up a notch."

Trent wanted to signal a time out. His brother's sex life was not an interesting subject, and since the tabloids followed the Hightowers, Trent had never picked up the locker room talk habit out of concern that his words might end up in print.

"If you love Luanne, then why pick up women in bars? And what does it have to do with my sperm?"

When Brent looked at him, Trent saw a vulnerability he'd never seen in his brother's usually cocky face.

"Luanne has wanted kids for years. And we tried. But my plumbing wasn't…up to snuff. When she suggested we ask you for some of your identical DNA, I kinda lost it." He took a swig of liquor and stared into the mirror behind the bar. "That day I realized for the first time why you always dumped your girlfriends once I'd been with them. There are some things a guy just doesn't want to share with his twin."

But Trent realized he'd fallen in love with Paige even though he'd believed she'd been with Brent first. He didn't know exactly when that had ceased to be important—except for the fact that their entire relationship had been built on a lie.

"I'm sorry, Trent. Until that moment I'd always thought it funny that 99% of women couldn't tell us apart. But then to have Luanne say we were the same and it didn't matter who fathered her baby…" He finished his drink. "That hurt. Bad.

"Anyway, after Luanne suggested that we separated for

a few weeks. And like an idiot, I tried to prove my…manhood with other women. Only I couldn't."

Trent wanted to know. And he didn't. "Couldn't?"

"Get it up."

"For Paige?" Impossible.

"For any of them."

"How can that happen?"

"I know I don't have to explain the birds and bees to you. Your little black book resembles a phone book."

"Brent, you're young and healthy. You don't smoke or drink to excess. How can you have…a malfunction?" It had certainly never happened to him. Especially with Paige. Damn, all he had to do was think about her and his blood caught a tailwind south.

Brent shrugged. "I guess my heart knew I didn't want to go there and played chaperone."

"I'm not following here. Get back to why you needed my…help."

"I have a low sperm count."

"But Luanne is pregnant and I didn't—" He made a crude hand gesture to indicate something he couldn't put into words connected to his sister-in-law.

"Luanne got the name of a fertility specialist from our sister and we…made an appointment. The doctors worked some kind of magic with a centrifuge or something. He concentrated my stuff, and voilà. I'm going to be a daddy." Brent's wide grin said more than words about his happiness.

"Congratulations."

"You know, that's the first time you've said that."

"I thought you were making a mistake. Now I can see you're not."

"No. I'm not. I love her, and I want to raise a family with

her. So how about you? How did you fall in love in... How many days did it take?"

Trent scrolled back through the days of Paige's wicked, daring smiles, the challenges she issued in her slow, Southern drawl, her blunt honesty and the way she crawled into his head and tried to play amateur psychologist. He couldn't pinpoint the moment. "I don't know. Five? Six?"

Brent punched his shoulder. "A little slow on the uptake, aren't you, bro? Well, welcome to the club. The love shack is the best place to be when things are going right and the worst kind of hell when they're not."

Brent threw an arm over Trent's shoulder in an unfamiliar offer of support. "Now all we have to do is come up with a plan to win her back. Are you game?"

Trent looked into his brother's eyes and for the first time, experienced the sense of teamwork Paige shared with her sister.

"I'm game. And this is a game I don't intend to lose."

"Do I need to go back there and castrate the bastard?" Jessie growled the moment Paige swallowed the last sip of her Margarita.

"Hey," Kelly interjected, "I said no questions until she calmed down."

"If Senor Patron's best tequila won't calm her, nothing will," Ashley drawled.

Paige raised an eyebrow at her oldest sister. "And when did you give that order?"

"While you were asking the valet to hail our cab. You looked shattered when we found you, honey."

Shattered. Definitely.

Paige shook her head. She should be grateful her sisters had allowed her a drink and time to gather her thoughts before beginning the inquisition. "I guess that's why you gossiped more than the church choir during the taxi ride even though you know I hate gossip?"

Four heads nodded in unison. Her sisters had whisked her out of the hotel and applied their version of first aid without once asking why she needed it. They'd been there for her. No questions asked.

Jessie covered her hand. "So, about numb nuts... Do we need to hurt him?"

"No. Just let it go. He's leaving tomorrow anyway."

"Always the peacemaker," Ashley said in disgust. "C'mon, Paige, slug somebody for once. It feels good to release all the tension."

Paige shook her head and laughed despite her aching, breaking heart. "This from the E.R. nurse who spends her nights cleaning up the messes other people make when their emotions overrule their heads."

"Yes, well, that's them. This is us—*you.* Have another drink and fill us in." Ashley signaled the waitress of the swanky restaurant they'd dragged her into for another round of drinks.

"Hey! I haven't even had breakfast yet."

Kelly pointed to her glass. "There's lime juice, a slice of orange and a cherry in here. That's breakfast, but if you insist, we can order food. Although I have to admit the meal we had on the plane was amazing. But first I have to know, is the gorgeous blond hunk the guy who paid our way out here?"

Paige blinked. She wasn't drunk yet. Was she? "Wait a minute. The four of you didn't just decide to fly out here and surprise me? When I saw you I thought...Sammie's call... She made sure I was going to be here. When I saw you in the lobby I thought this was my Christmas present."

"Not exactly. Trent Hightower of Hightower Aviation

Management Corporation sent his private jet for us. Is he the jerk we saw you talking to?"

Her surprise. Paige gaped. "Yes."

"He also reserved rooms for us at the Bellagio," Sammie added.

Confused, Paige crumpled her cocktail napkin. "I can't believe he did that."

He couldn't have given her a more perfect gift, but why had he done it? Probably to get her out of the way before his brother arrived. Or maybe out of guilt for being such a liar.

"What did the bastard do to warrant all the money he's throwing our way?" Sammie asked.

"It's a long story."

Ashley slung an arm over Paige's shoulder and hugged her close. "The good ones always are. 'Once upon a time—' Now you fill in the rest."

Paige took a deep breath. "It all started when David dumped me."

"The rat bastard," Sammie chimed in.

Paige smiled at her baby sister. "Hey, I just realized this is the first time I've been drinking with you. You weren't old enough last time I was home."

Sammie swirled her straw. "Nope. I'm finally twenty-one and of legal drinking age now. But don't change the subject."

Busted. Paige grimaced. "I couldn't face the whispers. Every time I came home to visit I saw curtains twitching and fingers pointing. So…I ran. The Vegas job gave me the perfect way to leave South Carolina without losing face."

"We know that part. Get to the good stuff," Jessie prodded.

Paige stalled by sipping her fresh drink. "I wanted to start over in Vegas as…someone besides Good ol' Paige, the girl next door. That's why I borrowed Jessie's hairdresser and had the makeover right before I left. When I arrived here I added sexier clothing, satin sheets and a bunch of other stuff that I wouldn't want to be caught buying at home."

She toyed with the fruit clinging to the side of her glass. "But the Vegas singles scene isn't like home, and I didn't have you all along as backup. Two months after I started my job at the Lagoon I met a hotel guest who said his name was Trent Hightower. He was good-looking, friendly, easy to be with. But…there was no chemistry."

"Are you kidding me? That guy oozed sexy from his pores," Jessie said.

"It wasn't that guy. He has an identical twin. I decided to try to have my first one-night stand with him because he wasn't threatening or scary. He was fun, and I wanted—*needed*—to get over David. Anyway the night was a disaster." Sharing had never been her thing.

"Don't you dare start editing this story in your head. Spill it. All of it," Kelly ordered in her bossiest oldest sister tone.

Paige shrugged her stiff shoulders. "He couldn't… And I wasn't… So we didn't. Last Sunday I bumped into him—or at least I thought it was him—again. Only this year he was drop-dead sexy and we had a chemistry like nothing I've ever experienced. I decided to try again."

"You go girl." Jessie punched a fist in the air. "But…?"

"He pretended to be the same guy I'd met last year. He didn't tell me he'd never met me."

"That's weird. Why would he do that?" Ashley asked the question of the hour.

"Maybe because his brother—last year's guy—is married."

"Another rat bastard. The world is full of them." Sammie viciously stabbed the cherry in her glass with her cocktail skewer.

"How do you know this?" Kelly asked.

"I met him and his very pregnant wife in the lobby this morning on the way to the front desk. They're in town celebrating their twelfth anniversary."

Jessie sat back against the semicircular banquette. "And all this time I've been thinking you were bored out of your mind and lonely here in Vegas and too proud to admit it. Your life is more exciting than mine. Twins, for crying out loud."

Embarrassed that they'd pegged her life so accurately, Paige stiffened. "Hey, I only slept with one of them."

"The hot one," Jessie added and lifted her glass in a toast. "He looks like he'd be amazing in bed."

Heat seeped through Paige's pores. "He is."

Time for full disclosure. "My life isn't nearly as exciting as I've led you to believe. I mean, I love my job, but you're right, Jessie. I've been sitting at home alone most nights because I was too intimidated by the singles' scene." She took a deep breath. "So all those places I talked or wrote about…well, I haven't exactly been inside them. I've only driven past."

Ashley tightened her arm, hugging Paige close. "We know that, honey, but we also know you needed time to get over the butthead, so we let you do it your way."

"You knew?"

Four heads nodded in unison.

"And you don't hate me for lying?"

Jessie reached across the table and grabbed Paige's hand. "We knew you were trying to keep us from worrying about you. That's the thing about you, Paige. You're always there for everyone else, but you won't let anyone be there for you. But we are, y'know? We'd do anything for you."

"Including castrate the rat bastard." Sammie's bitter comment yanked a laugh from Paige's throat.

Kelly brushed back Paige's hair. "You tell us what you

want from us and we'll do it. We're the McCauley girls and nobody messes with us."

Paige's eyes stung as she scanned the faces around her and found unconditional love. She realized she wasn't the only strong McCauley girl. Her sisters would always be there for her and for each other. They were a team, each other's sounding boards and their anchors in stormy seas.

"Thank you. How long are you in town?"

"Until Wednesday evening," Ashley answered. "But maybe we shouldn't use the rat bastard's plane or let him pay for our hotel rooms."

Jessie shook her head vehemently. "Are you out of your mind? Let the man pay for his sins. So…do you really have to work over Christmas or was that you saving face again?"

Paige grimaced. "I have a week's vacation starting today, and I think we need to see everything Vegas has to offer."

"I'm in," Sammie chimed without hesitation.

"We're all in," Ashley added. "Ladies, let's tear this town up." She laid her hand in the middle of the table. The other McCauley girls did the same. Paige covered them all with both of hers.

Maybe by the time her sisters left her heart would be healed. Maybe not. But one thing was certain. She wasn't going to avoid going home anymore. She had her sisters in her corner to keep her strong. Even if she failed to handle the encounters with David and the gossips with grace and dignity, her sisters would still love and support her.

She didn't have to try to be Perfect Paige anymore.

Eleven

Trent stared at his brother across his hotel suite Monday evening. "How can five women completely disappear?"

He'd spent the day futilely searching for Paige. She hadn't been to her apartment and the suites Nicole had reserved for her sisters at the Bellagio were empty although the staff assured him the women hadn't checked out.

"Vegas isn't exactly a small town, bro." Brent rocked back on two legs of the dining-table chair. "You need to pack if you're going to make the board meeting tomorrow. Your crew's been on standby for hours."

Trent didn't want to leave. He had a sick feeling in the pit of his stomach that if he walked away without settling this he'd never see Paige again. That same gut feeling had kept him alive during some of his more asinine adrenaline junkie stunts.

"Screw the board meeting."

Brent's arms windmilled as he almost tipped over in the chair. "What did you say?"

"I'll cancel it."

Brent shot to his feet. "Are you out of your mind? What about your expansion plans? You've yammered about striking while the iron is hot and the economy is cold for months. It's the perfect time to take advantage of our floundering competition's losses and obtain their assets at rock bottom prices."

"I'm not leaving until I've talked to Paige."

"Trent, come on. HAMC is your baby. Don't drop her now."

Paige's words echoed in his head. She'd walked away so that her sisters could learn to handle their own issues. She'd trusted them to make the right decisions or, worst case scenario, learn from their mistakes. His siblings had accused him of being a control freak and always looking over their shoulders more than once. Maybe it was time to loosen up and trust them to do what was right for the company.

The decision lifted a weight off his shoulders. "You go."

Brent gaped. "Excuse me?"

"I'll call the airport and have them ready your jet. If you leave tonight you can be back tomorrow night. You'll be gone twenty-four hours tops. Luanne can spend that much time in the spa. She's always nagged you to ask for more responsibility—"

"You knew that?"

"Of course. Now's your chance. You present the expansion plan to the board."

"But…but…but…what if I screw up?"

"You're a born salesman, Brent. There's nobody better. Sell the idea. I'll sign my proxy over to you, and instead of me voting your shares the way we'd planned, you'll vote mine."

"And if I can't convince the board?"

"Then we've lost nothing." Except a goal Trent had worked toward for years.

His brother's expression filled with empathy. "You really have it bad for Paige."

"Yeah, I do. I know it's too soon to know if this will last, but being with her feels right. I've never— Nothing has ever felt this right. I don't want to live with regrets for the rest of my life because I didn't give us a shot."

Brent hesitated so long Trent thought he'd refuse. And then his brother straightened with heel-clicking military precision. A new respect entered his eyes. "I'm in. Do you have your presentation with you?"

"On my laptop. I was going to work on it while I was here, but…I spent time with Paige instead. It might need a little polishing. I'll e-mail the files to you and give you my handwritten notes."

Brent nodded. "I'll read them on the flight and be ready to present them by the time we land. Trent, thank you for trusting me. I won't let you down."

"I know you won't."

Home sweet home.

Paige stared at the family tree Christmas Eve morning. The branches sagged under the weight of the heirloom decorations either made or collected by various family members over the decades. How could she have ever thought them less than perfect?

Her sisters had convinced her to fly home with them on Trent's plane yesterday. The crew had been surprised by having an extra passenger, but they hadn't objected.

She had one more item on her checklist to clear up, and then her slate would truly be clean. The only difference was, she knew she didn't have to try to be more like Jessie. She could be herself—plain ol' dependable Paige, assistant hotel event manager and future world traveler.

The doorbell rang and her nerves tightened like guitar strings. David. She'd wanted their first encounter to be a private one.

She crossed the living room, took a bracing breath and opened the door. David's familiar face filled her with warmth, yet seeing him didn't make her pulse jump, but neither did it hurt to look at him the way it had hurt to look at Trent after she'd discovered his deception.

"Hello, David. Come in."

Wariness clouded his dark eyes as he glanced around. "Are your sisters here?"

"No. They're giving us some privacy."

"Oh. Good. Merry Christmas, Paige." His hug was awkward, stiff and blessedly brief.

"You, too. Thanks for coming by."

"Uh, yeah." Looking ill at ease, he shifted on his feet. "Look, Paige, I'm sorry for the way I ended things. I—"

"Don't be, David. It was the right thing to do. We'd become a habit. Don't get me wrong, I do love you, and I probably always will." He stiffened. "But like a really good friend. We grew up together, and we learned so much together. Those will always be special memories. But I'm not in love with you, not in the passionate way a husband and wife should be."

Painful lesson or not, she had Trent to thank for that realization.

David looked both relieved and disappointed. "No hard feelings?"

"No. None."

"So…can I buy you lunch or something?"

She searched his face, checking to make sure a meal was all he wanted to share, but she saw nothing remotely romantic or wistful in his expression. Then she thought about going to the local diner and eating under all those prying eyes. The grapevine would be humming before they opened their menus.

How many times had she told her sisters the only way to solve a problem was to face it head-on? The best way to quiet the gossips would be to prove they had nothing to talk about.

"I'd like that."

"Lucky for you our momma decided to have the family join you in Vegas for Christmas this year," Lauren, Trent's half sister, said as she slid onto the bar stool beside his. "It's not her usual exotic locale, or so I hear."

No, and he wasn't happy to have the family witness his misery. "Lauren, I'm not in the mood for company."

His plane had left Vegas with the McCauleys last night as scheduled, but with an extra passenger. Paige. The crew hadn't notified him until after they'd safely landed. He couldn't go after Paige because the rest of the HAMC fleet was committed elsewhere.

"Your plane has returned, but your crew's maxed out on hours. Our sister says you're in desperate need of a pilot. I'm volunteering."

Given he'd resented the hell out of Lauren when her existence had been sprung on them earlier this year, and he'd made her life…difficult, her offer surprised him. "You'll miss your first Christmas with Gage."

The love for his best friend in her smile choked him up. "Who do you think suggested I volunteer? You're family, Trent, and sometimes you're a bit of an ass, but Gage loves you and that's good enough for me. If you want to go to South Carolina, I'll get you there. It gives me an excuse to get my hands on that hot plane of yours again."

"Smart ass."

"Undeniably true. So what do you say? Wheels up in an hour?"

Gratitude tightened his chest. "I'll be ready."

Two hours later they were in the air, when Lauren's voice came over the speaker in the passenger cabin of his jet. "Trent, I need you in the cockpit."

"Why?"

"Get. Up. Here."

The strain in her voice had him hustling forward. "What's wrong?"

"Sit down. Strap in." She pointed to the copilot seat with one hand and covered her mouth with the other.

"I don't—"

"Do it."

He debated reminding her who was in charge, but her pallor and the sweat on her brow alarmed him. For the first time in over a decade, he entered the flight deck and strapped in then put on the head set. "What's going on?"

"Take the yoke."

"I can't fly."

"Yes, you can. You have your license even if you don't use it."

"Lauren—"

"I've engaged autopilot." She threw off her seat restraints and bolted for the back of the plane. The door to the bathroom slammed closed.

What in the hell was going on?

Adrenaline plowed through him, sharpening his senses and making the fine hairs on his nape stand on end. He shouldn't be here. Heart-pounding minutes passed while he waited for Lauren to return. He studied the three liquid crystal displays of the instrument panel and listened to the quiet whine of the twin turbofan engines.

He flexed his fingers then curled them around the yoke and scanned the horizon through the wraparound windscreen.

Memories surged through him. His fingers tightened on the controls and it all came rushing back. His love of flying. His knowledge of the mechanics of the process.

God, he'd missed this. He was tempted to disengage the autopilot and test his skills. But he wouldn't.

"You okay up here?" Lauren slid back into the pilot's seat. She had slightly more color in her cheeks. She smelled like mouthwash.

"Yes." And he meant it.

"Gage said you used to be a top-notch pilot."

He and his best friend had flown almost everywhere. "I was good. But that was a long time ago."

"Well, you're going to get a refresher course this trip." She yawned. "I need a nap."

"The hell you do. What's going on?"

She gave him a what's-your-problem glare, one he'd been on the receiving end of dozens of times when he'd been giving her a rough time, then she ruined it by smiling brilliantly. "If I tell you, you have to swear to keep it to yourself. It's a surprise. Even Gage doesn't know yet."

"Know what?"

"Jeez, you'd think a smart guy like you would figure it out. I'm nauseous and sleepy. I'm pregnant."

The news winded him and then a surprising twinge of jealousy twisted his stomach. He'd never thought about having kids. But he liked the idea. With Paige.

Would her brown eyes ever glow with the knowledge that

she carried his child? He might never get the chance to find out. He blinked away the choking emotions and focused on his half sister. "Congratulations. Gage will be thrilled."

"I hope so. I mean, this wasn't planned, but I think he'll be okay with the idea. Our mom, on the other hand, is going to *hate* being called Grandma. Can you see the immaculately dressed and always perfect Jacqui Hightower as a granny? But she'll have a house full of grandkids by the end of next year, so she'd better get used to it."

Lauren yawned again then she leaned back in her seat. "Keep an eye on the sky and the instruments. This baby is set to fly herself to our destination, but it never hurts to pay attention. Wake me before we land, and I'll talk you through it."

Her eyes closed.

Shock rippled through Trent. Lauren was going to trust him to bring them in safely? Then he recalled that she spent half her time as an instructor. She was used to putting her life in the hands of others.

The knowledge was humbling. He had trouble putting anything in the hands of others.

His grip tightened on the yoke. He couldn't wait to tell Paige she'd been right. He never should have walked away from what he loved. Flying or roller coasters. He wasn't his father. He'd shown no sign of being unable to handle the downtime between highs.

If anything, the adrenaline rush was an asset because it sharpened his reflexes, memory and skills.

"Lauren?"

"Mmm," she murmured back sleepily.

"Thanks for getting me up here."

Her lids fluttered open, revealing the same Hightower teal eyes he saw in the mirror each morning. "Trent, like me, you have flying on your DNA, and when you're born with a gift you can't walk away from it. Love is one of those gifts. When you find it, you can't let go."

How was it that the women in his life—specifically the ones he'd treated badly—had a better handle on reality than he did?

But he planned to take his sister's words to heart. He wasn't about to let Paige go without a fight.

From the sidewalk, Paige waved as her past—David— drove out of sight, leaving her free to face her future.

A future that seemed a bit bleak at the moment, but one that held potential. She shoved her hands into her coat pockets.

Her mother joined her. "Are you okay?"

"Yes. Very okay. David and I made peace. I'm sorry I put it off for so long. It's one of the reasons I avoided coming home."

"You needed time to heal, Paige. We each do that in our own way. Of all my girls you were always the most private, the one who needed to hibernate while you tended your wounds. We were trying to give you time and space. We knew you'd come back when you were ready."

A sad smile tugged Paige's lips. "'If you love someone, set them free. If they come back, they're yours. If they don't, they never were,'" she quoted her mother's favorite Richard Bach line.

"Yes. Exactly." Her mother's gaze sharpened on a white luxury sedan creeping down the street. "An outsider."

"How do you know?"

"Baby, I know every car in the neighborhood and almost all the ones in the town—at least until tourist season. That one's a rental. See the front plate?"

The setting sun glared on the windshield, blocking Paige's view of the occupants, but her heart went a little wild when the driver pulled to the curb in front of her and turned off the engine. Dread knotted in her stomach.

The driver's door opened. A dark blond head followed by the rest of Trent's tall, muscular body unfolded. His intent blue gaze locked with hers over the roof.

The urge to run bolted through her.

"Someone you know?" her mother asked.

"Yes."

"Want me to stay?"

Running solved nothing. "No. I can handle this."

"Holler if you change your mind."

Paige nodded without taking her eyes off Trent as he came around the front of the car and toward her.

"I'm sorry," he said before she could unglue her tongue from the roof of her mouth. "I should have told you the day we met that I didn't know you. I had reasons. At the time I thought they were good ones. But I was wrong. Please let me explain."

She hated unanswered questions. But did she dare risk letting him rip another chunk out of her heart by listening to him?

She looked at her house. Her entire family would be watching and waiting to come to her aid. Then she glanced down the street and caught a couple of curtains twitching. No matter where she went someone would be watching.

"Let's walk. There's a park a short ways down the street."

Trent fell into step beside her. Electricity hummed between them. How could she still want him, still ache for him when he'd lied to her? She inhaled deeply, filling her lungs with his cologne.

They'd passed three driveways before he spoke again. "I

didn't correct you the day we met for purely selfish reasons. Telling you my married brother had slept with you—"

She flinched. "I didn't sleep with him."

"I know that now. But from what you said that day I thought you had. Brent's wife has threatened him with a very nasty public divorce too many times to count, and he'd recently signed over half his HAMC stock to her. All I could think about that day was the bottom line and how much his screwup was going to cost me.

"I want to expand HAMC. To do that I needed board support, but the board is of the opinion that if I can't control my family members and keep them from making stupid mistakes, then I probably can't control a company the size of HAMC, either."

"You're not your family's keeper, Trent."

He slowed his step and faced her. "I know that now. Because of you. But then…" He shrugged. "I tried to control them. You're right. I needed to let go and let them learn to sort out their issues or learn from their mistakes. While I was scouring Vegas for you I let Brent handle the board meeting. I'd never given him that kind of responsibility before. He pitched my expansion plan and he did well. He probably sold the package better than I could.

"Paige, I lied to you. By omission, yes, but it was still a lie. A relationship should be based on total honesty. When Brent came on to you he and Luanne had separated. He was nursing his wounded ego by trying to pick up women. But if you want my sister-in-law to know what happened I'll make Brent tell her.

"But please keep one thing in mind. They're happy. They've worked out their problems, and they're expecting their first child."

"Why would I want to destroy that?"

"I'm hoping you won't." He reached out and took her hand and her breath caught at the zing of electricity between them. "I've fallen in love with you, Paige, and I want a future with you—one based on truth and honesty. And in vein of full disclosure, you need to know I've been called a control freak. Other than my wealth and my success as CEO of Hightower Aviation, I'm not a great catch. But I'll do whatever it takes to convince you to give me a shot."

His beautiful eyes glowed with sincerity and…love. She pressed her fingers over her mouth.

"I love you, too. And you're wrong. You are a great catch, Trent Hightower. You're sexy and funny and smart, and you're the only man I've ever met, other than my daddy, who cares as deeply for his family as I do. You might claim you're bossing them around for selfish reasons, but I don't think you're giving yourself enough credit. You do it to protect them."

He cupped her face and she burrowed her cheek into his palm. Her heart was so full it felt as if it might burst.

"You taught me something else, Paige McCauley. Confronting my fear makes me stronger. You challenged me to ride the roller coasters, and today, my sister made me fly my jet. It felt good to conquer what I'd considered a weakness."

She glanced up and down the street and smiled at the quickly dropped curtains of her nosy neighbors. "Conquering demons is something I've had to work on myself."

"I want to be strong for you, Paige, but I don't want to smother you. I know you love your job, and we'll find a way to make us work if you want to stay in Vegas. But I'm hoping you'll let me use my influence to help you find a position in Knoxville. Then during our vacations I'll show you the world. Marry me and let's spend the next few decades facing the rest of our demons together."

Happiness welled inside her, making her want to laugh and cry and sing with joy simultaneously. "I'd like that very much."

"We could always fly back to Vegas and do the deed. That is where we met."

She couldn't keep the smile off her face. "I don't care where as long as our families are there."

"You got it." He snatched her into his arms and kissed her in front of her entire neighborhood.

Let 'em talk.

She threw her arms around Trent's shoulders and kissed him back, pouring her love into the embrace for all the world to see.

* * * * *

Desire™

THE MAVERICK by Diana Palmer

Ranch foreman Harley Fowler is in the midst of trouble and mayhem—with an unexplained need to safeguard Alice Jones…

MAGNATE'S MAKE-BELIEVE MISTRESS by Bronwyn Jameson

Secretly determined to expose his housekeeper's lies, Cristiano makes her his mistress to keep her close. But little does he know he has the wrong sister!

IN THE ARMS OF THE RANCHER by Joan Hohl

Hawk agrees to a short-term marriage to shield Kate from her dark past. Yet as the time nears for the arrangement's end, their desire may be all too permanent.

HIS VIENNA CHRISTMAS BRIDE by Jan Colley

Posing as the fiancé of Jasmine Cooper, playboy Adam is happy to reap the benefits between the sheets…

CHRISTMAS WITH THE PRINCE by Michelle Celmer

Playboy Prince Aaron is determined to show reserved scientist Liv how to have a little fun—outside *and* inside the bedroom!

RESERVED FOR THE TYCOON by Charlene Sands

Brock's new employee is planning to sabotage his Maui hotel for revenge, but their attraction is like nothing they've ever felt…

On sale from 19th November 2010
Don't miss out!

*Available at WHSmith, Tesco, ASDA, Eason
and all good bookshops*

www.millsandboon.co.uk

111

2 FREE BOOKS
AND A SURPRISE GIFT

We would like to take this opportunity to thank you for reading this Mills & Boon® book by offering you the chance to take TWO more specially selected books from the Desire™ 2-in-1 series absolutely FREE! We're also making this offer to introduce you to the benefits of the Mills & Boon® Book Club™—

- **FREE home delivery**
- **FREE gifts and competitions**
- **FREE monthly Newsletter**
- **Exclusive Mills & Boon Book Club offers**
- **Books available before they're in the shops**

Accepting these FREE books and gift places you under no obligation to buy, you may cancel at any time, even after receiving your free books. Simply complete your details below and return the entire page to the address below. You don't even need a stamp!

YES Please send me 2 free Desire stories in a 2-in-1 volume and a surprise gift. I understand that unless you hear from me, I will receive 2 superb new 2-in-1 books every month for just £5.30 each, postage and packing free. I am under no obligation to purchase any books and may cancel my subscription at any time. The free books and gift will be mine to keep in any case.

Ms/Mrs/Miss/Mr _____ Initials _____

_____

Surname _____

Address _____

_____

_____ Postcode _____

E-mail_____

Send this whole page to: Mills & Boon Book Club, Free Book Offer, FREEPOST NAT 10298, Richmond, TW9 1BR.